WOMEN
OF MESSINA

By Elio Vittorini

A VITTORINI OMNIBUS
WOMEN OF MESSINA

WOMEN
OF MESSINA

by Elio Vittorini

Translated by Frances Frenaye
and Frances Keene

A NEW DIRECTIONS BOOK

131425

Italian original © 1949, 1964 by Casa Editrice Valentino Bompiani
Manufactured in the United States of America
First published clothbound (ISBN: 0-8112-0496-0) and as New Directions
Paperbook 365 (ISBN: 0-8112-0497-9) in 1973.
Published simultaneously in Canada by McClelland & Stewart, Ltd.

New Directions Books are published for James Laughlin
by New Directions Publishing Corporation,
333 Sixth Avenue, New York 10014

Elio Vittorini's Hoping and Nonhoping

Cyril Connolly thought there was only one reason to write a novel: to write a masterpiece. Sometimes at the height of his powers and belief in himself Elio Vittorini seemed to think so too. "I have never aspired to write books," he said. "I have always sought to write *the* book."

Vittorini first published *Women of Messina* in Italy in 1949. Then he proceeded to revise it some fourteen times and forbade the republication of the original version. He wanted to perfect it. Which accounts in part for the fact it has taken this long to get it to the United States—nearly ten years after his death. Whether we have a masterpiece in *Women of Messina* is open to question. Perhaps it is unimportant anyway. Masterpieces may be unbecoming to the anti-idealism of the sobered twentieth century. What we do have in *Women of Messina* is a novel of grand scale and ultimate ambition. Vittorini wanted to tell us all he knew about how and why human beings behave as they do. Parts of everything Vittorini stood for are in it. When he first published *Women of Messina* he had survived the disease of Italian Fascism and taken heart at his country's rise from the Dantesque ruins of World War II. He revised it and revised it in the mood of disenchantment with Italian Communism's ability to effect social change. Finally as he struggled to give *Women of Messina* the scope of a lifetime, Vittorini himself was dying of cancer.

Women of Messina was to be a parable of Italy's resurrection from the war and the story of displaced men and women who believed in one another. It was to be a story of an awkward romance and Vittorini's statement of what men and women need from one another. It was to be Vittorini's comedy of bumbling authoritarianism subordinated to his larger vision of human beings reaching beyond themselves for a common good. In various versions and with assorted expository side trips, *Women of Messina* became Elio Vittorini's hope and resignation, his childhood and memories, his battle with language and his quarrel with contemporary Italy. Vittorini strove to push his art to its outer boundaries.

Time will show where Vittorini went. At the moment *Women of Messina* asserts itself like a peak above a darkened plain. It is a novel of large ideas. Even its flaws are so big they cannot be quickly forgotten. Continually striving to find primary human truths in the war wreckage of lives, Vittorini at the least dramatized emotions and drives we immediately recognize as our own. And he tells us a story of reaching, grasping, letting go that parallels the cycle of life itself. The scope of *Women of Messina* belongs to a different order from Vittorini's other fiction published in the United States. *In Sicily, The Red Carnation,* and *The Light and the Dark* were all parts of "the one truth" Vittorini sought to express.* *Women of Messina* attempts to bring all the truths together and make a coherent whole of them. It is the kind of novel a man writes once in a lifetime, never finishes to his satisfaction, and surrenders rather than completes.

Vittorini came to literature the hard way—perhaps the only successful way—by looking for something better or surely more humane. He had little formal preparation for it; yet he became one of the most consequential intellectual forces in modern Italian letters. Born in 1908 in Syracuse on the coast of Sicily, where his father worked for the state railroad system (railroads and Sicily habitually work their way into his fiction), Vittorini spent most of his childhood in "little railroad stations with wire grills on the windows and the desert all around." He finished five years of grade school. Then he went to technical school to study accounting because his parents wanted to advance him into white-collar respectability. But numbers were not for Vittorini. After three years he left without a certificate, borrowed his father's railroad pass, and set out to see the available world. After a couple of years of

*Both *In Sicily* and *La Garibaldina* (one of the two short novels composing *The Light and the Dark,* 1962) are now included in *The Twilight of the Elephant and Other Novels: A Vittorini Omnibus* (New York, New Directions, 1973).

traveling to and from Syracuse, he left for good, landing in northeastern Italy at Gorizia. During the 1920s he worked on road gangs, helped build bridges, and tried writing. His sympathies were, as his experiences, proletarian. And so when he began to write, his stories were published in the anti-Fascist literary journal *Solaria* published by leftist intellectuals in Florence. "I became solariano," he later said, "and 'solariano' was a word that in the literary circles of those days meant to be anti-Fascist, European, internationalist, antitraditionalist."

Vittorini became a linotype operator, and by 1930 he had found a job as a proofreader on *La Nazione,* a daily newspaper in Florence. There he worked from nine-thirty at night until five-thirty the next morning. It was not, as he said, a job good for the health. But it was fine for the mind. It was a job that helped change Vittorini's life. For in his spare time, sitting in the proofreader's cage at *La Nazione,* Vittorini taught himself English. He did it by translating *Robinson Crusoe* a word at a time from a dictionary. Within five years Vittorini became internationally known as a translator and critic of American literature. He translated Hemingway, Faulkner, Steinbeck, Saroyan, Caldwell, as well as Poe and D. H. Lawrence. During the early 1940s, Vittorini edited and wrote the prefaces to a definitive anthology of American literature, *Americana,* commissioned by the Milan publisher Bompiani. Because it was too friendly to the United States and Vittorini had overstepped the lines drawn by the Mussolini regime, it was suppressed by the police before it was published. The book was distributed only after Vittorini's prefaces had been removed. By the end of World War II, however, *Americana* had become Italy's best-known book on American literature.

If Vittorini's translations—and those of his friend Cesare Pavese—changed American literature from a curiosity to an intellectual presence in Italy, the effect on Vittorini's own fiction was still greater. A splendid synergism took place. The translations rose as literature because Vittorini was also writing fiction. And Vittorini's delicate novels and stories of social sensibility and moral concern gained density because the Americans seemed to speak to Vittorini about his own directions. He found in American literature the defenses he needed against the inflated rhetoric and social barbarisms of Italian Fascism. There had to be alternatives in speech and thought to the official absurdities of the time. Vittorini saw them in the elementary rhythms and simple language of Hemingway, in the elementary drives and raw needs of Faulkner's and Steinbeck's naïve heroes. The innocence and incompleteness of the American experience told Vittorini that history could be made, not merely repeated.

Altogether Vittorini wrote seven novels and short novels, a book of stories, and a huge diary. Best known and perhaps most important is *In Sicily,* a short novel about a young man's spiritual malaise and his return home to see his mother. Its debts to Ernest Hemingway are especially large, but the impact of American fiction on all of Vittorini's work shows itself continually—in Vittorini's speech, the pace of his narratives, his choice of characters. Vittorini felt a deep empathy toward America, a country he never visited. Perhaps there is a message for us in his life. He was most productive when he found the greatest meaning in American history and art, and as he labored under a hostile political regime. Both were essential to Vittorini's art: something to value and something to oppose.

Vittorini was for human fulfillment, and he found plenty to hope for in the organic naturalism of his American contemporaries. In an article published in 1933, Vittorini drew a line between two kinds of writers. He said there are those writers we read and then say, "Yes, that's the way it is," and other writers we read and then say, "I had never supposed it could be like that." Vittorini wanted both. But especially he wanted the latter. He wanted fiction that would lead to a new understanding of existence. Fiction as a formal method of teaching is an activity destined to depress its practitioners, as Vittorini learned. But he tried to make his fiction a way of understanding life and a method of engaging it. *Women of Messina* is Vittorini's largest aspiration in that direction.

He wrestled with the existential proposition. The world is a brute. It is indifferent to human need and offers no moral guidance. Yet, man lives, and not alone. He must choose from the alternative means of survival and, almost by intuition, find a moral order. He must invent morality. Vittorini, the workingman turned intellectual, found his moral order the only way anyone finds it, from experience. He invoked human interdependence and social justice. He put his art in the service of his beliefs. If the art sometimes suffered—and it did in *Women of Messina*—Vittorini would pay the price and total the cost later.

Vittorini was the artist as self-propelled activist. He believed, as Sergio Pacifici said, in "solidarity and action as effective antidotes against all forms of tyranny." At the outbreak of World War II, he decided to oppose the Mussolini regime at any cost. Vittorini joined the underground, operating with it in and around Milan. From this experience he wrote two novels, *Men and Non-Men* and *Women of Messina.* The first described Italian partisans' struggles with Germans and winter weather in 1944, insisting that men were ordained to be happy. *Women of Messina* suggests how two years later men and women like those in *Men and Non-Men* might find a new way—or is it the oldest way of all?—to happiness through co-operation and a sense of community.

World War II is over when we enter the elementary world of *Women of Messina,* and we know from the start that what we find in it will strive for the majesty of allegory. For Vittorini fixes time and then fogs it. He stops through his narrative to ponder how the world runs. He speaks to us in a Whitman-esque voice about his people—a voice he frequently summons to confirm history as his witness. It is 1945 and 1946. The Germans have been driven from Italy and have left their mine fields as mementos of contempt. The Americans are still there, racing their jeeps on narrow roads. Some sort of poorly organized, semicivilian authority has taken charge of Italy, but it's a no man's land of confusion and doubt awaiting any man's imposition of order. Victims of the war, refugees from the cities and countryside, bands of decommissioned partisans, runaway soldiers, rejected girl friends are wandering through battlefields and clogging roads.

Vittorini is particularly interested in one such group of men and women. They give him the means of reorganizing society and studying individual behavior within a new structure. When we meet Vittorini's chosen losers they are stranded on a road in the Apennine mountains in central Italy.

Their truck seems to be broken down. Their inertia and puzzlement, their aimless expectation suggest they are waiting for a miracle—or maybe Samuel Beckett's Godot. They are Vittorini's new Italians who have the opportunity to create a harmonious society from the social and economic wreckage of defeated Italy. They have no other choice, it seems. They cannot think of anything else to do. They move into a deserted village. Within a few months they have made housing out of the ruined buildings, planted crops on the mountain slopes, renovated the ancient truck, and brought electricity up from the valley.

There are other Italians driven in other directions by the war. Some are simply trying to find those they have lost. One of these is Uncle Agrippa, who is related to both the narrator of the novel, whom we never really meet, and to the romantic heroine, whom Uncle Agrippa never sees. (Vittorini prospers on such exotic confusions.) A remnant of the old Italy, the defeated Italy, Uncle Agrippa rides trains up and down the country searching for his daughter Siracusa. But Siracusa has joined the commune in the Apennines. Uncle Agrippa's travels take him to the fringes of many lives, but not to Siracusa. The old Italy and the new Italy coexist. They do not converge. Telling the story of her flight from her home, listening to other travelers' speculations about the life Siracusa led as a camp follower, Uncle Agrippa hears the words but does not fathom the meaning. Like the old Italy, his psychological reality no longer exists except as habit.

But it is the village that dominates *Women of Messina.* The village stands at its center, creates its drama, prevails over the behavior of its characters, and carries Vittorini's message. It also accounts for Vittorini's melancholy at the end. Seventy-nine men, women, and children build a new society of shared work, affection, and hope. To see it happening is to share Vittorini's sense of elation. We believe it all because Vittorini has the gift of conviction. The arrival of a wandering girl with a cart is like the invention of the wheel. The decision to grant one another domestic privacy is tantamount to establishing a new human right. We come to see, as Vittorini wished, that to start a society from ruins may be a greater leap forward than to perfect one from an old social structure. If Vittorini's characters lose their identities in the collective personality of the commune, that is what he wants. Cause over personality quirks. But not always. Vittorini's childlike use of physical characteristics for names helps him draw lines between his people: Black Nail, Red Kerchief, Ugly Mug, Carlo the Bald. And he gives them voices and feelings in diaries and journals of the building of the village. They speak to us—sometimes as from Thornton Wilder or Edgar Lee Masters with Italian accents—of struggle, discord, difference, but always within the bond of achievement.

Novels of utopian idealism, even one bound to reality by Vittorini's sexual primitivism and crusty people, must either float off into fantasy or return to cruel earth. Vittorini's comes down in strange fashion. It cannot have escaped him, passionate student of history, that the commune peters out under drives and yearnings so rooted to mankind's past that the very existence of the commune was an event of anti-history. External political authority begins to assert itself on the village in the guise of property rights. But more importantly, Ventura, lover of Siracusa and the village's engineer, becomes the object of a manhunt as a result of his Fascist past. The "hunters" from a still newer Italy bring stories of hot music, cold beer, and paying jobs in Bologna and Modena. The commune does not collapse under attack. It withers and shrinks because its men, having given themselves to mutual interest, turn to self-interest. Even the women of Messina, the tough, refugee Sicilians who put guts into their men and plows into the fields, grow fat and plant grapevines. Under pressure the village rose on the spirit of community and the pain of struggle. Under the softness of success, the village merges into the old history it had declared void.

Women of Messina tells us how much Elio Vittorini loved ideology and how troubled he became that ideology alone produces no change in the world. He revised the novel the last time disenchanted with both the purifying strength of America (our postwar military adventures depressed him) and the dogmatism of Italian Communism. He gave us his wisdom and his confusion as well. He settled for a hymn to aspiration sung with ardor in a novel churning with social movement and alive with the voices of human need. Vittorini stumbles and halts as he tries to understand these needs. He even loses track of them during his moments of ideological exhilaration. But Vittorini always writes from within. He never makes errors of emotion that tell you a novelist is writing to be writing.

Elio Vittorini cared deeply about how we become more than bundles of reflexes and imprint ourselves on our time and place. To read *Women of Messina* is to enter the company of a writer who takes command of your faculties. He tells you a story that, it seems, you must hear even when you grow tired of it. It is important. You know this instinctively. And Vittorini moves you to the necessary next step for art. Reality. You must believe his story. Everything has been altered. The reality is not immediate. The reality is inside you. What Vittorini imagined in an Italian village decades ago is the essential human condition.

WEBSTER SCHOTT

PART ONE

1

I know how someone who has never traveled the length and breadth of our country might imagine it, someone who has only seen its long profile on the atlas pages: high stretches of dry, red earth between two seas that mark east and west, arid land, treeless, seared by the wind and the breath of the sun, the breath of salt; and so it is, over great stretches of it, as soon as one goes above a thousand feet on the trip from one to another of its towered and cupolaed cities—it is arid over great stretches, naked over great stretches, high, with red earth between Emilia and Tuscany or between Siena and Rome, the way the desert is desert between its oases.

Crossing the desert, men are travelers, and in the same way our people are nomads as they cross our highlands; they go back and forth from the south heading north or from north to south on long trains from whose windows they look out, standing for three or four or even five days, wondering what this land is—everywhere alike—that binds together places as different from one another as Bari and Bologna, Catanzaro and Genoa, this land that calls itself Italy.

I am from Apulia and could find no peace until I began this run back and forth from Molfetta to Milan, which, at every station, shakes me from my lethargy as a baggage-rack straphanger and shows me, once more through little windows smudged with weariness, a plateau without a blade of grass, like the one along the Murge, here where we are near the drop down toward the river Po.

Or I am from Milan and did not want to stop on my great plain of a thousand trades; I wanted to see if I too could traffic in lemons, enter into the back-and-forth life of the long train that flaps a greeting with all its curtains to the loneliness

3

of sun and stone of the land through which it runs, both when we are between Parma and La Spezia, along the Apennines, and when, in a dawn that smells of ricotta cheese, we are along the border between Campania and Calabria, or when, on a late afternoon, we hear the crickets, louder than our train whistle, crying for help all the way from Catania to Syracuse.

Or I am a Ligurian from Bracco and could have been satisfied working in the shipyards of Sestri; I am from Emilia, from the Val di Taro region, and could have been satisfied churning cheeses on the outskirts of Parma—instead, I wanted the back-and-forth life, and I've earned my bread a bit everywhere, in Terni, in Naples, in Messina, perhaps for no other reason than to make my six or seven trips, my chest prickling with sweat, up and down this land which I see by the lights of my own trip stretching in curves as the rock curves in the moonlight; I see it in just such a way as I believed, when I was a boy, that only my Bracco had jack rabbits, or only my Val di Taro had shepherds, and I see that, yes, the land is there just to be traveled, made on purpose for a man to want to climb aboard a train and cross it, climb aboard a train once more and cross it again.

2

To this plateau nine hundred and more miles long, the last war brought wretchedness, cutting the country into two parts, so that people were stuck for two years half on one side, half on the other.

For two years, I could not push myself beyond Bologna; and another man like me for two years could not manage to get above the Roman line. We were stuck in a desert for two years; we were in Milan but we could not get home to Reggio Calabria, and we were in a desert; we were at Trani, at Barletta, at Taranto, but we couldn't get a train for North

4

Italy. Our long trains did not run back and forth any more, their curtains flapping; they told us they were burning in the yards, under the overhangs, and that our rail lines had been erased from the stone face of the plateau, the shining track wrenched loose, the bridges down.

Who among us did not rush to the station and the trains as soon as the war was over? An even more intense traveling to and fro over the high ground of Italy began anew;

on foot, thousands of ragged people came from Apulia, looking here for news of a soldier, there for a runaway girl, or for a certain store that used to sell oil and wine, all of them determined not to find what they were looking for until they had reached, say, Milan, and seen a certain Milanese street after the desert they had seen on their long walk, or the line of vegetable carts of their countrymen, or spoken with their townsmen who had long since emigrated to Milan;

who, in turn, were traveling in the opposite direction seeking news, in turn, of a soldier who was a relative or a friend, news of an old mother, an olive grove, four sheep, or a dog, even news of no more than a dog, determined, in turn, not to accept as fact any news until they had heard it in the square of Bitonto or Trani, or until they had found themselves in front of a certain closed door;

and all of them on foot, in turn, crossing at an altitude where the weeds, growing between one stone and the next, catch fire from the breath of the sun by day, and where one sleeps in the ditches by the roadside at night at only one step below the snow line;

or on trucks, caught in the excitement of the check points, no matter which way they are going so long as they take us south, east, north, west, seated on sacks or oilcans, on suitcases, scrap iron, our faces into the cutting wind, our hair in the wind like the little curtains of the trains, and our jacket collars turned up about the nape of the neck, collars into which we huddle, feeling an evermore acute need for consolation;

more acute, the way our own identity is more acute when we arrive at our destinations, when we say we have arrived and, instead, we can give ourselves no peace except for a month or a year, for three days or ten years, scarcely time

5

enough for each of us to reaccumulate the small sum needed to permit us another change, and another crossing of Italy in all its length, another long trip, on foot, by truck, or on the train, and another liberation from the solitude in which we bury our knowledge of the fact that, one day or other, we shall be still, with no more possibility of movement.

They rushed to the bronze doors that were swinging open and they beat on them, all these men and women who had been stuck for two years on one side or the other of the Gothic Line; and there was not one of them who did not take or plan to take a little trip at least a day long, of at least fifteen or twenty miles, at least on an oxcart, to see someone or something again.

But what?

Certainly not always was it one's own mother, not always one's wife or one's husband or children. It was not always something or someone already known, or the city where one had been born. But it was the re-establishment of contact with the *other* within us, with the *rest*, and this meant finding the mother in the mother and the house in the house even if, for two years, we had never left them and were only leaving them now.

Godspeed, good-by. . . We said good-by to our dear ones who had been our imagined company in the two years of our solitude, and we ran to embrace people who were unknown to us, to find in them our return to the world and the return of the world to us.

Little by little, the trains, too, began to run again. At first over short stretches, Florence–Pistoia, Urbino–Pesaro, then over the entire length of the nine hundred miles of dry earth, with a shrill whistle because each one was carrying ten times more people than any of our trains had ever carried before and because of a pleasure in traveling that was ten times ten more childish, beneath the sun from the narrow windows, than it had ever been in our trains even when we could stretch out our legs on the opposite seat, when we passed stations without stopping, and with only a slight variation in the noise of the wheels on the track.

There began again that great to-ing and fro-ing of people thanks to which Italy is a single country instead of thousands

6

of countries. It was in the spring of '45, in the summer; and it grows now in '46 and continues to grow, that back-ing and forth-ing of Northerners and Southerners who are looking to settle down, of veterans who are looking, ex-deportees who are looking, partisans who are looking, decent people and people who are not decent, all of whom are looking for something . . .

3

Since April '45 all my people have been constantly on the trucks and trains, and in the caravans of walkers with broken boots, with bound feet, with bare feet;

in one train there is even my mother seeking news of me, traveling seven days from our small town in Sicily, and my grandmother may even be traveling with her, swapping places with her every so often on the armrest they have managed to obtain, eating from a basket an omelet made of two eggs divided between them over seven days, cleaning their mouths with a bit of orange peel after each meal before using their napkin;

in a truck there is my brother Rosario, who was a partisan above Piacenza, among heather and stones, and searching a year now for a bakeshop where he can start as an errand boy, traveling by truck, as I'm able to think of him, with his knees fast in his arms, and his face high even in the chill of the ride, not crouched, always serious, always without a thing to say;

and there is my cousin Gaetano in the gray-green rags of a veteran; he has now reached the level of the Amiata above the Siena clay pits, he and his five comrades afoot trying to get to Sicily yet, at the same time, trying to find a spot to stop and work;

and the little old man who has lived in a truck or on a train for a year and a half, his head like that of an old sparrow, with the frightened glance of a sparrow, and wearing an old black suit with a scarf around his neck in which he hides

7

his face at night like a Bedouin in the desert, hides it up to his little eyes that even in sleep do not stop fluttering, he who has been seen on the train between Syracuse and Milan, Syracuse and Venice, Syracuse and Turin, some thirty-six times since April '45 and whom everyone who has traveled between north and south in this year and a half knows at least by repute, he too is one of my flesh and blood, almost like my mother to me, her brother, the son of my hundred-year-old grandmother who travels with her.

"Marinese," he introduces himself on the train.

But I want to make it clear that he is only one of many, only typical of people, people who have nothing special about them and nothing that, in the family, one should be ashamed of. The to-ing and fro-ing that has begun again has, as I have said, continued to grow in intensity, it doesn't slack off, it grows; and it does not seem to be able to level off either. Every day new people join this back-ing and forth-ing; new unemployed, new veterans; and of the earlier ones there are few indeed who have found a place to stop in. And of those who did stop, how many have not taken a train again? I know of far too many who stopped out of weariness or rage, stopped right in the desert itself where the stones beneath the sun and the red earth were mined on both sides of the road, where the village in sight at the curve was rubble, and where the fountain on its outskirts has been these eighteen months without water.

4

"I'm stopping here," said the older of two men who had just finished eating quietly together, from the same loaf of bread and bottle of water.

The scrawnier and younger (though he was a good forty) took care of the provisions; he kept a parcel of food in one pocket, the bottle in the other; and it was always he who spread the napkin in front of his friend or ran, during the stops, to fill their water bottle wherever there was a pipe.

"Here?" he said. "And what's here?"

It was open plateau country, with curving, naked heights, red in its nakedness, and there were cicadas singing. The road, from the point where the eye caught its rise to the place where it went out of sight in a series of descending curves, shone here and there because of the asphalt, shone as if it were wet, and so looking at it was something of a relief. A relief too because, of course, it came from somewhere, from houses and woods, and because it was going somewhere else, to some hole that was not this desert.

He gave him a long look: "And what's here?" he said again. He opened his arms wide, letting his gaze wander, and pointed to the left and to the right. "Thorns! Nothing but thorns!"

He indicated the scrubby vegetation a short distance away: it was low and covered with small white tips out of which grew needles that trembled and shone in the sun. "Thorns, see? And more thorns! Nothing but thorns!"

"But I'm stopping here all the same!" the older man almost screamed. He was seated on a milestone, in his shirt sleeves, his jacket across his knees, wiping the sweat from his head which was covered with short gray hair that showed under an old straw hat he had raised with one hand while, with the other, he wiped it and once more wiped it with a small rag. "Thorns!" he exclaimed. What did it matter if they were thorns? And, if they had not been thorns, what did it matter either ?

He stopped drying the sweat, and stood up, shook out his jacket and pulled up his pants. "Thorns!"

"What of it?" Thorn answered. He pointed them out in all the thousands of folds in the surrounding land, in the spears of grasses poking up on the brow of the hills, in the fields that disappeared with the sun and that re-emerged along the valleys. "That's what they are and that's all there is to it. We might stop a bit farther on, if you really want to stop."

"Ahhh!" the stocky older fellow cried. His weary face was distorted; then he added slowly but firmly: "As for me, I've had enough!" And he let out a harsh, loud whistle.

This whistle always underscored his decisions.

9

"A bit farther on?" His eyes queried the friend of the thorns. "It's been quite a while we've been going a bit farther on, and we've even gone as far as the Straits several times in our wish to go just a bit farther on. A man fights, old boy; that's why he's strong, so he can fight, and he can be whatever you want him to be, even for years at a time. But a man gets tired just the same, he's weak enough, aside from being strong; that's his weakness, and he wants to sit down and rest, then work, have his own house even if it's in a wolf's lair, he wants to be able to let himself go in his own way, let's say he wants to let himself go at believing in God. I'm a good fifty years old and you've seen me on my feet ever since we met. Haven't I been on my feet all the time?" his eyes asked Thorn. "And now I want to let myself go," the eyes said. "No more of your 'let's go a bit farther on.' I want to sit down. Sit down right here, because I don't believe in that 'bit farther on,' at least not for the moment."

He held his jacket by one sleeve and swung it, dragging it against the asphalt, while his eyes talked; then he threw it over one shoulder, still holding it by one sleeve, while his eyes went on talking, drifting every so often—on either side of Thorn's face—toward the countryside or even pausing, now on men and women like them who had thrown themselves down on the opposite side of the road; now on the truck where it had stopped nailed to the spot by engine trouble or lack of gas, its shadow beneath it; now on the group of four or five who had stayed aboard the truck, stretching out in the space that was now all theirs, an old woman on her feet to see as far as she could see, and a small boy running back and forth with a hammering of little feet.

"I don't deny a word of it," Thorn's eyes said in reply. They were lost and, remembering what had happened, they foresaw what might lie ahead.

Could they deny? They did not do so. "But here what kind of letting-oneself-go can there be? A man sits down in a place where there's a little hope. What hope is there here?"

His eyes too looked into those of his friend, and they were lost too, in the same drifting; they too pausing on the truck, on the figures who were on the truck, on the men and women

10

who were along the roadside, seeing them more than the thorny countryside, and not denying.

"You don't have to stop," the other one said at last. "I'm not telling you that you have to stop here! You can go a bit farther on . . . !"

"Here there's not a living soul," Thorn said. "Christ! Not the shadow of a living soul."

"And you're going where there are living souls, is that it? Go on. Go a bit farther on."

"There's not a trickle of running water."

"You just go a bit farther on."

"Not a blade of grass to pluck."

"Just go a bit farther on."

"No shelter for the night."

"Just go a bit farther on."

The man who had whistled said nothing except that Thorn should go farther on; sleep on the steps of a church where there was shelter against the night, eat his bread in a town where there were inns and drink his bottle of water where wine rang out in voices and glasses behind closed doors; he himself preferred to have these things on this very spot rather than go a bit farther on, and he was telling Thorn this by dint of telling him to go farther on. "There are cities farther on. Can't you go a bit farther on?"

For a minute or two he had been walking toward the spot where the truck was stuck, and Thorn was following him.

Thorn shook his head. He had not made himself clear, nor did he know how to do so. What he had been able to say was not at all what he meant.

He had gone on wearing his cotton jacket because of the things in the pockets, but now he took it off after having taken the parcel and the bottle in one hand. He stopped, his back all sweaty, and held the bottle up. "That's so," he said to himself. At least he was talking.

"What's so?"

"The bottle."

"What's the matter with the bottle?"

"I was wondering how you'd make out without it, if I went farther on alone."

11

The older man whistled once more. "I piss on the ground," he said. "Not in a bottle."

He went on now with a stride that made the asphalt ring, like the noise of going straight to make something, or break something. He had made up his mind; he whistled a third time, harsh and loud, a scornful whistle; and he slammed his jacket down on the ground, climbing with one bound aboard the big truck.

The little boy up there stopped running when he saw the face with the straw hat appear, and the old woman dressed in black looked for a moment at him instead of at the far reaches of the countryside.

Thorn, from below, noticed his scowling face as he bent here and there to pick up his things. He was quick about it. He stood up and tossed down everything, old clothes and cook pots, in a single bundle.

"That's one hell of a whistle!" Thorn grumbled.

But he stooped to pick up his things for him and carry them to the edge of the road.

5

The old woman, from the top of the heap of boxes on which she was standing, once more glanced at Whistle.

"You getting down here?" she asked him, without surprise.

"I guess so," Whistle answered.

"You seen it?" the old woman asked him.

"No," he said.

What was *it*? He imagined it without wanting to know the answer. But then he raised his face little by little. "What is it?"

The old woman pointed through the air.

"It's a village," she said.

Whistle drew near her by the two or three yards that separated him from the pyramidal pile of boxes.

"It's all broken," the old woman went on.

Broken? She meant that there were windows with no rooms behind them, and walls open to the sun; rubble of war. But he saw only a bit more road, with the scrap iron that had been a tank at one turning, then more scrap, this time a cannon, and a second and a third tank scattered along the curves of the rising road.

"It looks uninhabited," the old woman added.

"Why?" Whistle said. "I can't tell."

"Nobody's walking about."

"Isn't there a whole house standing?"

"It doesn't seem so. There's a piece of roof only on a church."

Whistle climbed to the first level of boxes. "Which way d'you see it?"

But the old woman was higher still. He had to climb to the second level, and there she was on the single box at the third level, her hand resting on the roof of the driver's cab.

"Over there," the old woman said.

Whistle watched her hand mark a direction in the air, and was about to get down again when he seemed to hear a muffled gurgling from the very distance she had indicated.

He stopped. "Didn't you hear?"

"Of course, I heard."

"And it's there?"

"It's there."

"Then it's inhabited."

"No, that's water running down behind," the old woman exclaimed, but slowly.

"Oh Christ!" Whistle said.

He climbed to the second level; he was higher, overlooking a wider circle than the bare red highlands scored with white patches of sunlight that befogged them. He planted himself up against the packing case from which the old woman looked out over her dead village.

"Isn't it rather the sound of people?"

"It's water running below there. I've seen it for the last half hour."

"Well, I don't see a damned thing," Whistle grumbled. "That is . . . ," he corrected himself. And he looked, keeping his straw hat brim turned down to shield his eyes from the sun. "I see a thread of brook that runs along a sort of gully."

13

"That's it," the old woman said. "Follow it."

Whistle looked. "It gets lost."

"Follow it on this side."

"But it still gets lost. Those hills, the ones in front here, hide it."

"Farther over, it comes out once more. And then right away there's a bridge."

"There's a bridge?" Whistle said. The old woman had a pair of eyes like binoculars. "I don't see any bridge. Is it a broken bridge or a bridge that's still standing?"

"It's whole, but just beyond it there's a big building busted wide open that must have been a mill."

Whistle gave her a quick glance as if to check that she did not really have binoculars. "The far side of the water, you say?"

"The far side of the water. And on this side there's everything else."

"Ah!" Whistle said then.

Finally, and all at once, he saw in the quivering haze what looked like houses; high walls, holes breached in windows with nothing dark, nothing enclosed behind them; everything wide open to the sun and as if erased by it, by the countryside, by the colors in the surrounding reddish nakedness of the countryside: a big village that must have numbered many inhabitants before the Gothic Line passed that way.

"I thought you were going there," the old woman told him.

"There?"

"I thought so."

"Well, I'm not going on with this trip any farther."

"I saw you'd put down all your gear."

"I put it down, and now I'm going to put myself down too . . ."

He let himself slip down from the top level of boxes, and from the first level he dropped to the floor of the truck while the people gathered aboard watched him.

"Did he say he was getting down here?"

"He said he's tired to death of waiting."

"He's right. What are we waiting for?"

"He said he's going on foot."

Whistle stopped once more, on the tail gate of the truck,

14

and wiped the sweat from his forehead with the back of his thumb, then shook his hand.

"Hey," Thorn called, his face turned upward.

"I'm coming down, coming down."

"But what does she say there is over there?"

"There's a village."

Thorn shoved his lean face upward.

"Toss me down my gear, since you're up there." And he stretched out an arm.

"That broken-down suitcase of yours?"

The old fiber suitcase, held together with string, made its way down to Thorn's hand.

"Nothing else, is there?"

"Nothing else."

Whistle got down, letting himself slip to the ground and even making a little hop backward.

"So," he said to Thorn, "you're stopping here too." His eyes had softened, they were talking once more.

"But didn't you want me to go a bit farther on, by myself?"

They picked up their things. Whistle found his all ready to carry like a rucksack, as he used to do on long walks; each put his jacket over one arm, and they started on the road downhill. As they passed beyond the truck, Whistle called out to the old woman: "Say hello to them all from us, Barbèra."

"We'll see each other again," the old woman answered.

6

A young man with good shoes and a still bright-red partisan's kerchief around his neck leaped up from the bunch of people squatting by the roadside and called loudly:

"Hey, you! Hey, you two!"

Thorn and Whistle turned around.

"What are you going to do?"

The voices rose, thin and strident, like those of field hands calling from field to field.

"Sick of staying put," Whistle called back.

"Going on foot?"

"We're going on foot."

"Well, I'm coming along with you."

Whistle and Thorn did not wait for him, just slowed their pace and turned around every so often. While the young man made his hurried, confused preparations—jumping aboard the truck, then down, then aboard again—almost every man's and woman's head was raised from the rest by the roadside, and almost every face watched him.

A man with a wan face got up from where he was seated, thus taking the shade of his small body from a woman behind him. He came toward the truck with his trousers open, unbuttoned over his white shorts up to the buckle of his belt.

"He's always unbuttoned," his wife told those near her. "There's no way to get him to remember how he goes around."

Meanwhile the young man, still busying himself on and off the truck, called out from time to time to a comrade of his also wearing a red neckerchief. The comrade was perhaps the only person who had remained motionless, his head resting on the hard ground of the roadside, his cap over his eyes, and one leg crossed over the other with a foot in the air.

"Hey, Toma! Hey, Toma!" he called.

The woman rose up on her knees and stretched her bare arms wide. "Mind you, I'll not settle for walking," she yelled at her husband.

"Do we have to go on foot?" he asked Red Kerchief.

"Of course not!" said Red Kerchief. "Is the truck going on foot? You can stay with the truck."

"But will the truck go on?"

"Why ask me? Certainly the owner won't want to leave it here forever."

"Those two are taking off on foot in the meantime."

"And I'm following them," said Red Kerchief. And he opened his young mouth to call his comrade once more. "Hey, Toma! Let's go, Toma! I've got down your gear for you," he cried.

Toma's blond head moved from the ground.

"You going?" the woman asked.

16

"I don't know," he said, already sitting up with his hands before his eyes to shield them from the light.

Red Kerchief was all ready; he slung his sack over his shoulder. "Hey," once more he opened his young mouth toward his companion. "Hey, Toma!" And his fresh voice rang out on the air. "I'm going to catch up with them and go along."

"Whereabouts are they going?" Toma asked the woman next him.

"Going on foot," she answered. "I never was one to go anywhere on foot."

The little, unbuttoned fellow behind Red Kerchief asked him: "Will you be taking the same road as the truck?" He could imagine the truck catching up with them after they had walked such a long way.

But from the top of the truck a woman answered, "Of course not! They're going down to the village."

"There's a village?" Unbuttoned announced to his wife: "There's a village not two steps away."

"D'you hear that?" Unbuttoned's wife said. She went on talking to Toma who was touching the back pocket of his trousers, feeling for something. "They've gone to look at a village nearby."

Word of the village spread. And Toma found on the ground what he had been looking for, a notebook and a thin wallet. "I'm going to take a look, too."

He was on his feet already, already running.

"But they'll come back," Unbuttoned's wife told him.

"We'll come back," Toma said. He was running, and he paused at the truck no longer than the time it took to grab up his sack.

"Now that's a fine boy," Unbuttoned's wife said to another woman.

"You're telling me?" she answered.

Meanwhile, others were calling out: "Hold on!"

"Your husband wants to go, too."

"It's a village destroyed by the war."

Unbuttoned waved his arms from his place on the truck, with all his belongings piled up at his feet.

17

"He knows I'm no good at walking," his wife said. But she had gotten up and paused only to chivy the girl. "Who do I complain to if he looks at you?"

"I can't bother about everyone who looks at me."

"That's because you only like fellows with ugly mugs."

"What's wrong with that?" the girl said.

She looked about her, and a man who had never spoken before smiled at her. Did he have an ugly mug?

The girl shrugged her shoulders and turned back to watch what was going on over by the truck.

7

Toward evening a few cars began to reach them and pass them coming from both directions, announcing their presence afar off by the rumble of their motors on the upgrade, and then popping into view from behind a curve, all unsuspecting, as if nothing else existed in the world, so busy were they with their own rumble. But they would pick up speed as soon as the stalled truck was sighted, with its many passengers trying to stop them with cries, gestures, half runs. Then, making a quick getaway on the downgrade, they would slip off to the next curve without so much as the sound of tires, until, at the next rise, the motors let out their breaths in a mixture of scorn and relief.

First a limousine, in dark green and chrome, came from the same direction as they had come.

Second, there was a jeep from the same direction, with a Negro driver who turned around to look at them and laughed.

Third, three military dispatch drivers one after the other who spread a film of dust from the high gray panels of their trucks as they jounced by on the pitted roadbed.

Fourth, a little Fiat Topolino.

Fifth, a dark, powerful Augusta.

And a sixth, a seventh, an eighth . . .

Last came a truck like their own, a trailer truck, and the trailer was filled like theirs with tightly packed people, standing. It was when the sun had already set and a chill was in the air that touched one's hands without a wind having risen, and turned all the landscape that had been reddish during the heat haze to white and shadow. The truck had made itself heard a good half hour before it appeared, and they could see it climbing at a man's pace for a quarter of an hour in the dusk of the long curves, coming on, with head lamps lit, from the very direction in which they themselves wished to go.

Their truck driver got down this time from his seat behind the wheel in which, his legs propped up, he had been filling out crossword puzzles ever since they got stuck. He signaled with his arms, and the oncoming convoy did not pick up speed at the crest of the hill from which it could finally have caught its breath for the descent; instead, it stopped, but it had no fuel to spare. The most it could do was take on whatever strays managed to clamber on top.

Once the convoy had passed, with two of their people who had gotten aboard in order to go back down, night set in on the road and in the surrounding countryside in earnest, turning colder and colder from the naked whiteness of cold of the highlands, and stretching its solitude ever wider in the great solitude of darkness that covered the earth.

A child cried, the little boy who had run up and down, hammering his little feet on the floor of the truck, and it was not the same as when a dog barked, it was no sign of life, but rather a cry of abandon beyond any words. A truckload of people is full of hope, even crossing the Sahara, so long as the truck is in motion. But if it is stock-still in the night, it is no longer anything; it is a seal on its own nothingness, a chair in the middle of the desert.

"They've lighted a fire," a voice said all of a sudden.

Men and women were all gathered on the truck and its trailer, in groups stretched out under the rags they shared in common, waiting with bated breath for the child to finish his crying against his mother's dark breast. The voice startled them, and they recognized it: it was old Barbera's.

What the devil! Had she stayed up there staring into the

night to make out what she could in those distant solitudes?

They looked up to seek her with their eyes, their diviner of signs and happenings, seeking her in the shadows where the brightness of the boxes was interrupted. But up there along that sharp line the whole sky was shadow, without a single star to mark by its gleam the empty openness of distance.

Yet anyone who raised his head above the truck sides could see that in one spot there was a strong glow.

"Those must be the lights of Bologna," someone exclaimed.

"Foolishness," someone else said. "Why not the lights of Milan? Or Rome?"

"Aren't we in the Bologna area?"

"We're also in the Ancona area, if fifty miles more or less don't count."

They found names and animation once more, and the possibility of discussion. Only the girl who had given Unbuttoned's wife a cheeky answer did not raise her head. She was curled up in a corner on a coat, motionless, her cheek on one hand and her eyes wide open.

The man they thought attracted her was not near her: the one they said had an ugly mug. He was behind her with two people in between, minding his own business and closed in the silence he had never broken during those days of shared traveling except to offer one person or another, but always without insistence, his bread and grub. He too had pulled himself up now to look for the city glow everyone was talking about.

"It must come from some hamlet on that mountain," they said.

"D'you think there are hamlets on that mountain?"

"The war can't have destroyed them all."

"Oh yes! And even the big farms that were there are all destroyed . . ."

They were talking almost under their breath, as if not to disturb anyone who might want to go to sleep, and it was the old woman who once more seemed to wish to break the silence or rather the whispering that had taken its place.

"*They'll* have lighted the fire," she said.

They? The subdued chatter had started again among the people beneath the boxes. They, who?

"She means those who went off on foot."

Then they said once more that they had gone to the village, and people spoke of this fact, of a village in these parts that had been hit by the war.

"Suppose they've found shelter?"

The women who were part of the group around the child were talking, too; they had been on the truck the whole afternoon.

"Who knows?" one of them said.

And another: "It's certainly a big village."

"Is it big?" they asked her.

"Barbèra told us it was," a third answered. "She said there must have been three hundred houses."

The old woman said that if they had found a roof to shelter them, they would not have lighted that fire out of doors.

This was true, they remarked. But that did not mean there were no houses standing. There might be some that lacked only a door, or panes in the windows. Each one hazarded a guess as to what might have been left of a town of three or four thousand people. They spoke of other villages, their own, through which war had passed. And it was of people they were speaking, everyone, even the young man whom they said had an ugly mug.

"And it's a big fire," the old woman said.

"Can you really see the fire?" they asked her.

"Of course," she answered. "They've built one bigger than this truck."

That meant they must have a lot of wood. Of course, they did: they must have joists and crossbeams. Two or three of them stood up; they wanted to see the fire, see for themselves if it was high, if it was in a square, and what they were doing about it.

"Where is it?" they asked. And still others kept on getting up to try to see the fire itself, not simply its glow. They asked the old woman, "How do you manage to see it?"

They could hear someone climbing up the rampart of boxes.

"D'you see it?"

Someone else could be heard climbing up, and the first one must have clambered still higher already.

"By God, if you don't see it!"

"So it's really them!"

"And is it really a big one?"

"By God, a real blast furnace . . ."

They were all yelling now, as if they could all see: an "ah!" in unison.

"And you can see the houses."

It was a mason speaking. He had not worked since a year before the war at a wall for a house. He saw by that distant firelight walls of rubble, and he saw them as if they were all walls under construction: that's the way they seemed.

"You know?" he cried. "I'm going."

They were all standing now, even the woman with the child who had been crying a little while ago.

"You mean you're going there right now?"

The mason came down from the top of the heap of boxes, and did not answer.

"Why not?" the old woman answered for him.

8

Once every two weeks the little old man with a head like a sparrow's whom I have referred to as my blood relative takes a train going north or another going south not far from the places which, that night, were lit up by the flames rising among the ruins of the abandoned village. Once he'll go north on the train that passes toward five in the morning when it's already daylight in summer or black night in winter; and then again he'll go south in the train that passes between twelve-thirty and one A.M.

You cannot see the railway from the road on which the big truck was stuck; at that point, it passes underground through a long tunnel from which the train emerges whistling, whizzing by so fast that you can barely notice in the mornings between May and the end of August that a big mountain village lies over there six or seven hundred yards higher up the hill, bathed on one flank, in a wide swath of white pebbles, by the same blue waters that, down below, stifle the sound of the train as it crosses the short wooden bridge beyond which it enters into another tunnel.

My uncle, his face wrapped in his Bedouin scarf, passes sleepless through the long whistle which, from the outer edge of the two tunnels, pierces the sleep of the inhabitants of the mountain village, once at half past midnight and again at five o'clock in the morning; it is a sure thing that he does not look out into the night. He can only look up, at the luggage rack full of suitcases and packages dimly illumined by a bluish light, or down, at knees, legs, hands, elbows. Or he can look at the faces of those sitting across from him, some of them fallen on their breasts, in the shadows, others caught between darkness and the wan light, exchanging smoke and breath in the gentle undercurrent of men's melodious night talk on trains.

My uncle, as well as being short, is a very thin man. He always was even when we were children, and his name, Uncle Agrippa, was synonymous for us with "Uncle Stick" or "Uncle Bean Pole." Wherever he sat down, there was always room for another person. Consequently, as now in his travels, he is always squeezed in between two others, one of whom takes up three quarters of his seat. He leaves Syracuse or Milan, Genoa or Rome, in a seat next to the window he has picked out hours earlier. But half an hour after the train starts, some big fat character jams himself in between my uncle and the window. Then, pushing him toward the next traveler, crushing him against the man or woman who happens to be sitting on the other side, little by little he deprives my uncle of all his space on the seat.

"Excuse me," my uncle says.

He draws back a hand that has been crushed under a fat buttock and smiles at the usurper to show that he is not annoyed. Thus he tried to make himself comfortable between his two neighbors and keep the peace. He talks to them; he talks to everyone in the compartment, sometimes perched on the edge of his seat when his neighbors lean back, sometimes disappearing behind them when they lean forward. But he can never look out at the night, for to do that he would have to press his face against the window and wipe the steam from the glass.

Besides, someone is always standing between the seats blocking a good part of the window. The aisle in the middle of the car, too, is always full of people sitting on their own baggage or on the floor. And my uncle, who manages to sleep only through the first hours of darkness, endures periods of paralysis during these long nights in which, while no one talks, he must sit with his little body and his little head quite erect. His face covered to above the nose by his striped scarf, he observes the others opposite and beside him with eyes that, no longer sparrowlike, have become a Bedouin's eyes, sharp and narrow like those of an old Arab nomad.

9

The silence has not lasted long—it must have been only fifteen minutes—and the train has stopped. A man who has been sleeping across from my uncle wakes up.

The train begins to move again. The man's arms are crossed on his chest. My uncle is still looking at him as he did while he was asleep. But when the man looks at my uncle in turn, Uncle pulls his scarf down below his mouth: "Marinese," he says to him.

The man raises himself a little, while my uncle stretches out his right hand.

"Marinese?" asks the man.

And my uncle: "That's my name."

"Ah," the man exclaims.

He brings his large bovine face forward, and his eyes and cheeks are shadowed by the hat brim he pulled down when he went to sleep. He yawns. Did he say "Ah," or did he just yawn? He uncrosses his arms and, as he lowers his stubby hands to his knees, my uncle catches one of them in his.

"Ah," says the man, "pleased to meet you."

24

He hastens to scratch an ear, and replaces his hands on his knees.

"We hadn't introduced ourselves," my uncle says to him. And the man: "That's true."

"It was already night when you got on," my uncle says.

"And I had to stand up quite a while," the man answers.

"An hour," my uncle tells him. "The gentleman whose place you took got off at . . ." He asks, "What's the name of that place?"

"I don't know," the man answers. But he adds, "I was lucky that man got off."

"Somebody always gets off at one station or another," my uncle tells him. "Even at two in the morning. Even at three."

At this point he pulls his scarf back up above his mouth and meditates for a little. At two in the morning! At three in the morning! They get off at a little station whose name the conductor doesn't even call out, and then good-by! The train goes on while they stay behind. Strange travelers! What will they do in a little country station at two in the morning?

But there are even people who get on at that hour! My uncle looks at the man facing him, studying the shadow his bovine face casts on his chest. "Isn't it strange?" my uncle says to him, for *he* always takes the train where it starts and gets off only at the end of the line.

"Ah," the man replies.

This is what my uncle wants, to be able to talk while he cannot sleep, just to have someone awake with him who will at least say "ah" now and then when he says something.

"Oh, is that so?" the man says, as my uncle tells him of the days and nights that his trips last and tells him too how each of his destinations is always, sooner or later, the place from which he must again depart.

"Do you know why?" he asks.

Since the man with the bovine face does not pick up the question, he himself does. "Why?" It is extremely important that the question be asked because the answer is the long story my uncle has been telling about himself ever since he made his first trip. He loves to tell this story, he wants to tell it. And if each new person he meets on the trains does not ask him the question, my uncle asks it of himself.

25

"I'll tell you why," Uncle says.

"I suppose it must be on business," Cow Face says.

My old uncle hesitates a few seconds as if it really were, in some sense, on business. Then, tilting his head to one side, he says, "Not exactly."

"Ah, no?" the man says.

And my uncle: "No sir. I have nephews and grandnephews and my working years are past. I live on a pension."

"Lots of people go into some kind of business after they've been pensioned," observes Cow Face.

"I, instead, had to get away from work altogether," my uncle says. "I had the kind of job that tires a man. I was a railway road worker. I had forty years of shoveling on my back, and was I happy to be given a chance to rest!"

"But if you travel, you can't be resting. You must hope to get something out of it."

At this, my uncle stops holding his scarf. It is down under his chin now, and his little old face is snuggled into it from his sharp jaws around to his ears. He meditates without covering his mouth. He smiles.

"Maybe I'll get something out of it in the end. But it's business of another kind," he says. "I had only nephews and nieces, all children of my sister's, and everyone called me 'Uncle.' But what's an uncle? No man in the world can be satisfied to be just an uncle. You see a beautiful girl and you're nothing to her, you're only her uncle. You can be sure she doesn't care a fig for you. On the contrary, she likes to make fun of you, whereas she fears and respects her father and pays him all kinds of attention. So I thought sadly about my old age, when I would be just an uncle."

"Lots of uncles are respected," the other man says.

He speaks this way, a little vaguely, as if he were hoping to drop out of the conversation as soon as my uncle leaves him in peace. "While," he adds, "many fathers are not!"

"Yes," says my uncle.

He is well able to agree with anyone who has judgments to make about life. Any philosophy can be his, too. But he goes on at once:

"Finally, after ten years, my wife died. She'd been barren, but I thought perhaps I still had time to remedy the situation.

26

I was forty, but I remarried, and three years later my daughter was born and began to grow."

Cow Face yawns. His broad jaws gape open, and he tries to cover the sound of the yawn with words. "It's better to have children when you're younger."

"That's right," says my uncle.

Hadn't he thought just this all his life? But he was happy at forty-five to have a child who was going to grow into a beautiful girl, and he no longer thought sadly of his aproaching old age.

"Men are egotists," observes Cow Face.

My uncle does not go on right away. Egotist? It's not a word with much meaning for him. He looks attentively at the man who said it. He might be inclined to agree with him.

"Sure, we are," he says. "I was like a bridegroom with my daughter, and, as I'd always imagined, it was a happy old age. I had my supper prepared by my daughter. I had my white collars ironed by my daughter."

Cow Face begins to get interested.

"You see?" he exclaims. "Men are so egotistical that you probably wouldn't have liked it if she'd got married."

He lowers his voice toward the end of his sentence. He still has not made up his mind to stay awake for the whole trip. But my uncle's answer rouses him.

"Never," my uncle answers. "I would never have permitted it."

"You see?" he exclaims. He's roused by this answer and irritated at being roused. He clenches his hands on his knees. "By God!" He beats his fists on his broad knees. "At least you're honest!"

"Always have been," my uncle answers him.

Now he is speaking pensively; his striped scarf has slipped up again and covers his mouth, but he goes on talking without pulling it down, in a voice smothered by the wool and still gentle as, in his absorption, he himself is gentle.

"Why should she have left me?" he says. "She was so young. She was twenty-two in 1943. She could have waited until I was dead before making a new home."

He talks without looking at the man; now it's the other, the big foreman, who is looking at him.

27

"Certainly, I don't deny," he observes, "that any man would enjoy having a young daughter at his side until the end . . ."

"Who can deny it?" my uncle says to him.

"But today young people have their own ideas, too," the foreman continues, "and the first thing many men look for in a wife is a girl who has an independent attitude toward her parents."

"I don't know," says my uncle, "but in any case my daughter was quite independent in her dealings with me . . ."

Here Cow Face interrupts him. "You mean to say she's dead?" he asks point-blank.

"Oh, no," my uncle answers.

"You spoke of her as if she were no more."

"Yes," says my uncle, "for now she isn't with me."

Cow Face does not let it go with a simple explanation.

"Well," he mutters. "It was bound to happen." And he looks at my poor uncle, studies him, is at last curious about this little person.

"Disappeared," says my uncle. He does not look at his questioner now, but he himself knows that he is being looked at, that he is an object of curiosity; he is embarrassed, he lowers his eyes yet he wants it this way. He could easily have avoided telling anyone his business . . .

Or does he talk about it to see what he can find out? He certainly cannot ask after his daughter if he does not tell the story first.

"Are you looking for her now?" Cow Face asks, genuinely interested. "And you're a railroad pensioner?"

He looks my uncle up and down, studies him in detail. There is a look of satisfied amazement in his no longer sleepy eyes.

"I think you're the uncle I've heard about," he says. "Haven't you been traveling back and forth since '43 looking for your daughter? Haven't you been to Milan fifteen times since the end of the war?"

10

Now the young man who is standing against the middle window, bracing himself by holding onto the wooden railing above my uncle's head, lifts his face which had been buried in his arms.

His eyes, dark with weariness, can be seen searching about desperately in the feeble light. He sees the big man in front of my uncle and mutters; he sees my uncle and mutters. Then he buries his face in his arms again, dragging on the railing, while his body, limp with fatigue, twists against the rack into a new and therefore somehow comfortable position.

"What's the matter with him?" Cow Face asks. He is at ease now, awake and delighted to be awake, a lively traveler.

"Him?" answers my uncle. "He's been sleeping on his feet since before you got on. If he hadn't been asleep he could have taken the place where you're now sitting."

Cow Face laughs heartily, though his laughter sounds choked.

So that is how it is. A bond of confidence is sealed between him and my uncle. And with his stubby hands, he squeezes my uncle's knees through his baggy trousers. "So?" he says.

But my uncle needs no encouragement to go on talking. He is ready to repeat what he has been repeating ever since the first trips he made in November and December of '43 between Syracuse and Messina, Syracuse and Palermo, Syracuse and Salerno, Syracuse and Bari, Syracuse and Naples.

"Do you think she was kidnapped?"

"I've never considered such a thing. Why should anyone have kidnapped her?"

"I imagine she was a beautiful girl."

"She certainly was. Rather on the order of my sisters, who don't look at all like me. They're tall and full-blown. They took after our father; I'm like our mother, who was a bit like an old broomstick, and a little like the bristles, too!"

"Tall and full-blown! That's saying quite a bit. At twenty-two she could easily have caught the eye of some passing soldiers. You had the Moroccans in these parts. You had the Poles, too."

"Not in our part of the country. We only had the Americans. And in any event, my daughter wasn't the type to give people ideas like that."

"Oh, well, for soldiers it's enough to watch a girl walking from behind! If she's well upholstered, they get ideas, all right. Didn't she have something . . . underneath?"

"She had more than that to attract their attention—her eyes, for instance. And whoever looked into *them*—good-by! Even if he'd had the kind of ideas you're talking about, he would have forgotten them."

"That doesn't mean . . ."

"Yes, it does. You know something? Any man would have wanted her as I had her: as a daughter, or else as a wife or a mother, whatever you like, but not in order to mess her up. For that matter, my daughter had fingernails and knew how to use them. No one in the world would have been able to touch her if she hadn't wanted him to."

"So you think," asks Cow Face, "that she wanted to?" He sounds a little afraid, but he asks the question just the same.

"What?" my uncle exclaims.

The young man holding onto the baggage rack moves slightly again. And another sleeper stirs; a woman moves.

But the face of the standing youth is different from the one he had revealed before; it is no longer dark with a tortured need for sleep, only troubled, as if he had not been able to close his eyes since he last stirred. Nor is his body soft any longer, like that of a man hanged from a noose of sleep. It is soft in a more self-aware way. And looking down, he murmurs with greater coherence. It is a jeer coming from the obscurity of his mouth, while he leans against the rack, thrusting his head back and grasping the other railing too.

"To disappear, yes," answers Cow Face.

"Oh, of course," my uncle says. "She wasn't the kind to disappear unless she wanted to."

"So you put all the blame on your daughter?"

"I blame her for having wanted to leave me alone."

"And you don't blame her for all the rest?"

"What all-the-rest?"

"Why, everything a girl's likely to do when she runs away from home."

"What could she have done? Go first to one place, then to another . . ."

"Surely, you don't think she travels alone . . . She must certainly go *with* someone."

"It doesn't matter whether she goes about alone or with other people. I think she left with a truckload of them."

"Soldiers?"

"Soldiers."

"Then she must be with a soldier. She must go around from place to place with him. Maybe even one place with one of them and another place with another. That's how these things go."

"Sure thing, she'll go now first with one, then with another. If she doesn't like the place she happens to be, she's the kind of girl to find somebody right away who'll take her somewhere else."

"Then you know the kind of life she must be leading . . ."

"I know, I know. Not a suitable life for a girl of twenty-two."

"Twenty-five by now. She might easily have taken sick . . ."

"She was healthy and strong. But I don't deny that she might have taken sick."

"Of course. It goes without saying!" Cow Face shakes his head in commiseration. His face is quite dark by now, shaded by the overhang of hat and nose, broad lips, and chin. "You're looking for her all up and down the whole countryside! And you want to find her! What would you do with her if you did find her? What if you found her in a hospital? What would you do with her then? Would you take her home, even if she were rotten with some disease?"

My uncle, though small and thin, is not a nervous man. He never gesticulates; whatever he says, he remains quite still.

"Of course," he says. "Why shouldn't I take her home if she were sick?"

Cow Face looks at him attentively. "You're the first man I've met who'd be willing to take back a daughter with a shameful disease."

My uncle asks: "What shameful disease?"

"Those, . . ." answers Cow Face. "What would you like to call them? There are those diseases, after all, which tell the shame of every girl who goes to bed with men."

"But my daughter," says my uncle slowly, "doesn't go to bed with men."

"Ah, no?" says Cow Face. "Extraordinary!" And he looks at my uncle intently. "She runs away from home after men; she goes around the world with men, yet she doesn't go to bed with men!"

"Why should she?"

"But did she run away or didn't she?"

"She wanted to, yes."

"Isn't she running around with one after another?"

"She might like that, too. She'd be seeing the world."

"Then she must go to bed with men."

"You shouldn't talk like that," my uncle says mildly. "Do you know her? No you don't. She wasn't the kind who'd want to do that. And she's never done what she doesn't want to do."

"But," says Cow Face, "excuse me if I insist. One can learn to want something, too."

"No," says my uncle. "My daughter was against that. She didn't know anything about it, and she didn't want to."

"You must admit," says Cow Face, "that the men she found herself going around the world with knew about it and wanted to continue to know more about it."

"I admit that . . ."

"But this means they must have wanted to with her, too . . ."

"What could they have done with someone like her? They couldn't help seeing that she was an innocent baby, and then they would certainly have changed their ideas about her. And they would have lost all their taste for it, too."

My uncle, at this point, has the look of one who considers himself profoundly wise.

"Things of that sort are pleasant to do only with people who like to do them." And he draws his striped scarf that makes him look like a Bedouin up to his eyes, which have suddenly gone hard.

But the big foreman cannot agree with him.

He pays no more attention to him. The foreman looks up at the young man. He hears him murmur again and sees that now he has thrust his hands into his pockets inside his bundled-up person. And he sees that the others have woken up in that dismayed silence of those who wake up on trains. He sees the woman wake up too, the one who had turned in her sleep. As he observes them in turn, he says:

"Extraordinary! This little man has a daughter twenty-five years old who spends a little time here, a little there, in the company of men, yet he pretends to believe she doesn't go to bed with them . . ."

"Who?" shrieks the woman. But then she thinks it over, "Oh, yes, of course," she says. "Uncle Agrippa!"

11

But at the time in which a bonfire was lit among the ruins, in the beginning of July 1945, and my uncle was making his speeches on trucks or trailers exactly like the one that had been stuck for hours and hours by the roadside, no trains had started to run again out of one tunnel and into another along the side of the hill with the village on top.

When dawn had scarcely broken, Whistle and Thorn sat against a shattered wall on either side of gashes that still linked the remains of many houses, and now they were looking at the water that trickled erratically along its tortuous little bed among the stones of the niggardly stream, now they looked at the small, undamaged bridge under which the water passed, a little more swollen; now they looked at the smokened mouth of the tunnel that opened a little beyond the bridge in the early-morning mountain; and, turning back from it, their eyes cast down, they looked at the no longer shining rusted rails that, overgrown every so often by heavy thorns, still bore witness to a time of trains in history, trains running along double rails and scarcely starting to take the curve when they entered the other black mouth of that other no less early-morning mountain.

The sun was on the latter; shadow instead was cast and

33

indeed fairly gushed forth from the former, covering even the bridge and a stretch of track. Thorn, following the shadow's outline, let his eyes wander to the point where it cut the tracks.

"Look," he said.

But this was what his comrade was already doing, looking.

"Do you see anything special?"

"There's a man and a woman."

"I caught sight of them, too, a minute ago. Where are they now?"

Thorn pointed him out to Whistle.

"I see. I see."

"The woman has stretched herself out on the track."

"What's she want to prove?"

"Perhaps she wants to take her own life . . . under a train."

"She'll have to wait a fat lot to pull that off."

"But the man seems to believe it. See how he's bent over her?"

"I've got an idea the woman's leading him on."

"Sure, she's leading him on. But he's looking all around, behind and in front of him at the mouths of those two tunnels just as if he thought a train might really pop out of one of them."

"A train, or somebody else. Perhaps only somebody else . . ."

"Think he wants to make out with her right there in the middle?"

"There in the middle, or any place else. Take a look at them. He's raising her head from the tracks."

"He's trying to pull her up . . ."

"The woman wants to stay where she is and he wants her to get up."

Whistle and Thorn kept quiet a few seconds.

The fresh cry of the stream could be heard rising from the shadows below, almost unpleasant at this cold hour. Whistle and Thorn swapped glances that told each other what they were now seeing: the woman, in letting herself be pulled up, had broken away from the man's arms and was running away along the tracks; the man was following her, a second

34

after recovering from his surprise, as if he were calling her at the same time.

"Now what's she stopping for?"

"She's stopping and she's turning around. She's waiting for him."

"No. She's started to run again."

"Oh, great! When he's almost caught up with her."

"Now they're talking quietly together. I don't get any of this."

"'Bye, kids! They're going to the other side of the tracks."

"D'you know if they're any of our people?"

"Couldn't say. I don't recognize them."

"The man is the fellow with the ugly mug."

"What about the woman?"

"She's that girl who was fairly well dressed. Don't you remember her? The girl who was thirsty tonight in front of the fire, the one I gave a drink to."

"Who? Siracusa?"

"Her name's Siracusa?"

"That's what I heard Unbuttoned's wife call her."

"Where have they gone to? I don't see them any more."

"They'll have gone down the other side of the embankment. And if they don't reappear farther on down, it means they'll have stopped somewhere behind there."

12

Pushed up against the embankment, the girl struggled to hold off the young man's face so that he could not possess her mouth. But she struggled far less against him with the rest of her body, as if it did not matter to her. As far as this was concerned, she simply kept her knees together, so that the young man said to her, after a few minutes, "I told you I'd have you, and I will."

"Fat lot of good it'll do you!" the girl answered, once more fleeing his mouth.

"It would do me a lot of good . . ."

"There's more than a few who've had it."

The girl struggled, but her legs were no longer hers alone, nor did she manage to pull herself up and away from him with her abdomen as she would have wanted.

"Now I'm in," the young man said, "be a good girl."

In this position, still struggling, the girl managed to rear back with her upper body and to rain blows on the young man's face in order to repel him; meanwhile, eyes closed and lips compressed, he still sought the contact of her mouth.

"Fascist!" she yelled at him all of a sudden.

Immediately, the young man reopened his eyes.

"What?" he asked as if he doubted having heard correctly.

The girl was puzzled. She did not answer him, but then too she did not struggle any more. And he could caress her head, embrace her waist, help her fall down on the blades of dry grass.

Only now he was not so cocky. The girl saw him raise himself from her, little by little, his face deep in concentration, funereal, and kneel and raise himself again, just as Whistle and Thorn from the top of the slope saw his chest rise above the embankment, plunge behind it once more, and reappear.

"I think that fellow's forcing her," Thorn remarked.

"You mean," Whistle cried, "that perhaps she doesn't want it?"

"That's it," Thorn said, and he jumped to his feet. "I feel that she doesn't want it, and he's forcing her to it."

"Never let it be said!" Whistle yelled.

He was already running down the slope over the yellow weeds fresh with dew that covered the ground in tufts, making it all the more hazardous. Thorn ran behind him; he had taken off almost regretfully, but he was gaining on him, being the more agile and bold of the two. And Whistle kept on repeating, "Never let it be said!" once every thirty, forty, or fifty yards, thus expressing his thought that such a thing should never be allowed to take place before his eyes.

"What d'you intend to do about it?" his comrade Thorn asked him just as he was drawing alongside and passing him.

They kept on running, Whistle in the way a man of fifty runs and Thorn, although of lighter weight, in such a way as to indicate he feared having to stop soon, with a stitch in his side. They were both yelling.

"Never let it be said!" Whistle yelled.

And Thorn yelled at him not to yell in order to save his breath, if he wanted to keep on running until he reached them.

13

But it was not easy for those down there to hear them against the voice of the stream.

The girl was now seated, and busy stretching her legs straight out before her, with her hands clasping her calves. Her glance was so downcast that he could not see even a part of her face.

"Well, then," he began, "why Fascist?"

The girl raised her face, though not toward him but sideways, and only after she had let her glance stray over the entire solitary view from where she sat did she turn, brusquely, to face his eyes.

"Why?" she said to him. "Because that's the word for it. Because it's the way the Fascists would do!"

"Fascists would do what? Just because you attract me and I want you?"

The young man almost laughed as he said this, but with too much effort and too bitterly.

"It's nothing to laugh about," the girl said, simply. She was still puzzled by the way he had reacted to the word. And she added, "You can't expect a person to stay with it who doesn't want it."

And here it seemed she wanted to finish the conversation, get up, and start walking . . . She even stretched out a hand for him to pull her up. But he did not take it.

"Is this being Fascist?"

"Oh, let's not keep it up."

"No, no," said the young man. "I'm interested. Can't we talk about it a minute longer?"

"All right. It's certainly this too."

"This too?"

He was deeply serious, and there was even an element of fear in his voice, although the smile behind which he seemed to be hiding—perhaps only out of long habit—gave his repetition a mocking tone . . . But Whistle and Thorn were already upon them.

The young people heard them, thanks to the stones they kicked up along the tracks, and then they saw their faces full of hostility, saw that they had been running.

No one on either side said a word. The young man stretched out his hand to the girl and she took it, both of them then climbing up to where the two men had stopped between the tracks, Whistle with one foot on a rail, Thorn immediately behind him.

"Do you need anything?" Whistle finally asked.

"Nothing," the girl answered. And she looked at them, then turned to look at the young man.

"Didn't you scream?" Whistle went on.

"No," the girl answered. Yet she hesitated, looked once more at the young man, and added, "No, truly not. I don't believe . . ."

Whistle started to wipe the sweat from his face. "We made a mistake," he said to Thorn.

He turned then to the young man, just to look him over, and they all three found themselves looking at him at once, Whistle, Thorn, and the girl, as if there were something they shared in which the young man as yet had no part. He seemed emotionally excited. He was radiant, in his dry way, just as before he had seemed funereal, behind the same mocking smile. Was it all because of the girl's answer?

"You're lucky," Whistle concluded. And he made a vague gesture with his hand.

"Not till now," the young man said. "But if I can stay with you . . ." He broke off, as if he had thought better of it. Then, just the same, he took up the idea anew. "I mean, with your group."

38

But Whistle did not seem to think that there was such a group. He looked sidelong at Thorn, asking with his eyes if it really existed.

"Aren't you stopping here in the village?" the young man kept on.

"It hasn't been decided yet," Whistle replied. "But it hasn't been excluded yet, either." And his eyes that had been glancing sideways at Thorn now looked up toward the village, encircled by its desert morning.

14

Then there was an explosion that seemed to take place high up in the vault of the sky. It interrupted even the sound of the stream.

"I think there's been a rockfall," Thorn murmured.

"In the village?" the girl asked.

Whistle did not answer them. He remained on the alert, as if he heard or was waiting to hear something else, and did not take his eyes from the face of the young girl, who appeared the most shocked.

"As for me," he said finally, "I think it was some kind of mine."

He saw the young man, who was looking at him, nod his head vaguely.

"A mine?" Thorn exclaimed. "You mean they're blasting rock? Or are they working at a stretch of road?" he added.

"But it seemed right behind the village," the girl put in.

"That's just where it was: right behind the village," the young man said.

"D'you think that one of ours could have walked on it?" Whistle asked him.

"Oh!" said Thorn, "do you mean that kind of mine . . ."

"Yes, that kind of mine," the young man replied. "And this whole place may be full of them. Let's go back. Let's go back."

39

They all went, with their eyes raised to the slope which might be full of mines. Whistle and Thorn had just made it at a run. They climbed back up with their eyes on the houses above, and Thorn closed his for a moment.

Then the young man moved outside the track.

"I'll go ahead," said Whistle. "It's better if we return the same way we came."

"Or by our route," the young man said.

He took the lead, with Thorn third and the girl last, as if a heavy thought were weighing down her knees.

"A little faster," the young man called back to her, turning around and adding to Whistle: "I know something about mine detection. We should hurry."

He started ahead once more, then once more looked back and saw that the girl had caught up with Thorn and was walking abreast of him. "No," he said, "single file's best, and only walk where I have already passed . . . And leave a little distance between you."

15

When day begins to break on a train it is unlikely that many people can go on sleeping, at least in third class.

They look outside; those beside the windows see things, bushes, stones; and those inside, far from the glass, see on it no more than a white hand as the opaque light of the little bulb overhead flickers out in its old age.

The compartment in which my uncle is seated (he is as stunned now as all the others, with his little round eyes open wider than ever on the great whiteness outside the windows) is divided into four quarters with places in each quarter for four passengers, but there are almost twice as many people, not counting those seated on their suitcases, who block the passageway.

My uncle is not looking at the little windows in his quarter but, for a while now, he has been looking at those of the quarter opposite, immediately across the aisle, since they show more light and the light is turning from white to blue. A voice reaches him from the fringe of that light.

"Mines!" it says.

Who is it?

Uncle Agrippa finds whoever it is just as he saw him yesterday, a man who was listening from over there, his face, with eyeglasses, leaning on his hand, as Uncle told his story and that of his daughter, and every so often, raising his head a bit, he would utter a comment to his still young wife seated facing him, in the manner of a man given more to reading than speaking.

"Mines!" he read now.

He must have read it just now, outside the window, on some wooden sign planted at the foot of some slope. In the livid reverberations that precede the dawn, "Mines" is the name we give our desert today as we pass it by on the train.

"Mines?" his wife asks him.

The face of the man with glasses is outlined in a glow against the windowpane, and he lowers his head with that meek expression of the so-called educated.

"You can see for yourself," he tells her. And he turns his face toward the outside, he points outside. "There's another sign there on which it's written. Just look there. It looks like a cross."

"But what does it mean?" his wife asks. "That there really are mines around?"

The man beside her would like to join in; he has such high shoulders that he half conceals her; his face and hands are those of a rough fellow, but he has been polite to her every time they have spoken. He nods his head. They do not see it. Then he raises a hand, and the thumbnail is entirely black. "Ma'am," he says. "Yes, there are. And there are even more without signs than with signs."

The husband with the glasses opens his mouth. He began to look at the man as soon as he spoke, and he smiles at him now as if to wish him good day; in fact, he almost bows to him. But, now that his mouth is open, he says: "The sign means it's a mined zone."

"That it is, Professor," Black Nail answers. "All along the

41

line. Yet the signs are posted only here and there. Why's that?" He raises his hand with the black thumbnail, then cuts the air with it down to his knee. "You said one of them looked like a cross, didn't you? Yes, you did. And a sign is a cross!"

A boy is seated beside the professor, and beside the boy a woman who is surely his mother, with an old handbag on her lap and the neck of a bottle sticking out of it. They woke up just in time to hear that a sign is a cross, and they stare at the man who said it, their expressions half offended, half stunned. They have come to after their sleep, but not so much as a hair has moved. Nothing has changed from when they were asleep except their wide-open eyes.

Instead, a fellow from the passageway who has perched on the arm of the seat next to the woman agrees heartily with Black Nail's simple words. Nor is this the first time my uncle has run into him on this line. He has sat across from him and been able to observe him, he has spoken with him and knows that he carries a folding double yardstick in the back pocket of his pants. He must be a road- or bridge-builder's assistant. He has heard his friends call him Carlo, and remembers that his sunburned forehead was bald when he saw it under the hat that he often pushes back when it is very hot, but never takes off.

He whispers a brief answer to someone who has spoken to him, standing behind him with his fist closed tight around the slender iron column that rises from the stanchion of the seat-back. As he answers him, he lights a cigarette; then, holding the still lighted match, he makes a gesture as he tosses the match to the floor, as if to say he doesn't want to be bothered or something of the kind.

Then he listens again to Black Nail's conversation.

". . . The marker," Black Nail is saying, "is placed where someone was blown up."

The professor's wife exclaims, "Dear God, couldn't they have put it up sooner?"

Black Nail is patient with her: she is so tiny and a woman.

"Ma'am," he says, "where a man's been blown up there's sure to have been a mine, and that means there are others around the same spot. That's why they put up a sign. But they can't know if there are mines where no one has passed and nobody's been blown up."

He lets his eyes light on the man he calls Professor, passes them over the boy and his mother, noting that they are not batting an eyelash, and raises them to Bald Carlo.

"Right?" he asks him.

Carlo the Bald nods vigorously. But his spoken reply is not exactly an assent.

"Completely right, no," he says.

"Why not?" asks Black Nail.

16

Outside, the blue light is now warmed with yellow and rose. It is the subterranean march of the sun as it draws near the surface of the foothills, returning to them from distant lands, and a cockcrow is in the air, even here in the midst of the desert of mines.

The train slows down, a red streak spans the sky in the direction toward which we are going. It is like a long stop sign suspended above the solitary curve of the horizon, just hovering over the still dark earth. And the train stops without so much as a whistle.

Where are we?

A window is lowered but we can see nothing; there is no station. From the opposite side of the car another window is lowered, and from there too one can see only the long profile of the train with windows lowered like mine and people staring out as I too am staring.

Yet one stays in this position, standing with his face staring out, looking at that long red streak and the dark earth beneath it that, little by little, is growing lighter and revealing its wounds.

The professor too is on his feet, his face turned to the freshness of the open world. His wife tugs at his sleeve.

43

What? He leans down, returns to his seat but leaves the window open. The air is not cold; he finds Black Nail gaping at him.

He picks up his conversation: "Here, for example." Carlo the Bald nods assent.

"Here?"

"Here, by God! Here and farther along."

The professor's wife asks: "But why don't they take them out?"

Her question makes several people stare at her. Even from the other side of the seat facing her a face pops up with a broad grin on it, gives her one long look and disappears. Then a farmer who is seated in the passageway on a sort of foot locker beside the rough-spoken fellow exclaims: "Easier said than done."

So once more Black Nail comes to her rescue.

"Look, Missus, we've been fighting mines for over a year now, from here to La Spezia and as far as the shores of the Adriatic. You're right to ask why they aren't taken out. But who's to do it? The Allies have little mine detectors that can do the job without any danger. But they didn't do it, it's not their job, and they didn't have their German prisoners do it either. What's more, they didn't give our government any of those little contraptions so that they could do the job . . ."

Carlo the Bald, who has been in agreement until now, interrupts him. "They don't have any to spare."

Black Nail stops with his hand halfway through his usual gesture.

"What I mean to say is," Carlo the Bald goes on, "those contraptions are delicately made and they have very few of them."

Black Nail concludes his sweeping gesture. "That's why," he picks up, "the government is helpless. So who's to do the job? If mine detectors aren't available, perhaps farm animals would do: sheep, pigs, cattle, horses that a farmer could drive ahead of him . . . Do we have them? I wouldn't say we had any farm animals to throw away. They too are delicately made."

44

"Heh! Heh!" the farmer chuckles, a bit behind him.

Carlo the Bald nods vigorously and grunts assent.

"For God's sake, let me finish!" Black Nail says. Then he continues for the exclusive benefit of the professor and his wife, turning as directly toward them as possible.

"I know something about mines because mines are part of my business," he tells them. "I have mines on my land, land where I used to know every crop from alfalfa to wheat, from feed corn to potatoes. I knew them all and so of course I have to know what my land has for a crop now. It has mines. The job is left up to the farmer; it's his job to take the mines out of his land if he ever wants to work it again. Here beside me there's a farmer. Hey, farmer!" The farmer gets on his feet.

"Do you want to go back to farm work?"

The farmer wants to, and he will challenge the mines. There's a way out for everything in this world. For example, you can take a long piece of iron, sharpen a point on it, and shape it so that it will penetrate into the earth without pressure and, armed with this, you can go over your field yard by yard.

"Have you done that yet, farmer?"

The farmer has done it. You can do all right with a foil, if you can find one. The blade of a foil whips into an arc at the least resistance. Instead, a piece of iron stays straight and that's why it's more dangerous.

In either case, if the point meets resistance or scratches something, it may be a mine. You dig around it with your hands and sometimes it's only a stone. But at other times it's a mine, all right.

The professor's wife says, "There, I told you so!"

"There!" Black Nail says. "The farmer has tested the ground step by step, he has felt it, he has dug into it, he has found resistance, once more he has felt it, once more he has dug into it, and now he has found the obstacle and it's a mine, and we say: There! Do you know how a mine is made?"

Carlo the Bald throws in, "There are several different types."

45

"Even our friend the farmer here," says Black Nail, "knows that there are different types. What do you say, farmer?" he asks, turning to him.

The farmer is quick on the uptake.

"How many types of mines are there?"

There are Italian mines and there are German mines. There are antiman mines and antitank mines. There are those that look like turtles. There are those that look like spider webs. Black Nail, his hand raised like a cleaver, suggests taking notes on the different types.

"The mines that are like spider webs can't be dug out. You find them usually along the banks of streams or among thorns or nettles and they have long slender lead lines that lead in to the main charge of explosives. The first to walk into one of those threads—good-by! The charge goes off and so does he. Yet they're the easiest to get rid of when you're clearing ground."

"Oh, yes!" The young boy interrupts.

The young boy?

Black Nail turns his eyes toward him. "Let's hear what you have to say about it."

But the boy has fallen back into his former attitude, looking at the man without batting an eyelash, and has once more buried deep inside any possibility he had of saying anything. Will his mother speak for him?

Standing above her, Carlo the Bald is smoking. Black Nail waits.

"We set fire to them," the woman says finally.

"That's right," Black Nail says. "If there is dried grass anywhere around, set it on fire. Fire destroys the thin lead lines as it passes, and little charges go off at various spots all at once, raising earth and gravel. True, farmer?"

But he wants the farmer to explain what the common, Italian, antiman mine is like.

"They're like little iron strongboxes. Rusty iron, at that. Three times as long as they are wide. And the tops aren't always closed tight. Sometimes tight, sometimes not so tight. And how do you go about picking them up? There's a little

46

lever inside that you can feel. You have to switch it off. Then you can detonate it later . . ."

Black Nail stops the farmer. There's more to say at this point and he himself wants to say it.

"You see," he says, "when the farmer has found a mine, he knows that to the left or right at approximately the same distance there will be two more. So he goes after the other two . . . Do you know this, too?" he asks the boy. He had been looking at him casually and had watched his eyes flicker with attention, but he cannot get out of him so much as the batting of an eyelash. "One mine alone," he continues, "doesn't mean a thing. It's when you've got all three that it means something. But let's go on with it."

The farmer has tramped the length and breadth of his field; he is sure of himself and leads out his cow; he hitches her up to the plow and lets his whip whistle over her head.

The plow digs into the earth which for two years has not been turned over. Perhaps he should have used a pickax. But the plow shatters, and *It* is revealed. What had shattered the plow is an antitank mine.

It's a mine? It's a mine of the heaviest type, hidden deep down in the earth.

"And right where the farmer had tested his land," Black Nail says, "they put up a sign that says *Mines*. All his work was in vain. The farmer died all in vain. See what I mean, Professor?" He looks from Carlo the Bald to the professor.

"A fellow comes along with a cigarette hanging out of his mouth, a surveyor's yardstick in his pocket, and where that old cow died in vain, he plants his sign: *Mines*."

The farmer who is beside him in the passageway sits down again on his sort of foot locker. He turns his back and his neck away from the man beside him and leans against the armrest. He is close enough to feel the movement against his head when Black Nail raises or lowers his hand. Meanwhile, he repeats: "Easier said than done!"

"And what's it all for?" Black Nail goes on. "A farmer can go over his field with a fine-tooth comb so long as he doesn't see any signs posted. But once he reaches a signpost with

47

that warning on it, he stops and makes the sign of the cross. So we've got a fine solution: he turns his back on it and goes back to the farmhouse, where he's dying of hunger. Not even a dog shows up where those signs are to be seen. See what I mean, Professor?"

"It seems perfectly understandable to me."

"The land that has one of those signs on it has been cursed. It's like having a cross growing out of it. And there's no point in talking about the crops, no point in talking about the wheat . . ."

Outside, very slowly, the deserted fields glide by.

For the last few minutes we have been moving again though there was no whistle, at least none that we heard. But we are moving, very slowly, with the wheels grinding.

"You see! All those fields are cursed. No one will ever set foot on them . . ."

Black Nail looks up at Carlo the Bald.

"Would you deny it? He would like to deny it, and yet no one has set foot on them. Just because of the signs . . ."

He points to a sign out the window.

"Wouldn't it be better if they never put up the signs? Those men with their yardsticks, there's just one thing they ought to do."

The train is picking up speed. The professor feels a cold wind, it is still early in the morning and he pulls his window back up. But he stops where he is standing, his back to the glass; nor does he bother to ask what it is the surveyors ought to do. The sun has begun to rise.

"What, then?" Black Nail asks. And he supplies the answer himself: "They should go rip them all up."

17

There is the sound of muttered comment in the compartment. Rip them all out! Rip out the mines? Rip out the signs!

Then the weak voice of the professor's wife expresses the

48

surprise they have all felt, while her husband looks at her wide-eyed. "But if they rip out the signs," she says, "anybody out for a stroll could be blown up by a mine."

"So what?" Black Nail replies.

The muttering increases in the compartment. A few faces poke up only to be withdrawn over the backs of seats. Almost every traveler shakes his head, a few of them nodding sadly. And Carlo the Bald, looking down from on high, has a thin sharp smile on his lips.

"No?" says Black Nail, looking about him. He looks at every face within the range of his eyes and little by little he turns red from the rage shut up inside him. He is boiling, seething, infuriated. Finally he looks at the face of Carlo the Bald, who is now smoking. And, raising his hand one last time, he says brusquely:

"Well, I'd better not say anything more on that subject."

Then he points the finger of his raised hand at Carlo the Bald. It is a challenge and a threat to all of them. "Let him speak," he concludes.

"Me?" Carlo the Bald asks.

He has one eye half closed against the smoke of the cigarette that he has left dangling from his lips. Is he still smiling? He may be smiling, or it may be that strange grimace of the half-shut eye which gives his face the appearance of a smile. Or he may really be smiling and the grimace tries to conceal it.

In any case, he says he doesn't have much to say. Now there's just one point he would like to make about clearing the fields of mines, which is not always as difficult and tragic as the gentleman makes out, but is sometimes quite easy, almost like a game, if one guesses the pattern or scheme by which the field was mined.

"What do you mean, pattern?" they ask him.

Carlo the Bald recalls what Black Nail said about mines going in threes. In taking out mines we have to bear in mind the motions of those who put them there, we have to think that while they were placing the mines they had to keep moving back and forth across the terrain where they had placed them, we have to think that they were soldiers and that soldiers move in groups as in a parade, with music in their heads.

49

The triple mine pattern means that soldiers placed the mines moving in groups of three. Don't they line up in threes to march? Well it's just the same when they go in threes to place mines.

First movement. The officer blows a whistle and a group of three executes its first movement. Second movement. Another blow of the whistle and, after so and so many steps, the three turn to the right or the left and execute the second movement.

It's a sort of ballet that could have its own music. And in order to keep in mind where the mines are placed, all the officer has to do is to note down two or three figures. With those two or three figures he can reconstruct the mathematical equivalent of any pattern.

In removing mines, wherever a mine has exploded, no special care need be taken except to locate the other two mines of the triad and to reach the point of the second triad. Once that has been done, it's as if you had the pattern that was in the hands of the officer: you measure the distance and position of the individual mines in a given triad in relation to each other, and then you measure the distance and position of the two triads in relation to each other.

"Then it's simple, is it?"

Carlo the Bald is interrupted and tosses away his butt.

"Certainly under these circumstances it's simple. It becomes a mechanical job."

The only thing is, he adds, the grimace now wiped off his face, that you have to have a point of departure from a single mine; and he adds that a place may have been mined for several purposes at the same time: it may have antiman mines, mines against light artillery, mines against the heavy pieces, and so on; or it can be mined with a border in a different pattern from that of the main design.

"However," he says, "if there's a man among them who's had experience of war, they can nearly always work it out . . ."

"Among whom?" someone asks.

My uncle is whispering in one of his neighbor's ears. His striped scarf is no longer around his neck but spread over his shoulders. He is speaking quietly but excitedly and he

50

has papers in his hands, even some photographs of his daughter at various ages.

Carlo the Bald answers the question: "Among those who clear the ground of mines! There are people who are going back to their villages here and there, and of course it's natural for them to clear the fields of mines first thing. The Allies didn't do it, the government can't do it, so the people have to do it for themselves, and if they have one among them who's actually been in the war, they'll make out . . ."

For a moment, my uncle has not been murmuring in his neighbor's ear. He has been listening to Carlo the Bald. And Carlo has got up from the arm of the seat.

"You see those heights up there?" he says.

He points out the window. "They're completely free of mines now . . . Women, old men, and children did it."

Black Nail slaps his thigh with one large hand; it is as if air were exploding between the hand and the thigh. And my uncle starts once more to mutter in the ear of his neighbor.

18

The train from which Carlo the Bald had pointed out the heights ran along at the foot of the village, coming out of one tunnel only to enter the other at five in the morning.

But I have an idea that the exact time when Carlo the Bald pointed to those heights was either earlier or later; at that moment we were not coming out of a tunnel nor were we entering another; and it may be that the heights he pointed out were not those on whose slope the village perches; or they might be the same but seen from another lonely angle, either farther north or farther south.

From the village you can see only one of these two heights, the southernmost from the village itself, after four or five ridges, which are in fact hills to be climbed, bare of any vegetation. They are called the "Solchi di Sacco," perhaps in earlier times Isaac's Tracks, since they run like furrows, parallel to one another, until they are lost to view. And it is beyond the last ridge that you become aware of the spot I am talking of: the train goes by in the open for quite a stretch, not like the brief span between the two tunnels; or you may see the rails gleam like shafts of light on a very bright, sunny day.

The northernmost height, on the other hand, is on the far side of that heap of dry, sun-bleached stone the village folk consider "their" hill, exposed for its full length to the point where, on the night of the fire, our people found a tree, the first tree they had found in the entire area although they had looked all day; a grand old one, with thick, dark foliage. It was of the oak family, a hardwood tree. Alone in the village, at its outer rim, and alone for miles and miles around, it looked more proud and almost more sacred than the Romanesque entrance to the church nearby. It was more imbued than the church with hopes, vows, projects, whispered at its feet for centuries of afternoons; with speechmaking, rituals, races, banquets, bands, hangings that took place in its great jagged shadows, which, after the noon hour, reached even the long, low wall on which men who had come back from their day's work sat or leaned, turning their backs to the pebbly stream-bed and the water below.

Now women, too, were coming back from work or were passing to and fro because of work, with wheelbarrows and pails, with baskets full of bricks, and it was at the foot of the great tree that they met, pausing there to give each other a last word.

Unkempt, with bare legs and feet, her breasts covered only with the fabric of her blouse, her skirt-band cinched in at her waist, drenched with the sweat from her armpits, one of the women who had stayed to mind the children on the truck the day it was stuck on the highway came out of one of the side streets in which demolition was going on and crossed the patch of sun to the tree, carrying her basket of bricks on a scrap of sacking that protected her naked shoulder. She passed the sawhorse at which a man and a boy were sawing old boards. The sound of the saw did not rise from the sawhorse; it was part of the sun and the tree. Nor did the woman look at what the man and the boy were doing.

The man said to her: "You women of Messina!"

The woman would not have heard him if he had not pronounced the name of the once-more destroyed city from which she and two other women friends had come with a little boy six years old and the infant to which she had given birth along the road. But when she heard the familiar name of Messina, she wheeled around.

"What'd you say?" she asked him.

Meanwhile, she had reached the pile of bricks where the oldest of the friends who had come up with her sat on the ground with her little boy, scraping the old mortar off the bricks. She put her basket down with care, and carefully tipped out its contents near to the big pile. Then she stood up straight, turning to the man.

"What'd you say, Cerro?" she asked him once more.

"I wanted to say you're used to it," he answered. His face was laughing; he wore a sweatshirt yellow with age, his skin was bronzed, and he thrust the other end of the saw toward the boy (who was laughing too) so that they could go on sawing.

"But what did you say about Messina?"

"I said, you women of Messina . . ."

"What have you got to say about the women of Messina?"

"I told you. Just that you're used to it."

"Used to what?"

"I told Carmela there the same thing. Used to what you're doing."

From her place on the ground among the bricks, Carmela raised her hand and shook it. It was true: he had something against the women of Messina.

"And what do we do?"

"You load and unload. You make bricks . . . With us, before the war, only men did these things. Now women do them too. But you women of Messina, you're used to it."

"We're used to it, are we?"

"You women of Messina always did it."

"We women of Messina stay at home . . ."

"But first you make your houses. And you go about unkempt. You load. You unload . . ."

53

"We do? In Messina? Whoever told you that?"

The man named Cerro guided the long saw over another board.

"Isn't it true that every so often in Messina there isn't a house standing!"

"That's because of the earthquake, every so often."

"The earthquake every so often. And every so often a war . . ."

"Now it's one thing, and then it's another."

"And so, every so often, you have to start from scratch, and you women, you work right along. You load. You unload . . . That's why I say you're used to what you're doing."

19

The unkempt woman dropped her basket and kneeled down to help with the bricks.

"To me, personally, it never happened in Messina."

"But even the song says so."

The unkempt woman sat down on the ground. Now she too was scraping bricks. But she didn't know any song that said anything like that. How did it go?

Cerro was not sure he knew the song, word for word. But he began with an *Alas!*—that much he remembered, and *'twas a great pity*, he said, *the women of Messina* . . .

So it *was* about Messina! And did Cerro know the rest? What else did it say?

It said *they were unkempt*.

The women of Messina?

And that to see them, *'twas a great pity*.

To see them unkempt?

And carrying stones and mortar, oh!

The two women's faces were grave, their voices grieving, and they said "Messina, Messina," and they said that right now the song should have said *bricks and mortar, oh!*

They looked at each other and nodded to each other.

It was a good song.

They looked at Cerro too, telling him with their eyes how good they found his song, then once more they picked up bricks in their hands and repeated the words of the song in hushed tones.

"Indeed it's a pity," they said.

"We're ruining our hands."

"And what about our shoulders, with the basket?"

"Doesn't it ruin the chest, too? What about the breasts?"

"And the sun burns us black as Negro women."

"It's the rain that really does us in."

Then they looked beyond the low wall to the heights, reddened by the sun and with a whitening pattern of thorns; and they followed up the seam made across the heights by the cleft of the road; a curve in the road; another curve in the road; and they said they didn't know why they had stopped at this place full of rubble, right out in the middle of the desert.

"Whatever for, when there are roads?"

"And trucks that make it over those roads!"

"And cities where the roads are going!"

"Cities with trolley cars, with sidewalks!"

"Where women stay at home!"

"And when they go out, they are well dressed."

"Not like here, all unkempt."

"Not like us from Messina!"

"Not with baskets of bricks."

"Not with pails of mortar."

They took up the bricks, picking them over with their fingers, but with their eyes fixed on the road over there with its recollection of trucks, while behind them the sad squeak of the wheelbarrow came to mingle with the other sounds.

Why had they stopped here? Why right here had they stopped? Here where there was only rubble? Here in this Messina?

And they looked toward the recollection of their trips by truck on the eternal road, traveling and sitting in the sun, traveling and sitting in the dark after a sunny day, in order to arrive one morning, one evening, one night a little before morning, in the very city one wanted to reach, and there

55

to try to be just what one wanted to be, a woman who lives in a house and goes out well dressed, or even an unkempt woman without a house to live in, who goes about all down at the heel, or even works as a servant in the public mess halls, and washes dishes, and scrubs floors . . .

Now Cerro was whistling. Was he whistling the tune of his song? They tried to hum singsong the tune he was whistling. And thus, singsong, they repeated the words of the song, Messina and unkempt, mortar and down at the heel, with the motif of the saw added now to that of the wheel-barrow.

"Indeed it's a pity," they said.

But wasn't the road right over there? They could see it. They could even get up and go where it was and make signs to passing trucks until one of them stopped.

"We won't stay here for the rest of our lives."

Carmela's little boy was running back and forth, carrying the bricks the women had cleaned.

"We have legs."

"We have our own two feet."

And the little boy repeated their singsong as he ran back and forth on his little feet, just as he had done on the floor of the truck a couple of weeks ago, except for the fact that the floor of the truck was wood and now his steps were muffled by soft dust laced with shade and sun . . .

20

At one far end of the long public square there was the single-arched bridge that old Barbèra had told Whistle was still intact that day the truck was stuck. The water beneath the bridge ran between two locks, a thin stream now, because of the long drought, threading its way into the black mouth of what had once been a mill and was now the "big building busted wide open" that Barbèra had also pointed out. Suddenly from over there a door slammed, a door that could not be seen, and out came an impetuous whistle, hard and shrill, such as no one but he could give, so that he had been called "Friend Whistle" ever since that day on the truck and, for a little while now, "Our Mayor," "Mayor," "Mister Mayor." This was a general designation that came to be accepted not because Whistle was more capable than the others nor because he was older, but because of a tendency he had, from the very first day, to support or negate, tolerate or disapprove everything that happened or was decided in this village of rubble—the whole of it weighed according to his own simple yet very positive moral standards.

He came out into the sunlight, his head tilted a little to one side under his old straw hat and a white tail end of handkerchief sticking out between hat and nape of neck. They all saw him coming after having heard him, and Cerro made a sign with his chin in the direction of the bridge where he had stopped for a moment to glance down at the water.

"So what's doing?" he called.

From the far end of the square Whistle raised the jacket he held in his hand and shook it.

"It looks good."

"Does it work?"

"It can work."

"But you didn't try to see if it does work."

"Christ! I found out that it *can* work."

Whistle had stopped beside the tree by now and, turning toward the spot where you could see the roof of the mill, he nodded.

"Tell us more."

From behind where Whistle stood, his friend Thorn, the man with the Gypsy face, came up pushing a wheelbarrow. He was crossing the bridge, in fact he had just crossed it and Whistle was nodding to him. They wanted him to tell them more? Instead, he started simply to enumerate the things Thorn had in his wheelbarrow. Nails, hinges, T-squares, heads of hoes, spigots, pliers, hammers, all sorts of scrap that he had salvaged from the heaps of rubble.

"Does he have your motor in his wheelbarrow, too?" Cerro asked.

Whistle cocked his head toward Thorn and repeated: "He wants to know if you're bringing the motor . . ."

Thorn guffawed for them all and went on pushing his squeaking wheelbarrow, without irritation or malice. Whistle now wanted to take the place of the boy who had been helping Cerro at the saw. He sent him off, tossing him his own jacket to catch. At last he said to Cerro:

"It's a water-driven motor that can, in its turn, propel any of the abandoned tanks around us. And if you don't hear it now, it's because the water trickles into it too slowly."

"You sure?" Cerro asked.

Thorn had come up to them and overturned his wheelbarrow.

"He's not sure," Whistle told him.

"Let's take him to look it over and then he'll be sure," Thorn said.

He shook out the barrow over the pile of rusty iron. He had raised a little dust, and other people were coming into view, moving from the demolished area they were working on toward the tree: an old man and a boy who sat on the low wall, women with baskets from which they unloaded bricks, and last of all Unbuttoned's wife dressed in a straw-colored slip tucked into an old pair of trousers belonging to her little husband.

"Well," Cerro asked, "is it only because of the drought? Only something that happens with the seasons?"

"And something that can be fixed. If we dig for mines we can dig for water."

Cerro's gaze was thoughtful, wide-eyed, and laughing as his mind dwelt on thoughts he had never harbored before. He looked at Whistle, Thorn, the wheelbarrow and, still preoccupied, he went over to the pile of scrap iron collected on the ground.

"A drill," he said to Thorn.

Thorn picked out a hand drill with its handle all eaten away and handed it to him. But Cerro was still preoccupied as he turned it around in his hands.

58

"D'you know what this means?" he asked Whistle.

"Depends on the strength it can generate."

At last Cerro smiled at the hand drill, like a happy child.

"And do *you* know what it means?" Whistle asked in turn. His voice rose. "It means that I can set up a forge in that cave! That I can fan a furnace! That I can set up a foundry!"

"And give me enough current for a sawmill?"

"And give you the current for a sawmill!"

"At least enough for a circular saw."

"And electric lights at night!"

The women listened, no longer scraping their bricks.

"Can these things really be done?" Unkempt asked.

Unbuttoned's wife, standing beside her, had dust all over her face and hair straggling into her eyes; she shook it back now, pushing it off her brow with the back of her hand, and said that she would be glad just to get on with the job at hand.

She stretched her arms above her head and looked at Whistle, then at Cerro, then at Thorn. She asked them if they didn't think it best not to look ahead to any other project until they had finished the work on the church.

21

Now they were building there . . . It had been a very big church with two rows of columns dividing it into three naves, with high windows now glassless, and the big rose window of the facade without glass, the apse destroyed, the altar destroyed, the cupola smashed, but the roof and the rest of it showing no damage, not even peeled plaster, above the three naves. That is what a certain *Register* kept by an anonymous person who certainly knew something about registries said, a register this person began to keep from the arrival of the new settlers, in old notebooks, found in what had been the Town Hall:

July 2, 1945—The church was cut in two: completely destroyed at one end, and the other in perfect condition.

They had used it from the beginning to sleep in. Didn't the soldiers use churches to sleep in during the war? They slept there, on old straw they had dislodged from under the rubble of a hayloft, in little groups that were disposed along the side aisles, each group setting itself off from the others, with the church benches placed in such a way that the pillars on either side were linked to the walls in so many parallel lines. The *Register* for July 3, 1945, says:

> *We need straw, covers of some kind to protect us a bit better. We plan to divide the naves into smaller areas with the benches . . .*

One does things like this to cope with immediate necessities, always in haste, always hastily, always in such a way that things could and should be better, but sometimes everything we do continues in the same awkward way, through endless transformations, while at other times, instead, it fits into the circumstances, and is rational and efficient.

That half church, with its white ceiling and the fire lit where the choir stalls used to be, was propitious to the settlers when they stopped between one heap of abandoned rubble and another. It was even better when, having found straw the second night, they started on the third day to raise the brick walls at the head of the naves, and on the fourth, when the walls had risen higher and they started to clear debris from the ruined apse, to plant a line of uprights across the mouth of the central nave, then to raise brick partitions where they had lined up the long church benches between the pillars and the lateral walls. The *Register* for July 14 says:

> *Today, finished four more partitions. They don't reach the ceiling. We are thinking of raising other partitions, facing these, with entrances, and then of covering them with wooden roofs that can open and shut like windows . . .*

And so holy church was good to keep them and to hold them together after the first one of them had been killed by a mine. And it was even better now that they were working to complete two rows of rooms, with wooden doors, windows and roofs, lining the two side aisles; better, in that it obliged them to seek elsewhere for services, for places to cook, eat, wash up, and so on. Good also, because it started them on a new way of life between one communal need and another, rather than between one man and another. This could become a better sort of life than the usual one, a more comfortable sort of life. Who knows how good the half church would be, even for later generations to which our children would transmit this way of life, these other ways of doing things that we found good enough to continue and so transform our customs in their antiquity, in their old age. Later, the *Register* says:

We have two rows of little houses inside this big house.

But it could not say so yet, and perhaps Unbuttoned's wife was just impatient for the day to come in which it could say so. She was the one who had said she did not like to walk, and yet she had walked. She always said she did not like to work, and yet she carried bricks back and forth. Or she said she enjoyed stretching out full length on the ground to rest, and yet she stood up even to gossip.

"Wouldn't we save time," she was saying now, "if we unloaded the bricks right in front of the church?"

22

But just then someone called to her.
"Giralda!"

And someone else called to her, too.

"Hello, Giralda!"

Toma and Red Kerchief were moving along the low wall, hot from walking, but their voices came from fresh mouths, and each carried an empty oil can; Toma had a strap they could use later on, when the cans were full, to carry the cans over their shoulders.

Giralda went to meet Toma.

"Hungry already?"

"And thirsty," Toma replied.

He had a voice that could speak both high and low. Red Kerchief, instead, used his voice as if he were on top of a hill, and now he yelled at Toma to get the water while he went to take care of the soup.

"That way I'll leave him with you a minute," he yelled at Giralda.

"What for?"

Red Kerchief winked at her. "To ask him for news of your husband."

Then he started off across the white dust of the square toward the area still in ruins, fearless once more in the sunlight.

"Oh," Giralda said, "I imagine he's still alive."

Cerro, meanwhile, from his place beside the saw, was asking the departing Red Kerchief for news of the mines.

How many mines today? But what did counting them matter, what did knowing the number and saying it matter, so many and so many? What did it matter hearing how many and how many? They had all worked at mine sweeping those first days, at least for a few hours a day, and they all had before their eyes the way their "engineer" had said firmly "There, there, and there," as he threw out three pebbles.

"I don't know how you put up with working with Ugly Mug," Giralda said.

No one answered Cerro's question; Red Kerchief was already out of sight, and Toma stood speaking to Giralda, a little apart from the rest.

"Why shouldn't I get on working with him?"

"If I were in your shoes, I couldn't stand it."

"If you were in my shoes you might change your mind about him."

"Not in your shoes."

"Yes, you'd be with him all day and you'd learn to respect him."

"Not in your shoes."

"If there's the least danger, he's always the one to go first."

"That wouldn't matter, or very little, if I were in your shoes. I'd never forgive him for what he did to you."

"I have nothing to forgive since he's done nothing to me."

"Ugly Mug's done nothing to you?"

"Stop saying the same thing, Giralda. You know only too well that he's done nothing to me."

"Ugly Mug didn't take your girl?"

"You know only too well he didn't take any girl of mine."

"He didn't take Siracusa? Don't tell me you weren't chasing Siracusa, and Ugly Mug took her away from you."

"I've told you a hundred times, Giralda. I wasn't chasing her because I was seriously interested . . . And anyway she was perfectly free to go with whomever she liked best. Should I bear Ugly Mug a grudge because she liked him better than me?"

"So you don't hold a grudge against Ugly Mug?"

"Certainly I don't bear Ugly Mug a grudge."

"Are you quite sure?"

"Certainly I'm sure."

"Come on, now!"

And she turned to the men. "Just listen to him. Ugly Mug takes his girl, and he says he doesn't bear him a grudge."

"Why the hell should he?" Whistle said. "And then," he added, "it's high time we stopped calling him Ugly Mug."

"Oh!" Giralda exclaimed.

"Oh, my foot! He's our engineer and he told us his name is . . . What did he say is his name?"

"He said his name is Ventura," Thorn answered.

"And you, there, you call him Ventura," Whistle continued.

"Oh!" Giralda said once more.

"The mayor is right," Toma told her.

"Yes, Mr. Toma," said Whistle.

"Well, to me he's still Ugly Mug," said Giralda.

"He's Ventura to you, too," Whistle told her. "And his mug's no uglier than yours."

63

"That means I have an ugly mug, that's all. But not that he doesn't have one."

23

Now Toma wanted to take Whistle's place at the saw.

"Don't you have to go draw some water?" Giralda asked him.

"It'll only take five minutes."

"Let our mayor work five minutes in peace."

"Tch!" said the mayor.

"Let be," said Giralda, intimating to Toma that she had something to tell him. "I'll go with you."

Toma picked up his oil can and they set out. They walked toward the bridge, in the heat of the sun.

"Well, what?"

"It's about your girl."

"Skip it!"

"You don't have to give up on that score."

"But I've already given up!"

"You shouldn't."

"Why not?"

"If you care about her, you shouldn't. Just see the way she behaves."

"It's her way of behaving."

"With never a laugh? Without even so much as a sign that she's happy?"

"That's the reason she attracted me."

"She attracted you for that and other reasons. A girl in love doesn't act that way."

"Perhaps she's not in love."

"Then you agree with me!"

"A girl can stay with a man without being in love with him."

"She's worse off than that. She doesn't even want to stay with him."

They were on the bridge by now, crossing it, and the mill was just in front of them. They had to pass all along the back side to draw water above the lock or just at the lock.

"Did she say anything to you?"

"She didn't have to say anything; it's obvious."

"Why don't you explain yourself?"

"That's what I'm doing. You have good reason to hope, Toma."

"Can't you explain yourself a little better?"

"They're never together."

"How's that?"

"I mean it: they're never together."

"But they sleep on the same straw mattress!"

"Don't forget, they're in a church."

"What's that got to do with it? It's no church any longer."

"It is for her. She can sleep in it, but making love in it is another matter."

They were now on the pebbly bank and, walking up it, they looked for a place with free-running water. They stopped by a freshet that spurted forth from a big rock poised on smaller stones on the bottom.

"Did she tell you she couldn't?" Toma asked.

He had knelt beside the water, one hand in it. Giralda placed first one and then the other bare foot in the water, maintaining her balance by keeping a hand on Toma's head.

"You know we sleep right next door."

"Do you worry about the fact that it used to be a church, too?"

Giralda withdrew the second foot from the water and stopped leaning on Toma's head. Now he watched her bare feet as they dried in the sun and then raised his face, looking her over from bottom to top.

"We know who worries about it," Giralda went on, "and we have seen that they do worry. She or he."

Toma had filled the oil can by now and placed it on the bank, but still he did not get up on his feet. He kept putting his hand in the water and keeping it in and letting it drift there. Every so often he would pull it out and bathe his face or the hot skin of his chest or shoulders. But he kept his eyes on Giralda's figure, from her feet to her thighs.

"The truth is," Giralda was saying, "she doesn't want to have anything to do with Ugly Mug. He isn't her type. And the business of being in a church is just a device to hold him off."

"Well, I'm not her type, either," Toma told her.

"What d'you mean?" Giralda said.

"I'm the type for you."

Toma did not touch her as he said this, not even the bare foot which was under the fingers of his damp hand.

"For me?" Giralda said.

"Of course! And you're the type for me, too; don't you believe it?"

"Just think of that!"

"I know you . . . like me."

"And what if I do?"

"You . . . I like you, too."

"And what if you do?"

Now Toma's hand came down hard on her foot; he squeezed it and looked quickly around. "Come up there," he said, "over the top of the bank, no one will see us at this time of day."

"And what'll you do to me when we're up there?"

"We'll be together, Giralda."

"I can be with my old unbuttoned fellow," Giralda said.

"Oh!" Toma exclaimed. "What's your husband got to do with it?"

"Can you do anything more than he can?"

"I have no idea what he can do. But I know what I can do."

"Tell me what you can do."

"Dear God in heaven!" Toma exclaimed. "That's what I'm wanting to show you!"

"And what if it's no more than the same as my old fellow does?"

"It won't be the same. You like me."

"I never told you I didn't like him."

"But you'll like me better," said Toma. "It won't be the same."

He released her foot and got up. "Come on—up this way,"

he told her. He had put a hand under her armpit. "Let's get moving."

Giralda pointed to the oil can. "Take the oil can with you."

"The oil can?" Toma said.

"The oil can," Giralda answered. "It's time for us to get back."

Red Kerchief's signal for Toma reached them then, across the dappled light and the fragile sound of the water.

"Hear that? Your pal is looking for you already," Giralda said.

Toma picked up the oil can.

24

Those first days constituted a period one might call "the age of the wheelbarrow": and not only because they had nothing except wheelbarrows to help them carry something from one place to another in their work, but also because they lived shut up within the radius of action of a wheelbarrow, without ever attempting anything that would have demanded the use of vehicles more evolved or complex than wheelbarrows, without ever going farther than where they could go with wheelbarrows and, above all, without ever seeing anyone outside of themselves, as they dug up mines or pushed a wheelbarrow from one place to another.

No more than three weeks went by before a new element was introduced. On the 19th of July, the *Register* dwells at some length on the first newcomer:

> *This evening a man came all the way up here. We were sitting at sunset over our evening soup, and we were eating when Thorn said: "Somebody's there!"*
>
> *We eat seated on stones, gathered around the shelter. We arrive and sit down before the soup is quite ready. Then, when the pot's taken off the fire, we line up to have our bowls filled by Barbèra. We eat without dousing*

the fire because very soon after the sun goes down it is
chilly. On this occasion we were about halfway through
our soup when Thorn said: "Somebody's there!"

It could have been one of our fellows who'd come up
late for supper, but had stopped when he saw us eating.
He held a twig of laurel in his hand. Now laurel doesn't
grow in our part of the country, so he must have walked
a long way in the course of the day. He was asked if he was
looking for anything, and he just pulled a leaf from the
twig for an answer. Then he put it in his mouth, and
watched us eat our soup.

"Would you like to join us?" Barbèra asked him.

Raising the ladle, she made him see that there was
enough soup for him, too, but he turned on his heels and
went away. Perhaps our voices had attracted him, or the
sight of smoke among the ruins . . .

Then the *Register* records frequent instances, sometimes
as many as four a day, sometimes at long intervals, of strangers
who arrived and moved on, or even of those who arrived
and stayed.

For example, on August 28:

Two who were headed for Tuscany to look for work
stopped with us. Toma met them on the highway . . .

And on September 5:

A man and a woman who wanted to go to Romagna
. . .

The entries get briefer, so that it seems unlikely that the
village showed any hostility to strangers. But some earlier
entries indicate uncertainty. For example, there was the inci-
dent of the young boy (*"threadbare and shoeless, burned by the*
sun, his head a tangle of hair") who agreed to stay on with
them but instead ran off in the night having stolen Whistle's
jacket and then stepped on a mine. The entry was made on
July 21 and 22 and written up in such a way as to reveal

perplexity, indifference, and even pleasure at having something out of the ordinary to report. And on July 26, perplexity is once more present between the lines in a note on Saint Anne's day marking the arrival of a young peasant woman in a little cart driven by a mule: *"handsome to look at,"* the *Register* reports, *"well proportioned, and with the round face of a child, but evidently four or five months pregnant."*

One can imagine the sound, like the chewing of pebbles, made by the iron-rimmed wheels of the cart as it advanced over the rubble; one can imagine how that sound was heard in the afternoon when people understood that it was coming their way; and one can visualize the scene of the long confabulation between her seated in her cart and them standing still around her, a confabulation that went on until dusk, thanks to their reciprocal diffidence mingled with aggression, their shared with to gull each other, and a shared fear of being gulled.

The young woman worked on a large estate at the edge of a city of the plain. The cart and mule belonged to her parents whom she had lost track of in their flight toward the plain during the war, and she still did not know what had become of them. Every now and again she had an impulse to go see if they had not gone back to their own village, they or some other relatives, and for that reason she came to the hill country, the cart laden with all her belongings as it had been on the day of their flight.

> *If that's the reason,* the *Register* goes on, *then the young woman comes originally from our village, and she is perhaps the only one to survive of its entire population, thus the single heir, one might say, to its ruins, though she spoke to us of peasants she knows in the city who are now making their living at other trades, or at black-marketing, or begging, or charity, or welfare . . .*

25

With the young woman's arrival, the village passed into its second stage or phase, which could be called the "age of the cart"; this, in turn, opened the way for the third stage, which we might call today the "age of the truck," to use the same parlance as we used for the first and second.

The cart did not take the place of the wheelbarrows in construction work; it only took their place in the collection of scrap metal left over from the war, but it speeded up this job so effectively that scavenging at once became one of the principal activities, with trips to town, and sales, purchases, exchanges, and other deals of the kind. The truck developed this new activity, and transformed it. But it was not brought in from outside or by accident. The skeleton of a truck had been seen from the very first day; it was lying on its side behind a heap of rubble, the farthest outlying pile of ruins on one side of the village. It had a red rooster painted on its hood, and at first it seemed to lack only wheels as it lay there on its side. In fact, however, it needed a new starter, a battery, two pistons, points, and brake linings. By dint of viewing it constantly, and returning after to examine and consider it, the men had managed to conceive of a day when they would have a truck—once the missing parts and wheels had been found. There was the day someone repainted the rooster a fresh red. Then, with trips to town in the cart, one by one the missing or worn parts were replaced and the search for wheels began. This was the start of the work that ended with the establishment of regular motorized contacts between the village and the outer world.

Instead, the step from the primordial age of the wheelbarrow to the age of the cart (with its medieval departures on August nights, and on into September and October, with the creaking wheels weaving slowness and distance ever more inaudibly together) this indeed was by accident, without previous thought or so much as a breath of energy or planning.

The decision had been reached that the young woman with the cart stay overnight, but Thorn began patting the mule as soon as the young woman had left it tied to the tree. Others who, like Thorn, were assigned to scavenging for scrap with wheelbarrows had hung about all evening, touching the mule and patting it.

"Aren't we going to turn in tonight?" someone would ask every so often.

"I'd just like to try him out," Thorn murmured. "What if she leaves with him first thing in the morning?"

Finally he went off to sleep, but an hour later the screech of the cart's iron-rimmed wheels was heard for the first time breaking the night stillness of the village. Everybody hurried out of doors to see the cart's old tail light thump-thumping between the wheels in the black, roadless distance.

For the first time . . . Since the next day it happened a second time, and after the second a third, and after the third a fourth; and the day never came when there was not one more time following another.

The Register has these entries on the subject:

> *August 2—Every evening the young woman bids us all good-by, thanks us warmly, and the next morning and all the next day she's still here because, once again, she can't find her cart and therefore can't go away. Thorn makes off with it regularly long before she wakes. We all think she is finally leaving when the noise wakes us in the middle of the night. Instead, the hours pass and the sounds of the cart reach us from one spot or another where scrap iron is still to be found, and this is the way we find out once more that the kind young woman has not been able to go away. Luckily, she is not in any hurry and is not too annoyed at staying on; we too don't mind having her with us one more day or keeping her cart with us one more day . . ."*

> *August 3—Thorn says that with the cart he can collect in one trip as much as he usually picks up in fourteen trips with wheelbarrows. The work is simplified, as well as speeded up. Fourteen times faster to load and carry. The simplification applies to three stages. The man who, for example, usually unloads the scrap now does not have to go back and forth with the wheelbarrows. He can unload without a break. This means that the total job is speeded*

71

up three times fourteen—or forty-two—times. Proof of this can be seen in the short time it has taken to fill up the annex to the mill where the scrap heap is kept. That is why Thorn is right when he says, "This is just what we need." And he says it every evening when he returns the cart to its owner, while who knows what she thinks every morning when she wants to harness up the mule to the cart and once more can't find them.

August 4—. . . She is one of the earliest risers since she wants to leave, and because of this she is one of the earliest at work, for she didn't sit idly by with her hands in her lap even the first day. She works the earth of the big field with old Barbèra and now it is in good condition, thanks in part to her help, and she seems happy enough to stay on with us a day longer and work the earth one more day. She looks to see if the cart and mule are there; she sees they aren't, and she takes it in good part, without wasting time over it. That's to say, she makes the best of it and goes to the field . . .

August 6—Our mayor asked Thorn: "Did you have to have a cart to make you work so hard?"

Thorn doesn't know what to say. He gets up at three, at two, and our mayor is the only one among us who tells Thorn that he should leave the young woman free to go on her way. According to him, she should take her cart and go wherever she wants. All because Thorn said one day that if he, Thorn, had had a cart of his own and mule of his own he would never have stopped here. In fact, he tells him this often. And Whistle gets in a rage and says that if he hadn't stopped here, he would never have had a chance to even touch a cart and a mule.

But a lot of us believe by now that the young woman would choose to stay here if she were asked to choose. If for no other reason than because this is her village . . . After all, she can't have been too upset at finding us here. It is certainly better than finding nobody. She wouldn't have been able to stay if there had been nobody here, while with us, instead, she can stay here as long as she wants, if she wants to.

72

26

It was at this point, precisely on August 7, not many days after the sort of hide-and-seek played by Thorn and the young girl, that the cart was used unexpectedly for the new event of a trip to town.

The *Register* says:

> *August 8—Today we had a surprise about the cart. Thorn took it to go to town instead of to work as usual. Evidently he had been thinking about a little fun in town. He must have wanted it. But he loaded the cart with scrap metal and told Toma to tell us that he was going off to sell it. But Whistle is beside himself; he says we let him rob the poor young girl blind, and quite a few people are worked up about it.*
>
> *"D'you think he'll come back?" asks our mayor. "He was looking for just a chance like this."*
>
> *But the young woman doesn't seem worried. She's been turning over the earth all day, just the same. And as to the remarks they've been spouting at her this evening, she just turns away and talks to Barbèra about spinach and leeks.*
>
> *August 9—Thorn hasn't come back. But it's almost twenty miles from here to town by the most direct route, and with a cart pulled by an old mule it must be hard going to cover the ground twice within two days.*
>
> *August 10—Thorn came back yesterday at dusk, having sold the whole cartload of scrap and bought three sacks of corn, plus beans, dried cod and stockfish, potatoes, a keg of anchovies, a demijohn of oil, twenty pounds of salt, and various tins of Allied army rations.*
>
> *"Now are you convinced?" he said to us.*
>
> *"But that's enough of it," is what our mayor replied.*
>
> *"What other way was there," Thorn asked him, "to take the scrap to town?"*
>
> *Then we all turned to look at the girl. She was seated behind Barbèra, and as we looked at her all of a sudden*

she gave the old woman's shoulders a sort of shove. "Eh,
what's up?" said the old woman. But we knew at once
what she meant. What we wanted was what the girl
wanted. Old Barbèra got up to tell us just that, and so we
all started to give each other's shoulders and backs a
jostling.

"And just why was Thorn the one who got to go back
and forth?" Whistle shouted.

Now the entire life of the village unfolded, in relation to
the cart, around one aspect or another of the cart's existence.
Even the girl's decision not to go away, and the attitude she
now took toward working the land, after having tried and
tried again haphazardly, so that she rapidly became Antonia
instead of simply the rather vague guest she had been, are
facts that might seem to have come about thanks to the cart
or from the absolute need of a cart. So they seem today,
especially if one does not limit oneself to leafing through
the *Register* and, instead, forces oneself to imagine happenings
as they actually were. For the *Register* shows greater interest
in the reactions of this one or that one than in the cart itself.
For example, it speaks only incidentally of the second trip,
while giving further details about Whistle's attitude:

August 15—Whistle continues not to trust Thorn, who
went to town yesterday with the cart for the second time,
but he doesn't want anyone else besides himself to cast
doubts on his friend. That's why he tells us one moment
that we were mad to let him go a second time, and says
a moment later that he was joking. "The time hasn't yet
come when he won't return," he added.

The tendency of the *Register* to go in more for psychological
anecdote than documentation doesn't, however, lessen the
importance of the cart in the evolutionary process of the village, and perhaps it even makes it mysterious, by virtue of
exaggeration. One guesses that this is the way it was, especially because of the notes on the way the truck was salvaged and
repaired.

The first of these notes is dated August 18:

> *Yesterday, Thorn went to town again, returning in the afternoon with a generator for a Diesel engine. Of course, we looked at him askance.*
>
> *"What are you going to do with that?" we asked him.*
>
> *He explained that, although the generator was used, it was good enough for his purposes. Then he took the mule by the halter—he was good and mad—and pulled it and the cart over to the old carcass of the truck, with its red rooster on the hood that someone had repainted when it still seemed the truck could be put back in order . . . But now Thorn had gone on his third trip to town in the cart at three or four miles an hour and brought back this generator, as if it were the only thing the truck needed to be put back in use. In fact, a fellow from Rifredi whose name is Spataro and who knows about motors told him: "Sure, you need the generator but only to see if she'll turn over. You'll need to fix the accelerator, and change the points, and you'll have to clean the starter valve, too."*

The next note, dated August 19, adds:

> *All the rest of yesterday afternoon Thorn worked with Spataro inside the hood of the truck.*
>
> *Red Kerchief went to fetch the cart in order to gather scrap iron, but there was no way to get Thorn to let it go. It was as if he were afraid we'd break the cart on him or lame the mule, and then he wouldn't be able to go on with the job of repairing the truck. He may be right there. Because he left for town last night with the starter valve, which he says has to be looked at and the points that need changing . . .*

Other notes, on the 21st, 23rd, and 24th of August refer to the way the motor got put back into running order. It was discovered there were two broken piston rods, and Spataro went to town with Thorn to look for new ones. The notes always put things in such a way that one can't forget the fact that, behind every step and every impulse, there was the cart.

Then, for twenty-odd days the *Register* says not a word about the truck. Instead, it speaks of Antonia, of the great ground-breaking and clearing Antonia was doing, of the sowing of the wheat, of how she brought back some survivors from the village who had been in the city since the last year of the war. Or it speaks of digging, demolition, reconstruction, and so on and so forth, mentioning Thorn, too, who was once more in the thick of things, rather than just looking for and trying out parts for the truck, as if for that project he had lost his enthusiasm. Whatever the *Register* refers to, whatever the impression it gives of that whole period, even into September or into October, and no matter how that impression varies, there's always the cart—now clearly playing a leading role, now just a thing of passing or minor importance—as a recurring element. The cart. The cart. The cart . . . Certain it is that ninety per cent of the people were busy from morning to night clearing mines, building houses, digging for water, and all the rest. Yet we must speak of the cart and not of mines and houses, as soon as we stop to think that every job would soon have seemed useless and have been abandoned (and the village itself would have been abandoned) if it hadn't been for the cart, a means of locomotion, a means of covering the distance between a prehistoric time in which one wished simply to survive and a historic time in which, with the truck, with electric power, there could be the guarantee of a better tomorrow.

27

The most notable among all the events during that period between August and the beginning of October was without doubt the one of which Antonia was, indirectly, the prime mover: the sowing of wheat over a large part of the land that had been cleared of mines; and then the return to the village of some fifty-odd survivors, people who had sought refuge in the city during the worst of the war along the Gothic Line.

The *Register* opens with the list of the seventy-nine men, women, and children who reoccupied the rubble of the village; in this list, the designation of peasant or farmer is used just three times for three names that do not figure until Antonia's arrival:

a man of Cattaro, from Friuli, listed as a veteran of the First World War, and a resident for the last fifteen years of a reclamation project in the Pontine Marshes;

a man of Cattaro, from Friuli, listed as a veteran of the listed as a loner without wife or children;

and a Sicilian whom one pictures as having a long face, a man dressed in heavy black clothes, because the comment reads, *"he never speaks"*—which may be a justification of the unpronounceability of his name;

but it all goes back to Barbèra, although she is listed as a housewife, if any beginning of cultivation of the land took place in those five or six first weeks.

Cattarine, Minervino, and the Sicilian worked the earth only because Barbèra had the set idea that, in some way or other, something should be got out of it. The others, who came from working-class or lower middle-class backgrounds, and after the many years they had spent largely as wanderers, or the men simply as soldiers, would have assigned a Cattarine to a worker's job instead of hoeing and manuring. From the silence in the *Register* on their account until quite late in the month of August, and from the facts that then appear concerning their reactions to the question of wheat, we may guess that the three of them were inclined to consider their status of farmers a thing of the past and that they accepted it anew because of Barbèra, but without involvement, with the idea of doing it on the side and temporarily.

Was it the nature of the group in which they found themselves that led them to wish to be something else? It was certainly also due to everything that had happened during these last two years. But there is no doubt that in the world of our village, during its "wheelbarrow" phase, there must

77

have been such a confused concept of work and the purpose of work—a laborer's concept of a titanic task—that the job of a peasant, slow to come to fruition, seemed like a luxury, almost beneath a man's efforts and good only for old men and for women.

This implies that, in its first stage, the village was counting on being able to live by selling off relics of the war. Yet there was as yet no vehicle that permitted the transport of iron and other scrap to the city to sell. The vehicle appeared, oddly enough, and was put to use at the same time as agricultural work and the produce of the earth began to be taken more seriously.

Was this because the vehicle was of agricultural origin?

Was it because everyone saw that this was Antonia's responsibility, Antonia's worry, Antonia's activity, since she had brought the cart with her? This area had been until then considered a mania of old Barbèra.

At any rate, it is certain that agriculture took a prominent place thanks to casual circumstances; this shows that the fate of the village was uncertain, despite the best intentions, until almost the third month.

From Carlo the Bald's remarks in the train, for example, it would seem that the idea of sowing wheat on these mountain ridges occurred almost because of a misunderstanding.

Carlo talked of "them," the ones who had cleared the village and the surrounding heights of mines. He often inspected the area. And it was on the second or third visit he made to the vicinity of the village that he noted the many tracings in the earth; where a week before it had all been uncultivated, there were now fresh furrows along the rock falls. A woman in a blue apron was looking at him, her face turned in his direction although her body remained turned in the other, and Carlo approached her to ask what had been going on. "Ba . . ." the woman answered. Carlo said that "Ba . . ." was what sheep said and that he was interested only in knowing what was new.

"What's new about tilling the soil?" the woman exclaimed.

"The novelty is that in a week you've been able to turn over so much of it."

From one question to another and one answer to another—after he had pleased the woman by wheedling her into telling her own personal story of how she was a widow from this place who had been in the city the past year because of the war and had now been back a week—Carlo managed to find out that all the land had been prepared for the planting of wheat.

"Wheat?"

"Yes, wheat!"

The widow looked at Carlo now as if he had been a person who should know all about wheat and told him that the people who came from the village did not know what to think of it since before this they had never put in anything but fodder crops. She asked him for his opinion. "Do you think it won't grow?"

Carlo didn't think anything; he knew only by hearsay that there were types of wheat that could be planted at an altitude of three thousand feet, and he ended up by saying that the people who had come from the place must have had good reasons to let those who did not decide and carry out whatever was done . . . But the widow answered that it was Antonia who wanted to sow the wheat. "And Antonia is one of the ones from here that have come back now. Not one of the others."

The widow also explained that Antonia had worked for a year on a farm on the plains, at the gates of the city where she herself had been. In those fields she had seen that they sowed wheat, and so she had said that the earth could be sowed to wheat.

"But did you people decide to sow it because she told you to?" Carlo exclaimed.

The widow replied that she and the others from the village had not yet arrived, that Antonia was the only one originally from the village at that time. She must have spoken of the wheat she had seen sowed and harvested on the plains as if she had seen it sowed and harvested there all the years of her life.

"And they decided to sow wheat for that reason alone?" Carlo exclaimed.

"They must have thought she knew what she was talking about," the widow answered.

Carlo said that the people from the village must have known that wheat had never been sowed there. But the widow told him that they would not have sworn to it, after they had talked with Antonia. That is why Carlo says on the train that the wheat was put in almost because of a misunderstanding.

"So," he says he said to the widow, "are you going to go ahead and sow it?"

"Why not?" was the widow's answer.

28

But we have the *Register* too to keep us informed on the subject, we have more direct witness than Carlo, and it may be worth while to consider the situation in the light of all the news we have about it. The *Register* notes with increasing frequency toward the end of August what Antonia was doing with the land as it was being progressively cleared of mines, and what old Barbèra and the three others who were in the farmers' category were doing along with her. Then all of a sudden, it tells us, Antonia became ornery, and she worked the fields almost as if she were showing off, with the doggedness of one possessed.

From then on, any communication between Antonia and the others, the *Register* mentions, took place through Barbèra. The younger woman fell asleep as soon as she had eaten, although the others were talking; and it was Barbèra who made herself Antonia's mouthpiece.

"What's up with her?" someone asked her once.

"The same thing that's 'up' with me," Barbèra answered.

"And what's biting you, then?"

"I've told you over and over, lunkheads . . ."

So the old witch began again. Was it once more the story of the land?

"Of course. The truth is, you don't know what to do with it, and that truth turns up over and over."

"But we already have over twenty acres under cultivation."

"You have twenty-five, plus twelve more we're readying now—but you people don't know it, and that's why you also don't know that you could have a hundred, or that you could have two hundred, just because you don't know what you could do with them . . ."

Whistle was not far off and he came closer. "You mean we don't do enough about it?"

Oral testimony reports it as if everything took place on a single evening, but the *Register* mentions it, although summarily, on three successive dates, so we must conclude that the discussion went on for three evenings running, with people having time in between to think over what had been said and what was left to say.

The first evening may have concluded with Whistle's question. Were they not doing enough with the land they already had? Whistle turned to the three who were qualified farmers, and the Sicilian with the long face did no more than shrug his shoulders; Minervino had to start talking about all the things they did with the land in his part of the country. Even Cattarine had a lot to say on the subject. He knew what they did to prepare the soil in Friuli, and what they did in the Pontine Marshes.

"So you think we're not doing enough?" Whistle asked once more.

The two of them began again, first one then the other, and they kept on saying the same things—finally deciding that it might be said, yes, it might, that they weren't doing enough. But when Whistle drew it to their attention that none of them had ever mentioned it before and that they were saying so now for the first time, they both said that they wouldn't have known what to say.

Minervino: "What could I say? This isn't land like in my part of the country."

And Cattarine: "It's not like Friuli . . . not like the Pontine Marshes . . ."

Indulging them was time-consuming. It's a fact that the

second step was not taken until the second evening. Whistle insisted upon hearing from them whether there was more that could be done with the land.

The two of them began again. Yes, of course, there was more that could be done.

"What, exactly?"

But they couldn't say. "More right now?" Minervino scratched his head and didn't know. Cattarine smoothed his white mustache and didn't know.

Much more spinach, they opined. And more cabbage. And potatoes in March.

At that point, Barbèra interrupted them.

"D'you know what Antonia says?"

Antonia was sleeping in the same circle of people around the fire, seated on the ground like them, her head on her arms.

"She says that this is the season," the old woman went on, "when we should begin to prepare the soil for wheat."

A silence followed in which each one slowly raised his head, then Cattarine said that in Friuli they sowed wheat in October, and Minervino added that in Apulia they sowed it even in January. The important thing was to have it in the ground before the snow fell. They had seen snow in Arignola the last time in 1929. But in those hills snow often fell every year. Perhaps in November, they said. Perhaps as early as October. That was why, they said, it should be sown in September.

Whistle began to shout. In September? Within the month of September? None of them had ever said that. Only now did they mention it, when September was about to begin.

Cattarine shook his head, and so did Minervino. They smiled. They could scarcely have been expected to tell anyone to sow wheat on these mountains . . .

Whistle was going out of his mind.

He asked them if they meant that wheat would grow in the mountains. And then each one who came from a mountainous or hilly part of the country, that is from Tuscany or Liguria, from the Marches, from Umbria, from the mountains of Romagna or Abruzzi or Molise, from the mountains of Latium or the Samnites, from Basilicata or Calabria, or

Sicily, each said that he had seen wheat at eighteen hundred, at two thousand, at twenty-five hundred feet . . . The important thing, said one fellow from the hills of Macerata, was to sow it on the side of a hill exposed to the southern sun. Another, who was a veteran from the Russian front, said it was a question of sowing it a little deeper, if there was danger of a frost. And Cattarine told how he had seen wheat sowed at twenty-five hundred feet in Friuli.

"But you said it wouldn't grow here," they told him.

"Me?" he exclaimed. And Minervino put in that one could never be sure anything wouldn't grow.

"No?" Whistle cried. "You didn't think it wouldn't grow? You didn't think it wouldn't?"

The two of them insisted that they had never said it wouldn't grow.

Word of mouth would have us believe that Ugly Mug came into the picture at this point, but it is more plausible to suppose, as the *Register* indicates, that a whole day elapsed while Whistle consulted seriously with Ventura, and that both of them talked with others and then questioned Antonia. It was no light matter to count on a harvest for the following July. And with Antonia who said they could manage it, and Cattarine and Minervino who didn't say they couldn't, the only question was were they still in time for the sowing. It was already the first of September; there was not enough land that had been cleared of mines—more must be cleared, the same amount, perhaps, or twice that much, three times that much, and then the whole acreage must be plowed and manured. He must have come into the picture on the third evening, Ugly Mug-Ventura, and said they had an exaggerated idea of their prowess. "Instead, there's so much we should have done and haven't done."

He called on Antonia to say how it should have gone. That third evening Antonia had not gone to sleep. And Ventura said that now it was a question of making up for lost time.

Were they all in agreement?

Not everyone agreed; Cattarine was of two minds about it and so was Minervino, but when it was put to a vote there was a majority and they went on to discuss how they should do it all in time; they decided to double the work of clearing the fields of mines and turning the earth, meanwhile reducing their loads of work of other kinds. "And you'll bring in the manure with the cart," Whistle told Thorn.

"Daydreams," Thorn replied.

"Daydreams?" Whistle told him. "You'll see what sort of dreams these are!"

But the trips to town were not suspended. The grain was not yet on the spot to be sowed; it had to be bought, and a few extra tools had to be laid in, another harrow, one more plow; in order to buy them, more and more scrap had to be sold, so Thorn could not stop his trips to town, back and forth and back with his cart, always threatening that one day or other he would not come back.

But now he threatened darkly, his glance surly, his eyebrows puckered, and he acted this way not only with his friend Whistle but with anyone who came within range, even Antonia. The *Register* notes that it was because people provoked him . . . Moreover, no one left him in peace for a single moment. The new job of transporting the manure was simply added to his old chores; and it happened that, as soon as he arrived after a long night spent on the road to the accompaniment of the creaking wheels, each turn of which only covered a fraction of a mile, he had to drag himself on foot toward the fields and there, halter in hand, lead the now reluctant mule up and down to the tune of more creaks, each of which meant only another thousandth part of a mile.

It was all very well for them to tell him, "For this part of the work, we don't need you. You're dead tired." Or to say that he should go off somewhere to sleep, that one of the "youngsters" would look after the mule.

Thorn said that "his" mule was dead tired too, and that he couldn't leave him just when he most needed care and attention; he couldn't leave him in the untried hands of a "youngster." "Because the time will come," he threatened, "that we'll take a good spell off, him and me. Just the way we're sharing this here sentence at hard labor."

They had all noticed the lugubrious way he said this, but after the twentieth, and then the twenty-first, and then the twenty-second time they had seen him turn up just the same. Only Whistle still seriously worried that one day or other he would not turn up again, and no one thought to assign one of the other fellows as a companion to spell him on the road, for it was he and he alone who had elected himself, you might say, to do any job that had to be handled by the cart—with the exception of that trip, among the last, that he and Antonia made to look for the group of former villagers whom Antonia knew.

29

Less was written in the *Register* about this than about the decision to sow wheat; as if one were the consequence of the other.

Not two weeks had passed since the planned change of activity in the village, when the young woman, Antonia, had snapped, ill-humored and sullen, "Here we ought to have the people who were here before."

"Why?" she was asked. "Were they able to do things so much better than we?"

The young woman said that had nothing to do with it. "There'd be more of us, and we'd get more done," she answered.

On this point people ended up by agreeing that more would be accomplished if there were more people, and it seems they discussed the mere possibility, which many questioned, that those who had fled the village might want to return. Or were they all of them out of commission?

They reminded Antonia of this too: that they needed people in good condition, not half dead from hunger; but in any case Antonia left the next time Thorn took off at night, only to turn up a day and a half later with a woman with oily hair and a rolled-up mattress and a goat. Then for four or five days little groups turned up: of a father and a young boy; a mother and a young boy; an elderly couple; three sisters and two boys—with bundles and tools, or with just an old dog, or pushing four sheep before them. They turned up until there were some fifty of them who had come on foot or on bicycles, all by their own means, yet with a repetitious rhythm as they appeared on the road below, as they climbed up to the town, as they introduced themselves all around, and the movements repeated were those of the first arrival of the cart.

"So these are your people?"

This is what they kept saying to the young woman from the moment of the first arrival. They showed plainly that they were worried, from the third or fourth day, that the constant trickle of arrivals might not end but might continue with the same rhythm, even with people from more distant cities. "Are these your famous people?"

"They're not all here yet," was all the young woman would say.

But she had no need to say anything after they saw that work in the fields redoubled and was even continued on a night shift thanks to these people's return.

Now there was no longer time to ask a question or to answer it.

Cocks and hens strutted about the mined fields of the farms destroyed the summer before. They had returned in a wild state, and our people had caught one every so often with traps or gunshot. The cocks started to crow during the last hour before it was light. A man (or woman) of the straggling line bent to the ground would straighten his back as this harsh cry rent the air in the fading dark. It was one or the other of the survivors; he stretched; and if, on hearing that there were really cocks, he happened to ask why everyone was in such a hurry in September, and with the earth in that condition, young Antonia would make him shut up. Wasn't he glad to be back? And all the other survivors made him shut up too. That is, they refused to go along with him when he happened to ask why . . .

Had they learned in town not to want to know why? There are always some fifty of us out of a thousand who wander like strays after every exile, upheaval, or flight; these wanderers were like the fowl wandering without their chicken houses over the mined fields; and what we and they learn is not to want to know why.

Thus a man would settle for being told to shut up. There

were creaking sounds as the cart could be heard from afar. He could look up and about him in the flashes of the lantern. And his work at night made no further sense than that of the cart, or of the night itself.

30

In July sunset is toward eight-thirty, and the train that goes from north to south enters a vast station where it lays over some fifty minutes and then leaves, shorter by a passenger car or two and beefed up by the addition of an engine at the rear.

The people who are getting on are already on the platform; they crowd around those who are getting off at either end of each car. There are always those who clamber in through the windows hoping to find a place to sit while a crowd is still pouring off and the doors are not yet accessible to the reverse flow of the many who are fighting to get one.

My old uncle, who for once has a seat in the corner, is happy to have it; he looks happily, his face all puckered, at the crowd through which the train jolts at a walker's pace before it stops. There he sits, untouchable, above all those stunned faces. He is like a little pope: no one can touch him, although the world around him is in turmoil; it is only natural that he should enjoy it, that he stick out his birdlike head and enjoy it; or simply sit there listening . . . and enjoying it.

Little by little, listening, he hears one voice or another detach itself from the general babble.

"Carlo," someone calls.

The caller is several cars behind him, and now, as he moves forward alongside the train, the name rings out again: "Carlo!" Then he moves farther ahead and repeats:

"Carlo!"

Two of them are calling. But why Carlo? This is the name of the bald one who has the folding double yardstick. And the voices are country voices like his own. Could it be that they were calling him? My uncle could stick out his head and find out. Instead, he preferred to stay where he was and keep on listening. The two fellows are talking to each other, they call out, and one says to the other:

"Uncle Agrippa is here. Uncle Agrippa!"

They are asking him: "Haven't you seen Carlo?"

"Are you looking for Carlo?"

"He has to catch this train and he's not here."

They do not have to leave with Carlo, but they have brought him his brief case and have something to tell him.

"Isn't there a place you can keep for Carlo?" they ask him.

One of the two grabs a hold, pulls himself up and, for a moment, my uncle has the man's fat face close to his, looking from side to side.

"Did nobody leave this compartment? No?"

The face drops down, then glances up with an opaque, sneering expression. My uncle catches sight of Carlo, his hat pushed back on his forehead, standing among his comrades, both of whom are talking. They have *double-entendres* in their eyes, their faces are ironical, and so is that of Carlo the Bald who, with his lean cheeks sucked in, seems equally mocking.

"Well, hell!" they wind up.

"If you want to get a seat . . ." my uncle manages to say.

Carlo the Bald is suddenly aware of him at the window.

"Oh!" he greets him, "good evening."

He bows, and my uncle bows in turn.

"Do I have a place here, with this gentleman?" Carlo asks his companions.

"Just as well here as anywhere else," they reply. "There's no place to sit down . . . Couldn't you have gotten here a little sooner?"

The bald fellow makes a scornful grimace.

"You'll find a place here next to the window," my uncle tells him.

Carlo grimaces again, but it is a grimace of politeness. Then he grabs the lowered frame of the window and quick and light as a cat, he is up and over. Once inside, he turns back toward his friends, who hand up a brief case from below, then another brief case, and a roll of folded newspapers.

88

A moment later, he starts to take off his hat to get more air; he raises it; he shows that he is indeed Carlo the Bald with a scattering of freckles all over the skin of his skull. But in the very middle of the gesture of raising his hat, his hand pauses and lets it fall back where it was.

My uncle sees the shape of the double yardstick sticking out up from beneath his jacket in the back pocket of his trousers. He can call to mind exactly what it looks like: the yellow wood sticks folded every six inches.

What is it for? Why does he always have it on him? He could carry it in his brief case. Why does he carry it over one buttock like a revolver?

31

When the train starts to move after its long pause, lights are already lit under the platform roofs, but there is daylight in the sky that rises as the train picks up speed, light on the housetops and the fields, as far as the edge of the hills.

Darkness lurks on the slopes, but not only there; it is a quality of the earth that now, little by little, gushes forth from the grass as if it had been just cut, and darkens one field within another. Louder than the sound of the train is the chirp of the crickets that runs along with us like the hum of the high-tension wire. We look about us into the air to see where it comes from, and then we see that the air itself is darkening, and then we listen, and then we realize that we have been paying attention to these things only because there is no light around us in the train.

Carlo bares his wrist to look at the time. His wrist is outside the window and yet he cannot see; he leans close to his wrist but he sees nothing.

"What the hell!" he says.

He turns back into the car, his eyes on the ceiling. My uncle does the same, raising his little eyes to the ceiling. Perhaps all of them, in the compartment sitting on their facing

89

seats, look up at the ceiling to the spot where we know the overhead light should be, but the dark inside the car is now so dense that no one can see who is sitting opposite him.

Uncle Agrippa murmurs: "They haven't turned the lights on yet."

But someone pokes his head out the window, Carlo the Bald is at the window, and looking out they all see the reflections cast by the lights in the other cars of the train.

"We're the only ones without light," someone cries out.

Right after him everyone's voice is roused, like the bellow of cattle jolted from side to side in a cattle car. By God! It is always a maddening experience even if it is a frequent one. Or just because it is frequent. We can curse our mothers.

Carlo the Bald grinds out between his teeth: "Some dirty trick!"

And my uncle, hearing him, feels a little guilty.

He can see him standing against the last thin light from the compartment window. Why did he get into this car? Out of politeness. Just to be with someone he already knew. If only he had a place in which to sit . . .

My uncle touches Carlo's arm.

"Is there something you want? Perhaps you'd prefer to sit down."

"Sure, I'd prefer it."

My uncle offers him his seat. I can just see it, as if it were I getting up when, at thirteen, I was a student, thin from studying.

"No, I wouldn't think of it," Carlo tells him. "What an idea!"

"Aren't you tired?"

"Yes, of course I am. I've been going all day."

"Well, I'm tired of sitting."

"In that case . . ." Carlo says.

He sits down while my uncle leans against the half-lowered glass, his shoulders to the open air.

"Thank you very much," Carlo says.

"Not at all. You'll rest sitting down and I'll rest standing up."

"Whenever you'd like to sit down again, just tell me."

My uncle is satisfied. He protects the nape of his neck from the air by raising his striped scarf a little higher, and he asks himself which is better for a traveler: to stand in a compartment where there is light or to sit in one where there is darkness. He would opt for one with dazzling light, for his own pleasure. But he would also opt for a good place to sit down. He is without light, and Carlo has his seat. Thus he no longer feels guilty, and he leans over just enough to talk.

"This is the fourth time we've met, isn't it?"

"Only the fourth?"

"Or possibly the fifth."

"More likely the fifth. I often travel this line."

Someone who cannot see calls out, "Who does? Carlo?"

"Yes," my uncle answers. "Our Mister Carlo."

Perhaps Carlo nods in assent. His face, at the same time exhausted and mocking, cannot be seen, nor the slight motion, but it can be remembered. He says once more that he often travels our line but not always, because it does not pass all the places where he must go, and then he travels by motorcycle.

"By motorcycle?"

My uncle is delighted to have given him his seat. He likes to talk to him, to talk and to make him talk, and now he can indulge himself without let or hindrance. Carlo the Bald tonight is, as it were, "his."

Once more he leans over.

"Are there many places you have to go to?"

Carlo answers: "Yes, many. There's no spot from here clear across the mountain range to the other side where I haven't a job to do."

"That'll save me from having to go to them too," my uncle tells him.

"How's that?" Carlo says, surprised. "What do you mean?"

Almost laughing, my uncle asks him, "I imagine I can count on you."

"Of course you can."

"If you were to see my daughter, wouldn't you let me know?"

"Of course I would."

32

My uncle can talk endlessly about his daughter, yet Carlo the Bald does not have much to say when he describes her. Hasn't he already said whatever he could say? And my uncle not only wants to talk, he wants to listen.

"Have you gone to sleep? You spoke of the women who clear the mines . . . You know, I've been thinking about that."

Carlo the Bald starts to talk about the village built of rubble.

In the darkness of the compartment, people have started to talk almost everywhere; there is no longer a general silence; people are talking low, in little groups, and matches are lighted, cigarettes are lighted; the men have become aware of one another in a different way from before. They do not remember what it was like when they could see each other; they are caught up in one another's breath, contacts, pressures; and each one becomes a creature that one hears, plus the smell of a trade, plus a gleaming cigarette.

"And they took it over," Carlo says.

His conversation is no louder than that of the others. But it seems to be more closely listened to: it obtains greater attention.

"They say . . ." someone puts in.

"Have you heard it mentioned? People are talking about it now. But last year," Carlo the Bald goes on, "people just said that village had been wiped out."

My old uncle seeks a more comfortable position against the window. He moves, and then Carlo the Bald breaks off; he urges him to remember that his seat is waiting for him whenever he wants it.

"No, no," my uncle says. "I find the conversation interesting."

He has been listening in silence, his scarf across his mouth and a hand holding the scarf in place. He has not uttered a single question or remark. He has listened to the questions; he has listened to the remarks.

"Now what about those women?" he asks.

"They're the women who belong to the men," Carlo the Bald answers.

"Their wives? Their daughters?"

While my uncle was speaking, he stretched out a hand over Carlo's head, trying to grab the rail of the luggage rack. One end of the scarf is loosed from around his neck and flaps in the air; it flaps in the dark air and flaps toward Carlo the Bald.

"They say," repeats the man who had spoken before.

But Carlo the Bald interrupts him once more. This time there is no Black Nail. It is Carlo who has the floor on our line. And Carlo does not go in for "they-say's"; Carlo knows; Carlo the Bald has seen with his own eyes.

He has seen that there are three big dormitories: besides the one within the walls of a tumble-down church, there are two others, identical and completely new; he calls them dormitories because they serve for sleeping, but they are buildings with many rooms . . . It's the simplest way to build when you want to do a quick job. Just as it's simpler to build one big kitchen for a hundred people than a hundred little kitchens.

In the dark, the others seem to approve with the lighted tips of their cigarettes.

Is it because they are traveling in the dark? Is it because they enjoy a story?

My uncle is thinking rather than listening, and the words of the others voice his fantasies, his thoughts. In fact, he is thinking and listening at the same time. He knows that the others' words are there. But he cannot tell which are his thoughts and which are the others' words.

"But what did they live on while they were doing all this?"

"There were the remains from the war." And Carlo tells of the carcasses of planes, of tanks with their motors, of cannons, of abandoned gear. All this belonged to the "Italian people." It was up to the people to make use of it. They appropriated it, selling it or turning it to their own ends. And by doing so they had committed their first abuse. A fairly accurate list had been drawn up on the basis of his observations.

His? My uncle turns to look at him in the smoke lit by the tip of his cigarette.

He has duties. He has his folding double yardstick with

which to measure. But we must be objective and, if they have been able to rebuild the village, clear the mines, cultivate the fields, and so on, it has all been due to the lack of scruples with which they disposed of public wealth.

"Wealth?" someone questions. "Was there all that much?"

"Enough for them to eat in those first months. And then animals to raise. And then a truck . . ."

"They say," observes the "they-say" fellow. He would like to tell what "they say" about the truck when it comes to town: with a man who is all eyes driving; another behind him whose eyes are even bigger, big enough to be scary. And each time there is a new woman aboard with very big eyes and more or less disheveled hair; once even an old woman who got down and wandered about among the market stalls, and looked in the shops, looked in the doorways, then went back to sit beside the driver, and all they ever bought was corn or cornmeal.

But Carlo Fiery-Tip picks up the thread; he will not let him say more than "they say." He knows what the sum total amounts to. And while some people steal for their own personal gain, these fellows at least stole for the general good, which in the end benefits the place itself and the region.

Did they steal? My uncle finds his thoughts separate from the others' words. Now he can ask questions, make observations, contradict. It is as if he had slept for a few seconds and returned, after a little sleep, to himself, lively and emboldened.

33

It turns out, then, that someone among those wretched people got rich. Someone has a truck. Someone has cows.

"But you people don't understand," my uncle says.

Carlo the Bald stops him by touching his arm. He had been unwinding himself while the others were talking. My uncle was aware that he had brought his legs out from under the seat and stretched them.

"But you've not understood."

"It's just like Uncle Agrippa says. Either you people haven't understood or I didn't make myself clear."

Carlo the Bald meant to say that he had come on the scene to clear this thing up.

There is the fellow who says "they say" who could really say it. What he means is that things are the other way around, and that the shocker, in town, is that it is so.

that the truck should arrive with its trim all shining in the sun of the market place, and that, shining, already cleaned, yet with one of the two men with big eyes still cleaning it up and asking for water and washing it off, it stands there belonging to no one, or to so many, to a whole village, while every stall in the market belongs to this one or that one.

But Carlo the Bald explains that they can own things in common. And not because of a principle.

He can laugh at the idea of a principle. They do not have principles, and perhaps they do not even know of principles' existence. They only understood that they had no choice. Either they owned things in common and they worked for the common advantage, or they gave up staying there and went back to the trips up and down, back to vagabond times, to the migrant who picked up a week's work in one place, a week in another, to the cheapest black market, the meanest stealing.

Here my uncle breaks in. "You say those people come from that?"

"I wouldn't take it on myself to say. Only they say so themselves."

"In a word, they were like Gypsies."

"Exactly like Gypsies . . . That's the very word."

And the fellow with the "they-say's" could say that was just the impression they made in town: that they were always like that, they were Gypsies, from the first moment their truck showed up; earlier than the cock's crow, with that red rooster painted on the hood.

"So maybe Gypsies have principles!" Carlo the Bald added.

He insists that he has more than one proof of what he is saying. But without its sounding offensive to anyone. He means it as a compliment when he says a fellow hasn't principles. He means the fellow's not stuck up. It was pure necessity, "and not what they say," that made those Gypsies work together, with everything owned in common. Because if one or two sharp fellows had built themselves up to be bosses, they would still never have been able to keep the others there, given the conditions under which they were living. That is the truth about today: wherever you are, if you have to start from scratch without any immediate reward and facing risks and efforts, there is no other way but to do everything in common.

"I've been convinced by watching them," Carlo the Bald says. "And studying them, because it was my job . . ."

At this point another glowing butt is lowered, another cigarette removed from the lips, another mouth has something to ask.

"How did they go about it? One job at a time or lots of jobs at the same time? And if they tackled one job at a time, which came first, and which second?"

"But, sir!" Uncle Agrippa exclaimed. "We have to sleep and eat every day . . ."

Carlo the Bald did not let him finish. "One must admit that at this they were past masters."

He had seen them at many stages and had asked questions about how they did it; he had even managed to get some of them to talk. (All because of his job. A rather dreary reason, but one which, nonetheless, gave him an opportunity to clarify his ideas on life.)

"Well, how did they go about it?" He would say in the most rational because the simplest way in the world . . .

They had to accomplish certain essential operations at the same time; this was clear. And from the very first day, they set about doing things at the same time: at least the most elementary things. Only they knew how to change the order and the pace of doing these things according to circumstances.

There was always Carlo the Bald's admiring refrain: "Everything points to the fact that they never had any definite purpose or the will to carry out the wild ideas that people have attributed to them."

Carlo does say that there was a time when, realizing that they were surrounded by mines, they wanted to break a path through them. Then, from a stage in which their only purpose was to survive they passed to a stage of lesser tension, when they dug up the mines not just for the sake of digging them up but in order to have more land. "And so now, logically enough, they don't intend to go away."

In the darkness of the compartment exclamations arise even from the seats farthest away. Now Carlo is standing up. He throws his cigarette butt over Uncle Agrippa's head into the black air, which scatters it in sparks along the way. The sound of the train whistle is scattered in the same manner, and a bridge is shaken by the noise. Outside the window a valley opens up, between the darkness of the mountains and the darkness of the sky, which is dragged along behind us, with our train.

34

Carlo the Bald does not sit down. He and my uncle are standing in a space not meant for two. Carlo leans on the lowered glass of the window frame, and the whiteness of his hand can be seen pointing to the empty seat, as if to invite my uncle to sit down.

"But how do you explain it?" they ask him.

"It's because of the group, the community feeling," my uncle answers.

"The group?"

The business of small bursts of flame that appear and disappear begins again, and nervous little matches light up the men's faces.

"That's what's usually lacking . . ."

"The sense of community?"

"Why, yes. What is it men need when things go wrong? They need a sense of community."

Someone says that perhaps my uncle is not making himself clear.

"I'm making myself perfectly clear," my uncle answers. Then he tried to make himself clearer.

"Take me, for example. I had no daughter. I had only a wife. I was always unhappy. And why was I unhappy?"

"Because you hadn't any daughter."

"It was because I belonged to no community. And it was the same afterward. I had a daughter, I was happy, I'd never been so happy, and yet I wasn't happy."

"Why was that, if you had her and she hadn't yet run away?"

"I was uneasy. Why? I was afraid. Why was I afraid?"

"Well, why were you afraid?"

"It was all because I wasn't part of a community. I was too much alone. I was too wrapped up in my daughter . . . Oh, I'm aware of it."

"That can happen," they told him.

"So my daughter disappeared. And why did she disappear?"

He let the question hang in the silence that followed, in the sweet smell of the valley outside the window.

"Who's to say?" someone commented behind the glow of a cigarette butt.

"Because," my uncle went on, "there was no community. There were only the two of us. While if we had been in the midst of something like what Mister Carlo here is talking about . . ."

The train starts to whistle and loses speed.

"Sit, sit down," Carlo the Bald says to my uncle. He says it to him as if to say it was better to sit than go on talking.

"Yes," Uncle Agrippa answers.

And he sits down but he goes right on talking while the whistle continues to sound desperately—the whistle of a train that has stopped.

"We've stopped at a signal," says Carlo.

"What signal?" my uncle asks him.

He pokes his head out of the little window beside him,

he sees the still night and the motionless valley, and he sniffs in the direction of the mountains.

"It seems to me we are at just the spot," Carlo the Bald says, "where last time you pointed out the places they . . ."

Carlo too is looking out into the night.

"Perhaps," he answers. "Anyway, we're in that area."

He points with the whiteness of his hand. "It's up that way . . ."

He adds that to get there you would have to leave the train a couple of stops farther on.

"Why not get off here?" he says half to himself.

He goes on saying what has come into his head: "I'll sleep at the stationmaster's house, and tomorrow I'll get up early . . ."

"You have to go up to where they are?" my uncle asks him.

"Because of my job," Carlo the Bald tells him. "Job" is a word like the folding double yardstick: you pull it out of your back pocket. And all of a sudden Carlo has made up his mind; he lowers the window still farther and hoists himself over the sash.

"I'm trying to get on their good side."

As smoothly as he got aboard, he has dropped down onto the siding.

"Thanks," he calls out to my uncle. "Have a good trip!"

The gravel can be heard shifting under his creaking boots.

"Take care!" my uncle calls after him. But when he draws near the window, with another fellow who wants to call after him, he sees the red light for which the train has stopped. It doesn't let him say another word. It blazes away there without lighting up anything: a heart of flame among the points of light.

"Mister Carlo!" my uncle calls out.

The train has started up, and the night starts to move again; they pull in their heads, and the two or three weak lights of the station slip by.

"They say . . ." the man who had waited so long finally says.

35

It was during the second half of September that Carlo the Bald came to our village for the first time. Our people had been there less than three months, and among the rubble things did not look very different. But even from a distance the figures of the men could be seen working at something in the earth, following the cracked furrows of the surrounding acres.

The day was white all over the sky, as if the sun had not come out; and there was no chance that the sun would come out now if Carlo, who had left toward seven-thirty, had been on his motorcycle about an hour. It was cold, too; the wind might have had no more velocity than that of his motorcycle, but certain details of rocks and ledges on the heights could be seen that were only visible when the wind was blowing. Carlo could tell one wall from another as soon as the rubble came into view, not much higher than he was, on the opposite slope of the valley where the roadway dips down and rises, and once more dips and rises, always running several miles distant from the village even at those points nearest it. He stopped to look, because it is almost hidden even from the eyes of anyone looking from the road to the level where it rises on the valley wall; and he saw that there were big holes made by the demolition, big square or rectangular piles of stones, a new brick wall. You could tell from the occasional black hole of a window that a house here and there had been covered by a new roof. In this fact alone there was a marked difference from three months before, but Carlo looked with an eye at once derisive and half asleep, the eye of the petty official for whom everything in sight is not what it seems but is in itself suspect and valueless.

The engine of the motorcycle bothered him with its nattering, the object of his interest prolonging within him the impressions he had had on his trip; he turned it off, and thus at last had this detached world to himself, and could even feel that the wind was wind once more, moving slowly along the ground, but with a high velocity above, where the passage of great white clouds filled the sky.

He saw among the rubble that something had shifted, as it often seems to do in any inhabited place seen from a distance. He saw the same thing at a spot in the red earth about a mile to the right. Then in other places still farther on the right, and on the left, and down below. They were lumps of turned-up earth with black curved lines traced on them every so often, lines that disappeared in spots. But he could make out the difference between what was a first step toward cultivation of the earth and what was an excavation.

He traced a plan, with sketchy lines, in a notebook, and put a cross where the excavation was. This particularly interested him, as if it were a sign of some grim scheme. He went back to the cross, in fact, and made it blacker; then he looked among the curved lines nearest the village for the spots where they were working on the mines, and he found them and smiled but without marking down anything special on his leaf of paper. Instead, he was very curious about a great dark covered object.

"Aha!" Carlo said.

He looked at it a long time, and he looked away, and exclaimed again. He was taking notes meanwhile, with little circles and crosses.

Then he grabbed the handlebars of his motorcycle and started off, against the wind, still looking toward the heights, which were more brown than red in the sunless air. Now great piles of clouds were forming. It was not going to rain until evening, however, until evening or the following day; but Carlo the Bald was undecided; he started the engine, settled into the seat, and acted as if he could not make up his mind whether to go forward or back.

He had a little cycling cap, not a motorcycling helmet, on his head, instead of his usual hat. It hugged the nape of his neck, forehead, imprisoning the upper rims of his ears, and he pulled it down over one eyebrow; then, when he heard a car drawing near, he started downhill at a modest pace, accelerated, braked for the curves, picked up speed again, and did not slow down until he had reached the point where the asphalt national highway crossed a dirt road.

He turned onto this and rode uphill to the level of the surrounding fields of thorns. Among the thorns, he noticed a sign with a skull on it. And he heard the car behind him turn at the crossroads onto the highway. Little by little, he found himself shrouded in the dust he was raising. Higher up, all that he could see about him was convex red earth streaked with rocks. He slowed down, slowed down, and then suddenly turned off the motor.

He seemed highly satisfied, engrossed now in what he was doing, what he had seemed almost on the point of not doing before, as if he had considered it more or less of a bore. Now, obviously, he considered it a pleasure. His job was done, and he could indulge in his favorite sport, drop the motor-cycle and leave it without so much as removing the key, and run downhill on tiptoe with his cycling cap on his head . . . He heard hammering on metal. He heard voices.

36

It was Thorn, standing upright in the cart, who warned of the stranger's presence.

"Fellows!" he called out.

Only after he had called out three or four times did they hear over the sound of the hammering.

Someone asked without turning around, "What's up?"

Thorn called him by name, "Cataldo!"

This is the name of a saint to whom many churches in Apulia are dedicated. There is even a small town named San Cataldo, in Capitanata, I think. The fellow named Cataldo did not turn around, but Thorn told him and the others to look.

"There's a guy over there!"

Finally someone looked up. Then a second one looked and a third, and Cataldo turned, too.

"What's he after?"

They all saw the guy who was Carlo the Bald with his cycling cap on his head, tipped over one eyebrow in the wind. He was a bit beyond the cart and a bit up from where they stood among the white outcroppings of rock that burst through the red earth.

"Looking for someone?" they called out to him.

In reply, he mumbled a few words they could not make out.

Our fellows murmured in turn among themselves. "Oh well. . ." they said to one another. And one of them shrugged his shoulders, another did the same, a third went back to hammering.

The hammering was followed this time by a movement of the metal itself, and everyone in the little group was suddenly busy.

"Hey, Thorn!" Cataldo called. "Come on down and give us a hand."

Thorn ran to join them, but he had not got the stranger out of his head.

"Now he's smoking," he said.

They were all moving back, bent over the heavy piece of metal they were carrying slowly toward the cart. They threw out an odd word here and there, between one effort and the next.

"Smoking?"

"I swear . . . Smoking."

But they were not really making much noise, and so everyone heard the question that finally reached them, loud and clear, from the stranger.

"What are you doing?"

Each one wanted somebody else to answer, then the one called Cataldo straightened up.

"What are we doing?"

"Yes," Carlo said. "What are you working at?"

"You can see for yourself."

"Were you breaking something?"

"Working it loose."

"A piece of iron?"

"Part of a gun battery."

"You're breaking down a gun battery?"

The others asked Cataldo to ask him why he wanted to know.

"Ask him yourselves," Cataldo muttered.

"What?" Carlo the Bald called.

"Nothing. Nothing."

The others mumbled several things for Cataldo to say. Why not tell him the fellows all felt like a smoke? That they had not had a smoke for two months. That not having smoked for two months is like not having eaten. That he should remove their temptation to play him a dirty trick and take himself off.

"What are they saying?" Carlo called out again.

"We're just talking to one another," Cataldo answered.

Then he told his comrades not to talk like a bunch of idiots.

"But I'm dead serious," one of them said.

He was young and dark, a tall fellow who still worked stripped to the waist, even in the sunless air, and sometimes even in the rain, almost always in the wind, those last days of September.

"Then tell him yourself," said Cataldo.

He turned away to bend down, and in the distance they heard a stone rolling.

"He's coming," Thorn warned.

He did not see him, but almost immediately he heard Carlo's voice from nearby .

"Was it an antiaircraft battery?"

He looked about him, standing now in their midst, and he looked at the weight they were straddling; he looked at them and beyond them at the remains of the hulk they were taking apart. He offered Cataldo a cigarette.

"Oh!" said Cataldo, "give it to him." And he indicated the fellow with the bare chest. "I can do without it."

"I may have enough to go around," Carlo said.

His face had assumed a particularly mocking look as he

104

made the offer. He proffered the freshly opened pack, saying that, alas, it was his last. Cataldo handed it around.

"What kind of cigarettes are they?"

The men concentrated all their capacities of acceptance and thanks on the quality of the cigarettes themselves. The brand name was repeated by each one of them, even by the bare-chested fellow who flushed as if he had been slapped all over his bronzed face. In the same fashion, each of them repeated the fact that they were American cigarettes.

"Say," Thorn asked, "are they easy to get?"

They turned them around in their gnarled fingers, and then Cataldo wanted to return the pack with those that were left, but Carlo told him to keep the rest for his companions. He waited for each of them to get a light from his own hands. He used little wax matches, the most delicate there are, yet he knew how to protect the flame from the wind for an almost indefinite time.

The men lit up, each intent upon his first puff.

They did not see insolence in his face. They did not see his face. They only saw his hands, so carefully cupped around the flame of the little wax match. And the fellow who was bare-chested lit his from Thorn's who had gotten a light from Cataldo.

Meanwhile, Carlo kept on with his questions. Seated on the gun emplacement, he looked at the way the smoke rose from their mouths as they dragged on his cigarettes, he clapped his knee with his hands, and he was a man in the midst of anticipated pleasure.

"But why are you stripping this thing down?"

"And where are you taking it?"

"And when you've got it to town, what will you get for it?"

"And what will they do with it in town?"

Thorn leaned toward Cataldo's ear.

"Seems to me we're talking a bit too much here."

Cataldo answered that he did not think so, and Thorn said the same thing to the bare-chested fellow. "Don't you think we're beginning to talk a bit too much around here?"

Once the cigarettes were out, or set down on a nearby rock, they settled the big iron plate on the floor of the cart.

The bare-chested fellow watched Carlo with expressionless eyes. He was trying to make out from his face why he was rattling on like a fool. "It's always better to say nothing," he observed to Thorn, but once he had picked up his cigarette again, he told Carlo that surely he knew they bought other things besides cabbages in town.

Here two or three of them laughed.

Carlo too transformed his ironic smirk into a little laugh.

"You beginning to catch on?" someone asked him.

"Yes, I am," Carlo said.

He looked thoughtful for a moment, then he got up and nodded his head.

Our fellows could not make out if they were having him on or if he was having them. And it seemed as if the first situation would have been no more pleasant than the second.

Carlo had not stopped nodding. He had also taken to moving first one arm and then the other. It was almost as if he were making a speech without words. Behind him was the gun platform, while in front of him were the men with the cart and the mule, now ready to take off. At last he said:

"Well, keep up the good work . . ."

37

The rain, that end of September, fell only one day every so often, and never for more than an hour or two at a time, but in October it began to rain all over the Apennines and all over upper Italy, one day yes, one day no, three yes and one no, and even five, six days in a row. It rained in Bologna, La Spezia, Ancona, from Milan to Rome, and on the trucks as they made their way from Milan to Rome, a rain so fine that one was unaware of it even against a nearby windowpane, and yet so unremitting that night after night the sidewalks of our big cities sparkled with reflected lights along the interminable streets. Dark and pounding were the waters of the Po, and yellow and pounding were the waters of the Arno, and yellow and pounding were the waters of the Tiber.

It is magnificent, under such rain, to have one's skin dry thanks to money; it must be the same as having a hearty appetite and everything one can take or touch, and a house with many rooms where even the floors smell good, a court-yard from which the gleam of the damp leaves can enter, and where one can stand behind the tall glass of the windows, or where one can go and open and shut closets in which camphor is the smell of happiness accumulated during one's mother's childhood and one's grandmother's childhood.

Then it must be like a hearty, young appetite,

to be able to go from room to room over waxed floors, and rugs, to light lamps and turn them off, take down and put back books, crystal glasses, records, and to feel that the street lamps and leaves are still outside there in the rain,

and to want to go out together, hear voices laugh without reason, and to see people run without reason, push each other without reason, and to laugh, run, and stand in a long line of shiny black umbrellas or gleaming automobiles . . .

It can be the greatest appetite . . . Just to see, and to sense the smells, sounds, and steam of the espresso machines as they are wafted out of crowded, fragrant café doorways, the wetness of the throngs standing in front of moving-picture theaters, promenading under the arcades of Bologna or look-ing at the food shop windows along the Via Speronari, where bright lamps play, even in broad daylight, on steaming lobsters and slices of smoked salmon, still rose-tinted by the river estuaries where they were fished. It is a total sensation to walk or run under an umbrella, amid a mass of other um-brellas, opened up over Milan; over Genoa, huddled around its invisible bit of sea; over Ancona and Livorno and Rome,

and, at the same time, it is, or may be, a feeling of possession, that is of appetite aroused by the possibility of possession.

In our cities, even if you are poor, you can enjoy the rain: there is the same happy appetite for life, indeed more magical, more deeply felt because it is expressed in a shout of joy for a sheltering umbrella and even for soggy, water-logged shoes and for the strident bell of a trolley car that skips a stop because it has no room for any more riders,

or for a trolley car that does stop but you cannot clamber

107

into it, for the one where you finally load your drenched signs and posters, under the newly lit street lamps, in the course of a life which is a continuous improvisation,

until you find a connecting thread,

which may come from a trolley car triumphantly clanging over the tracks of a long route where the rooftops are even more glistening than the umbrellas raised during the week of rain that caused both streets and rails to glisten in Milan, Rome, La Spezia and Bologna.

But not all of my people are on these brightly lighted streets, and for one of my brothers who is there, others are absent;

my mother and grandmother are not there,

Rosario and Gaetano are not there . . .

Where they are, the streets distil emptiness; the houses and rooftops distil mold. They are towns with fifty thousand dark windows that are never lit up except by a candle in honor of the dead;

they are roads traveled by trailer trucks, where the drivers neither eat nor sleep, as if they were already journeying toward the other side of the grave;

the sections of the town where every wall is the negation of a wall;

the last stops, where you get off the trolley to go home but, instead, you sit down on an iron bench, even if it is raining.

This is no fabricated story. The sun rises, and it is always the same sun; the rain falls for a week, and it is the rain of the last eighty centuries. The sun is the mummy of eighty centuries of sunshine, and the rain is the ditch out of which the sun rises.

And yet I know that this comes from no emptiness of heart.

Do I know my own flesh and blood or don't I? I lived just under twenty years with my mother and grandmother, and I know that no mold has gathered on my grandmother's hundred-year-old heart. And what about the hearts of my mother and Rosario? I know that they long for change, for something new and imaginative; I see their travels, the disastrous week in a truck, or the journey by train. They say it is all because they wanted to come to see me, but the fact is

108

that they were after a happier way of earning their daily
bread, a ration of lightheartedness;

exactly what I wanted to give them, by removing them from
the mystification of journeying to and fro;

what they were looking for in the village crossed by the
Gothic Line, where they were drenched by a week of rain, rejoicing in the fact that it was raining on the seeds of their
wheat and in everything else that is signified by rain: the way
you can run through it, the sloshing of bare feet, the yellowish
steam rising from the soaked twigs, the long-lasting smell
. . .

38

Carlo the Bald had made his second visit in order to view
another aspect of their efforts, and his third and fourth visits
as well, as if he wanted to get to know the motley group
in its single parts, one by one. Or was there a contradiction
between the execution of his job and his curiosity about how
far these men's illegal enterprise would take them? Or was
he naturally inclined to turn study into pleasure and thus
to mitigate the harshness of a task otherwise very vaguely
defined?

"Now to the mine-digs," they said every time.

He noted the importance of the excavations in his notebook, since it seemed to be a sign of serious intentions. They
were the first things to be shut down, evidently, if he must
shut down something. But must he? He asked his superiors.

"Weeeelll," they answered. "How are we to say?"

"I've taken a look and reported," said Carlo.

That, they said, was, for the present, all that was necessary.

"To take a look and report?" he queried.

To wait and see what happens, they told him. In the hope
that order would be restored, that there would be a working
government. "Wait until spring," was their conclusion.

This did not mean suspending his visits. And it was without asking whether he should or should not make it that Carlo set off on the third one of them.

"Now to the famous mines," he said to himself.

He landed up, instead, on a newly plowed piece of land, where he met the widow with the light-blue apron and learned about the wheat. This bit of information seemed worthy of reporting to his superiors.

"Listen to this," he said. And then he told them. "The wheat may really come to harvest."

"Well, well," was the only answer, one not unlike that of the widow.

"You mean 'Wait until summer,' is that it?" he retorted.

Meanwhile, the rain had set in; for a week Bologna and Modena flew drenched red flags, and Carlo could not be sure of being free on the day when the sun came back. Nevertheless, he managed to make his fourth visit and to reach, finally, the place where they were removing the mines. There was one group in front, one in the middle, and a last one, composed of three men, at the end. When he had over-taken this last group, Carlo paused and said hello, shoving his cap up from his forehead. Then, after clearing his throat, he said:

"I see that you know your job."

The sun threw a long shadow at his feet and at the feet of every one of the three men to whom he had spoken. But they were pallid shadows, and it was a pallid sun, and it seemed as if, farther along, neither shadows nor sun existed. The men were standing on a height, without any visible world around them. The length of the height extended as far as the eye could see, while the breadth was hollowed out in its solitude. A man holding his head in his hands might be solitary in the same way. Carlo sat on the ground, digging his fists into his forehead and his elbows into his knees. Was he still looking at the shadow that he cast before him? In any case, he no longer saw the shadows of the three men to whom he had spoken, who now were within the space of the extinguished sun. They were black bodies; the men of the middle group were black sticks, and those of the third group black dots. The lightless space was punctuated by black

110

amid the billowing, reddish folds of the earth. He made a black mark for every bush, but the drifting voices might have come from any one of the black marks. They were digging up and defusing mines, just the way Carlo knew they ought to do it. It was as if he were digging them up himself or teaching someone else how. "Old men, women, and children . . ." He got up on his feet.

Did he think the things he said on trains?

He began walking toward the edge of the hilltop, and a heretofore invisible world rose up to greet him, with ranges of hills on hills, among which the village was insignificant. Every place else was filled with silence as the slopes rose one out of another until they were wreathed in solitude and blue sky. Carlo went up to the group of men, which had moved a short distance away.

"Don't I know you already?" he asked Cataldo.

"Good day. I recognized you too," Cataldo replied.

Carlo went right to the point; he said he did not know why they were doing it. The other two men had worked at taking apart the gun battery as well. Carlo saw that they were the same ones that had said with their eyes: "Why does this fellow keep showing up?"

"What I wanted to say . . ." he added, "was that you're doing something worth doing."

Already a message had traveled from Cataldo's eyes to his companions: "You ask him." But all three of them had lowered their heads, one wielding an iron rod, another a pick, another a shovel. They went on with their work, paying Carlo no heed, until they had dug up one mine and moved on to another.

"I could tell you the exact spots where they are, one by one," said Carlo, "as if I'd laid them myself." He followed them, pointing to the right and left. He had taken a notebook and pencil out of his pocket and was tracing lines on a page. "We're here . . . That's north and that's west . . . And here are the mines that have still to be dug up . . . A1, A2, A3, B1, B2, B3 . . ."

The men stood around him and took each page as soon as Carlo had filled it. They studied them and then threw them away. Even Ugly Mug, they said, could locate mines that way.

111

"You mean there is someone that could do this for you?"
Carlo asked.

But to a direct question, Carlo won no reply, or only an
evasion, and he had to phrase it differently.

"What about your cart?" he asked.

All three men had resumed digging. Cataldo stuck his long
rod into the ground, the fellow with the pick loosened the
earth around it, and the third shoveled the loose dirt away.

"The cart with the mule, and the little man that drove it,"
Carlo repeated.

Again he saw in their eyes the look that said: "Why does
this fellow keep coming to stick his nose into our affairs?"
But Cataldo raised his head.

"He's no longer with us."

"Is that why he's no longer to be seen in the city?"

Cataldo laid down his rod, and the three of them conferred.
Then they put aside the other tools and knelt down.

"Pull its tooth before you remove it," Carlo admonished
them. Then, looking into the hole he said, above their heads:

"Does the fellow that can locate the mines for you let you
take them out of the ground without defusing them?"

He got only mumbling for a reply and changed the subject
back to the man that had gone away.

"Did he take his cart with him? Another one of you would
surely drive the cart into the city if he hadn't taken it away."
And he added, insistently: "Isn't that so?"

Finally, they gave him the satisfaction of saying:

"We have a truck now."

From this source (and from the *Register*) we know that,
toward the middle of October, the cart age came to an end
and the truck age began. Carlo started to ask about the truck,
how they got it, and so on. But he saw a hostile look in their
eyes and said only:

"Strange that he should have gone away."

"Strange?" they answered. "Here everyone's free to come
and go as he pleases."

Carlo the Bald looked with mock attentiveness into the eyes
of the fellow who made this last remark.

"And to take something that doesn't belong to him?"

39

For another week there was rain, a chillier rain every day, prophetic of snow, and Carlo began to think that his fifth visit would be the last until the following spring. He went, somewhat heedlessly, to the center of the village, where he was seen by Ventura and spoke, by chance, with Cerro. He did not wait for perfect weather. When he woke up in the morning, it was not raining, and he went, with two of his men, to the station, to make a tour that ended around noon in a tavern, where he was transformed from a railway traveler into a motorcyclist. He disappeared somewhere behind the kitchen with his hat on his head and came back through the front door wearing a sporty cap.

"You fellows, go back to the city."

"What for?"

"I have something else to look at up here."

After an hour's ride through puddles and holes in the road he came to the place where he always stopped to have a look around. The sky was clearer, and light swept in from the north. Across the way, Carlo saw the village in a northern light, which bared details that he had never noticed before. There was the tree, the bridge, men, or rather black dots, moving to and fro from a shed to a puddle, from a puddle to the tree, and from the tree to somewhere else.

Back on his motorcycle, he coasted along the curving road downhill toward the square, which had momentarily disappeared, along with the rest of the high-perched village, behind the mountainous terrain. "I'm on my way, all right," he said to himself several times over, in a joyful rhythm attuned to that of the engine.

A great white flower of a cloud, blooming across the western sky, against the reddish, brown, and black stripes of the highlands, seemed to be running in time with him. Below the fast-moving, flowerlike cloud, Carlo saw the village reappear. Apparently, he wanted to make his presence known, for the insolent clatter of his motorcycle increased as he drew near to the houses at the summit. Faces stared out of huts and reconstruction projects, but Carlo merely glided among the ruins, dodging the puddles. He was like a man on horseback, unable to check his mount's wild gallop, as he rode, as if under a spell, through every one of the village streets, with a visibly radiant expression on his face, and signs, also, of scorn and provocation.

He slowed down, but made no less noise, as he came to the square. Here, while little groups of staring people gathered around, he uttered words that could not be heard because of the noise of the engine. "What the devil is he saying?" they asked one another. And Carlo passed among them again, more slowly, shouting what he had to say before once more stepping on the gas:

"What's the name of this place?" he shouted.

Finally they understood. "Why doesn't he stop if he really wants to know?" they wondered out loud. No one had a name to give him; that was why they stood and stared, with wide-open eyes and long faces, and made no attempt to reply. Or else they threw out their arms, in a gesture of futility, and smiled. Carlo seemed to be inhabited by spirits. Stepping hard on the gas, he rode on, crisscrossing the village again and then coming back to the point of departure. In the end they laughed every time, as he stopped to ask again: "Is there no way of knowing what place this is?" Yes, it was laughable, and they laughed and went on laughing, even after, first one and then another, they were left with upraised faces staring into space.

Carlo saw streaks in the puddles and felt drops fall on his hands, and he too raised his face. Rain was pouring from the darkened, low-hanging sky. Leading his motorcycle with one hand, he took refuge in the shed near the tree in the middle of the square. Men who were busy planing and sawing stopped work for a moment to look at him. He shook himself, unbuttoned his waterproof jacket, and asked:

"Isn't there something like an inn where I can stay?"

"In summer we work in the open air," Cerro told him. "We set up a trestle at the foot of the tree. Now we have a shed, sixty feet by forty-five, and in a couple of months we may have an inn as well. But first we want to make a glass wall around the shed."

He seemed to be clowning, but he gave a rational explana-

114

tion of the state of affairs, pointing out which side of the shed was sixty feet long and which forty-five.

"Make yourself at home," he said. "You're not disturbing us."

As the rain—or perhaps hail—beat down on the roof, he observed that it would not last for more than a half hour.

"This isn't the first time you've come to these parts, is it?" he added.

Carlo was taken aback. He would have liked to continue the game of riding up and down the village on his motorcycle.

"No hurry to answer," said Cerro. "Take your time and think it over."

"There's no need to think it over," Carlo said after a short pause. "It's not the first time, no. Why shouldn't I say so?"

A yellowish cold air was blown in by the rain as it fell straight down, parallel to the shed's four walls, wiping out sight of everything outside, including the wall along the stream. It was only natural to pause before speaking up.

"Perhaps you know someone here," Cerro continued.

When two people talk, they look at each other. And the difficulty of looking someone straight in the eye obliterates silences, no matter how long they may be. Thus Carlo the Bald was able to stop and think without seeming to.

"Who it is I came to see, is that what you were asking? The fellow that drove your cart . . . I was sorry to hear that he's left you."

"Oh well, he may come back. How long has he been gone, now? Let me think. Ten days or two weeks."

"He was gone already on the fifteenth of this month," Carlo interrupted. "So it's nearer to three weeks."

"Three weeks, then. That doesn't mean he won't come back, does it? Let's give him time. He may have had an accident. Perhaps they arrested him and threw him into jail. Or he may have been kidnapped by bandits."

"What kind of a load did he have?"

"T.N.T., to be sold, perhaps, all of it to the same man. That made it simpler. One time he carried T.N.T. and another time scrap iron."

"Since he was coming to meet me, it's strange that he should have been carrying T.N.T. Because I deal only in iron."

115

"Were you the buyer? Anyhow, he left the addresses of the people to whom he made deliveries. And we continue to make them with the truck . . . How does it happen that no one has delivered to you?"

"Does your truck carry special identification? In our work we can't trust just anyone. A trucker we don't know isn't the same as a carter we do. I preferred to wait and see."

"But the trucker didn't just linger, to wait and see. And he's never told us of having any trouble, or of having to go to new addresses."

"As you know, the transaction is made at an outside meeting-place, not at the storehouse. Maybe someone else picked up what I failed to get. Some people are more ready to run risks than others."

"Do you want to clear the matter up? To hear from me where the trucker is delivering his loads of iron?"

"Why should I?" asked Carlo. "The truck is covering the same ground as the cart. I only wanted to be sure that the trucker was in the direct line of succession to his predecessor."

"And are you sure now?"

Carlo said that he was. Then he changed the subject and asked, admiringly, about the shed, about where they had got the wood and the roofing, and how they intended to mount the glass walls.

"Why are you so interested?" said Cerro. "Do you want to build something of the sort yourself?"

They continued this banter, ingenuous and insinuating, evasive and provocatory in turn, until Carlo realized that it was no longer raining. He got up, pointing to the now silent roof above their heads and to the outside, where, among the gutters, there were signs of the first gusts of a distant blue wind.

"I must take advantage of the clearing," he said, starting to lead out his motorcycle.

It was then that Ventura saw him. He had come into the shed from the opposite side, but now he made an abrupt stop and wheeled around. His hand, which was covered with blond hairs, grasped the handle of a shovel. With his head bent to one side, he raised his hand up into the air and examined it. Water dripped from the hair hanging over his forehead onto the lapels of his jacket. He was thin, with big, deep-sunk, sparkling eyes, momentarily veiled by the rain. While he stood stock-still, staring at his upraised hand, he did not shake the water out of his hair. His expression hardened, and became funereal and malicious.

40

"What's the matter?"

The speaker was the girl called Siracusa, who had come a bit behind him and stopped at his side.

Ventura did not answer.

They could hear the motorcycle's engine, although it was not yet in motion. Ventura was still looking intently at his hand. The girl began to look at it too, yet she did not stop looking at his face. "I know that expression of yours. What's the matter?"

His hand looked as if nothing were wrong but, as she took hold of it to look at it more closely, she felt it contract in a gesture of evasion. Then, as the motorcycle got under way, Ventura slowly raised his eyes, which grew larger as their gaze returned to normal.

"Well, what was wrong with your hand?"

Ventura showed her that nothing was wrong, and the girl examined it, opening and shutting the fingers.

"Why did you hide?"

"I just stopped in my tracks."

"But you turned around and lowered your head."

"I was looking at my hand."

"But since you say there's nothing wrong with it . . ."

"There was something wrong."

"Didn't you want that fellow to see you?"

"Leave off!" Ventura said. "I didn't even notice him."

The girl turned and started to leave.

"Wait," Ventura called after her.

She went out of the shed, but at a slow pace, picking her way around the mudholes. Ventura could see that her steps were not purposeful and that she did not mean them to be. He started to walk after her.

"Wait," he repeated.

Evening was coming on. The blue wind of far places lay over half the distant hills. But over the other half it had eased into a bright blue breeze. About four-thirty? Or five? Ventura had to work a while longer, and it was the girl's turn in the kitchen.

"Wait."

"Don't think I'm angry," she answered him.

She was on one side of a big puddle, he on the other. Ventura looked at her reflection in the water. He looked her up and down, and then could not take his eyes off her. She, on the other hand, was looking at his drenched hair and drenched clothing.

"You should come along and dry yourself. Besides, you know that even if I was angry . . ."

Then Ventura slowly crossed the puddle.

"Are you going to dry yourself?"

He walked along in her reflection.

"I'm going to dry myself."

They had arrived.

It was a little darker under the subdivided cover-all roof over the line of dwellings among which, from the very first day, they had had theirs. Beyond the threshold it was darker still. He closed the door carefully, as if he were replacing a lid on an opening.

"And now you want us to be together?" the girl said.

Her face could not be seen, but her eyes were visible. "Her wicked eyes," Ventura might have said. He placed a hand on her back.

"I just want to help you."

He began to undress her, then to give her a rubdown.

"You get undressed, too," the girl said.

He undressed kneeling. He left his clothes on the ground without even disengaging his feet. But then, when he had stood up, he held her to him, trembling a little.

"You said you only wanted to help me."

"But this is better. Yes . . . we quarreled."

118

"I don't say I don't want to. I'm just repeating what you said."

"It's better if we do it."

"Then let's hurry."

The girl gave herself to his still damp body, letting him lay her down on the straw mattress and tenderly embrace her.

"We quarreled," he said again, immediately afterward.

"But you know," the girl said, "you know why you can always do it."

"Why?"

"Don't believe it's because you want it."

"Tell me why."

"It's because I like it."

"Yes?" Ventura said.

"And that's why you can always have me even when I'm angry."

"You like it even when you're angry?"

"It's better for you to know this: no matter what happens between us, you can always come on me and take me . . ."

The girl's voice sounded in the darkness the way her eyes had shone.

"Yes, on me, on top of me," she went on. "That's the word. Hand me something to dry my belly."

Ventura bent over her with the towel.

"Even if you should hate me?"

The girl took the towel from him.

"Of course," she almost cried out. "Light the light."

"Then," Ventura said, "I could never know when . . . when you hated me."

"Of course not," the girl cried. "But you should feel it, somehow."

Ventura sought out her face in the dark.

"Tell me," he asked her, "you don't hate me now, do you?"

At last the girl spoke in the same tone as his. "No, no. Of course not."

"Could you say you loved me?"

"Of course I could."

Ventura paused. "I know that I can say so." Then, after

a moment, he went on. "Don't you want me to say it to you?"

"If you want to."

"You tell me first."

The girl's face eluded Ventura's touch, and her voice was once more strong.

"Light the light, will you?"

They had a lantern. Both of them knew where it was, and Ventura knew where to find the matches. He lit the lamp. Then between the low brick walls and the external wall made of stone, they got dressed again without another word. Because of the noises coming from the nearby rooms and reverberating under the vaulted roof, they might even have been unaware that each was silent.

"By the way," the girl said when she had finished dressing, "I wanted to thank you for the mirror."

"You did?"

"It was a good idea to have someone buy it for you. My handbag mirror is too small."

"Tomorrow we'll see about hanging it."

"So we have a real mirror. Besides the chair . . ."

"Cerro promised me a second chair by Saturday."

"He'd promised us beds."

"We'll have them . . . And I think that toward the twentieth of November we'll all have tables."

"So," the girl said.

"So?"

"So nothing. We'll be all set up."

Ventura dawdled over his dressing, and the girl combed her hair. She had finished, but she began again. "I'm not saying I'd like a kitchen just for us two, or to do everything on our own. The way things are has its advantages. But this room . . ."

"What about the room?" Ventura turned. He was fastening the belt of his Allied military jacket.

"I'd like it away from here," the girl cried.

"You mean isolated?"

"Even a hole where we could be by ourselves once in a while."

For some time now they could make out words among the noise beyond the bricks, and steps sounded as they went to and fro. The girl put down her comb. The steps sounded now as if they were going away. They echoed, and so did the voices.

"The new dormitories," Ventura said, "are already a bit better."

"I'm speaking of a separate room," the girl answered.

"We're supposed to build separate rooms, and we can have one."

Once more the vaulted roof reverberated outside their thin walls. First it had been an echo, but now it was a whole wave of sound; and then, little by little, there were new steps and new voices. Pounding on a distant wall. The beat of a hammer on a faraway wall was reproduced in ghostly poundings on ten other walls.

Ventura and the girl continued more quietly.

"Why would you ever be making separate rooms?"

"Because we'll have storage areas of one kind or another, and stables to keep an eye on."

"Rooms for watchmen."

"Like the one in which Whistle sleeps down at the mill."

He could have added: and Cerro with his little hutch under the shed . . . There were already several examples.

"And can we have a room like that?" the girl asked.

"If you want one."

Once more the voices and steps drew near, and someone knocked on the door; a woman's voice was speaking to them.

"Have you forgotten it's your turn in the kitchen?"

"Tell them I'm just drying myself and I'm coming," the girl answered. "I haven't forgotten."

The woman's voice was talking to the others now, to men.

"She's drying herself, she says."

A murmur of voices.

"They want to know if Ugly Mug's with you."

"He's here, too."

"They're looking for him."

Ventura spoke up. "I'll be there in half an hour. I'm drying myself off, too."

Words and more steps, and grumbling, and then they went away. "Hurry it up in there." The fullness of the echo returned to them.

121

"Why," the girl asked, "did you say half an hour?"

"Don't we have to get dry?" he asked her.

41

Ventura cast the girl a melancholy but not embittered smile. There was often a smile of this kind on his face, which they continued to call ugly, or an expression equivalent to a smile. A smile indicative of something like happiness and at the same time of an obstacle to happiness, of an effort that he had to make in order to attain it. But this expression was that of a good man. Whereas, when his face was radiant with triumph, it took on a dark, hardened expression. Was it one and the same face? A metal of the same kind?

Now he said:

"We were just beginning to talk."

"Do you feel like talking?" the girl asked.

Ventura said he was. "Why not? I can want to talk, like anybody else."

"You should save it up for when I want to talk too."

"Because right now you don't want to?"

"I didn't say that. I meant that you should save it up for when there's more time."

"Not so long ago," said Ventura, "we quarreled."

She was aware of how, ever since the morning when they first woke up together, he had persisted in a smile which was, essentially, an effort to be happy and at peace. Her attitude could not be all that helpful, either. But wasn't his effort, his struggle, concerned primarily with her?

It must irritate a girl to feel that she is the object of an effort and a struggle instead of an outgoing, simple affection. And perhaps this girl was, as she seemed, a little prickly and rough in her reactions, not so much because of her character or the vicissitudes of her existence but because, in this new relationship with a man, she was unable to give him rest, relaxation, and release.

122

"You can't seem to loosen your tongue unless you imagine that we've quarreled," she observed.

Ventura shook his head. He was sitting in the only chair while she stood in front of him. Wasn't that it? No, it wasn't. It absolutely wasn't. His smile was melancholy because of the thousand and one things that he might well recognize for things as they are. There was, for instance, from that first morning, his way of watching over himself, almost fearfully, lest he somehow offend her. Did he think that he had actually offended her on that first morning? Obviously he believed that he had a capacity for giving offense that might from time to time recur. Against this he seemed to be perpetually on guard.

Never, when they were momentarily alone, did he put a hand on her breasts or hips, as any man does when he is alone with his woman, or search her out under her skirts, grinning from ear to ear. A girl may look at a man in a way that encourages such intimacy. But if her look is at the same time resentful, as if his expectations seem to her offensive, then he can no longer follow her reasoning.

Ventura never took the initiative. Because he was so scrupulous, he left it up to her. At the same time, he demanded that she take it. He looked hard at her and staked out his demand. So it happened that she was rough and rude. Every time she had to peel off his reticence, and that was hard work. Hard work, not to let his reticence contaminate her, and hard work to have to take the initiative. So it happened that she had turned to look at him across the puddle and to start a conversation.

What sort of a conversation? Well, we have overheard it. "If you want to, I'm ready," or: "Why don't you do it?" Or, once and for all, that she was willing for him to do it even when he had reason to think she was angry with him.

"So, no talking?" she said.

Ventura shook his head, with a smile rather than a laugh. Then he leaped to his feet, suddenly aware that he was seated while she was standing, and pushed the chair in her direction.

She put her hand on the back of the chair.

"Did you want to talk about that fellow?" And his face hardened, just the way she had thought it would.

"What fellow?"

"The fellow with the motorcycle."

The hardening of his face gradually relaxed as he fought to master his feelings.

"Yes, among other things."

"What do you mean, 'among other things'?" she asked, nonplused by his answer.

"The fact that I avoided him, for instance."

"But I never meant to question . . ."

"Why not? You have a right to know if you want to."

"I don't want to, particularly."

In her surprise, she was touched by the fact that for her sake, he could so master his feelings.

"I don't want to know!" she shouted. "Have I ever asked you to tell me anything? I don't want to know, I tell you!"

Did she mean that if he started to talk about the fellow with the motorcycle, he would go on to speak of a lot of other things that were on his mind? She took her hand off the back of the chair and then replaced it. Again she said that she did not want to know.

"It's not on your account," she explained, "it's on mine. I have no wish to talk about myself, and that's why I don't want to know about you." Speaking in a tone of voice alternately normal and shrill, she added: "Did I ever talk to you about my affairs? No. And you continue not to talk to me about yours. You never did and you never do."

"All right," Ventura interrupted. "What I actually wanted to talk about was how happy I am."

"Happy?" she exclaimed.

"Yes. What I wanted to tell you was exactly how and why."

42

For some time now the voice of Carmela had been heard outside.

"Littèriooo!" she was calling from far away.

Doors slammed, walls echoed, and the cry of a newborn baby in the tunnel had the sound of an underground stream. Was there a knock at the door? No. Once more it was echo's flying hand. And behind it was the hammer. It was the muted echo, from a dozen other walls, of the beat of a hammer against one wall.

Now came a grumbling sound from out in the open, as if, across its solitude, the road were singing. In spite of everything, it was easy to identify. The road was singing as it wound upward, with a rabbit running from an automobile's headlights, singing of the hunt and of the return home. Voices met at a faraway point and became more clear.

"Ilaria!"

The road laceratingly penetrated the drumlike entrance of the tunnel. Was it the truck with the red rooster? With so many doors opening, Ventura and his girl burst forth too, in the light of the headlights, the smell of gasoline, and the roar, rising and diminishing. The light came from four head-lights, two above and two below. In it there darted to and fro, with their heads between their upraised arms, slithering like swimmers, Carmela's child and another, and two or three older ones besides. Men and women walked along the edge of the glow thrown upon the road. One of them crossed the road directly in front of the lights, a great black shadow that was first immersed and then emerged, but did not make as great an impression as the laughing boys. A young woman plunged in and then came out abruptly, shrugging her shoulders and laughing and throwing herself at the first man to come along. The window of one door had been lowered, and Elvira from Messina was laughing out of it. And from another similar window, a hand was tirelessly waving . . .

All this was a good thing.

Elvira from Messina seemed to be happy. Ventura and the girl guessed it from her face, just as she might have guessed the same thing from theirs. And all this was a good thing, just as it is a good thing to see the faces of an animated city crowd.

A good thing that just then a truck made its arrival, that its blinding headlights played upon the two rows of houses under the tunnel, on their doors and windows, that Spataro the Trucker made no effort to dim them, so that the broad glare rested on every face, in turn, that came into its path. It was good, while the men were unloading the truck, to have the light, and good that the truck should stop there and remain all night in the nave of the former church, with its body weary but not yet dead, and smelly.

Wasn't it a good thing to sleep with a truck in the passageway? Men have slept with a dog, even a lion, in the passageway. Now they could sleep with a truck, lulled to rest in its smells. Wasn't it a good thing?

Good, too, were the noises when Spataro the Trucker was working on the truck, talking to the boys who gathered around to help him. And his nighttime departures, when the motor woke up, awakening everyone around and keeping them awake for a full half hour until it was fully awake itself, ready to elbow its way with its glaring headlights into the world outside, to disappear into the distance, transformed into the singing asphalt of a singing road.

And yet, fundamentally, it was a bad rather than a good thing, just as the cart was bad as well as good.

They could remember the insomnia of which the cart, at one time and another, had been the cause. Now the truck, in its turn, produced its bad results. Ventura could have read them on his girl's face at the moment of the truck's arrival; indeed, he could have deduced them from his own state of mind.

He might have admitted, for instance, that it was *not* good to have the glare of double headlights in the living quarters for as long as it took the men to unload the truck. And equally *not* good the drumbeat of the motor against the tympanum of the houses, as it reiterated the story of its travels. Why did Spataro leave the motor on for hours after his arrival? And did he really have to let it sing its song all over again, in a key of clanging iron, just before he set out on his travels again?

Yes, every good had something that was *not* good to balance it.

Yes. And it was comprehensible that an individual should want a room of his own and separate himself from what was good and from what was not good, both together.

126

But what is a "room"?

A man wants a life of his own and says that he wants a "room." Certainly he was born to have a life of his own besides the life he shares with others. And he has a right to a "room." But for all too long he has had a "room" and nothing more, and this is the cause of his sickness and his death in a lonely bed. He must be healed, because he wants to be healed rather than to die. And to want a "room" may be as equivalent to one thing as to another.

It may be a sign that he is unable to recover, that he is shutting himself up in his sickness and his death and reposing in them. Or else he may be impatient to progress beyond his sickness.

Man has come to this point in these dormitory years. Behind him is his old private room, and he may well want no more than to stay in it and smoke solitary cigarettes. Before him is the prospect of a room in which he is no longer confined and condemned to die, but rather one where he can go in and out, or even simply affirm his desire to possess it.

And what did it mean to the girl?

Just now her face was similar to the face of Elvira from Messina and to that of Giralda. Ventura turned around, abruptly, to look at it. She was talking and gesticulating to various people. What was the significance of her having stated her wish for a "room"? And the significance to Ventura of his having admitted her wish?

Did it signify a denial of the impoverished community from which they both derived a minimum of joy? Or did it support this community in its aspiration to a more perfect happiness?

43

The red rooster painted on the hood of the truck was lit up and so was the inside of the cab, where Spataro the Trucker sat idly at the wheel, his eyes laughing.

Men with large eyes went to and fro, unloading, and from

the truck a large-eyed, disheveled woman, with her hair flying, lent a hand. Whenever she had a chance to stand up straight for a stolen moment of rest, she looked proudly down at the bystanders.

"I was about fifteen miles away," Spataro was saying. "Three quarters of an hour if you calculate the speed I make in second or third gear . . ."

"What's that? About twenty miles an hour?"

Four or five of them were in the shadow of the truck.

"You know the kind of motor I've got, part of it from a car and part from a tank. Haven't you seen the speed of a tank?"

They laughed.

"Tanks walk on their knees, boy, not with big feet, like those of your truck."

"Anyhow, I'm all the time in second or third. It's not good at climbing hills. And the fellow came at me on his motorcycle, his eyes tightly shut because of my headlights and his mouth half open like the slit of a piggy bank. Right then and there I thought of a piggy bank in this connection. And my other thought was that . . ."

"That you'd drench him?"

"That it was inevitable. There was that puddle, a mass of water only about ten feet away, enough water to supply the horses of a whole cavalry regiment. He wasn't in it yet, but he was coming on . . . Didn't I have a right to keep going?"

"So you drenched him, is that it?"

"I shut my eyes, as if the impact of the water were striking my body as well as his. Then I saw the visor of his cap pushed back over his ears. I practically drowned him."

His listeners showed pleasure at this idea. A child's cry was heard among the rest: Litterio was not playing with the other children in the glare of the headlights.

"So are we supposed to be glad or be sorry?"

"Wait a minute . . . I must admit I wept for him. I sat there with my head down between my shoulders . . ."

Litterio was crying again.

"Give him what he wants, Mother," said Spataro.

"He wants to climb up into the truck."

"Into the truck again? Hand him up to Ilaria . . . Oh no! Just wait!"

With a gesture, he stopped the mother and child.

"Do you know what I brought back with me?"

"What?"

"Glass!"

"How did you find that?"

Ilaria was looking down, momentarily erect in all her glory, nodding and half laughing.

"That's my load for today. I found it and cut it."

"Is there all we need?"

"Ask Ilaria, she knows. How many panes are there, Ilaria? How many square feet?"

Through the flood of light, with his eyes tightly shut against it, came Red Kerchief, with Toma just behind him, his hands in his pockets.

"Hello there, Toma! We have the glass."

Other men were now helping to unload it.

"Fellows," Spataro called down to them, "aren't you interested in the end of my story?"

"Is there a story?" asked Red Kerchief, raising his head.

"Shall I tell it again from the beginning?"

"Yes, tell it."

Even Toma held out for a retelling.

"Go ahead!"

Little Litterio was crying again.

"What a pest! He'll have to wait until that breakable glass has been put away. Mother, give him to me."

The child was passed from hand to hand to Spataro. His lips were tightly compressed, his eyebrows scowling and his little body as stiff as wood.

"If you're a good boy," said Spataro, "I'll take you on a trip with me for your birthday."

And he started again to tell his story.

He was on a piece of road studded with holes, all of them filled with a week's rain. He was literally fording his way, at times between showers of water as clean as if they had just fallen from the sky, at others choked with mud. It was among these deep puddles and the showers of water raised up from them that he had nearly run into the fellow on the motorcycle, had drenched and nearly drowned him.

"Lit-té-rio," Carmela was calling from below.

"Litterio tried to free himself from Spataro's arms, and his little face grew purple.

"What the devil's got into him?" Spataro exclaimed.

"All right," said Ilaria, "hand him to me."

Spataro was happy to do so.

"I stopped," Spataro went on, "got down, and went to look for him. It was pitch black, or so it seemed, because I'd been looking so long through the eyes of my headlights. I got wet, too, when I jumped down from the truck. This, I thought to myself, will bring us closer, brother! But before I'd covered half the ground between us I heard him yelling.

"How could you hear?" asked Red Kerchief.

"I don't know. But the interesting thing was *what* he was yelling: 'The working class! The working class!'"

"The working class?"

"He said that my driving was symbolical of the working class of the future. He didn't yell, really; he talked loudly. He said that, once upon a time, great folks' carriages used to splash people, and that, from now on, we and our trucks would . . ."

"By 'you and your trucks' did he mean the 'working class'?"

"Us . . . Our trucks . . . He said that we hog the whole road, leaving no place for anyone to walk, that we're heedless of bicycles, motorcycles, and any other vehicle that isn't a truck. He says the size of our trucks swells our empty heads."

"Well, I hope you filled *his* empty head with something," said Red Kerchief.

"By this time I was right in front of him," Spataro continued. "He was wiping the mud off his piggy bank mouth, and he asked me if I had got down from my truck in order to see what I'd done to him. 'Yes, fellow,' I told him."

"That must have got his goat!"

"Not a bit. He pulled his cap back into position and said that insolence might have passed from one social class to another, but it was still insolence . . ."

"Would you recognize him if you saw him again?"

"If my headlights were on him, yes. There'd be the same

130

expression on his face. But it was dark when we were talking. He asked me, quite calmly, where I came from and where I was going."

"At that point didn't you jam his cap down over his eyes?"

"I told him I was going to New York."

"New York?"

"That was the name I chose to give to our shed. And the funny thing is that he understood. 'Ah,' he exclaimed, pointing in this direction. 'So you're one of *them,* are you? Take it easy, and we'll settle accounts later.' "

"You settled them right way, I hope."

"I asked him what he meant. Meanwhile, Isidoro came along . . ."

"Did you let him have it, Isidoro?"

"Look here, boys," said Spataro, "there were only two of us, three if you count Ilaria. Did we have to prove our point?"

"He deserved it . . ."

"Listen, boys, if we're the working class, I think we can hold off. But at that point he said . . . Tell me, Isidoro, what did he say?"

Litterio was running up and down on the hood of the truck; every evening his little feet hammered as insistently as they had in the sunlight all day, and Carmela continued to call after him. The world is full of such repetitive things: running children, calling mothers, mothers and children that shout and cry, men that crumple under a head blow, clanging coffin lids. And yet the world changes. Now the truck came in every night and went away every morning, and the motor was left running under the feet of Litterio, as if to teach him.

"What do you want?" shouted Isidoro.

He was another man with large eyes, and he too was on the truck, leaning now toward Spataro.

"You tell them, Isidoro," Spataro repeated. "Tell them what he said."

"You mean the fellow on the motorcycle?" Isidoro asked, scratching his head.

"Him, yes."

"Something about people that might yet do us in."

"That's it," Spataro assented, "that or something like it."

131

For a moment the hammering of the little feet were silent. And all around they were talking again about the glass. Someone went to look at the panes, and Red Kerchief and Toma followed. Only Ventura remained leaning against the fender. His head bent over the headlight, but he did not blink.

44

Then, for more than five months, from November until the middle of spring, there were no more visits from Carlo the Bald; the village was cut off for almost four months in its winter; and the things that happened there until February, and from February to May, are told by the village's inhabitants during the long summer evenings, to refresh their memories or to inform now one and now another, a friend or a new acquaintance who asks about what went on.

They tell it like this:

ZAIRA FORZINELLI, WIDOW BILIOTTI

"I was born here. I came back in September, a war widow, when Antonia persuaded us to come and picked us up, and four lost creatures we were . . .

"In the first days of November there was a little snow, then it melted; then the rest of the snow fell and stayed on the ground till the beginning of March, and by then we had to harvest the spinach and cabbage by shoveling away the snow. For Christmas, the last ones we'd taken up were nibbled by the frost. Our hands too were nibbled by the frost. But we had a good stove in the mess hall, and under Cerro's shed, after it had been enclosed by glass, there was a good stove, in fact two good stoves, and we farm folk who rest only in winter wanted to sit close to the stove all the time.

"Instead, Ugly Mug told us: 'No, not on your life! The wood we have will never be enough for all these stoves. We'd have to cut three times as much in the woods of Sacco. And we can't do that in this snow. Keep yourselves warm with your work.' "

MICHELE CATERINI, CALLED CATTARINE

"Only he came forward afterward to explain things to us. Whistle and Mime the Mason who were the first to tell us no, and old Barbèra along with them, just told us we should keep warm by working. They started it and kept it up, so that every other minute someone was telling us to keep warm by working, as if they were masters and we were servants. Doesn't it make sense that we were annoyed?

"Besides, personally, there's the fact that I'm old. We people of Friuli, we have our habits. I already had to change mine in the Pontine Marshes. Then I was supposed to change 'em again for the third or fourth time. And besides, we had less and less to eat; we had no bread . . ."

WIDOW BILIOTTI

"We had cornmeal mush and nothing else for two months straight, without so much as a bit of drippings. They could have bought salt pork instead of that window glass. After New Year's, we got together. But we didn't rightly know what we wanted to say; we knew only that things weren't going well and here it was only the start of the winter, and they told us we'd get a slice of baked cornmeal mush every morning to last us all day, and no more soup, and they said the milk would have to be kept for the babies, even if some of us, like myself, had our own goats . . ."

POMPEO MANERA

"Ugly Mug really got to us with his explanations. But we farmers, we'd already been rubbed the wrong way for over a month and we didn't feel right, I because I'd been born here and I came back in September, called by Antonia; now I felt put down, and that's how the ill will there had been during the past month between us farmers on the one hand and the various workers on the other grew into open discord.

"We never have Sundays. There wasn't a day between March and November we don't work. And yet it's only in winter we can take a rest. The earth's asleep and there's no way to wake it, and we too are shut up in our shacks, with a little fire, a little wine, a few chestnuts, to enjoy our only days off during the entire year."

CATALDO CHIESA

"That's the point. Farmers drink and do nothing all winter long, and here too they wanted their wine, they wanted to be warm and do nothing. They say we have our Sundays. But when have we ever had Sundays off here? They say we also have Saturdays, they say we have a whistle that blows at five o'clock every day . . . But when have we ever heard a whistle to stop work here?

"Here, instead, work and no thought other than work has been our secret. It was the one way not to let ourselves be overcome by the wish to drop everything. If work hadn't existed, we'd have had to invent it. And so we have to thank our lucky stars that there was such need to build: storehouses, silos, stables, dormitories . . .

"There was also plenty of sewing for those women who knew how to sew. We had bought a good quantity of cloth after one of our sales of scrap metal. It was meant for aprons, overalls, blouses. Instead, they told Ilaria that she should have bought beans and salt pork. They all but suggested that we resell the cloth. They didn't understand, they began to gather at the old stable, they wouldn't work any more, and they grew melancholy . . . But there was no discord."

ELVIRA LA FARINA

"We poor women of Messina kept on with our bricks and mortar, the walls went up but the mortar didn't hold, the rushing stream was frozen over, the mortar froze, and even Siracusa and many others, and even Ugly Mug had switched work to give our teams a hand and speed up the work and prevent the walls from falling, but when they thought we should be happy about this we weren't, and in the whole long day there was not one hour in which we were happy; there was no gasoline, so the truck didn't go back and forth any more; there was no more nothing; we would get together to eat, but it was no longer the way it had been; we no longer said anything to each other, and we no longer heard anything through the snow except the blows we struck as we worked; we no longer thought of the cities with their shops and the lights behind their glazed windows, the way they are in winter and the way we knew we'd find them, shining with ice too, if we'd still been on the roads that lead to the cities, roads black under the passing trucks, gray by day and black by night, and then all of a sudden those cold lights wrapped in ice fumes that mark the edge of a city, when it breaks like a fair upon the traveler's vision."

CARMELA GRAZIADEI

"Yet we saw how we were running down. I told Elvira how run-down she looked, and Elvira told me how run-down I looked, while first one of us, then another said we were dying.

"This was an ugly thought, especially if it came on one of those nights filled with snow. As if our job had been not to build us our Messina but to build our cemetery. We could think of ourselves turned to solid ice, lined up in so and so many rows with our faces like the tops of the mountains, and with the black crows that wanted to peck at us flying and swooping and trying to peck at us and managing only to peck away slabs of ice from our faces. That is how I almost took my Litterio by the hand and went off with Elvira and the other of us three women of Messina, with the other baby, to wait by the roadside for a truck to pass and take me no matter where.

"We'd never have thought of such a thing if it hadn't been that others we knew were thinking of it, and that set us thinking back to when we were traveling the roads, with all that happened to us then, and the cities we passed through before we stopped here, where no one had even thought of stopping . . ."

Widow Biliotti

"I'd spent all my winters in these mountains, except for the last two I'd spent in town, and I'd already passed more than one winter hungry. But then everyone fended for himself and didn't give away the milk of his own animals to feed the children of others . . . You could make cheese out of it, you could make butter . . . Now I'm not saying it wasn't fair, here, under the circumstances. The animals were mostly goats, although there was one cow, bought with everybody's money. And the children, there were so many of them. But I couldn't help thinking that if the grownups were to die, the children wouldn't be able to survive. So I used to say: 'Let's kill a goat and eat it.' I went so far as to propose my own goat, even if she was about to give birth to kids (and later did, to two of them). She wasn't giving any milk, and for that reason she wasn't indispensable. Other people offered their goats, also, not too enthusiastically, but *they* made no answer and, on the day we finally picked for slaughtering mine, Siracusa pointed a gun at us from one of the stable windows . . ."

Pompeo Manera

"Trifles, just trifles. We were wrong to think of killing off one of the animals. Females shouldn't be killed, and if we'd gone ahead with it we'd have been sorry. They may very well have been right to keep us out of the stable, although our plan to kill a goat was an excuse rather than a reason. Actually, I think, they shut us out in order to force us to follow their example.

"Because they thought we were lazy, in spite of the fact that from September to December they'd seen how hard we worked. And they weren't content to merely hint at this opinion. They voiced it in no uncertain terms, and called on us to help them with one job and another."

Cataldo Chiesa

"We called on them because we needed them and others besides, if there had been any, because we wanted to distract them from their ugly thoughts, which we might have shared and did, indeed, share.

"The way we treated them was, I admit it, too rough. But they made us waste our time watching over them; they were childish, and if we told them they were slackers it was in order to needle their pride and bolster the pride of us all in the face of the temptation to let everything go and run away. The trouble was that they took offense; every day they wore a more disgruntled expression, as if there were a deep disagreement between us. Instead of their following our example, we followed theirs."

CATTARINE

"We peasants, too, need to be forced into a change. This is the third change I've made so far. I left Fruili in the autumn, because there was no place left where I could sow. Minervino, from Cerignola delle Puglie, went away in the summer, he says, for the same reason.

"A peasant's disgruntled facial expression may have meant that he had in mind to go away either in the summer or autumn. But if, instead, he managed to sow his seeds and the winter was freezing cold, then his disgruntled expression meant that he was cold and hungry and out of sorts, but he didn't want to go away and let everything collapse. A peasant who has sowed his seeds has somehow committed himself and so he stays where he is and broods over them. If I left the Pontine Marshes in the month of April, it was because the Allies landed at Anzio, which caused my irrigation ditches to break down and destroyed the seeds I had sowed."

POMPEO MANERA

"That's what happened to me near the Gothic Line, when they placed mines among my potatoes . . . For two years, in the city, I played the wine expert. I sat at a table and tasted wines, but all the time I was wanting to be a peasant rather than a wine expert . . .

"What do you want?" they asked me. "Do you want to be a wine expert?"

137

"If it wasn't Barbèra that said it, it was Antonia, and when it wasn't Antonia, it was Ilaria. Someone was sure to say it.

"Troubles are like the hunger and frost that may come upon a peasant after his sowing, when there's nothing he can do about them. So it was that none of us thought for a single second of going away, no one made any such suggestion and no one carried it out, although a lot did think and speak of it and do it.

"Who were they? Let them speak up for themselves. They even spoke of going to the city—as if it were a winter resort—for a couple of months and then getting together again here in early April. Who they were? A lot of people were discouraged and turned back, people that had left us early on. And who were they?"

ELVIRA LA FARINA

"I don't know where the idea came from that we could go to the city and stay until April, but it did come, somehow, and made the rounds. Everyone said it, and no one wanted to work, except for six or seven or perhaps a dozen of us that stubbornly kept on working, including Whistle and Ugly Mug and Cerro and Siracusa and Ilaria and old Barbèra and Spataro (even without the truck that had run out of gas) and Toma and about half a dozen more.

"Every one of them had his piece to say. Some said that going away or not going away didn't make any difference, because we'd all die of cold and hunger anyhow. Then, one day, all of a sudden, someone would be missing, and people would call attention to the fact that he'd gone and that a truck had stopped just below us on the icy curve of the highway. The highway was snowy miles away from us, but we all knew where it went, with its slow, icy miles, gray and then green in the course of the day, and black at night, when it was struck by automobile headlights. At a certain point, as we knew, there were city lights, lights upon lights, lights in a dazzling row, outshining the sporadic lights in the windows of delicatessens, fruit-sellers, cafés, moving-picture theaters and, finally, behind the glazed panes of dining rooms and bedrooms, gleaming white bathtubs and toilets, white kitchens in which we never set foot . . ."

CARMELA GRAZIADEI

"The *second* one to go off in the same way was Manfredi Spagna, a Neapolitan from Sparanise. He disappeared just like the other, while all of us were wondering where he was and whether he too had run away and how.

"The *third* was Nardo Delitala, who had worked in the steel mills of Piombino, and with Whistle, and played a harmonica.

"Along with him went Santina Garoglio, who slept with him and others but who had learned to work at roofing, more efficiently than a man. The more she slept around the better she worked, so that when Mime wanted her output to increase, he told her to go sleep with someone and then come back to work.

"So Santina Garoglio was the *fourth,* and the *fifth,* who went off on the evening of the same day, was poor Biagio, the oldest of us all, a brickmaker and hod carrier, who had been chewing, ever since July, on the same cigar butt, which no longer had any of the properties of tobacco.

"*Sixth* was a boy called Saverio, who had worked with Biagio, an orphan born in Busalla. But he came back the next morning, half dead, and four men rushed to the place where he said poor Biagio was waiting to be pulled out of the snow. They found him, all right, but he was frozen stiff; his clothes and the cigar hanging from his mouth were stiff with ice, his face and staring eyes were icy, just the way we imagined that all of us would be some day.

"I made him the *fifth* and Saverio *sixth,* although Saverio came back. If I were to count all those that came back, the number would swell considerably.

"The *seventh* was . . ."

CATALDO CHIESA

". . . They were ours, all of them, for sure. Some had been workers, others apprentices until they were drafted into the army, but now they were acquiring skills among us. None of the others, the farmers and peasants, gave the bad example of going away or trying to go away.

"What does that add up to?

"The first really bad example was not working. *They* were the ones to set that. And if, subsequently, our people got scared and started to run away, it only shows that we are quicker to follow our words with action. Now, one was dead, five had gone, and others went and came. But it wasn't proper for *them* to count everyone who turned back in the wind and snow and to shake their heads. *They* had no right to disapprove or pity them . . ."

CARMELA GRAZIADEI

"The *ninth* was Mariano Santarosa, who comes from around Massa and Carrara. He works now with Cerro and knows how to cut and carve marble.

"Number *ten* was Savina Maiocchi, from Milan, the one who always talks about the time when she had a stall on the Via Melzo and sold fruit and vegetables and brooms,

and number *eleven* was Filiberta, her friend, although she comes from Giulianova in Abruzzo,

and number *twelve* Liberata La Grua, a friend of both of them, from Sicily, who sold Sicilian-type bellows and hand-warmers.

"All three of these women came back, and so did Santarosa; the three women almost immediately, and Mariano three months later, in April;

"Basile Moncada, on the other hand, didn't come back, although no one had ever expected him to run away. He had worked like a dog on Whistle's motors and in the mill, until they told him Whistle was gone, and three men ran to look for him, but in vain.

"Basile was number *thirteen,*

"and Arduina la Cortese, because she was in love, ran after him. She wasn't bad looking, although in spite of our starvation conditions she was too fat, and she cared more for him than he did for her, and she was number *fourteen,*

140

"and she was found by the three men who were looking for Basile, sitting in the snow, to rest, or to hide while she heeded the call of nature, with her face rosier and redder than ever, and her fat slightly lightened, although she suffered from chilblains for a whole month thereafter.

"We counted them, one by one, as they went away—*eleven, twelve, thirteen*—although we noticed that most of them came back, and in very poor shape, after a single day or a day and a night. Either they never got to the highway, or they got lost on a road where no trucks went by, or else they were sorry to have left our company and retraced on foot the road they had traveled by truck. One fellow, Guerrino Cucuzza, whom we called Guerrin Meschino, came back after a whole week, bringing butter and cheese and a two-gallon can of gasoline, slung over his shoulder, for the truck.

"up to *fourteen* we counted, and *fifteen,* and we looked one another in the face, Elvira and I, and the disheveled Giacomina—five of us we were altogether, with Giacomina's brat and my Litterio. Giacomina calculated that her child and mine would make *sixteen* and *seventeen,* when I told her to skip *seventeen,* because it's unlucky, and to start counting us five from *eighteen.*

"but when *eighteen* came along I couldn't make up my mind,

"and I stayed here alone, counting Giacomina as *nineteen,* her child as *twenty,* and Elvira as *twenty-one,* although one Barbèra eventually brought her back from a village tavern, where Giacomina had left her in the weakened condition of the fifth month of her pregnancy . . ."

45

They have a story to tell, we said. They remember, and speak of what they remember. Or else someone that was not there with them that winter wants to hear about it, and they tell him.

141

"They came back weeping with rage, struggling upward for an hour or more through the snow over a distance that ordinarily they could have covered in five minutes. When we saw the condition they were in, we shook our heads in despair. If it hadn't been for us peasant women, for Barbèra, who is fundamentally a peasant, too, and for Antonia, I don't think they'd have survived.

"I had the idea we could cook the onions, and that way we had something hot again every night and managed to take care of them, every one. We even gave them half the milk set aside for the children, although Whistle, our mayor, and Ugly Mug were dead set against it.

"Toma had been a medical student before the war, and the Germans turned him into a vagabond. Taking upon himself the role of a doctor, he told me we had to feed them up.

" 'Shall we kill a goat?' I asked him.

'Take it easy,' he answered, 'That wouldn't do any good. Give them a double ration of cornmeal mush . . .'

" 'And a double ration of soup?'

"At which he suggested hot milk, at least for a few days.

"I gave them milk, stretching the children's ration with water. But two women protested to Whistle that I was diluting their children's milk; in fact, they said that we peasants were plotting a Massacre of the Innocents, so that we could have the milk all to ourselves.

" 'God, no!' I told him. 'We don't want the milk. We've been giving it to the returnees.'

" 'What?' Whistle shouted, 'to those saboteurs?' "

POMPEO MANERA

"I appreciate Ugly Mug; he's a good fellow. And so are Whistle and Toma and Cerro. Separately, I appreciate every one of them; I'm ready to put that on the line.

"But why did they have to be so hard-boiled, to keep on thinking up jobs to be done, when they could have done the job that took three months in one, since we had good

142

weather and every other circumstance in our favor, including the comradeship there was among us? I don't know what got into their heads, what they saw during the days when it was snowing and we were content to fold our hands and relax. The devil that's what they must have seen. They were in cahoots with Spataro, the truck driver, that old witch Barbèra, Ilaria, Isidoro from Livorno, Guerrin Meschino, and some others, all or most of them good people, but wanting to force us into their rigid pattern. Life was quite hard enough without their trying to make it any harder. Well, never mind . . .

"That's what led to dissension. From the end of January to the middle of February they were constantly bickering, more among themselves, actually, than with us . . ."

WIDOW BILIOTTI

"Whistle went out, and because I thought he was going to get Ugly Mug, I went to find Toma. I told him what was up and said I didn't want to face the two of them alone.

" 'I'll be with you,' said Toma.

"We met Siracusa with her gun. Toma said hello, and I said hello, and Giralda, who happened to be nearby, made fun of us with a military salute and said hello twice, once for Toma and once for me. I didn't know what might be going on between Siracusa and Toma, but I knew about Toma and Giralda. Anyhow, Giralda followed us, still teasing, and Siracusa came after her.

" 'Listen!' I said to Toma.

"I heard Whistle shouting and knew he must have come back. Meanwhile Giralda, from just behind, mockingly repeated: 'Listen!'

"Inside, just as I thought, we found Whistle and Ugly Mug.

" 'What's up now?' Whistle asked me. 'What's got into your head?'

"Giralda came in, and so did Siracusa. Ugly Mug was telling me that the returnees were deserters.

" 'Saboteurs, I call them,' said Whistle.

"Giralda mocked him, too. '. . . teurs,' she echoed."

143

"We were lazy dogs and they were saboteurs and deserters, that was the story. They insisted on getting up on their high horse, but no one could get it out of my head that everything would have gone more smoothly if we'd fallen in with Nature and spent the winter in a natural way. It's natural, after all, in winter, to take it easy.

"Everything indicated taking it easy rather than being in a hurry. The flow of water from the dam was blocked by ice and the motors couldn't turn over, but they insisted on trying to pour the cement three times over rather than relaxing and letting others relax. They wouldn't let even the children alone. So I can't help fearing that the division between us, who are called idlers and saboteurs, and them, who are miracle workers, may lead to more trouble between us."

Widow Biliotti

"Ugly Mug is usually reasonable and accomodating. He knows how to set a good example instead of speaking from the soapbox. He works rather than talks and finds the best way to do one thing and another. Then he goes to his girl and asks: 'What do you say?' He seems to be asking her approval, while she seems unwilling to give him satisfaction, although she tacitly admits that he's done a good job.

"Even on the worst days of the winter, I've seen them acting out the same scene. Ugly Mug looked at her as if asking whether he wasn't a fine fellow, and she looked at him as if she were about to say no, but at the same time she smiled, and that set him up proper.

"Then he became quite different. He said that the milk was for the children and so it must continue to be. Obviously he was going to follow Whistle. And Toma seemed afraid to speak up. He looked at Giralda and then at Siracusa. Obviously he didn't want to cut a poor figure. 'Hold on,' he said. 'I ordered milk for them because they need it.'

"Giralda was gesticulating in such a way as to lead him on. But Ugly Mug wheeled around: 'You did, did you?' he said to Toma. They stared at each other without speaking, while Giralda gave a low whistle and made gestures now to Ugly Mug. 'You did, did you?' she echoed.

"I saw him from the back and Toma from the front. So I had a full view of the slap he gave Toma on the face, leaving a mark of shame upon it."

CATALDO CHIESA

"Such quarrels didn't prove a thing. What could they prove? There was nothing serious behind them, no fundamental difference of opinion. They were trifles, womanly trifles. The women provoked them, and then the women caused them to blow over. And Toma was always involved.

"The worst disaccord was between him and Red Kerchief, who nonetheless remained his friend. They rolled and tussled in the snow, got up and tussled some more. At first I didn't linger on the scene; I shouted to them to lay off and went my way. And if I came back, it was because I thought they were giving quite a good show. 'Still at it?' I shouted.

"By then they had shed the shirts and undershirts from their backs and were rolling again in the snow, leaving dark streaks behind them."

WIDOW BILIOTTI

"Toma was unusually prudent for his age. Or perhaps Ugly Mug's girl had more sense. I thought to myself that they would butcher each other. Then I saw Siracusa come between them and pull Ugly Mug away. Suddenly he was pale-faced and docile, as if he were aware of being in error.

"'You Fascist!' she said, but calmly rather than with anger. I didn't see any sense in the word, but I saw that he was shamed and that Toma no longer minded having been hit in the face.

"This time Giralda clenched her lips and made no signs to anyone. Ugly Mug turned from Siracusa to her and then to Toma. 'I'm sorry,' he said. He was genuinely ashamed and said that it was right, after all, to give the sick and weak people milk, even if they had only themselves to blame for their misfortunes. To Whistle he said: 'The best thing is for them to recover as soon as they can.'

"Then he came over to Siracusa, who was standing near me, and looked at her out of his earnest eyes. Was his look reproachful? It seemed timorous."

CATALDO CHIESA

"Giralda crouched in the snow, looking at them, with her hands under her folded arms. I became aware of her because of the steam coming out of her mouth. Otherwise I'd have thought that there was only a pile of clothes on the ground, where they had thrown them. She was peacefully absorbed in the spectacle, and probably had been even before I passed by for the first time.

"When I saw her I thought that the two boys were fighting more seriously than was really the case. I resented the idea that they were wasting energy that should have gone into their work. So I called out to them to lay off, I threw snow in their eyes and tried to force them apart. 'Let's go,' I said. 'You've done enough. And what for?'

"To Toma I said: 'You've broken his nose. Quit it.' And to Ugly Mug: 'You've smashed his face.' "

WIDOW BILIOTTI

"I can't say that Ugly Mug had it in for Toma or that there was any personal question between them, since I'd never seen any sign of it. Ugly Mug was rough only because he was angry to see us take thought for the returned fugitives when he wanted to punish them. The trouble is that he has the mentality of a soldier; he must have been in the war. This explains, too, the remissive way in which he reacted to the epithet his girl pinned upon him. On second thought, he didn't really want to think and act like a Fascist.

"His girl must have more of a head on her shoulders. Like Giralda, she's the kind that likes to dominate men and to stand above other women. These are grounds on which women can always agree, while men lose their cool, make an outburst, and then are taken for a ride, as were, that day, both Ugly Mug and Toma."

CATALDO CHIESA

"But both boys wanted to claim a victory.

" 'O.K.,' I said to Red Kerchief, 'you won.'

" 'The hell he did!' put in Toma.

" 'So I told Toma, too, that he was the winner. One of them wanted to win on the girl's account, and so, actually, did the other. Finally I put it up to her.

" 'What's that?' she said. And she added that she hadn't egged either one of them on to win. That's why I say that nothing serious was at stake. She went her way, and the two of them started laughing. All the other winter quarrels went the same way; they all ended in laughter from both sides."

ELVIRA LA FARINA

"But Red Kerchief and Toma weren't fighting on Giralda's account; they were fighting over me. Red Kerchief had been after me for some time, and Toma too, ever since old Barbèra brought me back from the tavern and I came under his care because he was our doctor.

"Red Kerchief resented my having tried to go away without telling him good-by, but Toma had nothing against me. I told Red Kerchief to be good to Toma, because he was taking care of my pregnancy, now in the fifth month. I told Red Kerchief to stop showing his resentment, but he kept right on. Then I let Toma stroke my belly the way he liked to, and I told Red Kerchief about it so that he'd lay his resentment aside. That's the reason why he picked a fight with Toma.

" 'You don't ever stroke my belly,' I told him.

" 'Who does, then?'

" 'Toma.'

"And that's why he hit Toma in the face."

CARMELA GRAZIADEI

"Did they fight over Giralda? Did they fight over Elvira?

"In any case it was a good thing, because after that things began to change. A lot of things happened, whereas previously we did nothing but count how many people had gone away: twenty-two by such a day, then twenty-three and twenty-four . . .

147

"It was twenty-four on January 29, including the thirteenth of those who were coming back. A few days later, on the feast of San Biagio, the sun shone on the snow, the ice began to melt on the dam, the stream once more had the sound of water, the mill had the sound of a motor, and on February 15 there was electric light, as Whistle had said there would be, gleaming from every window of the shed.

"I counted a twenty-fifth man going away and a fourteenth coming back; a twenty-sixth going away and a fifteenth coming back. Eventually the only ones to be counted were those coming back. The shed was lit up like a railway station, as if our village were one of those big cities to which we used once upon a time to travel, a line of lights visible for miles away on snowy nights and calling to those who journeyed through the night.

"Number fifteen of the returns was that of Elvira on January 30. I could have counted her as number twelve, when I saw old Barbèra go after her and Giacomina. Red Kerchief already had it in for Elvira for having gone away, and he hung back, unable to make up his mind."

ELVIRA LA FARINA

"And I was waiting for him! Yes, waiting for him!

"I had done wrong, I admit, not to tell him that I was going away, but after I had gone I was always thinking about him, especially at nightfall. I was tired from walking over the white ice of the country road, which never arrived at the gray ice of the highway, where trucks were passing by that might have stopped to pick us up.

"Giacomina was always in the lead, and she would turn around to talk to me, but I was thinking only of him. I was walking only in order to keep my feet from freezing, and if I wanted to get to the highway and grab a ride on a truck, it wasn't because I was so keen, now, to go away, but simply to snatch a moment of rest. I was already sorry about going away; thinking of him I could have cried, thinking of him and the others, our mayor, our Ugly Mug, my Barbèra, my Carmela, the truck when it came back every night, our house and its kitchen and all the work we'd done to no purpose,

148

the baskets of bricks and the bags of cement, all lugged in vain. If I was happy to see the headlights of an approaching truck it was because I was tired, not because I was happy . . .

"That truck didn't pick us up, though; it was another, and the driver laughed to see that I was pregnant. He asked me to tell him how I got that way, and to show him. Tired and feverish as I was, this was a drag, and in the tavern where we stopped in the morning I did nothing but cry. Giacomina and the two men were fed up with me, and they left me there, not knowing what I should do and wishing he'd come fetch me and waiting for him, until, instead of him, in came our Barbèra . . ."

Carmela Graziadei

"By now, for every one that went away, another came back. Number sixteen was the Maiocchi girl from Milan, bringing vegetables with her and sweeping away the snow so as to set up a stall like those on the Via Melzo in Milan.

"Filiberta brought something back with her too, pulling it with a rope. She ploughed her way through the snow a hundred yards farther than the Maiocchi girl; she was number seventeen, and at every step she fell onto her knees in the snow and moaned.

"Liberta La Grua was number eighteen; she was the third of their group, pulling a wooden case full of fruit and a foot-warmer and a pair of bellows, with the same idea as that of the other two, of setting up a stall like those lined up on the sidewalks of Via Melzo, Via Lazzaro Palazzi, Via Plinio, and Piazzale Lima in Milan, where they display apples and oranges and warm themselves over fires lit in trash cans, in the space between the grimy houses and the white snow . . .

"I went on happily counting; the next was number eighteen. I stopped counting those that were going away and counted nineteen, twenty, and twenty-one of the returnees. On February 6 or 7, I counted Thorn, who had left with the cart months before and now came back on foot, jumping in the snow and sinking into it, and clambering out and sinking in again, and crouching there until he recovered his strength, and then jumping again and pushing forward, his head and shoulders covered with snow, until the others went to meet him and pulled him home . . ."

46

And the fellows with the nicknames? And Whistle? And Thorn? And Siracusa? And Ugly Mug? And Toma? Of course Whistle and Thorn had a story to tell. Each one had something within his own experience to say. Toma, for instance, had his own story, and so did Giralda. And Siracusa and Ugly Mug might have had theirs. What was the story?

WHISTLE

"I knew he'd come back.

"There were three possibilities. That he should come back with the cart. That he should come back with the money he'd got from its sale. That he should come back after having spent the money. But that he shouldn't come back at all was out of the question.

"If I didn't run after him and grab him by the hair when he ran off in September, it wasn't simply because I couldn't interrupt work on the powerhouse. It was because I was sure he'd turn up one day or another, with the hypocritical expression on his face of a man who's done nothing wrong.

"I knew last summer that the cart and mule were too much of a temptation, and I said to myself that he wouldn't last long, that he'd surely go away. I said that because I knew him. And, because I knew him, I said that he'd come back. He can't resist temptation, but at the same time he can't resist being sorry. Besides, he can't stand on his own two legs, he needs to lean on somebody else.

"That's why I waited tranquilly for him to return. I knew that I could mete out his punishment on the spot."

"What a sight! If Ugly Mug hadn't intervened, he'd never have come out of it alive. But he deserved such a close shave. After all, he'd not only robbed us, he'd cheated and deceived us as well.

"For three or four days we'd all been happy, because the sun was shining on the snow. We were anxious to get started, to clear the snow from the village streets, from the paths, and even from the road leading down to the highway. Above all, we wanted to stay in the open air. Every now and then there was noise, like that of a holiday celebration, which meant that one of those who had gone away had come back. I've never seen such happiness as there was on the day of Thorn's return. Everyone shouted out his name, and Whistle hugged us all, saying that he'd said so all along.

"Thorn was all smiles as he came up through the snow, which now was like foam on the hillside exposed to the sun. The rest of them went to meet him and shake his hand, but soon they began to hit and then to kick him every time he fell down. Whistle shouted a protest:

" 'Bring him to me alive!' "

"Finally he took off his belt and made his way into their midst.

" 'I didn't mean to take a step for you,' he said, 'but I want to give you your due before they devour you.'

"And he beat him with the belt, whose buckle caused streaks of blood to run down his face . . ."

THORN

"And to think that I believed in the story of the Prodigal Son!

"Right away they all seemed very happy, including Whistle, who wanted to take me to see the progress of the powerhouse. He claimed that he hadn't done anything to my legs that could prevent me from walking. 'What did I do to your legs?' he kept asking.

"All this was very different from what it had been when I went away. Then, even when I came back with all sorts of riches in the cart, they pulled long faces. Then they were incapable of being happy, now they couldn't seem to worry. They'd nearly killed me, and it made no dent on them; all they could do was joke and laugh about the shellacking they'd given me.

"What caused such a change? According to what they said, it was the fact that the winter was over, that they had successfully come through so many difficulties and privations. But good luck doesn't make for that much of a change of attitude, not until you've enjoyed it for a long time. So, in spite of what they said, they must have been pretty well off all winter. They had put on weight, I saw that. And a slice of cornmeal mush a day wouldn't have made them any fatter. What's more, their clothes were in order. I ask you: would they ever have had time for mending if they were living through difficulties and privations? Hard times don't leave you carefree, and they were models of good cheer and assurance. They were so carefree that they might have killed me, if it hadn't been that a few of them had common sense. Ventura had the most of that and had undergone the most radical change. He was another man from the one they had named Ugly Mug."

"Another man?

"Yes, another man from the one I had been two years before. Anyone who knew me before could have testified to that. Sometimes I wished I could tell them the way I used to be so that they'd tell me the way I was now. That I could at least tell *her* . . . Certainly, I'd already begun to change when they first met me, in the days immediately after I was still changing, and a month later I had changed some more; you might say I changed, if only a little, every day, in spite of the fact that, as one thing and another happened, I felt that I hadn't changed at all since a year or two years before . . .

"Those were our best days, in February, with the sun turning the snow into white velvet on the hilltops and with cessation of the fear that we'd be scattered, since they were coming back instead of going away. But there were still difficulties, because winter was still there. In those days I couldn't help

152

changing, even in her eyes, that is, unless she was the one to change, to think differently from the way she had thought before and to judge things in a different way . . .

"Only a few days before, I'd lost my cool with Toma, but this didn't seem to stop her from thinking I'd changed. She made an outburst, too, when she called me a Fascist, and the result was that we didn't break up, in fact our relationship continued to grow as it had been growing ever since the day when the village heard the motorcycle approaching."

SIRACUSA

"Finally his black granite mold began to melt, and the funny thing was that, although I had liked him for it because it was such an essential part of his make-up, only now did I realize that I was in love.

"I mean his essential quality had attracted me, but it was when I saw it melt that I began to feel more tender toward him.

"In him I now saw what a man ought to be, stubborn in struggling against reality but at the same time gentle and understanding. I don't mean only me. Would I have had the same feelings if he'd been that way with me alone? I'd have seen that he could be gentle and understanding. But his being good to me wouldn't have convinced me that he was really good. What touched me was not only to think of him as being good but to see him working on his good behavior.

"December and January went by, and he was always coming to me as if to ask for my approval. That was how we came closer together.

"He could have asked me: 'Am I doing all right?'

"And I could have answered: 'Yes, you are.'

"He kept up his good behavior, and perhaps he had always been good, really, and there was no sense in my telling him so, and I didn't tell him, or else I told him, meaning to say that he had been that and more, that is, kind as well, as it would have made more sense to tell him if only we had been close to each other in the way that's necessary to bring out words of that kind.

"He seemed to understand, and stopped asking for my

153

approval. His whole manner changed. He approached me
half boldly, half jokingly and asked:

"Do you still think I'm a Fascist?

"Our closeness was suspended, and I didn't reply. Moreover,
one time Giralda Adorno heard what he was saying.

"She asked whether I wouldn't rather think of him as a
Red Kerchief or a Toma, and that's why he took advantage
of the first opportunity to slap Toma in the face."

TOMA

"I never said I didn't like to chase the girls. I had chased
Antonia and, before that, Elvira. But if a girl turns me down
I never push it. And I respect anyone else she chooses to
care for, if he deserves respect.

"I put Siracusa out of my mind in July, as soon as I saw
that she'd chosen to go with Ventura. Everyone can bear witness that it was as if I'd never so much as looked at her.
Unfortunately I didn't fully understand what sort she was;
I kept thinking she wasn't like other girls, and that's why,
months later, I had her on the brain again. At a certain point
it seemed to me that between Ventura and her it was all
over. Of course, that was wishful thinking. I had the bad
luck to look as if I were waiting for her. And I had, for the
second time, to endure the shame of withdrawing. And to
make the effort, all over again, of putting her out of my mind
and of not holding a grudge against Ventura. And of not
showing that I wasn't happy, as all the rest of them were, in
the month of February.

"But why did she let me believe that I wasn't so objectionable
to her, after all?"

SIRACUSA

"The trouble between us was quick to pass. I wasn't concerned for Toma, I was worried about Ventura. And I knew
that a slap given in a moment of exasperation wasn't all that
important. Still, I didn't let it go by easily. I wanted him to
come back but, after what had happened, I wanted him to
suffer a bit. For instance, I told him that he shouldn't make
a fuss if I wanted to go with Toma.

154

"'*Do* you want to?' he asked.

" 'I don't want anything,' I said. 'But if I do, don't think you can stop me.'

"In other words, I told him that if I didn't go to bed with anyone else it wasn't becauce I was afraid of him or even because I didn't want to do him wrong; it was simply because I didn't want to.

"And he said that I could have conveyed the same idea with many less words.

" 'That is? . . .' I said.

"This was my last weapon for making him suffer. We were walking along, I in front and he behind, after supper, with snow underfoot and around us all the way to the snowy distances that we could see by daylight, and instead of wondering why it was so clear I was wondering whether we could make love outdoors without having to lie down on the ground.

"It seemed as if we had no house in which to take shelter, and no time. And yet I had time to notice that the snow was blue and very hard, like ice, as if it would produce sparks, like those of flint, if one were to strike it. I didn't know that, beginning the next day, I wouldn't see the snow that way again.

"We saw lights above us. The sky was clear, and the lights were stars, twinkling in the wind. The sky would be blue the next day; we could see just how it was going to be, and in our impatience for dawn to come we couldn't sleep.

"We had a room of our own behind the stable, a few hundred yards from the village. That was our house. He kept going to the door to look out and see if the sky was still the way we had left it. I wanted to see too. And halfway through the night, after he had looked out a number of times, he couldn't resist running to tell the others that there was a sky which boded a sunny day to come."

TOMA

"If I felt ashamed it was because of him, of the way he continued to treat me just the same way as before. For instance, the night before that first sunny day of the winter, he came to the dormitory and I was awakened by his calling my name: 'Toma! Toma!'

155

"He was knocking and calling, calling by name for me rather than for anyone else.

"'What's he want?' I asked myself. And when he went on I felt ashamed.

" 'Come see what's up,' he was saying. And he told me to rouse Spataro and all the others and to come see something new.

" 'What is it?' we all asked.

"We heard him go on to knock at another door and call Cataldo. But he had called me first, and this was like a wink that recalled all the things we'd done together.

"He said that there was sun, and for a minute I almost hoped that he'd gone mad. The windows were dark, and my wrist watch said that it was only three o'clock in the morning. But outside the darkness was blue over the glistening snow, and the sky was filled with twinkling green stars. He wasn't mad; the sun was on the way, and I was ashamed not be happy about it."

SIRACUSA

"This was what made me feel tender toward him, to see him not self-satisfied or happy for himself, but happy for the possibility of happiness for the village.

"It was as if he had to create happiness among the others in order to have some for himself. He even seemed to think that I couldn't be satisfied with him unless I was satisfied with the way things were going for all of us or at least with our efforts to make them go . . . That was how I acquired a soft spot for him, for all the times, like that night, when he made it clear that he couldn't be happy unless sharing the happiness of others.

"So February was a wonderful month, a month of the winter sunshine we'd dreamed about, with the satisfaction that even Thorn had come back and with the electric power that, one evening, lit up the whole village. A month that brought us a new cause for satisfaction every day, and was followed by March, when we planted the potatoes and saw green stalks coming up where we'd sowed wheat, and then finally Easter,

156

when the stalks were higher than the snow had ever been, and we killed some lambs . . .

"I came to have a soft spot for him, I was saying . . .

"I realized that he couldn't be happy, and good, and relaxed, and human any other way. It was as if he had to get a feeling of his own identity from others, from outside, as if otherwise he had no identity, or else that it had been paralyzed by a bullet shot into him during the war.

"And as if he were on guard lest his love for me come from inside him. This love was somehow thorny . . . That was it . . .

"But this was what melted my heart, the idea that he had to make such an effort to soften up and at the same time to be a man, since it was impossible for him to act in the same simple, spontaneous way as anyone else . . ."

VENTURA

"February, and then March;

"in February the electric power, and the light bulbs, and the light that suddenly blossomed in all our houses;

"and at the end of February the patches of red earth among mounds of snow that melted away without ever losing their whiteness, and the earth that had to be fertilized and ploughed, and joy in the fact that although the winter wasn't over, it was no longer such an enemy . . .

"April, too, was a wonderful month, with our relationship growing and growing, because of the way she was with me, the way things were going for our land and our village, and the way it was with all our people.

"I was able to believe that I had really changed. I felt happy, and I couldn't have felt that way if I had been the same man as before. For some time I'd been asking myself: 'Am I happy?'

"For a while I found no answer; then there came a period when sometimes I could say I was happy and sometimes I couldn't. I was afraid of not being happy, and I tried to be happy even when I wasn't. Then I found myself able to tell her and show her that I was happy, and then I really was. I don't know if it's clear what this meant . . .

"You have to remember how we first got together. This group of people could have been a good thing or it could have been a bad one. Every one of us had the power, in his relationship to others, to influence them for good or for ill. Every one of us was, you might say, ambivalent. Only I seemed to be one-sided. I could wish for something good and work at it harder than anyone else, but my heart wasn't in it; the impulse didn't come from inside.

"That's why, even while the community was becoming more and more of a good thing, I was still asking myself whether or not I was happy. Did I really care how things were going? Sometimes I did and sometimes I didn't. But from the end of February to May I was really happy, happy to be a part of it. And what did that mean? Didn't it mean that I had changed? The growth of the relationship between Siracusa and myself seemed to indicate that I had. I helped plant potatoes in earth still cold from the snow with a joy that was that of a new man. And my reaction to the sight of the green stalks of wheat and the odor of boiling milk and burning twigs when we started to make cheese told of a change in me as well.

47

Ventura and Siracusa might very well have said nothing. And what we heard, as it were, from their own mouths, could have been mere supposition. But for everything we imagine, there is confirmation on the part of those who speak or have spoken . . . Of Widow Biliotti, Carmela Graziadei, Whistle, Thorn, and Pompeo Manera.

WIDOW BILIOTTI

"Every four or five days, beginning with the end of January, a lamb or a kid was born, so that by the end of February

158

almost all the ewes and nanny goats had milk, some already in October, November, or December. I was the first to say that we should make some cheese and also some *ricotta*.

"Do you know how to make *ricotta*? The cheese is sprinkled with salt and set to drip in a wicker basket in which it takes shape and dries out. The pot below fills up with whey, and the fire is no more than glowing embers, until twigs are thrown on to make it flame higher. Meanwhile fresh milk is added to the whey. With the addition of a small amount of milk, you get only a thin layer of the finished product. But the more milk you put in, the higher will be the layer of *ricotta* that forms at the surface.

"Shepherds usually make *ricotta* early in the morning, but we made it at dusk, so as to enjoy a bowl of good soup when our work was done. But we began when there was still sun in the sky, since the twig fire can be built only outdoors, not in the kitchen . . ."

CARMELA GRAZIADEI

"Just the way we made it in Sicily, outside the caves where the shepherds keep their sheep. Here, in the beginning, before we had any kitchens, we cooked even our soup outdoors, and sat down on rocks to enjoy it.

"By now, of course, we were eating inside, but for the *ricotta* we proceeded as if it were July, standing in line (I held Litterio by the hand) and passing in front of the pot, where two women were serving, one skimming off a slice of *ricotta*, the other spooning out some of the whey.

"We ate it just as they do in Sicily, too, outside the caves, with chunks of bread tossed into the pot. Here, unfortunately, we had no bread, only baked cornmeal mush, but it was good enough, with steaming *ricotta* on top of it and the pale green whey, poured through an opening in the surface of the *ricotta*, which stood two, three, or even four inches high . . ."

POMPEO MANERA

"But if you want the *ricotta* to be tasty, you have to see to it that the fire is built with twigs that have an aroma. The degree of heat is important also. The flames must rise high as soon as the fire is started. Splinters of faggots, broom, and rushes won't do, because their flames are too sticky. The dried stalks of weeds are better . . .

"But beware of a cemetery smell, of anything that grows underground or close to the ground. You need vine shoots, heather, or wormwood, all of which catch fire quickly but without too much crackle, because their twigs are sharp-pointed and wiry. The thornier they are, the better, especially if the flower is thorny and dries up together with the rest of the plant, so as to form a silver rose or a silver geranium and to make, in the fire, a silvery crackle.

"Or else laurel branches, which burn as they should even if they are still green and were cut down only a week before."

VENTURA

February and March, those were our best days, each month in its own way, without ups and downs, and all of April and part of May, in spite of some inevitable difficulties. The difficulties were almost agreeable, whether produced by our own affairs or by nature, as when there was a high wind and fog, which we feared would dampen the growing shoots, or the weeks of continuous rain in April.

"By now we could call ourselves well organized; everything that had come to a halt during the winter was again in motion. The truck resumed its trip to the city, although not as frequently as before. War scrap had to be gathered farther away, and the men had to ride on the truck in order to load it; sometimes they met up with other scavengers, working in organized gangs for big city buyers.

"In connection with the truck, there was rejoicing when Guerrin Meschino brought back a two-gallon can of gasoline upon his return from the exodus. And also, as proof of the solidarity of our group, when Thorn extracted from his jacket lining an amount of money even greater than what he might have obtained from the sale of the mule and cart he had stolen from us five months before. He produced it when it became apparent that the truck couldn't go on functioning, after Guerrin Meschino's can had been emptied, without the purchase of more fuel. For one thing, he wanted to drive the truck, as he had driven the cart.

"This was, to me, such a good sign of the merit of our enterprise and such a confirmation of my happiness in belonging to it, that I persuaded the others to let him take the wheel when we drove one day into the mountains to gather some laurel bushes for transplanting."

WHISTLE

"I was the one to get the money out of Thorn's jacket; he didn't surrender it of his own free will! If I let him take credit for it, it was because it would have been a blow to my prestige to have a friend that insisted on holding on to the fruits of his own crime.

"He began courting the truck from the very first day of his return. He got to it as soon as he could and starting running his hands over the hood and the painted rooster, the fenders and even the tires, just the way he had caressed the mule brought by Antonia.

" 'Do you remember,' he asked me, 'that I know how to drive?'

" 'I remember,' I told him.

" 'I've still got my license, right on me.'

" 'Where?'

" 'Sewed into my sleeve,' he said, touching his arm.

" 'So what do you want?' I asked. 'To do with the truck what you did with the cart? Perhaps you'd better let me keep your license; it might be a temptation.'

"Of course I didn't wait for an answer. I jumped on him, and we scuffled, but I tore his jacket off his back and sat down on the running board with it lying across my knees.

"He didn't try to get it back, but sat down on the ground facing me, in his shirt sleeves. We were under the roof of our first shelter, which now served as a garage. Nobody else was around, and we stared at each other. I didn't want to lay hands on the license; I turned the jacket around in my hands, but didn't finger the sleeve to which he had pointed.

" 'I'll get it out,' he proposed.

161

"'I can do that,' I retorted.

"I gingerly ripped the sleeve lining out of the jacket, noting that it was new although the jacket was old. He observed that I might not be able to rip the seam without making a tear.

"'I might not be able myself,' he admitted. 'Perhaps we should get one of the women to do it.'

"'I know how to sew and how to unsew,' I said. 'I leave women out of it.'

"'I don't feel that way any more,' he told me. 'You overdo it when you think of women the way you do. There are things they can't do, but there are also things they do better than we do.'

"'For instance?'

"'For instance ripping a seam.'

"But many a time in the course of our travels, I'd patched a hole in his clothes or sewed on a button, I reminded him, and meanwhile I had ripped just enough of the seam to extract his worn driver's license, which I proceeded to put into my pocket.

"'Have you finished?' he inquired.

"I shook my head. I had just begun to pluck the chicken, and I wanted to finish the job, so I went on to rip out the padded front of the jacket. He held his head between his hands, sitting back against the wall, but looking up at me. Then he began to sing a different tune. He told me what I could expect to find, but I had already extracted it.

"'Look out!' he said. 'There are papers, and they're worth money. They are money.'

"As I pulled out the papers that were worth money he continued to tell me to take care, because they were thousand-lira notes, his savings for the months when he had worked as a carter, which he had sewed into his jacket in order to donate them to the truck.

"'To buy gas and keep the truck going,' he insisted.

"Carefully but thoroughly I ripped all the seams and got out all the money. The thousand-lira notes, as I stacked them up, came to be about a hundred in number. I must say that, at this juncture, even in the midst of such abjection, I chalked

162

up a point in his favor; after all, he had come back to us before spending the money."

THORN

"Whistle still had the same prejudices and shortsightedness. He always believed the worst, and was taken in by appearances.

"When it came to the money I had sewed into my jacket, he didn't take into account that it came to more than the going price of a mule and a cart, and he didn't let me tell the others that there were thirty thousand liras saved up from my trading. No, he wouldn't let me take any credit. He didn't understand my idea of earning money while I was away, in order that everyone should be happy when I came back, to make up for their sorrow at my departure. And he deprived me of the satisfaction of pulling out the money at the appropriate moment, that is, when a surprise would have boosted their morale.

"As for the question of the truck, he was positively childish. I'm not denying that I wanted to drive it. I said so, quite openly. But he insinuated that I was plotting to make away with the truck as I had done with the cart. As if a man couldn't have a change of heart, and as if I hadn't, after all, come back. As if, even were I tempted to repeat the business of the cart, I hadn't brought them more than enough for the price of a truck on the market. Never mind . . . Fortunately, the others had changed their ideas for the better, especially Ventura. He could see that I had changed and that they could trust me. He wanted to show Whistle how he felt, and so one day when he too was supposed to go in the truck, he suggested letting me drive.

" 'Thorn at the wheel!' he said. 'Let's see how he drives.'

"We were setting out for something like a pleasure trip, to go look for some laurel to transplant and make into a thicket."

GIRALDA ADORNO

"Things were going in a way I liked. We could take some rest, look around us, without doing anything except listen

163

to our companions tell their stories. I enjoy these things more than making a racket or having a party or even dancing to music. Taking it easy and listening to talk and putting my own word in edgewise. Making eyes, as if it meant something, even if it means nothing at all. Seeing somebody else get angry and excited and Unbuttoned jealous of me.

"Their idea of fun is to dash around. It's their way of snatching a little free time after so much hard work. Finally we had that time, and if they chose to spend it in their way, I was free to spend it in mine. I looked around and made mental notes, and I came to the conclusion that Toma wasn't really my favorite, even if he was the youngest among us.

"The bloom of youth may be the greatest asset in a man's eyes, especially in a woman. I'm glad I'm still in bloom. But I respect a man that says: 'I'm the boss.'

"Or acts the part, without even opening his mouth. Ugly Mug was the one that came closest to this ideal. As I watched him, I realized that Siracusa had had the right idea in prefering him to Toma.

"Not that I was envious of her or really wanted him. But I'd have liked to see her deprived of his attentions, and so I made eyes at him and chatted in order to rile her. And she *was* riled the day we went to get the laurel, more for the fun of it than for the laurel itself . . . Thorn, Carmela, Ilaria, Spataro,Toma, Red Kerchief, Siracusa, Ugly Mug, and myself, and Isidoro, who brought his accordion along . . ."

POMPEO MANERA

"Laurel doesn't grow into a real tree or provide wood, but it's a good thing to plant if you want to reforest.

"It takes root and spreads fast, it stays green all winter and has a good smell. We needed to reforest for various reasons, and we needed kindling. And laurel is easy to transplant; you don't have to dig down deep or use fertilizer, yet its roots grow strong enough to split stones.

"We had to find out where we could get enough of it to make a special trip worth while. We'd seen people pass by holding branches of laurel in their hands. And some of the old inhabitants of the village said they used to gather it. That

164

was why we finally decided to take a day off and go look for laurel."

48

It was June, however, perhaps halfway through June, and not on the day of this excursion that Carlo the Bald and Ventura inevitably met.

Carlo had resumed his periodical visits at the beginning of May. He came early in the morning, not by motorcycle but on foot, or else with two of his men, in a minicar, as if he did not want to be recognized after what he had said, in an outburst of anger, to the men on our truck when he went back to the city after his last visit in the fall.

By now it no longer seemed strange to the village when someone passed by for no particular reason. There were buyers of scrap and T.N.T., salesmen of agricultural machinery, and merchants of other kinds who, ever since the beginning of April, appeared on the square and made deals with Whistle. By May we had set up a wineshop, where no one thought of asking a customer whether he was there on business or just to pass the time of day. So Carlo the Bald's visits might have been unnoticed if, on account of his job, he had not asked so many very specific or strange questions.

Usually he asked the girl behind the counter, and when he repeated them for the second or third time, one June morning, she quite naturally said that she remembered having seen him in the village the previous fall. Carlo was wearing the hat in which my uncle had seen him on the train. He pushed it back from his forehead, which had a streak of red from the heat.

"Maybe so," he said laconically.

"How come?"

"My activities don't date from just this year."

"Do you work for the government?"

"Nothing to do with taxes, I promise you."

165

"You ask an awful lot of questions."

The faces of Carlo and his companions were shiny with perspiration.

"It's our job," said Carlo. "Can't you guess what it is?" They came from the Automobile Club, he told her. "We're writing a guidebook for the area." And he explained about the Automobile Club and its guidebooks, as if their purpose was to collect all possible information. But the girl would give him no more answers. And so the next day he said to his superiors:

"I think the time has come."

They looked at some papers spread out on the table.

"We need more data."

"We're no longer in a position to get any more. Either I lay my cards on the table or they lay theirs. And for our purposes, the first step is up to us."

His superiors eyed one another.

"At a time when the political sitution is so confused?"

Carlo maintained that the political situation had nothing to do with it, but they wanted to wait.

"How high is the wheat?"

"No higher than the poppies. But it's going to sprout soon. It's a dwarf variety that's well suited to the terrain."

"When would you say they'd harvest it?"

"At the beginning of next month."

"That's the time to show your hand. When they harvest."

Carlo's reticence seemed like approval. We saw that before, on the train.

"Or not much later," he added. "About a month from now, and in the course of a month there can be some variations in the rate of ripening. I'd have to make another inspection, on the q.t."

"Well, that's just what we need in order to fill in . . ."

The speaker put his finger on a blank spot on the paper before him.

"But there's a risk of messing the whole thing up," said Carlo.

Nevertheless, he went back, a few days later, perhaps because he himself was curious about the missing data. And just as he was leaving the village he ran into Ventura.

166

Between eight and nine o'clock the air was as fresh as if there had been no dew. On the plateau there was nothing worthy of note except the profusion of poppies. At a distance the wheat was still inconspicuous, no more than a golden glow on the slopes, and unsubstantial, as if the ears were empty. But this could not content Carlo the Bald. He could be content with no less than a rich harvest. And there was a look of satisfaction on his face as he rounded the last curve and saw signs of our people's accomplishments.

But suddenly his expression changed. He had walked up, seeming to have walked from a long distance, although there was no dust on his shoes, and he did not pause or turn back. The truck was on the square; its motor could be heard for a moment and then died away. A man was seated at the wheel, and other men were looking out of the rear. A man who was climbing up in order to take his seat beside the driver paused with one foot on the running board just as the motor gave out.

So it was that Carlo the Bald and Ventura came face to face. Ventura was standing with one foot on the running board, while Carlo the Bald approached from two hundred, one hundred, seventy-five, fifty feet away, until he was so close that he had to open his mouth and say something. In the rear, Isidoro was tuning his accordion. Amid the fragmentary notes Siracusa spoke up, very quietly and leaning toward Ventura.

"Isn't that the fellow on the motorcycle?"

Ventura made no reply, but, from the wheel, Spataro put in:

"The one I nearly ran down in the puddle." And abandoning his effort to start the motor, he looked around for Isidoro, who could have borne him witness.

"Never mind," said Ventura calmingly. "Even if it is he, what do you want to do about it?"

By now Carlo was no more than a dozen steps away from the truck and advancing toward the side of Ventura. Ventura said he would have a word with him and find out what he was after. He got down from the running board and turned toward the visitor. Carlo came to a halt and addressed them collectively.

167

"Good morning," he said. And, pointing to Ventura: "Is he one of your group?"

Ventura spoke up to say he was.

"I'd never have thought it," Carlo said to him. And then he added, in a general way, "We two know each other." And, advancing another step: "Or am I mistaken?"

"No," said Ventura.

In the back of the truck Isidoro was experimenting with a tune. He was so absorbed in playing his accordion that he took no part in the conversation. Others, too, paid it little heed, and one of them called out impatiently:

"When do we get going?"

"We'll go, we'll go," said Ventura.

Spataro stepped again on the starter and the motor began to turn over.

"We'll talk another time then," said Carlo. The sun was shining into his face, obliging him to keep his eyes half closed.

"When would that be?" asked Ventura. "I can't see that you have much of a reason for coming up here . . ."

"No more than you do for . . ."

"But I live here. I'm one of them."

"And are you *for* them?"

A worker's voice rang out from the back of the truck:

"He was hanging around here all the time last year, Ventura. You must have known him, but perhaps not enough . . ."

"You should set their minds at rest," Carlo said to Ventura. "Or do you think you don't know me well enough?"

Ventura said nothing, and Carlo turned to the others:

"How well do you know *him*?" he asked. Well, or not so well?"

From the back of the truck they all shouted, including Isidoro, with his accordion hanging around his neck.

"Listen, you!" called out the worker. "Do you know why I haven't come down to smack your kisser? Just because you're an acquaintance of Ventura."

"That doesn't wipe out the fact that you don't know much about him," said Carlo. He had to raise his voice in order to be heard over the general tumult. "Do you know where he comes from? What he has to his credit? And what he might get in return?"

168

Between one question and another he glanced at Ventura, as if measuring their effect upon him. But there was still an uproar from the back of the truck, and he concluded hastily:

"Your esteem for him probably has a sound basis. But he's had other merits in the past, even more considerable. And if I were in his shoes, I'd rely on the esteem I enjoyed before. I'd consider it very precious, I would . . ."

He stoped short, amid a general silence, broken only by the hum of the motor, which irritated his ears as much as the sun irritated his eyes. He stared at Ventura, giving him a chance to speak up; then, when he had no response, he added:

"Do you know the story of Cincinnatus? He was a Roman warrior with a great reputation, but at a certain point he asked to be left in peace to plough the land with his oxen. But if a man wants to be left in peace, he must have not only the understanding of his old comrades but also their permission, and he can't have this without consulting them."

From the back of the truck they shouted again:

"What's biting that fellow, Ventura? He's blackmailing you."

At last Ventura reacted, with a calming gesture.

"Ventura, you call him, do you?" said Carlo, "I'd forgotten his last name, and I'm glad to be reminded of it."

He had come close enough to touch Ventura with his hand.

"I'm not blackmailing anybody, you know that. You ought to explain it to them."

Ventura agreed that there was no blackmailing involved.

"But what are you getting at?" he asked Carlo.

Carlo pointed apologetically to the truck.

"I've delayed you too long already. We'll talk another time."

Ventura shook his head gloomily.

"He never did like me much," Carlo explained. "He doesn't relish the idea of my coming back into his life, and all I wanted was to make sure I could eventually find a way of talking to him."

He held his hand out tentatively toward Ventura, who kept his hands in his pockets.

"Until next time then, what do you say? Perhaps I'll come after the harvest. When would that be?"

169

"We'll be starting in about two weeks," Ventura answered.

49

Aboard the truck, as they drove in search of wood in the Solchi di Sacco, over the section of military road which they had chosen to use ever since the laurel excursion, Ventura talked only to Spataro, who was sitting beside him. It took him a while to realize that Spataro was talking to *him,* and that he would do well to make a reply.

"No," he said. "What kind of a trap could the fellow be laying for us?"

"Various kinds," said Spataro. "You know perfectly well that we could get in trouble for not having certain licenses or permissions. For the war scrap we collected and sold . . ." Their situation, he implied, was not exactly legal.

"What's legality got to do with it?" Ventura interrupted. "In Italy today, nobody's in a strictly speaking legal situation."

They could clear themselves with the law, he implied, when law came into the picture. And Spataro mumbled something as to how they should go about it. Then, at last, he came out with what was really on his mind.

"It's a mistake to be caught in an illegal situation if you find that you have enemies . . ."

Ventura seemed to be distracted by other contingencies, by the sun that shone into their laps and occasionally into their eyes, and by the hardened ruts in the road which caused them to bounce first one way and then the other. Suddenly he interrupted.

"We haven't trod on anyone's toes, we haven't hurt or robbed a single soul, so why should we have enemies?"

"All that may be very true," said Spataro. "These things have to be carefully thought out. I'm the first to admit it." He pulled some tobacco and cigarette papers out of his shirt pocket. "But all the same . . ."

"All the same, what?"

170

He took the tobacco and papers out of Spataro's hands and went about rolling a cigarette. He did not smoke, so it was on behalf of Spataro that he lit a cigarette and handed it to him.

"Don't you want it yourself?"

"I don't smoke."

"You don't smoke? You ought to. You're depriving yourself of a kind of companionship."

"What do you mean by that?"

"A means of communicating with others. When two smokers get together and light up cigarettes, they create an immediate understanding."

'I'd never thought of that."

"To think of it you have to be a smoker."

"So, if one fellow's a smoker and the other isn't? . . ."

"It's worse than if neither one of them were a smoker. One of them lights up, thinking of something he has in common with the other that will bring them closer together, and all of a sudden he realizes that, on the contrary, they're farther apart."

"It must be a curious sensation . . ."

"Well, the upshot is that he doesn't enjoy his cigarette as much as he expected to."

"I don't want to spoil your enjoyment," said Ventura with a smile.

Spataro shot him a glance and saw that he was starting to roll a cigarette. He too smiled, indeed he broke into laughter.

"Do you want to learn how?"

"I want to keep you company."

"Look out there! Fake companionship is worse than no companionship at all." And he laughed some more.

Ventura's smile was not long lasting. As soon as he had rolled the cigarette, licked the paper and lit up, he fell back into his gloom.

"Would I have be a dyed-in-the-wool smoker, the way you are?"

"That's what makes for companionship and understanding."

"The habit of smoking? The vice?"

"The extra something in common."

"A common experience?"

There was no reason for shame, said Spataro lightheartedly, in having a weakness or even a vice in common with a fellow man. In fact, the more of them, the greater the understanding.

"Doesn't your girl smoke?" he enquired.

Yes, she did, said Ventura.

"I've seen her smoking," said Spataro. "In fact, two or three times I've given her a cigarette."

He, too, returned to being serious, aware that these last words had a certain significance.

"What do you think when someone gives her a cigarette, or when you see her in the company of smokers and you don't smoke?"

His cigarette was down to the butt, and the smoke had caused him to half close one of his eyes.

"In your place, I wouldn't like to see her smoke if I didn't. I'd want to be close to her at all times, not to miss out on anything she has in common with others or on the possibilities of understanding that result."

He was drawing a last puff from the butt, seeming uncertain as to whether he should say more or let it go at that. Then he spat the butt forcibly out of his mouth onto the road.

"You know how to roll them, all right," he observed. "They stay together till the very end."

Ventura spat out his butt, too, although he had not smoked it to the very end.

"That shows you're not a real smoker," said Spataro. "Otherwise you'd know that the last part was the best."

"Do you know what I was thinking?" Ventura asked him. "How come you can understand me even if I'm not the same as you are?"

"It's the exception that proves the rule," Spataro said with presence of mind, once more smiling.

But Ventura had not finished.

"And if you see with your own eyes that I'm not the same?"

"If we both see it, you mean?"

"If you see it, anyway? If you know it, for sure. Because you do know, don't you, that I'm not the same as you?"

172

"To tell the truth, I hadn't ever noticed the fact that you don't smoke, for instance."

"And then? . . ."

"When you told me, then I noticed."

"Otherwise you'd have gone on thinking I was a smoker, when I'm not?"

"Well, now you're beginning to be one," said Spataro. "And that's all to the good, isn't it?"

50

They were proceeding slowly, at about twenty miles an hour, but rounding the curves fast enough so that the sun constantly shone first on one of them and then on the other.

After Spataro's last remark there was a prolonged silence. Then Ventura came back to the point where their conversation had moved away from its original subject. He took it up with a phrase that had originated with Spataro and that he himself had echoed in the form of a question, without receiving an answer.

"All the same? . . ." he repeated, as if the phrase had been spoken only a minute before.

"All the same, what?" retorted Spataro, wheeling brusquely around.

"That's what you said," Venturi said mildly.

Spataro's forehead wrinkled as he tried to remember why he had said: "All the same . . ."

"What did I say before that?" he queried.

"That I was right."

"Right about what?"

"That no one had anything against us or any reason to be our enemy."

"I said that idea of yours was right?"

"I explained it to you, and you seemed to be convinced."

"We might have enemies that have some old score to settle. Any one of us can have an enemy of this kind. You have that fellow, and I may have another. And because of our way of life, the enemy of one is likely to be the enemy of all. Do you see?"

"So that's what you were driving at," said Ventura thoughtfully. He seemed to agree either with Spataro or else with his own train of thought, and Spataro continued:

"That fellow seems to be dead set on settling a score of some kind. What was the connection between you?"

"I hardly know him."

"You said you did know him, though."

"We were together in the army."

"He was under you in the army? Is that what you mean? Perhaps you played some dirty trick on him without even realizing it. That must be it . . . And soldiers have a way of holding a grudge." He went on to speak of all the strange things that happen in the army, not only between soldiers and officers, commissioned and noncommissioned, but also between one soldier and another. And he revealed, incidentally, that because of his truck driver's license he'd driven a truck. "Where did you serve?" he asked abruptly.

"Here in Italy."

"I mean in what branch. Engineers? Artillery?"

"Paratroopers."

"Paratroopers? I thought that branch existed only in the army of the Fascist Republic of Salò. Were there any paratroopers before that?"

"There were."

"What a crazy idea to join the paratroopers! Brrr! And what was that fellow a paratrooper too?"

"Well, you know, we didn't spend all our time tumbling out of the sky."

"But there were plenty of occasions for you to play him a dirty trick."

"Him? You mean that fellow?"

"Yes, him!"

"I didn't like him, that's true. And I may have shown it."

"Well, it all depends on how. Meanwhile he's got it in for you, that's certain, and it explains why he's been hanging around. But how did he know that you were with us? Every time I think I've found an answer, the question seems to change before my eyes. He couldn't have known, really, that you were here. So what's his big idea? And why, that time, when I met him on his motorcycle, did he say that we had accounts to settle? . . . They say he came several times last fall."

Ventura let Spataro rattle on without interrupting, as if he were considering the sum total of his observations. Then, making an effort to smile, he said there was no reason for worry;

it was all very simple;

there was no reason for reading some deep meaning into it;

the fellow did have it in for him in some strange way, which might be slightly neurotic;

if he had come back so often, it was because he'd caught sight of him, Ventura, the very first time;

and when he came for the first time, it must have been because he'd learned from mutual acquaintances that he, Ventura, was somewhere around;

and if he'd threatened Spataro the day when he got splashed, it was only in a moment of understandable bad temper, etc.

In other words, his way of facing up to the situation was to avoid, at any cost, spreading alarm among the others. It was a matter of shoring up a situation that might collapse. And who would talk in terms of such a danger unless his personal existence were threatened? Carlo the Bald was not coming back until the harvest was in. He must know how to size the fellow up. Therefore, he was acting on an instinct of self-defense, which, whether he realized it or not, was stronger than his concern for the future of the rest of them, or of the relationship with his girl.

But it was strange that his instinct of self-preservation in the face of imminent danger should take the calculated form of exposing himself to attention and conjecture, of admitting that the danger, great or small as it might be, stemmed from his person.

That day and every day until Carlo the Bald's next visit, with anyone in the village, including Siracusa, this was Ventura's manner of answering all questions about him.

175

Sometimes he was reticent or even curt, at others merely elusive and cut and dried, but the manner was always the same, a day after the occurrence narrated above, or a week, two weeks, and three weeks later. He seemed resolved to obtain his own safety or salvation, lighthearted or slightly inebriated with this resolve, and at the same gloomy, even after three and four weeks had gone by. At a certain moment he even spoke of "blackmailing."

Spataro, toward the end of their conversation, had listened to him with a broad smile of something like relief on his face. Then he had seemed to concentrate on the road, at one side of which the terrain was of bare, porous clay. His hands constantly turned the wheel first one way and then the other as the truck approached a yellowish, clayey hollow. The truck ran at moments inside the rim of the hollow, at others outside it, while the outline of the road was so poorly defined that he had to guess where it was going. Meanwhile Ventura talked and talked, with an incrasing rapidity that made his speech obscure and futile. But when he uttered the word "blackmail" Spataro interrupted him.

"Did you say that he's blackmailing you?"

"I say that his visits are a sort of threat, not that he can really do anything to me . . . He takes advantage of knowing that I can't stand him, that the mere sight of him gives me the feeling of being persecuted . . ."

This was the interpretation he gave, from that day on, of the word "blackmail," which he pulled out whenever anyone happened to speak of Carlo. He spoke calmly and reasonably at some length, but at a certain point there were always two or three minutes in which he piled up words one on top of the other, disconnectedly, almost as if he were raving. It was then that he muttered "blackmail," during the days of the fourth week and even on the last one of them. And if he were asked for the meaning of the word, he gave the same explanation that he had given to Spataro, although there had been a long enough interval for him to think it over.

"If that's it," Spataro had said, "then we have only to prevent him from carrying it out. Let him come back, if he wants to, but we can tell him you've gone away."

Ventura shook his head.

"It's not all that easy," he objected. Then, abruptly: "Do you really want to handle him yourselves?"

"Why not?" asked Spataro.

"No, no!" Ventura exclaimed. "I must be here when he comes. I know what to say. After all, I know him, don't I? You must call me."

Then Spataro was the one to shake his head.

They were coasting downhill by now, at thirty miles an hour or so, from the rocky rim of the hollow through a changing landscape that was swallowed up in the distance by an expanse of woods, split (as far as the eye could see) between sun and shade into two, indeed three, levels of valleys. In short, they were arriving at their destination. The dry, thorny shoots along the road came alive and grew thicker; they changed into bushes and clumps of bushes, and finally there was a tree. But Spataro made no reply other than to shake his head.

Ventura was visibly pacified. He too took visible pleasure in breathing in the fresh air that rose from the shadowy woods. And, in the breeze, Spataro felt that Ventura's silence was no longer very different from his own.

"Why worry?" he heard Ventura say. "We can work out what has to be done. There's plenty of time . . . The fellow has a way of showing up later than when he's expected. He takes it easy, as if his chief enjoyment were in looking forward to what he was going to do, as if anticipation meant more to him than actuality . . . So we have a month or a month and half to think it over."

He breathed deeply, as if relishing the good smell of a whole month to go.

Had he really won a respite? Every day he should have struggled to win it. But until the very last day, he wound up every mention of Carlo the Bald in the same manner, saying that there was plenty of time. So that, in the end, everyone thought, at least momentarily, that there was something different about him, something not of his real self or of what he had been in the past.

51

Carlo had said nothing to his companions and superiors about Ventura; he had only shown satisfaction with the visit to the village during which he had run into him.

"I've got the situation in hand," he said, with no further explanation. When the wheat was ready to harvest, he said, he would lay his cards on the table.

Mowing, measuring, and storing in the barn are three simultaneous harvesting processes, that is, when you have a reaper. But if the wheat has to be beaten by hand or by mules turning in a circle, these processes are distinct one from the other. And Carlo seemed to think that the village had given up the idea of bringing in a reaper. Indeed, there had been discussion of this matter.

"Do we want strangers milling around?" asked Ventura.

But from one of his excursions in the truck, Spataro, smiling over the idea of so big a surprise, brought back a reaper and its driver, saying that it was a gift, or very nearly, from a co-operative and that the only payment required was one sheaf out of every twenty-five harvested.

Ventura stalked away, with an ugly expression. What was the matter? Spataro wanted to know but got no response.

"What's got into him?" he asked his friend Isidoro. And he asked Whistle and Cataldo Chiesa the same question.

Everyone saw that Ventura never took part in cutting the wheat; he always had some other urgent job to do all on his own. But wasn't he overdoing it? Others, for various reasons, had stood out against the idea of getting a reaper, but they had come around and worked with it. Why did he have to treat it as if it were a personal offense? Whistle and Cataldo Chiesa and Pompeo Manera all wanted to put the question to him. But Ventura's face was too forbidding, and finally they put it to Siracusa, asking if he was out of sorts with her as well.

"Yes, he's nervous and out of sorts," she told them.

What else could she say? When Ventura was silent and in a bad humor she stiffened in her turn; everybody could see it. For days on end she did not speak to him, but stared at him with an expression of perplexity or slightly sardonic disappointment or slightly sardonic disapproval.

Perhaps *she* was the one to put him in a bad humor, or at least to prolong it. Certainly, whenever anyone asked her if he was out of sorts with her as well, there was a hint that she might be in some way responsible. And that she would do better to give way, to show herself more reasonable than he was.

But none of them could fail to realize, after having lived so long together, that Ventura could only pull himself out of his gloom by dint of his own efforts, with the aid, perhaps, of favorable circumstances. His spirits never improved because of a word or an action on the part of Siracusa. Was she too proud to be the first to hold out a hand? Or was he so proud that he had to achieve self-conquest without any outside intervention? The mystery remained, and from one day to the next the reaping drew near to an end without Ventura's breaking his silence. Spataro had no rest.

"What a man!" he exclaimed. "He went all out for sowing the wheat, and now he won't allow himself the satisfaction of reaping it . . ."

Spataro was exhilarated, like the others, by the blazing sun and by the joy of driving the reaper; obviously he could not fathom why Ventura had deprived himself of the joy of participation. Finally, one day, he saw Ventura passing by. That is, he saw a dark figure outlined against the sun on the slopes, and the figure was that of Ventura. Spataro ran after him, calling out:

"Hello there, Ventura!"

He waved his arms and ran down toward him. Ventura had actually stopped in his tracks, and Siracusa told Cataldo to go join Spataro.

"And you, too," she said to Manera.

But in spite of her nervousness, the encounter between Spataro and her seemed to be perfectly calm.

"After all, it costs practically nothing!" said Spataro, going right to the heart of the matter.

"You call one sheaf out of every twenty-five nothing?" Ventura retorted. "That comes to four tons out of every hundred."

"But we'll never harvest a hundred tons!"

"Just the same, it's four percent."

"That's one percent less than the regular fee."

"Or one percent more."

"Why do you have to say something like that?"

"What I say is that we could have cut the wheat in no more time without paying out any percentage at all."

They had raised their voices, so that Cataldo Chiesa and Pompeo Manera and the others who were on the way to join them could hear them.

"Spataro!" Cataldo Chiesa shouted.

Spataro was pointing up toward the red machine, whose blades glistened in the sun with every stroke. When it moved, all its iron teeth glistened, but when it sputtered and ground to a halt, blades and all returned to the color of red sealing wax.

"What do you mean, without any percentage?" Spataro shouted. "You mean you don't want to see anyone new!"

"Exactly. We don't need anyone poking his nose into our business."

"Are we supposed to be in hiding? If that's what you mean, say so! But, frankly, I don't get it."

By the time Cataldo Chiesa arrived on the scene, Ventura had regained his self-control.

"Just look at your machine," he said more calmly. "We're in the mountains, and in the mountains such a contraption isn't much use. It can't climb, and it's always stalling."

He pointed to the motionless reaper.

"You wanted it, but it's given you nothing but trouble. You have to tag along after it, cutting the wheat by hand every time there's a rise or a hollow. Have you ever, for a minute, been able to leave it alone with the driver? So you can't say it has freed you for other work."

Actually, they had done other work during the cutting. Long lines of men, women, and children were piling up sheaves along the paths and burning the chaff. Clouds of white smoke, streaked with black, dimmed the bright sun. Spataro called attention to these things, but in a less combative manner, and meanwhile, from a row of wheat on a hilltop, the reaper emitted once, twice, three times, a harsh whistle,

180

calling for help. That evening, Ventura's arguments won corroboration, and everyone agreed that when the cutting was done, they would not try to deal with a thresher.

In vain, Spataro insisted that a thresher would be even more useful than the reaper. There was no hurry, the others replied; the weather promised to stay fair, and neither strong arms nor animals were lacking. So it was that, on his next visit, Carlo the Bald found the village just as he had expected to find it.

52

On that July morning, men and women with battered straw hats on their heads, or white handkerchiefs, which they occasionally dipped in a bucket of water, were working over stacks of wheat or around a rusty scale or going to and fro with sacks slung over their shoulders, their bare feet rustling the grass.

Carlo contemplated the scene for the time it took to smoke a cigarette, standing at the vantage point where he usually paused before going down to where the asphalt highway met the dirt road leading to the village. He was not close enough to see the mingled dust and sweat on the men's backs or under the women's blouses. What attracted his attention was the quantity of wheat piled up on the concrete threshing ground. Or the fact that "they" had so many sacks in which to carry it. "Where the devil did they get them?" he might have been wondering. There was satisfaction in his eyes and even in the way he puffed at his cigarette, not so much over the movement of the tiny figures weighing and carrying the wheat as over the amount of what they were weighing and carrying. His satisfaction, he appeared to think, was even greater than theirs.

He had come on his motorcycle, as in the preceding fall, and alone, as if wishing to display his insolence and vainglory.

181

No one hearing the put-put of the engine, as he rounded the curves, could have failed to appreciate the violence of his feelings.

But from the threshing ground, because of the distance and also because of their excitement, they did not hear. The bearers and the weighers were shouting, and Whistle was outshouting them all as he called out numbers, repeating them several times over and receiving shouted confirmation before he marked them on a piece of cardboard. The women hummed a tune, with the men sometimes joining in. No one sang any words, but the faces of both hummers and listeners seemed to say that there was no better tune in the world. All of them talked or shouted at once. Carmela kept calling "Litterio!" while Whistle repeated the weight of every sack. At one point, a woman jumped up to weigh herself on the scale, with Thorn jauntily assisting her. He shifted the weights and shouted: "A hundred and twenty!" Then, amid general laughter, he added that it was Agnese and not another sack of wheat, because Whistle was on the point of writing a hundred and twenty on the cardboard. It was with their eyes that they communicated the joy they felt in their achievement. In the spark of one another's eyes they read a tacit understanding. "*We* did it!" their eyes said, reflecting the "we" that was in their minds. And the unsung words of the tune began with this "we."

All of them had straws in their hair and wheat dust on their skin. Even the air some distance away from the threshing ground was filled with the dust. When a breeze blew, the golden chaff formed luminous clouds which, instead of scattering, swelled and floated through the air until the fall of the breeze allowed them to drop to the ground. They floated as long as two or three days before they rained down. The men's skin itched with the dust, on their faces, hands, necks, chests, and even underneath the belts of their trousers. Carlo became aware of the vibration of the chaff in the air, and the first man to hear the put-put of his engine mistook it, for a moment, for an increase of this vibration.

"Do you hear that?" he said when he recognized the put-put for what it was.

The nearest of his companions lifted his head. Everybody

stopped talking and listened, immediately alert to the fact that "he" had returned and was challenging them from his motorcycle.

"We said we'd face up to him, didn't we?"

They came out of the fields and moved toward the part of the village at the end of the dirt road.

"But Ventura wanted to be in on it."

"Can't we do anything without the permission of Ventura?"

From curve to curve the put-put of the motorcycle climbed up from the valley hidden by the glare of the sun. Finally it came into sight. The men stood with their jackets hung over their shoulders and forks and shovels in their hands.

"Stop!" they said.

Carlo veered to one side, as if to pass by. Then he seemed to realize that this would be a mistake; he got down and ran alongside the still moving motorcycle until he brought it to a halt. He said something about having an appointment with Ventura.

"Ventura isn't here any more," they told him.

"Good-by, then," said Carlo. "I'll be going back."

He had not turned off the engine, and now he threw his leg over the saddle, but without wheeling around. The men closed him in.

"Look here, fellows," he said. "It's half past ten, and I'd catch the full heat of the sun if I were to start now. And why should I submit myself to that? You have a wineshop where I can spend my money. I'll wait there until the heat has gone down."

"You'd better go home right now."

Carlo had got down again from the seat. Now he got up again and turned on the engine.

"I'll lie down in the shade of your laurel bush."

"No," they said. "Go back home right now."

Carlo started on his way. They saw him turn to wave his hand before the first curve that hid him from view; after that they only heard the put-put of the engine. They had told him not to show his face in these parts again. But wasn't it suspicious that he had given in so easily? Scowlingly they consulted one another. Then someone moved across the threshing ground, seeming uncertain as to whom he should

183

address himself. He saw the spark in their eyes and understood that it conveyed a message, but he did not answer. It was as if they were speaking a foreign language, and perhaps the fact that they were laughing and joking and the women were humming seemed foreign to him too.

Ventura began joking himself about the make of the motorcycle.

"So he came, did he? He was supposed to come a week ago, but we finished threshing before his arrival . . ." Then, choosing an interlocutor, he added: "So he came, and you took care of him, did you?"

"That's it," they said all together.

"He did come, then?"

"And we spoke with him."

"You took care of him, did you?"

They laughed.

"No, that's not it," said Ventura. "He thought better of it and didn't come. Every day he thinks better of it and postpones his coming."

Ventura was behaving childishly, and so were they. Because the enemy was not Ventura's alone. If one of the men was still scowling, this was the reason. He had seen that Carlo was the enemy of all of them, that on his face there was a declaration of war, and that the put-put of his engine was the trumpet call of a lone herald. With his trumpet call in the sun Carlo had come forth from an army, and to an army he had returned, with a loud noise and a wave of his hand. But is a lone herald really alone? No, he is the herald of an army.

The man with a frown still on his face paid no more attention to what Ventura was saying. As if to show his disdain, he took his jacket off his shoulders and slipped it on. What was biting him, the others wondered. In his eyes there was no understanding. Now he, in his turn, was for a moment considered a foreigner. He paused beside first one and then another; he paused beside Spataro. He spoke no more than five minutes with each one, but suddenly there were two, three, and four of them who no longer had in their eyes a spark of understanding. They did not stop their work, indeed they speeded it up. But, in a short time, those who

184

had not yet caught on somehow realized with astonishment that a change had come upon them.

The women, one after another, stopped humming their tune. No other woman mounted the scale in place of a sack of wheat. Whistle made no more jokes about the figures he was recording. When noon came, they ate lunch in the shade of the barn, while Ventura repeated, like a drunken man, his rigmarole about the fellow on the motorcycle.

"Even on the first of August he'll think better of it and not come. And he won't come the second of August, either, because he'll have thought better of it . . ."

Finally Siracusa stopped him.

"Can't you talk about something else?"

"Why should I? . . . Did he come?"

"He didn't come," said Siracusa. "But you might change the subject . . ."

Ventura rose to his feet.

"I'm going for a drink. Isn't anyone else thirsty?"

Two or three of them went along. And after them, a group of five or six followed.

"I have an idea," said Spataro to those who remained, "that we've wasted our time."

"How's that?"

"By doing nothing. By seeing things as Ventura sees them."

Many of them agreed, and some of them said so. And the men who had followed Ventura probably agreed too.

For Carlo was once more in the village. They had not heard the motorcycle again. But first his cyclist's cap and then his face and his body emerged behind a hillock from which, by slinking along an old wall, he had thought to enter the village unnoticed.

Carlo had dusted off his sleeves and trousers. He had looked down from the hillock at the land, now free of mines, lit a cigarette and smoked it. The men could have run after him, for he was no more than a hundred yards away. But they waited, and only when they saw him slinking along the wall did they move in his pursuit.

Carlo picked his way slowly among the nettles, and soon one, two, three, four, five of his pursuers reached the spot whence he had emerged and every other place he had touched

185

as he proceeded, walking more slowly but less furtively than he, so that there was always the same distance between them. The distance had not been shortened when, at a turn of the wall, Carlo saw that he was being followed. He stopped, as if to wait for them. But when he saw them pause, too, he went on at the same pace, looking back more frequently, until he came to where both nettles and wall ended.

"We have to remember the three fellows who stepped on mines," said Spataro. "They might call on us for an accounting. Perhaps it's a crime to run a risk without permission . . ."

He and the men to whom he spoke were continuing a conversation they had begun on the threshing ground, as they made their way toward the wineshop.

"We may be in for trouble."

"That's sure! But perhaps it's better that he should speak up and let us know how things stand. We've been living cut off from the rest of the world . . ."

"Do you think he's government?"

"Police, courts, local administration, everything that goes to make up government. During the year that we've been up here we've forgotten all these things. And meanwhile they may have got into gear again. For instance, the trains are running now, whereas a year ago they were strictly imaginary . . ."

Ventura and his group had arrived at the wineshop. Carlo saw them go in. Emerging from the shadows of the last turn of the path, he stopped in his tracks. Did he want to create an interval between their entrance and his? His pursuers were at the far end of the shadows from which he had emerged. Resolutely, he stepped into the sun.

53

Inside the wineshop the first thing noticeable was the smell of sweat. The next was the difficulty of seeing clearly. More sun than usual was coming through the slats of the blinds, cutting the semidarkness with bands of light crossing one another from either side. Ventura was sitting with a circle of men around him, the sun striping their faces. They fell silent when Spataro and his group came in and stood at the bar.

"So you concealed his visit from me?" Ventura shouted.

A translucent reddish mat served as a curtain over the door, and the shadow of someone else approaching from the outside was outlined against it. Ventura seemed to be waiting for the latecomer to enter. But the face that suddenly appeared was not that of just anyone, it was that of Carlo the Bald, with his cyclist's cap above it.

"It's not true, then, that you'd gone away," he said at once to Ventura.

"What's that?" Ventura exclaimed. "You told him I'd gone away?" He looked through the rays of light at his companions and then repeated, to Carlo: "They told you I'd gone away?"

Carlo had let the curtain fall behind him, but he did not come farther into the room.

"It's almost warmer in here than outside," he said. In the shadow in which he was standing, something like a smile seemed to be playing over his lips. "If you don't mind, I'll take off my jacket," he added.

Without waiting for an answer he took it off, revealing a thin body, bony, slender, freckled white arms, and a striped cotton T-shirt.

"It's better that you should be here," he said. "Your presence may facilitate what we have to say before these friends of yours and help us to add it all up."

A murmur arose from all those present. So they were in the picture. By twos and threes they began talking to one another, paying scant attention to Ventura's explosive reaction.

"What the devil have you to do with my friends? What can you have to say to them?"

From the tables and the bar they looked at Ventura with a trace of irritation.

"Come on!" they protested. "We can at least hear him out."

New shadows appeared outside the door, and men came in, men and a few women, raising first the right and then

187

the left side of the curtain, three, four, five, six. Carlo let them slide by him without budging, even when they bumped him as they went by.

"Please . . ." he said. Everyone stared at him as they passed, eyeing his striped T-shirt, and it seemed as if he were limiting himself to saying "please" because there was no time for all he wanted to say. One had hardly glided along the wall, breaking the web of sunlight, when another followed. Finally Carlo was able to say, touching his cap, that they must forgive him for having lingered.

"It's ninety-eight in the shade," he explained, "and you wouldn't want me to get a sunstroke . . . We could have talked even if he wasn't here . . ."

They interrupted to ask whether he had time to waste. Carlo bowed slightly, and said that he was available until such time as the heat of the sun had lessened sufficiently to allow him to start toward home.

But they spoke of having to go back to the threshing ground, where the wheat was waiting. They asked him to abbreviate the preliminaries and get down to telling them concretely what he was after.

"Concretely?" he answered. "You speak of wheat on the threshing ground. That's something concrete. Do you have any idea of the total weight? How much have you weighed and how much is still up for weighing?"

They exchanged glances of something like relief.

"Who are you to question us?" said one of the women.

"But they held her back.

"If that's all you want, you can take a look and see for yourself," they said.

Had he come to claim the government's share? They intended to hand over whatever they owed; it could be sent in the truck the next day. At this point they winked at one another.

That was it, and that was not it, said Carlo. There was more than that, and he would explain.

"But I'd like to wet my whistle first. May I order something?"

He went up to the bar, with the bands of light falling on the stripes of his T-shirt. As soon as he had given his order he paid for it, without waiting for the drink to arrive, and pointed to the tip that he had left on the counter.

Our people were divided into two groups, one tough and hostile to the point of ugly words, the other conciliatory, seeking to circumvent him and size up his strength.

"You came to provoke us, fly-by-night!" said the first. To them he was not an unarmed stranger, who had to be protected, but a gadfly that could easily be crushed. "Didn't you hear that we're pressed for time? And we're not long on patience, either."

They would have no sentimentality; all of them together mumbled a protest, and then one of them acted as their mouthpiece and put it into words. "If you don't hurry, we'll pick you up by the seat of your pants and send you flying through the air to the place where you left your motorcycle!"

But the other faction exhorted calm and good manners. "Come on, boys!"

Carlo smiled at these words, silently drinking. He listened only when the tone was conciliatory.

"Let's see, then . . ." What else could he want to know? About the potatoes, the government no longer claimed a share of them . . . or did it? They had gathered little over a ton the first time around, and probably the second gathering, due to take place in another week, would yield the same amount. The sum total was barely enough for their own needs. Then there was the corn. That would not be ripe for another month, and they could not calculate the yield. And there might be a storm. If all went well, there would be enough for the government's share. Exactly what percent was expected?

"Strange," said Carlo. "I thought your meetings were more orderly. You all talk at once; nobody can make himself heard above the rest, and so we're not getting anywhere."

Did he have to teach them the workings of a democratic community? He was surprised that Ventura had not given them instruction.

"All right, all right . . ." they answered. Even the conciliatory faction at times showed signs of annoyance.

"Shall we speak one at a time?" Carlo proposed.

189

"Of course . . . That's the way we *are* speaking."

Each one should have his say, and to this end Carlo proposed naming a chairman to keep order.

"Fly-by-night!" some of the tough ones protested. "Are you teaching us play acting? You have your say, and we'll have ours."

Others maintained that there was nothing wrong about Carlo's proposal. They knew what it was to have a chairman preside over discussions. If now they were to discuss, a chairman there should be.

"Isn't it so, Ventura?"

Through the sun dust Ventura did not bat an eyelash to signify either yes or no.

But the rest of them went ahead. How about you? You? they asked around. Finally one man volunteered to be chairman, and Carlo, glass in hand and one foot on a stool, asked for the floor.

"My God!" exclaimed someone. "Can't you see he's making fools of us?"

54

Whether they saw it or not the interruption was silenced. Perhaps it is a good thing to encourage an enemy to make a fool of you. Good because it leads him on to self-confidence and foolhardiness. Or, in this case, perhaps because they relished the aspect of comedy in the situation.

"So," said Carlo the Bald, "Do I have the floor?"

The "chairman," aware of Carlo's gaze, looked around him and then nodded.

"In short," Carlo began, "I suppose you know what the land office and its register are, and the maps of landed property. You may have seen them. Lands and houses, mines and factories, river courses, riverbanks and coastlines are all mapped out, with boundary lines to indicate who owns what, and hence who has to pay real estate taxes. The maps are so carefully drawn that not a single square inch, including the cratered summit of Mount Etna, is left without an owner. What doesn't belong to Tom belongs to Dick or Harry, and that which is not the property of an individual or business belongs to the public domain. In this last category we have riverbanks, the seacoast, and the craters of Mount Etna. Nothing is without an owner, so that there can be no misunderstandings, no private takeovers without rights acquired by inheritance, purchase, or leasing. Is that clear? Uncultivated land, marshy shores, a village where all the doors are unhinged or even the unlikely example of an entirely uninhabited province does not signify that there is no owner. Take a piece of land that is uncultivated because the owner, for personal reasons, chooses to leave it that way. Does someone want to cultivate it? Then he must find out who is the owner and offer to buy or lease it. And if the owner consents, no representative of the law will intrude. But if, on the other hand . . ."

Within the diabolical network of sunbeams, the men, sitting or standing, said not a word, but their eyes grew big as saucers, reflecting concentration, perplexity, and dismay reminiscent of the hardest times they had lived through together. Even Ventura had the same look of wide-eyed attentiveness. Only one peasant, with a droopy mustache, at the mention of an officer of the law, raised his hand. Did he want the floor? His face reflected the same wonderment as those of the others. But obviously he wanted to speak. Carlo shook his head.

"I haven't finished," he said.

He indicated that the "chairman" should call him to order, and the others looked at the peasant unfavorably. What the devil could he have to say?

"As I was saying," Carlo went on, "if a man desirous of cultivating uncultivated land regards it as an uncharted desert island which he is the first to discover and, instead of coming to terms with the owner, takes it over, brings in water, plants seeds, and makes it into a praiseworthy model of fertility, an officer of the law is, nonetheless, entitled to ask him for the piece of paper that authorizes this transformation. And what happens next? The officer of the law is empowered

191

to treat him like vagabond or a beggar. He can put a stop to the whole enterprise and arrest the executor as if he were a common thief."

By now our fellows were wriggling, shaking their heads and looking at one another. They might have realized from the start that theirs was a somewhat illegal position, but they had no idea that its illegality was so flagrant, that even deserts had an owner. The peasant with the droopy mustache falling over both cheeks, like the folds of a long-standing but refractory despair, was still standing up to indicate his wish to speak, and now, without a change of expression, he once more raised his hand. But the others stared him down as before, and he was left alone with his protest. What change could he make in the situation?

"What does the chairman have to say?" asked Carlo. "Will he give him the floor? I haven't finished . . ."

Hands waved a denial, and the man called for the fourth or fifth time by the title of "chairman" echoed their gesture and authorized Carlo to continue.

"Thank you," said Carlo, happy to acknowledge the recognition of his rights and ready to hasten his conclusion. "The owner of the land is, in this case, the one to have called in the officer of the law. But then, he takes into account what has happened. The uncultivated land yielded nothing but weeds and overgrown grass. Now it has produced potatoes, wheat, and corn, there are terraces and irrigation ditches, and he sees it transformed into a garden. And so he changes his idea of leaving it uncultivated. The new situation is to his advantage. Why should he prosecute the man who has brought it about? The man has trespassed, acted illegally and without due respect for the rights of ownership. Trifles! Such a man is too valuable to be lost; for his sake alone the land must not return to its former sterility. So the owner doesn't send the officer of the law. And what does he do instead? He offers the agreement which the trespasser should have solicited. There's still time. He calls in a trustworthy agent and dispatches him in the officer of the law's place. He offers whatever terms the trespasser prefers: an outright lease or a sharecropper's agreement, by virtue of which such and such a percentage of the potatoes, wheat, corn, etc., goes to the owner."

55

Carlo fell silent and sat down on a chair which he had shoved over near the curtain. With his face in the shadows he seemed to be waiting for answer, observing the indications of toughness or willingness to compromise on his listeners' faces. To Ventura he apparently gave no special attention. Obviously he was pleased by the murmur that greeted the end of his peroration as the two conflicting attitudes took shape. Which one did he himself hope for? Die-hard opposition, which would enable him to separate them from their land, or a conciliatory stance, which would allow him to purchase their labor? His superiors must have authorized him to make whatever arrangements he chose on their behalf. And when the peasant with the droopy mustache raised his hand for a third time, Carlo only smiled. The hand, sweaty with effort and from the sun beating upon it, paused in mid-air, chased away a fly, and then was once more motionless.

"I have a very different point of view . . ." he began.

Carlo again pointed him out to the chairman. Someone wanted the floor, and he himself shushed the assembly. But the others, as soon as they turned around and saw who was asking for the floor, waved their hands in the same gesture of dismissal as before and, as before, the chairman echoed their motion. The murmuring arose again, more loudly. Carlo and Ventura exchanged hard looks, until the former chose to say something rather than endure this tacit defiance.

"We'd do well to smoke peace pipes," he said. It's a praiseworthy custom among the prairie Indians. In the search for agreement, they gave this sign of good will, and thus they were able to reach it. We are men like them, and there's no reason why we shouldn't be friends. Why not exorcise the evil spirits and demonstrate a mutual trust that will lead, while we smoke, to the triumph of wisdom?"

He rose, leaving his jacket on the back of his chair, and began to circulate, holding out an open pack of cigarettes. The first men to whom he offered them accepted, and he himself gave them a light, with the wax match of the kind they had seen him use on a windy day of the previous September. Then one man impassively turned him down, betraying a negative intention. Carlo would soon be able to calculate how many belonged to the opposition. Perhaps this was the purpose of his peace pipe suggestion. Two or three were rolling their own cigarettes, but he offered them a light all the same. Smoke rose lazily into the sun-dusty air and coiled around the ceiling light, enveloping it in a thickening blue haze. Men half closed their eyes against the sun as they bent their heads to take a light from Carlo's hands. One brushed it aside and lit up for himself, then others took a light from their companions. Carlo did not stop in front of Ventura. "He doesn't smoke," he pronounced himself, but a moment later, to his surprise, he saw Ventura with a cigarette in his mouth, like the rest. Had he learned this habit here, too?

He went back to his seat, while the smoke traveled from one ray of sun to another, weaving in and out, as through a net, and then rising and falling apart in the air. At the rear of the room, men smoked with their backs against the wall—others leaned against the bar. The old peasant held an unlit cigarette, given him by his neighbor, in the hand which he was still waving. But Carlo was the one to speak, setting forward his peace proposals.

Everyone knew how sharecropping worked in regard to the products of the soil. For houses, taking into account the new taxes, rent would not be much higher than before the war. For buildings with an industrial or business function, the rent was higher. Likewise for the mill. Then there was compensation for the land used in digging for water and for the basin and dam that served the power plant, and so much for the consumption of water and electricity and for the rent of the truck . . .

"No," the men muttered.

At this juncture they were all ready to enter the discussion, to fight it out point by point, whether they were conciliatory or combative.

"The water's ours!"

"We produced the power!"

"Houses? Why houses?"

"And how does the truck come into it?"

They were humiliated by the fact that nothing touched or produced by their hands should be exempt from the claims of an outsider.

"'This is all a different matter," insisted the old peasant, still on his feet. But the others brushed aside his total negation and went on fighting point after point.

"No, no," they repeated, abandoning one contention to take a stand on another. Until Ventura shouted out: "Bunk!" and went on to say, categorically, that not only the land, but also the water, the houses, the electric power, and the truck were theirs and theirs alone.

Everyone was on the alert by now, and many faces reflected alarm, while some seemed to indicate that measures should have been taken, before this, to hold Ventura in check.

"Do you really think you could send the carabinièri in on us and that they'd come?" asked Ventura.

Carlo left his chair and began to move across the network of sun that hung over Ventura. "Ah!" he exclaimed, continuing to break through the bands of sun.

"They wouldn't come," Ventura went on, "and you know it. Because you and your bosses have known for a whole year what we were up to. You came last year and saw that we were clearing away the mines. You kept mum and let us go ahead. Then you saw us building houses and let us go on without saying a word. You let us plough the land and fertilize it . . ."

Carlo waved his hand. "Listen . . ." he said. He could prove that on these occasions he had come merely as an individual.

"You have no claim!" shouted Ventura. "And the carabinièri can't support you. Since when have they ever run a man out of his own house? You know all this perfectly well. If you're presenting these outrageous demands, it's on my account, to promote the blackmail you're trying to pull on me."

"What are you saying?" retorted Carlo.

Standing now, in the shadows, Ventura retorted.

"I'm saying what you heard me say." And, turning to the others: "He counted on scaring me and persuading you to give in. He was banking on me to bring you around. But I'm not going along with his game. Let him send in his carabinièri, and you'll see that the whole province will protest if they touch you . . ."

"That's it!" someone shouted.

Others held back, as if loath to choose war instead of a cheap peace. But everywhere there were cries of "That's it! There's the real point!" The old peasant no longer stood waving his hand, because he was content to join the outcry of the others. Even those who had wanted to hold Ventura in check, although they had not entirely changed their opinion, joined in the shouting. Carlo merely shook his head.

"So what about this fly-by-night?" the men said to Ventura. "What else have you got to say to him?"

"I think *he* has something more to say," said Ventura, sitting down and staring at Carlo. "Aren't you going to say it?"

Carlo shrugged his shoulders.

"Aren't you? . . ." Ventura repeated.

"That's not what I want."

Ventura's face darkened. Protected from the sun by Carlo's body, he could see the unaccustomed way in which some of his companions were looking at him.

"What *do* you want, then?"

"To talk to you in private."

Ventura searched his companions' eyes.

"I'll be right with you," he answered.

"You wouldn't want to go out in this sun, would you?"

"What do you say? Won't you be coming here again?"

"You might honor me with a visit, instead."

Under his companions' gaze, Ventura reflected.

"Where?" he asked.

Carlo mentioned a town some ten miles away. He went there every Friday afternoon, he said, to a café called Fidelio, where he played billiards.

PART TWO

56

By now we are at the same point with the village as we are with Uncle Agrippa in the search for his daughter. We are in the same summer.

Uncle Agrippa is still on the trains. He stops over only at the end of a line, at major stations such as Milan, Genoa, and Rome, or such minor terminals as Colle Val d'Elsa, Schio, and Matera. If he gets off at a lesser place, it is only to take some branch line, such as the Pontremoli-Fornovo, that branches off from Sarzana, or the Avellino-Salerno, that branches off from Benevento. If he spends the night at Cefalú or Porto-Maurizio, it is because he took a local instead of an express at Messina or Ventimiglia, but so far he has never stayed over in any place for a reason unconnected with railway timetables. So one may even wonder whether he is still looking for his lost daughter, whether he still wants to find her, or whether he has found, in trains, something that means more to him than she did, whether he has found, for instance, what he calls "community," and does not want to lose it.

So many people looking at one another and studying one another for hours on end, talking together without its mattering whether they know one another or not, and then getting to know still other people—this, in spite of discomforts and privations, is the joy of travel.

And perhaps my uncle, by now, travels just for the sake of travel. Why is everybody traveling? Why are we always so ready to jump aboard a train?

The fatigue of traveling, at least in this year of 1946, is greater than the fatigue of working an automatic drill. To take a train from Bari and travel for two days and a night to Bologna and then to Trieste or Milan, in a windowless third-class carriage or a freight car, is as wearing as to dig out sulfur under the ground for an entire week. The littler

southerner with his olive complexion, whom we call a black
marketeer, makes this trip in order to sell eight half-gallon
bottles of oil in two large suitcases on which he sits and sleeps
in the stations, sits and sleeps in the corridors of the train,
sits and eats, sits and looks, sits and talks, while his wan face
is further saddened by an unshaven beard. Whether he be
a Sicilian from Capo Passero or a descendant of the Greeks
from Metaponto or Cotrone, he barely makes his train fare
with the eight bottles of oil he has brought north and the
fifteen pairs of nylon stockings he takes back south. He brings
home no more money than he made from two weeks of harvesting olives or a month of cutting wood for an estate owner.
Day and night there is coal dust in his eyes and tunnel smoke
on his breath, and the locomotive whistle swells the arteries
of his forehead. Why, then, does he travel? He began, no
doubt of it, for a profit, just as my uncle began by searching
for his daughter. But it is not for profit that he goes on
and on. And similarly, it may be said of my uncle that he
does not go on merely for his daughter's sake. The traveling
companions he bumps into most frequently all say the same
thing.

For instance, on the train that leaves Venice at noon and
journeys during the heat of the afternoon through the Po
delta and the regions of Ferrara and Bologna. Or on the
train that is ferried across the Strait of Messina by night and
at dawn rounds the endless curve of Santa Eufemia in Calabria.
There is a fellow from Friuli with leather for Sicily, a woman
from Cefalú who finds him customers in Sicily, while he finds
them for her in Venetia. Every time they see my uncle they
make a fuss over him, offering him bread and cheese and
wine, and he responds with equal joyfulness, accepting a dried
fig as well. Sometimes, in their conversations, they forget his
presence and talk about him as if he were not sitting just
across the way.

"It's a strange way of searching . . ."

They point with their chins in the direction of Uncle
Agrippa, who is asleep with his head erect. The sun is rising,
and two or three of them are talking about him.

"Yes, strange, isn't it?"

The train is running beside a gray sea, over a succession

of bridges whose iron structure clanks every quarter of an hour. Uncle Agrippa, like a sleeping bird, opens his eyes, staring at his companions until one of them slaps his knee.

"We were just saying . . ."

And the fellow repeats what they have said:

". . . That you have a strange way of searching . . ."

He gets up, while the woman beside him starts to laugh, loosening her hair from the curlers in which she had put it up the night before.

"Isn't it so?" asks another.

My uncle is the sort that may not answer. We of the family know his ways. He talks and provokes others to talk, he leads the conversation, but only if he wants to. If instead he only wants to roll his eyes, then he rolls his eyes or, at the most, shrugs his shoulders and shakes his head.

Just now, has he shrugged his shoulders?

He rolls his eyes toward the leaden gray sea, toward the ashen gray sand, interrupted at every bridge by the whiteness of a parched riverbed. He hears the three of them talking about him. The woman with the curlers is talking uninterruptedly. "Chicken!" she calls, and Chicken starts talking. Then the man from Friuli chimes in. My uncle may turn slightly, make a sort of bow between his narrow shoulders and wear something like a smile on the lips partially concealed by his scarf. Through the windows on the other side, the light filters in from a range of mountains. In this light, the sea is no longer gray; it is covered by a white veil which opens on patches of blue water; there is sun in the air even if it does not strike the sand; quail and turtledoves cast shadows on the water. My uncle looks from the windows on the mountain side to the windows on the side of the sea, back and forth from one side to the other. Then his cheek rests against the window, and his face takes on the attentive expression of a man who is listening to the echo of the sea in a sea shell.

"What can he be looking for?" they are saying.

My Uncle Agrippa, they say, is always on a train; wherever he arrives, he spends no more time than that necessary for changing from one to another.

"He searches only on the trains," says the man from Friuli.

201

Rosina, having loosened her curls, is putting rouge on her unwashed face. She spits on a corner of her handkerchief and uses it to remove traces of smoke or hair dye. With a small mirror in one hand and a powder puff in the other, she jolts the arm of the man from Friuli and whispers into his ear.

"He's looking . . ." But her words are lost as the train goes through a tunnel.

"What's that?" asks Chicken.

"This good woman is asking . . ." says the man from Friuli.

"I wonder . . ." Rosina continues, "whether he isn't looking for a brakeman, rather than for his daughter."

They laugh, with conspiratorial faces, the woman more openly than the men. Then, as the train comes out of the tunnel, they lean back to talk more at ease, looking at Uncle Agrippa.

Unexpectedly, he smiles. There is an opening between bushes and rocks, an expanse of open countryside and, in the distance, mountain peaks interwoven with sun. Uncle Agrippa unwinds his scarf and enters the conversation.

"We're at Praia d'Ajeta Tortora," he says.

57

Or didn't we, rather, set out again from Rovigo and aren't we approaching, from one quarter of an hour to another of a mid-August afternoon, the Feast of the Assumption in Ferrara?

The leather man from Friuli and Rosina of the curlers may have started talking about my uncle in the station at Padua, with the sun to abet them, a sun that has taken over at least a knee or an elbow of every traveler. The countryside catches onto the train's coattails in a torrid wake buzzing with cicadas. And ever since Monselice, lunch baskets have been opened.

The man from Friuli, tossing his head from side to side

to get it out of the sun, is sweating through his unbuttoned shirt and cotton trousers. The other man is not the one who was on the train from the south and changed at Bologna for Ancona and Pescara; he is physically very different, frightened and with a forelock like a horse's, but Rosina calls him Chicken too. "You there, Chicken," she says. He leans down from a standing position, with the lock of hair falling over his forehead, to take food from her. Ever since Monselice, she has held her underpants in one hand, having deftly removed them, with the appropriate "excuse me." Now she brandishes them with the same hand that serves her for eating, calling the man from Friuli and even my uncle "Chicken" and holding out a stuffed tomato.

"Chicken!" she calls, and no one knows whom she is calling.

The compartment is glowing with sunlight, the fields are filled with ripe corn and red tufts, and the passage of the Po affords not the hoped-for breath of fresh air but only the clank of the bridge.

"Pontelagoscuro, Chicken! . . ."

Has Uncle Agrippa ever searched Pontelagoscuro?

Soon it will be three o'clock of the feast day in Ferrara, and although Rosina and the man from Friuli often get out to do business there, Uncle Agrippa has never left the train at Ferrara. What kind of a search is this?

They study his small face, dry even when he lowers it to escape the sun, and they cannot figure out how he can carry out his search if he is always in motion.

"You should look in the hospitals. That's the most important thing to do, to go to the hospital of every city that has one."

"Chicken," Rosina says to my uncle, but he does not realize that she is addressing him. She strikes his hands with her underpants:

"Have you ever looked in a hospital?"

Three o'clock, and the train has come to a halt. Heat waves rise from the bell towers; the sun treads with wooden sandals on every face turned up to it. But my uncle does not even say that this is Ferrara.

Has he responded all too often to Rosina's chatter? He gives no signs of life and does not even raise his head until a new voice says: "Is that Uncle Agrippa?" Someone who has pushed through the crowded car is asking for him, right and left, and my uncle is flattered by his curiosity. What he thinks is written in his eyes. He wishes that everyone's curiosity were of this kind, noble and respectful. His three fellow travelers are indignant.

"Just look at him!" they exclaim. "He seemed half asleep and, instead, he was waiting, in all his vanity, for a stranger to touch him with his little finger."

Now the finger is upon him, and he will find out how rough it is.

"Is it you?"

Uncle Agrippa modestly hesitates to come out of his shell. He does not admit to his identity; he blushes and tries to get up before making himself known. But the newcomer cannot allow him to put himself out. He is ceremonious, and my uncle is radiant over having a real gentleman to deal with. He makes a half bow, holds out a gray, dry hand, and says that he is honored.

"Are you looking for me?" he says at last.

The newcomer is perplexed and rolls his eyes in the direction of his companions to signify that they should hold back. Then he winks at the man from Friuli and his friends to show them that he is no fool. And he says to the old man that for a long time he has been looking for him.

"I've been looking for you, too," says Uncle Agrippa.

The man from Friuli is nonplused.

"You were looking for him?" he asks incredulously.

"The gentleman was looking for me, and I was looking for him," says Uncle Agrippa.

"Chicken!" exclaims Rosina.

"What I mean," says my uncle, "is that I should be glad to boast of the acquaintance of such a gentleman."

The man from Friuli and his friends drop their arms in resignation.

"Do you think that he too was looking forward to making the acquaintance of someone like yourself?" said Rosina.

Uncle Agrippa smiles, waiting for the gentleman to make a reply. The newcomer shoots lightning bolts from his eyes in the direction of his followers, and no longer bothers to wink at the man from Friuli and his friends.

"Why not?" he says to them.

Then he grasps the baggage rack, leans over my uncle, and gives him a chance to embark on one of the long life stories that have made his fame. Everyone that might have taken fun in teasing him finds it still more amusing to take him seriously. And my uncle, even if he has gone through long hours of discouragement, perks up and finds satisfaction.

58

Running into Carlo the Bald seems to combine, for Uncle Agrippa, the pleasurable feeling of meeting an old friend and the excitement of making a new acquaintance. At the sight of Carlo he almost yelps with joy, wriggling on his seat and gesticulating until the actual encounter.

"I'm coming," Carlo says.

There is a crush of people in the passageway, and he pauses to talk as he slips by. My uncle calls out to them to let him pass, saying that it's his friend and he has to talk to him.

"As if he were your only friend," says the man from Friuli.

But he laughs, and so do the other man and Rosina when Carlo finally makes it. Because Carlo asks my uncle bluntly:

"What do you want?"

Outside, people are walking with newspapers or wet handkerchiefs on their heads, and in the train they have also put newspapers in the window frames to protect themselves from the sun. My uncle is trying to explain that he would like to take up the conversation with Carlo where it left off before.

"To find out whether I have anything to report about your daughter?" asks Carlo.

He is accusing Uncle Agrippa of an ulterior motive, which Uncle Agrippa admits and at the same time denies. Carlo turns down the stuffed pepper held out to him by Rosina but consents to sitting down on the arm of the seat beside her.

"I've never seen so much as a photograph," says Carlo, "so I don't know how I could recognize her."

"I never showed you a photograph?" says Uncle Agrippa.

He loosens the shoelace bound around his old black wallet and talks out a first photograph, mounted on cardboard.

"You'll see," says Rosina.

She and her companions must have seen the photographs, and they are grinning in advance over Carlo's reaction.

"But this is a little girl," says Carlo.

"You couldn't ever mistake her for a boy, could you?" says Uncle Agrippa. "She looked like that from the first day, without the benefit of hair ribbon. When she was six months old . . ."

"And here," says Carlo, "was she six years old?"

"Five. That one wasn't made on any special occasion. I'd taken her to the fair, and a strolling photographer snapped it. Now this, with the smock and the book bag, was made during her first year in school."

"And this on the day of her first Communion," says Carlo.

"And this," Uncle Agrippa continues, "when she finished elementary school, with her classmates and her teacher."

Finally, there is one of a girl about fourteen years old, in mourning clothes, with her head bent over under a black veil.

"Was that when you were left a widower?" the man from Friuli asks mockingly.

"When she lost her mother," says Uncle Agrippa. "I had her picture taken, much against her will, because a new phase of our life was beginning, and because I wanted to remember how sweet she looked in her mourning clothes."

The train has started moving when Carlo hands back this last photograph. The newspapers cast reddish shadows and quiver in the window frames as a breeze is raised by the speed of the train; they flap and tear, opening a vista, through clefts in the banks along the tracks, of hilltop castles, macadam and dirt roads, and row upon row of waving corn.

"Haven't you got any more?" asks Carlo.

My uncle signifies that he has not, throwing out his arms, with the wallet and the shoelace in one hand and the last photograph in the other. As he lowers his eyes to look at it, they are suddenly smiling.

"You see?" says Rosina.

Carlo rises from the arm of the seat beside her and sits down on the one beside that of my uncle. He asks for a second look at the photograph that my uncle is holding in his hand. Why? For what purpose? Does he enjoy looking at is as much as if he were an old man?

They scrutinize it together, while rows of corn fly by in the glaring sunlight outside the window. They seem to be thinking along the same lines, until suddenly Carlo shakes his head. He begins, very softly, to criticize the technique of the photography, the fact that the subject is not shown standing up and that the face is hidden. It is as if he were throwing a cloak of calm and reasonableness over Uncle Agrippa.

Does he want to shield my uncle's naked innocence from those who would mock it? Nothing of the sort! And yet it seems as if my uncle's feelings for Carlo were in some way reciprocated. No one has ever known Carlo to second the tricks of a swindler. Is it for lack of time? Because the train always arrives too soon at Bologna? In this case, it would be inexplicable that he should take part in the innocence of Uncle Agrippa and fall in with it so completely.

59

Here is what happens if, in the compartment where my uncle and Carlo meet, no extraneous persons pay them any attention. The summer sun is like a chloroform compress applied to the travelers' foreheads; one head dips after another, or a cheek leans against the nearest support. But someone there will be able to tell the story. He must have known about them without their realizing it; now he suddenly wakes up and silently observes them.

They have divided the seat that my uncle was occupying

alone, and Carlo has pulled out a wallet. It is tan and squeaks because it is new, as do his tan leather shoes. While his eyes follow Uncle Agrippa's pointing fingers, he begins to extract his own photographs and mingles them with those of the lost girl. Himself with his schoolmates, himself playing Ping-pong or billiards, himself in the uniform of premilitary trainee. Of course he furnishes an explanation. "Here I am in 1932 . . . 1934 . . . The photographs are by now thoroughly mixed, and Unce Agrippa's daughter returns to view only after two or three versions of Carlo—on a bicycle or a merry-go-round or aiming a gun in a shooting gallery. On his face there is written the same satisfaction as on Uncle Agrippa's. Increasingly often, their satisfied smiles coincide. Both he and the girl were photographed in 1931, 1932, and 1933.

"What's this?" asks Carlo. "Is it from 1934?"

No, says Uncle Agrippa; his wife died at the end of 1936, and this must be from the end of that year or the beginning of 1937.

"That's when I went to East Africa," says Carlo.

It was in the autumn of 1936, he explains, when the Abyssinian war was already over. He was looking for a job, but he did not want one in Bologna. He wanted to see the world, and he saw Naples, Cairo, Alexandria and the shanty towns amid the mountains of black Africa. He tries to find some African pictures, but those that emerge are from the recent war.

"I saw Nice, too," he says. "Here I am in Nice."

He is in the uniform of a sergeant, looking proud to be in so famous a city. Next come two or three photographs that he apparently wants to skip, and Uncle Agrippa has to ask about them expressly.

"What are these?" says Uncle Agrippa.

"Oh, well . . ." says Carlo.

He no longer seems amused, and although he lets Uncle Agrippa look at them—one of himself and three officers, a second of himself and an officer against a background of snow, a third of himself and an officer beside a pile of wood—it is without any sign of sharing pleasure.

"You were always with officers," observes my uncle.

"Pretty often, yes," says Carlo, shrugging his shoulders.

Seeing the keen look on my uncle's wizened face, he makes a correction.

"Just with one of them, really; this one, don't you see?"

He runs his nail over the face of the same man in all three photographs. He has recovered the half bored, half mocking tone that he affects when he is talking to a group.

"Too bad, though," he says. And when my uncle asks if this was an exceptionally fine officer, he continues in the same tone: "Yes, but he did something silly. He was in an Allied prisoners' camp where the partisans couldn't get at him. But last May or June, he ran away and lost the protection of the Allies, not to mention the release that he might very well have got from them. And, as if that weren't enough, he did something even sillier. Not content with hiding out, he joined forces with a band of desperadoes of quite a different color and embraced a cause directly opposed to his own. That way he has kept his old enemies and lost his old friends."

"What's that? What's that?" sputters my uncle, not following the thread.

In a bored manner, Carlo says that he will explain.

"I've told you about a village in the mountains south of Bologna, do you remember?"

"Where you had a job to do?"

"Where I still have it. That's what keeps me so busy."

"And what point are you at?"

"Always the same. There's no agreement."

"But you said they were so able," my uncle puts in.

Carlo has to summarize the whole story. Other passengers want to know what it is all about, and Carlo has to spell it out, unwillingly to be sure, but with details, including the admitted merits of the villagers.

"So, you see . . ." says my uncle.

Yes, Carlo "sees," and for this reason he is doing his best to make *them* see the light of reason.

"It's to their advantage to come to an agreement, isn't it? All of us have to make compromises."

"And they don't want an agreement?" my uncle asks.

In his view, a reasonable agreement is sure to find acceptance. Has Carlo offered them good terms? Is he sure he can't offer them something better?

Carlo looks at him crosswise.

"The trouble is, there's one fellow among them . . ." And he goes on to say that every herd has a maverick, and so does this one.

"So!" exclaims my uncle.

At this point, Carlo could really keep his promise to explain. But my uncle has forgotten what went before and does not await an explanation. Not even of why this one fellow is the rotten egg in the basket. "So!" he repeats. He does not ask why, on account of this fellow, the others will not accept advantageous terms but hold out against their own interests. Apparently, my uncle understands how such things can happen. He says, instead, that Carlo should handle it more intelligently.

"Haven't you tried to get him out of the picture? That's the thing to do. Send him away. Then the others would see the light."

Carlo continues to look at him crosswise.

"Send him away?" he repeats. "Yes, there's a point. Send him away."

60

In the village, meanwhile, the discussion that had begun with Carlo's visit was carried on in the fields, the workshops, the wineshop, and over the dinner tables. One day after another, although they worked just as before, there was only one subject of conversation.

On almost every point, there were still the same divergent points of view. Even of Carlo's exact words there were different versions. He had said thus and so; no, he hadn't. And there was the matter of interpretation. And theories as to what those who had sent him really wanted to obtain and whether or not they could legally obtain it.

Always there was the same fundamental cleavage between those who wanted to hold out and those who—like the Widow Biliotti, Manero, Cattarine, and even Cerro and Whistle—thought it would be wiser to come to terms. There were infinite disagreements as to *how* to fight back and *how* to give in, as to what turn events might take and what opportunities might be turned to advantage. And if, occasionally, they all came to the same conclusion, the next day everything was once more brought into question.

Strange to say, no one ever commented on the behavior of Ventura. He was guilty of having concealed from them, for over a month, the danger that Carlo represented. And he had himself admitted the possibility of finding himself involved in Carlo's game. But no one seemed to want to find out why he had behaved as he had and exactly how he might find himself involved in the "fly-by-night's" purposes.

What had struck them the most was his exhortation that they should not surrender. Even the most conciliatory among them appreciated it. Those closest to Ventura were willing to overlook whatever might be his past, and the rest felt they should not stick their noses into his personal affairs; they chose not to be suspicious or inquisitive or to play the part of policemen.

This is not to say that there was not hostility on their faces. But it was a hostility that dissimulated mistrust and at the same time dissimulated the fact that they still held him in esteem, a hostility like that on the face of his girl which concealed the fact that she still loved him.

Although continuing to work side by side with them, he had fallen back into his former muteness. From the day after Carlo's visit until the following Friday, that is, for almost a week, they seemed indifferent to his attitude. They discussed the burning question among themselves without ever drawing him into the discussion. But Friday morning they began looking at him, and there was a question in their eyes. The question was reproachful and even accusing, but gradually it was transformed into mere expectation. That day they held no discus-

211

sions. Every now and then someone asked if it was Friday.

"What day is it? Friday?"

"Isn't today Friday?"

The answers served only to underline the question. Was it Friday or wasn't it? It seemed as if only Ventura could say, for they turned to stare at him, some carrying the weight of the question on their faces, others in the stiffness of their necks. Toward the end of the day, their questions became sarcastic.

"Isn't there a Friday this week?"

And they thrashed out again the question of giving in versus holding out, more bitterly than before. But between Ventura and themselves the ice was broken, and finally his girl asked him point-blank why he had not gone to keep the appointment he had made for Friday with the man on the motorcycle.

Ventura scowled.

"You think I should have gone?"

He was not alone with her; others were standing around. Ventura made a gesture of indifference, as if the appointment, kept or not kept, should have no influence over their course of action. It went along this way for several days, with the others shooting him hostile glances or even saying something to provoke him, while he gave vague or ambiguous answers and failed to respond to provocation. Actually, they were provoking him to reassert his old prestige, and he seemed to refuse to make any effort, as if he were too tired or unwilling to risk disappointment. Whenever he was drawn into the discussion, he remained vague or ambiguous and then slipped away. As soon as he had said anything, he dropped what he had been doing and walked off, even if he had said no more than a "yes" or a "no" between clenched teeth. He did the same thing when he was forced to enlarge upon his views of one detail of the question or another, or to repeat the opinion he had voiced before Carlo. For this reason, they never had a chance to say that he was the cause of some of their present difficulties.

"Do you see?" Spataro sometimes managed to put in.

But Ventura was already walking away, giving them no time to say what they thought about him. In the course of the second week, they grew less hostile and provocatory. All except the die-hards, that is, those who were on his side. On the contrary, the compromisers treated him more and more kindly. Was it because they saw him as a possible negotiator?

In any case, they all wanted him to meet with Carlo, the die-hards for one reason, the compromisers for another. And they all brought pressure to bear on him, the former with a certain anxiety, the latter with a perversity of their own. This time they started the day before.

"Isn't tomorrow Friday?" they murmured.

And all Thursday afternoon and evening they argued as to whether or not and why Friday was the next day. Ventura wearily shrugged his shoulders.

"What difference do you think it can make?"

"You *did* make an appointment with him," said Siracusa.

"We have to keep an eye on them, after all," said Spataro.

"We have to put out feelers," said Manero.

61

The next morning, Ventura was resigned and said that he would go in the afternoon. No one said a word, but it came out that Spataro was prepared to take him in the truck. Actually, he was going on business to a place farther away, and he would stop to pick him up on the way back.

"I'll come back on foot," said Ventura. "I may wind things up in a few minutes, and I don't want to have to hang around waiting for you."

After lunch he absented himself, with his girl, in order to get ready. From the truck he waved good-by and, on the way, he smoked, along with Spataro, giving the impression of a man that might or might not return. He insisted that Spataro let him search alone for the Café Fidelio, somewhere in the long, empty village. The doors were all unhinged and the insides of the houses, visible through the shattered windows, were in ruins. Twice he asked for directions, first from a girl leaning out of an intact window, and second from a man who was sprinkling water on the hot gravel in front of his house.

"Fidelio?"

Neither one of them could tell him. But at a curve on the shady side of the main street, he saw two green plants set out in pots beyond the line of the arcades. Of the village's two cafés, one was a wineshop as well, known as the Café Mercato; the other, because it had no liquor, was called "the Café." This, then, was the one marked by the two plants. A couple of steps led down to a dark front room where three or four men were talking in front of the bar. A woman was in attendance, and another woman sat at the cash register. In a second room, there was a ceiling light which played upon the green surface of a billiard table. The sound of one billiard ball knocking another was interrupted by that of shuffling feet as a player shifted from one position to another.

"What will you have?" Ventura was asked as soon as he came through the door.

"A glass of soda water."

The men standing with their hands in their pockets between the bar and the cashier did not seem to be the kind that might have been waiting for him. Were Carlo's men with him in the room beyond? Ventura emptied his glass. Among the shuffling footsteps he immediately recognized the squeak of Carlo's new shoes.

"So you've come," said Carlo as he walked in.

He was taking aim with his cue and made the shot before drawing himself up to an erect position. Unexpectedly, he was alone. He was wearing the same striped T-shirt as two weeks before, revealing his thin body and scrawny arms. But instead of his cyclist's cap, he was wearing the hat that Uncle Agrippa had seen on him on the train.

"Do you mind if I finish my game?" he asked.

He chalked the tip of the cue and moved to another side of the table. Hearing no answer to his question, he raised his head to look at the visitor.

Ventura was staring at him. He could feel sweat rolling down his chest and wetting his shirt, while Carlo was as dry as a bone in spite of the oppressive heat of the underground room. Carlo, he noticed, did not play particularly well, although he attempted difficult shots. Was he trying to exhibit his skill? To compete with an absent opponent? He went from one corner and from one side to another, often missing his shot and causing the balls to bounce back from the edge of the table. "Solitaire," he had said, but he was playing, with equal concentration, for two people, first for himself and then for his adversary. His footsteps squeaked, then shuffled as he slowed down and took his position; after the shock of the balls, they squeaked again as he went over to the blackboard and wrote up the points, both his own and those of the imaginary other player. Balancing the cue on one corner of the table, he pushed his hat back from his forehead, revealing a red line produced by the heat and the pressure of the brim.

"Well?" said Ventura.

Carlo picked up the cue and started to chalk it. But it was not the same one he had laid across the corner of the table; it was another. For he had been playing with two cues and chalk of two different colors.

"Well, well," he said.

"You asked me to come here."

"But it's you that have something to say."

Ventura looked over his shoulder toward the front room, where what little daylight came through the door at the head of the steps fell upon the men and the two women.

"What about them?" he asked.

Carlo seemed not to understand.

"Well, let's have a game," he said.

Ventura accepted. He had not played for some time, but immediately he took the lead. After his third shot, he paused to take off his jacket. But it was still his turn, and he returned to playing, making no show of his ability and not dragging his feet when he moved to a new position. His shots were clear cut; the ball rolled decisively, and unfailingly put the others in motion. Carlo made the conventional comments, which aroused no response. He spoke too quickly, before the ball had struck, and as often as not the result was different from what he had foreseen. "Short," he would say, and then it turned out not to be short at all. Finally, he fell silent. There was no sound except for that of balls rolling on the green felt, the impact of one against another, the ricochet from the edge, the fall of a ball into a metal pocket which closed over it, interrupted by pauses for chalking the cues and writing up the score, which showed Ventura still in the lead. At a certain point, Carlo's game improved. Without showing off, he caught up with Ventura. Pausing for a moment, he wrote up points indicating that they were neck and neck. Turning around, he called attention to the score.

"What do you have to say?" he queried.

Ventura shot and shot again, then paused to aim. Whatever he had to say, he observed, he had said two weeks before.

"You mean you're staying on their account?"

"I mean I'm staying, just as I told you."

Now they stopped playing.

"I'll be here again next Friday," said Carlo.

"Every Friday you're here?"

"Except when I come up to your place."

Ventura shrugged his shoulders and put on his jacket. He seemed to be about to say something, but all he said was "So long." He passed through the front room and went out underneath the arcade. Then he stepped from the sidewalk onto the middle of the street. From the back of the café, he could hear billiard balls striking one another. But he knew, without this, that he was not being followed.

He hastened his steps toward the end of the arcade. Once more he was among the destroyed houses and the occasional intact ones, in front of which water had been sprinkled again. He stepped lightly, and there was a satisfied expression on his face. He seemed actually to enjoy the streaks of water, quickly dried by the hot gravel, the burning sun that fell on the middle of the street, and the sweat that trickled down his chest. Yes, he enjoyed sweating and being free to sweat, taking off his jacket and walking in his shirt sleeves, with miles and miles to go and a whole week ahead of him in which to burn in the sun and sweat and walk free.

62

But the week to which he was looking forward was made up of staring faces, expectant of hearing the results of his conversation with Carlo. He would have run into their expectancy that very evening had he not lingered from hill to hill on out of the way paths until he saw the lights of his village go out, one by one, or had he not, when he reached home, sat down on the steps instead of going in, spending half the night with a cigarette which he relit from time to time, while Siracusa, in order not to show him that she was still awake, did not call to him to come in.

Hers was the first of the expectant looks that filled the precious days with perplexity and resentment—Saturday, Sunday, Monday, Tuesday, Wednesday, Thursday, and the nights when they all gathered together on the threshing ground. The eyes that irritated him the most were those of the men that had placed their hopes in him and his meeting with Carlo. They were the most upset by his obstinate muteness, and for that reason the ones that made it impossible for him to break out of it and offer a word of explanation. Hadn't he been able to achieve anything? This was the meaning of the staring eyes that turned away after posing and reposing the question and, in their humility, they were harder to bear than the eyes that bored holes through him.

What was so unspeakable about his colloquy with the man with the motorcycle? Why couldn't he come out with it? What was there between them that had to be hidden? The boring eyes told him that he had already got himself into enough hot water without further incurring their suspicion. Why didn't he talk, Siracusa's eyes shouted? Why this haughty refusal when he had a duty to come clean? What was this recurrent Fascist way of denying satisfaction to whom it was due?

He exchanged words with them of course, but only those necessitated by working and eating together. By Friday, even this minimum of communication ended. On Monday, Ventura did not apply himself to work; he walked, with his hands in his pockets, from one working group to another; even

Spataro did not raise his head when he passed, and Whistle failed to call out to him as he went by. Nevertheless, he got wind of the fact that there were hunters in the area. Every group was talking about them in almost identical terms.

"Hunters?"

"They have guns . . ."

"And why haven't we heard them shooting?"

A thirteen-year-old boy had been the first to spot a couple of the hunters lying flat on the ground near the dirt road, with their bodies exposed to the sun and their faces in the shade of the laurel.

"Hello," he called out to them.

Then he went on, stopping to look over his shoulder and scrutinize them. They were whispering together, their youthful faces close together, faces like those of Red Kerchief and Toma.

"What are you looking at?" one of them asked him.

"Nothing," he said. "I thought you were some of us."

"And instead you saw that we were strangers."

"Yes, I saw that."

"And who do you think we are?"

"I don't know." Then, noticing the guns laid out beside them, "Are you hunters?"

They raised themselves up on their elbows and looked at each other.

"Hunters, that's it."

"But you don't have a dog."

"Do you need a dog for hunting?"

"Of course you need a dog . . . You shoot, and the bird falls to the ground, but without a dog you can't find him."

And the boy told of an uncle who had taken him hunting before the war. There he had seen what a part the dog plays. He had run along with his uncle's little dog after the bird had fallen.

"But that was before the war," they countered.

The boy did not get it. What difference did the war make?

"For one thing, there aren't so many dogs."

The boy reflected.

"Really?"

Then he agreed that he did not very often see a dog or

hear one barking. A lot of dogs must have died under the bombardments and on the mines.

"Not to mention those that got eaten," one of the young men said.

The boy looked at them severely.

"You're pulling my leg," he said, turning around to walk on.

But the other young man detained him.

"The fact is," he said, "that we're not hunting birds."

The boy stopped in his tracks, looking again at the guns.

"It's the same thing with rabbits," he said. "Rabbits go on running after they've been hit, and you need a dog to track them down and find the place where they've gone to die."

"Maybe we're hunting animals bigger than rabbits."

The boy was miffed. He looked again at the guns and said, laughing:

"Lions, I suppose. Or elephants."

All of them laughed together. The two young men were not so very much older than the boy.

"We do have a dog," the young men admitted.

"A good dog?"

"For trailing game, yes."

"And for the rest?"

"So-so."

"Perhaps he's not a real hunting dog. Does he have long, hanging ears?"

And he described the little dog that had belonged to his uncle.

"Ours isn't so little," they told him.

"If he's big, so much the better."

He asked where the dog was, and the two young men raised their beardless faces and nodded in the direction of the hills behind them.

"Over there."

"Where?"

"Over there with the others."

"There are more of you?"

There were a lot of them, they explained, scattered in pairs and waiting for the signal to begin.

"Don't you want to stay and hunt with us?" they asked.

But the boy did not stay, and soon word got around the village that there were hunters in the area.

"We should hear the dogs barking," someone said.

Those who knew about hunting said that hunting dogs are not barkers. In the distance, there was something like the growl of dogs held back by leashes. They cocked their ears and waited to hear the shooting.

"There!" said someone.

There was a sound like that of a shot. Was it a shot or wasn't it?

Ventura asked in which direction the boy had seen the hunters, and when the latter traced a vague line, cutting the highway and the railway diagonally from north to east and also the rocky heights near the woods, he separated himself from the others and started walking along the dirt road.

Half an hour later, they saw him moving through the heat of the fields below, stripped to the waist and with his head bare, proceeding at a cautious gait or perhaps slowed down by the furrows. It is hard going on ploughed ground, even without the August sun. After another half hour, he seemed to have progressed no more than a quarter of a mile. Half an hour to cross three ploughed terraces? He must have stopped along the way. For a time he had disappeared from view; he must have walked leaning over or pausing to listen. Now he was at the boundary line between the last field and the laurels, looking around him, perhaps, and seeing nothing.

He began to walk again, disappearing at intervals among the distant shrubs or in the dazzling sun, and then reappearing. At ten o'clock they fancied they saw him as a black dot moving up the glowing, rocky hillside from whose summit a path leads down to the so-called Solchi di Sacco or d'Isacco. Was he going to those woods? Or where was he going? He had passed the edge of the area where the hunters were said to be. So he hadn't gone to talk to them, as they had imagined. Or, failing to find them, had he pushed on farther? Of course, the dot might not be him at all. But who else could it be? Many of the men had stopped working in order to question one another. Was it he or wasn't it? Might it be one of the hunters?

63

Meanwhile, when it seemed that there was no actual shooting, Toma decided to take a look for himself.

"I'll go with you," said Red Kerchief.

They did not put on their shirts but, for no particular reason, tied their partisan's kerchiefs around their necks in such a way as to cover their bare shoulders, as they had done in the village's early days. The kerchiefs were faded, but the red was still visible at a distance to both those who knew and those who did not know where they were going.

"Look!" one of our fellows exclaimed. "Partisans!"

"They aren't the hunters, in any case. It's Red Kerchief and Toma."

The two of them were searching among the laurel bushes.

"Nobody here," they said to each other.

"Either there never was anybody, or else whoever there was has gone away."

Finally, they discovered a fellow asleep, wearing the spotted trousers of a German army truck driver and an Allied summer jacket, his gun beside him and his hand around the barrel. They might have stepped over him and gone on, but they paused to observe the sweat running over the bare skin between the bottom of the jacket and the top of the trousers, with an ant trying to make its way through the salty rivulet to the dry cotton.

Peering among the bushes, they detected two more prone bodies. They were sleeping so deeply that Toma and Red Kerchief could have walked freely among them without danger of waking them up. Two of them, one with his head covered, were lying flat on their stomachs, the third on his back. He had black hair and thick black eyebrows, and the pimples on his cheeks showed him to be, like the others, no doubt, some nineteen or twenty years old.

"Hunters," Red Kerchief murmured, exchanging with Toma a glance meant to recall past summers. One of the guns was a Sten light machine gun, but Red Kerchief and Toma were still talking about hunting when the fellow with the upturned face half opened his eyes, rubbed them, looked up, and raised himself to a seated position.

"Good-by, game!" said Red Kerchief.

"What do you mean?"

"I mean that you're sleeping and the game is getting away."

"Getting away?"

"Well, the birds come around and recognize you as hunters, and then they leave you behind . . ."

The young man's companions had woken up and were looking, without alarm, at Red Kerchief and Toma.

"What's that?"

"If you sleep, you won't shoot so much as a sparrow."

"We were just resting."

"You've been here half the morning without firing a shot. Have you done nothing but rest?"

"Ugh!" said one of the young men, scratching his neck and stretching.

They asked him what he was expecting to find in the way of game. He made a face, and there was laughter in his eyes, but then a more alert expression came over his face.

"Anything that happens to be around."

There seemed to be no mistrust between the two groups. None of the hunters had reached for his gun as he awakened. And our boys talked freely to each other, turning their backs on the intruders.

"There's not much. Sparrows, plenty of them, and black-birds, and some larks, but very few since the middle of July."

"How about rabbits?"

"Did you come for rabbits? This is their season for love-making. And we've never seen any of them around here."

"Well, partridges, then . . ."

"Partridges, *here?* . . ."

Red Kerchief turned to Toma, as if to express a doubt that these three had ever been in the mountains along the Gothic Line.

"Partridges!" he repeated.

Toma smiled back at him, well aware that they were not really talking about partridges.

"I tell you what there is," he said. "Chickens."

"Do you take us for chicken thieves?"

Toma went on to tell of chickens that had run wild during the war. There were plenty of them, still, in the mined fields.

"You have to go to a spot where there aren't any more mines and wait for them to come by."

They talked, then, about mines and about where they had fought as partisans, of divisions, brigades, parachuted weapons, weapons they had been forced to turn in, and others—not the best—that they had managed to conceal. Suddenly, a fourth hunter burst into the clearing and rushed up to Toma.

"Toma!"

"Turchino!"

The two boys embraced each other, and handshakes were exchanged between Red Kerchief and the others. Then they all sat down on the ground, winked at one another, and talked again about hunting.

"Never in the world would I have thought . . ."

"To find me here?"

"To find you the way you are. Do you remember the day we said good-by?"

"I'll say I do! With that political fellow who spent an hour and a half explaining the situation and ended up telling us to cut loose, every one on his own."

"God, but you were scared!"

"Weren't you? And the others? Don't forget we had the Mongols at our heels as well as the Germans . . ."

"Now you're a Mongol yourself."

They all laughed, including Toma, who had brought the word into the conversation, and Turchino. But Turchino interpolated:

"That's what I wanted, at the time, more than anything. To be in command of the situation and set the tune for others to dance to."

"And you succeeded, didn't you?"

"Well, I had my satisfactions, I admit, at least for a while."

"Well," said Red Kerchief, "I looked into it myself, but I got fed up, and when they told me I could join the police I let the whole thing go."

A loud protest arose from the group of hunters.

"I mean I couldn't make up my mind," Red Kerchief added.

The hunters continued to vociferate; one of them stretched out his hand and pinched Red Kerchief's cheek, as if he were an impertinent child.

"We're not in the police," they said in chorus.

"No?"

"Of course not."

"But you're here on a police operation. You can't deny that."

The hunters looked at one another. There were mellifluous smiles on their boyish faces, and Turchino hesitated before he finally said:

"The police don't give a damn about political crimes. They're interested in petty thievery, and people come to us whenever they run into some suspicious character."

"To you? But the brigades have been broken up for over a year."

"The men who made them up are still around. When they haven't taken to growing lettuce, but are sitting on their weapons in view of a second day of reckoning to come, it's as if the brigades still existed."

Red Kerchief and Toma were scowling.

"If we grow lettuce . . ."

The others seemed not to hear, and Toma interrupted him:

"Drop it," he said and, turning to Turchino:

"What do you do with suspicious characters? You've no place to lock them up. And if you shoot at sight, you get into trouble with the law. Real trouble . . ."

Several of them together cut him short.

"There are different situations in different places . . ."

"It all depends . . ."

"There are dubious characters who've been in hiding since the end of the war . . ."

"So who's to know whether you nabbed them now or in 1945?"

To this, every one of the hunters reacted in turn:

"Nabbing them, that's what matters."

"So the police can't pretend not to know them when we bring them in. In fact, they have to thank us."

"Don't you see? We bring them in and send them to cool

224

their heels for a year or two in the jails their fathers and grandfathers constructed."

"Only for a matter of months, more often. Too bad . . ."

"But we do force their own police to put them in handcuffs and their own courts to judge them. Is that clear?"

Then they did have some official charge, observed Toma.

The hunters made wry faces, and Turchino protested. A "charge"? This implied that someone had charged them. And what they were doing was directed against any other group that might be doing the same thing, the Partisans' Association and the Communist party included. These last made more of a racket than a priest if a dead man escaped him who didn't turn out to have died long before.

Toma didn't get it. Why had they taken on a job as onerous as the one they were now performing? Just to nab an individual and turn him over to police? Or was it partly for their own satisfaction?

"Our satisfaction is always the same," said the hunters.

They talked, for another half hour, lying in a circle, on this matter, passing around a big bottle of Coca-cola. When it was finished, they threw it away and opened another. Their mouths were always in motion, talking, sucking, licking their lips or pulling them out with two fingers and, with every sentence, they looked at one another, as if what they were saying did not make sense without some sort of tacit understanding. They said they wouldn't know what their hunting was for until it was over, that they had to check the information with which they had been provided, that at least one informant would have to come forward to identify the person they were after.

Every one of their statements was contradicted or corrected by the next. One of them said that they didn't yet have data on the object of their search, another that they knew his story by heart. A third put in that the fellow in question wasn't such that they had to feel many scruples.

On this point there was disagreement. If they didn't even know his name! All they knew was that he was an officer in the army of the short-lived Fascist Republic and that he had escaped, between May and June of the previous year, from the camp of Coltano. If he had fled from an Allied prison camp, it must be that he was scared of the Allies' military tribunals. But there were cases of men who had escaped from a place like Coltano, and then it turned out that there was nothing against them except the fact that they had worn the uniform of those madmen.

On this score they argued three against two, and then four against one. This one finally admitted to meaning only that where the fellow in question was concerned, it was as easy as rolling off a log, there was nothing to fear.

Then they disagreed again. Was the case so simple? The flight from Coltano might have taken place in May, before the brigades were broken up, or in June, which was after. With the breakup of the brigade, the rules of war were suspended. No longer could a survivor be shot on the spot; he had to be captured and taken to the police, or else directly before the judges.

From four to one they returned to three to two. The most questioning among them passed to the offensive, recalling that, during the first months after the dissolution of the brigades, there had been an amnesty for deserters who had gone into hidings, taking guns with them. For a moment, it seemed as if the problem were resolved. An officer who had run away from Coltano must surely have been armed . . . But Turchino said it was no use wearying their brains with suppositions. By afternoon, he said, looking at his watch, they would know what to do. For the time being, the important thing was to have cut off the surrounding area. But opinions continued to vary, with one side losing its enthusiasm and the other regaining it.

"Well, are you having fun?" Red Kerchief put in.

What a question! they replied. As if fun entered into it! But then they admitted that yes, they were having fun, and one of them asked him to tell them his idea of a good time.

226

64

Meanwhile, in the village, they could be heard saying: "I'm not so sure that these fellows aren't in some way connected with Carlo."

This doubt kept cropping up. Some people voiced it as soon as they realized it was not merely a matter of hunters; it was expressed, thoughtlessly or with malice, by one or another, sometimes by several at a time, constantly recurring and on the basis of the same contention. Did they think the intruders weren't what they seemed? Or what the few eyewit-nesses—the young boy, Giralda, and Spataro—had branded them? Were they bogus partisans and not the real thing? After noon, there was the additional fact that Toma had recog-nized members of his brigade. This they had on Toma's word, on the news that he had embraced them. Was this mere inven-tion, or what?

The doubt was insistent, in various forms, although the qualification of partisans was generally accepted. "And then? . . ." "Would partisans necessarily have connections with Carlo? . . ."

A murmur was aroused by this last question, because it seemed to be inspired more by pity than by surprise, and it traveled from group to group during the hours of waiting in the sun, in front of the line of houses. "Do you know what they're saying? That even partisans have to do with Carlo." There were smiles and laughter and exclamations of "Did you hear?" and "What do you know about that?" and "Poor fellow!" But they would not let this last speaker alone. He might have spoken out of malice as well as ignorance. Every ten minutes or so, a man came from a job on the remote side of the village and wanted to have his say, which might or might not be pertinent. He had to be brought up to date by a repetition of everything that had been said before.

There had to be a repetition of what had been said about the possibility of the partisans having accounts to settle. About how they might proceed to settle them. And about what had caused them to mount guard in the village's fields.

"You don't suppose they have accounts to settle with one of us, do you?" No one supposed it. "Impossible!" To mention such a thing was only to exclude it. "There's nobody here but us," was the answer.

But one of the things most often said was that the man the intruders were after might be someone who had gone into hiding in the vicinity. Another was that the choice of their fields might only be a feint, a maneuver. Or a day's pause between two nights of hunting.

The last man to arrive was the most definite in his opinions; one of the myriad theories had won him over. The operation, he admitted, looked like a settling of accounts. But with whom? He was insistent, but the replies were evasive. No one had anything particular in mind or any name to bring forward except for that of some petty spy known only to the person that named him. The conversation broke up, and the group dispersed. Spataro took his friend Isidoro aside.

"Why did Ventura disappear?"

Isidoro made a face. He looked slightly embarrassed, but evidently he did not want to put it that way or even to think about it. And Spataro hastened to correct himself.

"He went away, that's all. And he didn't go so very far. I know where he is."

He pointed to the rocky hills on either side of the former military road leading to the Solchi di Sacco, sloping down, on the east side, toward the plain and steeper on the side of the village with its two separating cultivated valleys. But everyone knew that Ventura had gone up, up the ascending sunlit slopes, and that he must have stopped on the nearest and highest hilltop whence he could look down on the dirt provincial road, the thin line of the hunter's stations in the ditches, or among the bushes, where Toma and Red Kerchief sat in the hunters' circle, the terraces, with their ploughed fields and vegetable gardens rising up to the village, and the village itself.

But Spataro held to his point.

"I could show him to you if I had spyglasses."

He described Ventura, sitting with his head between his hands, at a definite place, just as if he could see him, and spoke of other places on the way to the woods, as if Ventura were or had been there. Isidoro asked if he had followed him on this itinerary. But Spataro paid no attention to this query. He looked thoughtfully at Isidoro for a minute and brought the conversation back to the way in which his own thoughts were leading.

"I don't mean to say that these fellows have nothing against him. We know his complexes; it wouldn't be the first time he's had a fit of nerves and broken away. What's strange is that he hasn't come back. It's after two o'clock, and I'd expect him to be hungry. Can he be waiting for them to go away?"

Below them they could see, every now and then, the tiny figure of a man coming out of a ditch or a row of bushes, stretching, or jumping like a goat, and then going along the road a way until he disappeared, doubtless into another one of the hunters' ambushes. Obviously, he was looking for company or for a cigarette or simply for a change of scene.

"They're bored," was the villagers' comment. "But they're not going away."

This was during the afternoon, after a couple of hours in which they saw nothing but the occasional gleam of metal or glass.

"They're eating," was the comment, or "They're sleeping." And there followed a discussion of Red Kerchief and Toma, who seemed to have forgotten that they had something besides sleeping to attend to.

Then news came that the hunters had indeed eaten—sandwiches with cold meat or tomatoes, sandwiches with preserved mushrooms ("Why haven't we put up any mushrooms?"), sandwiches with Gorgonzola ("There's something we never eat!")—and that otherwise, they continued to sit around among the bushes in groups of four or five, telling stories and yawning.

"They're bored," it was said again.

"And what business have Red Kerchief and Toma to share their boredom? They're stuck where they are. But our boys could very well bid them good-by."

It was said that there was no need to spend the whole day in discussion, no point in all of them being distracted from their work.

"And Ventura hasn't even eaten," one of them observed.

But they chose not to linger over the subject of Ventura.

229

"Oh, Ventura!" they said.

At this point, someone muttered something about the work on the dam, and went away. But another, who had done the same thing an hour or two before, reappeared, and the group that had broken up re-formed around him while he asked if they had noticed anything new among the hunters.

He had been in the direction of the rocky heights at which he was now looking back, at the steepest point of the path that they had seen Ventura climbing. When he asked about the hunters, did he really want to know about Ventura? He looked up at the heights, but he continued to ask about the hunters. What were they up to?

"They're bored," was the answer.

And they pointed to the tiny figure of a man who had come out into a sloping, open field on the other side of the road and was wandering or stumbling along on legs that looked no bigger than wires. His arms, too, were wires, and they seemed at times to bend and touch the ground, first on the left side and then on the right. At the edge of the road he stopped, leaned over, touched the ground, first with a hand and then with an elbow, and sat down. So the villagers said again that the hunters were bored. They emerged from their circles among the bushes, but all they did was to stretch out again on the ground.

65

Around five o'clock, when the sun was no longer so blazing and shadows were longer than the bodies that cast them, a man emerged from a field of stubble, with another man pursuing him. Amid the corn at the far end of the field there had been a sudden gleam of metal, and then the man—that is, the usual black dot—had appeared, leaving a slit among the stalks behind him. "So they were in the corn, too," the villagers commented. Before they could say anything else, the slit was broadened by the emergence of his pursuer, both

230

of them now running through the stubble in the direction of the road.

The pursuer was gesticulating; he seemed to be running with his arms rather than his legs; obviously, he was shouting as well. The first man did not turn back; on the other hand, he did not quicken his steps, so that the second soon caught up with him, even though he stumbled and had to continue the pursuit limping. At last, he caught him by the shoulder.

The first man seemed to tread water, trampling the stubble to the right and left. The pursuer was holding him back, but somehow he managed to drag him along to the boundary line between the field and the road. Here a third man suddenly rose up, halfway out of the ditch bordering the road. The two others came to a sudden stop, as if they had not seen him until the last moment.

The second man detached himself from the first, and the latter waved his hands, pointing in one direction and then another. Meanwhile, the second swayed and leaned over, seeming to search for an object that had fallen to the ground. Finally, he sat down at the other's feet, his face upturned to listen to his peroration. Every now and then, from his seated position, he was the one to wave his hands, while the other fell silent.

The third man rarely entered the conversation, and always in the same way, raising an arm from his side and moving it backward and forward. There was no way of telling with which one of them he agreed; perhaps it was with neither.

At a certain moment, the first man went down into the ditch, and he and the third man disappeared from view amid the overhanging laurels. The seated man did not attempt to follow. Perhaps he had sprained his ankle. For nearly ten minutes, he was the only human figure in sight, and in this time he made no effort to even get up.

Then a group of an undeterminable number of men came out of the corn, high-stepping across the field of stubble. They paused near the seated man, as if merely to ask him the name of a bird. All of a sudden, one of the two men who had gone away a few minutes before reappeared in the open section of the ditch. The group hesitated at the ditch's edge, then jumped down in, while he came out onto the road

231

and gesticulated in the direction of the man who was still sitting in the stubble. Was he the first man or the third? He waved his hands like the first one; it was not certain to whom he was talking, but he seemed to be pointing to the terraced fields in the background. The men of the group—they were four in number—came out of the ditch again to join them. They were all confabulating, when suddenly a big jeep appeared out of nowhere and drove slowly up to them.

"Something has happened," the villagers said to one another.

"Have they captured the man they were looking for?"

"Or have they received orders to go after him?"

"They aren't bored any more, that's sure."

"Or are they so bored that they're breaking up?"

"We can't be certain they're leaving. We know about only five of them."

"Six, if you count the one sitting down. And eight, if you count the two in the jeep."

"That's not all of them. And who knows what the seated one wants?"

"Have they quarreled?"

"Who can tell? There's trouble in the best of families."

"And the sudden appearance of the jeep! Who could have imagined they had one of those? They must have left it down near the riverbed in hiding."

The jeep was open, with three rows of seats and storage space behind them. Here a man stood up and began to load objects that the others handed up to him from the road: black wires like their arms, or else round.

Now the number of men—black dots—multiplied all along the three hundred visible yards of the slightly curving road. They emerged from the fields on either side and ran toward the jeep like a flight of sparrows. One of them was slower than the rest and seemed, in the sunlight, to have something that might have been red around his neck. Was it, perhaps, Red Kerchief or Toma? But there were three or four others who advanced with the dignity of a general staff. Two men recrossed the ditch and helped or forced the man seated in the stubble to come with them. Then a second, smaller, five-seat jeep drove up, very fast, behind the first one and was greeted by waving arms.

66

At this point, one of the villagers who had been busy regulating the irrigation of the corn and the vegetable plots brought up a piece of news whose meaning was contradictory to that elucubrated by the more distant watchers.

They were talking about the second jeep, of the fact that there were two jeeps, one large, one small, both of which had been apparently hidden in the dry riverbed. The total of eight plus five seats, they calculated, was insufficient; for five plus two equals seven; plus two, equals nine; plus four, equals thirteen; plus three, equals sixteen; plus one, plus one, plus one, plus Red Kerchief and Toma, who had to be added to the total. Even if three or four fellows could fit into the rear or onto the knees of their companions.

In any case, they were going away. They were going away because they were bored; they were going away because of orders received; they were going away because their day of waiting was over; the two jeeps, one large and small, had come to get them and, in conclusion, they were going away. They repeated these things, partly with relief and partly with disappointment, some of them looking up, with the same mixed feelings, at the rocks which they knew had been the goal of Ventura. Were their relief and disappointment due to the fact that nothing seemed to have happened?

It was at this point that they got the news from the man who had been regulating the irrigation. It was not true that they were going away. The truth was that some wanted to go and others did not, that the latter were trying to hold back the former and the latter to take the others with them. All this happened after lunch. They had been waiting for someone to come, a man with a key whom they called the "dog." They were expecting him at lunchtime; indeed, they

233

had seemed to be waiting for him to come eat lunch with them. This was why they had waited until after half past one to take out their sandwiches. Half past one, two o'clock, and three o'clock had gone by without his arriving. They had eaten, you might say, with their watches in hand. Half past one, quarter to two, ten after two, they seemed to be saying as they sat in circles, with their eyes on their watches. They finished their third round of sandwiches, opened their third cans of American beer, calling out the time as it went by. In each group, someone said that the "dog" probably was not coming. He did not come and did not come. Perhaps the "dog" did not exist. In every group, someone began to say that he had known it all along, that the whole thing was a farce, and he had been suspicious of it from the start, that the "dog" was nuts and the best thing was to forget about him. For three hours they had argued, in groups, as to whether to go or to stay. Even after they had come out onto the road, the discussion continued, because many of them had changed their opinion; some of those that had wanted to go now wanted to stay, and vice versa.

At this point, all the groups had converged into a compact unit; only the two men who went to help or force the man sitting in the stubble onto the seat beside that of the driver of the large jeep separated themselves from this assembly. The rest of them covered three quarters of the space between the rear of the first jeep and the front of the second, as close together as if they were holding a political meeting. Every now and then, the assembly widened its ranks, only to draw them once more together. In the course of one of these contractions, the two "helpers" turned to the others as if in response to a protest. After this, they helped or forced the stubble-sitter to get down from the large jeep, circle around the others, and get into the small one.

But the others seemed to be restless, swaying first in one direction and then in another, and seeming more like a football team than an assembly. And the lame man was obviously combatting the efforts to place him in the seat next to that of the driver of the small jeep. When the two "helpers" suddenly leaped down into the midst of the assembly, he jumped up and down and gesticulated wildly. The assembly swayed even more emphatically than before; its amorphous mass spread out toward the ditch on the one side and the opposite edge of the road on the other. There was a moment of stagnation, with openings on either side and in the middle. The two "helpers" hurried over to the small jeep, removed the lame man from the seat where they had just installed him, and took him back to the jeep where they had placed him before. Then they rubbed their hands as if to rid themselves of the trouble they had endured.

This was like a signal. Three, four, five, six men clambered from both sides into the large jeep, and one of them took the wheel and started the motor. Three men crowded onto the second seat, and others followed. One of them stepped over the lame man and squeezed himself in between him and the driver, another occupied an empty place on the third seat, and the rest fought to insert themselves among those who were already seated.

By now, the assembly was all centered on the jeep, and no one was left on the road. One man still outside leaned his elbows on the door, while others grabbed at it with their hands. From the third seat, a man leaned out aggressively. An argument seemed to be going on between those who were inside and those who were threatened with being left behind.

Then the man at the wheel turned around and made a gesture. Was it to say that he was getting into gear? Three men still standing between one seat and another were still struggling to find a place. A fourth man hoisted himself up but almost immediately dropped back to the ground. The jeep began to move, and those who could not climb aboard loosened their grip on the door while those inside waved at them. The man who had dropped to the ground made another try and managed to install himself behind the third seat .

Aboard the moving jeep, there were thirteen people, nine of them seated in orderly fashion, as if on school benches, three by three, one crouching in the rear and the others standing up and swaying. The jeep backed up in order to turn around; pointing its front to the left and its rear to the right. One of the three standing men managed to join his fellow in the space at the rear, another sat on the knees of a companion on the second row, and the last leaned on the back of the third seat.

67

"Do you see?" they said in the village, still with relief and disillusionment on their faces, and looking up at intervals at the knobby, rocky heights where they imagined Ventura. The affair had ended in the expected manner. The hunters, all of them, had gone away.

The large jeep left behind fewer persons than those who had seemed to be milling around it, a little group of four or five men. For a moment, they looked on as the jeep moved away down the road, which was by now almost entirely in the shadow, then, as if strolling down a village street, they walked the few yards that separated them from its smaller counterpart. They took a step and paused, took another step and paused again. There were five of them, and they fanned out into a semicircle when they moved forward, and fell back into close formation at every pause. A dozen times these actions were repeated, until they reached their destination and climbed aboard. One of them, judging from a wisp of red visible at his neckline and also from a vaguely familiar way of climbing up and sitting down, must have been Red Kerchief or Toma.

Yes, they were all going away. But was Red Kerchief or Toma going in their company? He—whichever one it might be—was one of the two sitting on the second seat, while the two men on the first seat turned around to talk, so that all four heads came together. There was an endless moment while it apeared that the fifth man was still on the ground, holding on to the door. The four heads drew apart, and he jumped onto the running board and held fast to the frame of the windshield. The jeep jerked into gear and, with two abrupt movements, turned around. Just then, a sixth man appeared and jumped onto the running board on the opposite side. Where had he come from? From underneath the jeep? For there had been only five of them before.

The jeep started off at a fast clip, as if it were going to catch up with the one that had gone before. But the presence of the two men on the running boards made it seem as if it would not go far. Red Kerchief or Toma was aboard, and the sixth man, the one who had sprung up from nowhere, looked like one of them too; he had the same red wisp around his neck and the same familiar motions. So both of them were there, one traveling on a seat, like a gentleman, and the other hanging onto the windshield frame like a factotum. No, surely the jeep could not go very far. It was not directed toward home base, like the first; it must be making a short trip in the immediate environs, with Red Kerchief and Toma as guides.

Guides? The villagers looked up from the road, overcast by shadow, to the rocky summits, still struck in their full length by the sun, the vantage point of Ventura.

"Who knows?" they said to one another.

When the jeep drew near to the curve where the provincial road crossed the dirt road, which rose on one side to the village and on the other, barely more than a path, wound around the sun-struck promontory, it neither rounded the curve, like its predecessor, nor took the winding path to the right. It turned on to the dirt road leading to the village, which made its way upward first among the fields and then among the terraced vegetable plots, in a succession of rises, as long as a quarter of a mile each, four on one side of the hill, two on the other side, then one on the first side, and three more on the other.

It ran below the level of the bushes on either side, and all that could be seen from the village were two black, or rather bluish, billiard balls, the heads of the two men standing on the running boards, which contrasted with the pale vegetation. Then the jeep reappeared in its entirety on an open piece of road, which described a wide semicircle, before another, higher curve where the road was once more out of sight, although it made a line between the cornfields and the terraces.

So they were coming to the village. But after the jeep had

disappeared at the end of the semicircle, considerable time elapsed before it was seen again. It must have stopped at some invisible point, because of a shortage of gasoline, a punctured tire, or some other such trouble. Or had it turned on to the path that rises from the far end of the semicircular curve through the terraced vegetable plots all the way to the dam?

The center of interest had changed place, and they could expect to see nothing more from the wall over which they had looked down all day long. Except for the next move of Ventura. A few of them lingered on. Out of curiosity? Or because they were tired? Without saying a word, they continued to scan the mass of rocks on whose highest point a ray of sun still played, overhanging the darkening valley.

The others, in loosely formed groups, made their way back, chattering, to the houses, the wineshop, the mill, and the former church, or walked along the wall, up to the underlying area of nettles where the east side of the village became the south.

But news that reached one group quickly circulated among the rest, those along the wall near the nettles, those around the mill, those in front of the wineshop, the former dormitory, which was also the former church, the community kitchen where on days of festivity or extra work they still did their cooking, on the old main street, now bordered by new houses, and Cerro's square, around Cerro's shed and at the original observation point, where some four or five people were still waiting to see if Ventura would come back, once his mountain was left without the last ray of sun that still capped it.

"Do you know what?" ran the first piece of news to arrive. "Red Kerchief and Toma have taken them to that piece of land we never had time to free of mines. They left the jeep on a curve and went by foot. One of them has a camera around his neck and was taking pictures. That is, he wanted to take pictures, and complained that it was too late, as he knew all along, and swore up and down. And Toma and Red Kerchief showed him and the others how we go about extracting the mines. They pulled up a mine in front of his eyes, and he took a picture of them, protesting that it wouldn't

238

come out, and they showed him the holes where mines used to be and the places where they still have to be uprooted."

A second bit of news came later, while they were still all excited over the first, especially by the presence of the photographer.

"What do you know! Red Kerchief and Toma took them to see the place where we dug for water, and the basin. They went all over the place, and one of the hunters has a Kodak and two Leicas . . ."

The third, fourth, fifth, and sixth bits of news followed at shorter intervals.

"Listen to this one!"

"Listen to this!"

"And this!"

"R.K. and Toma took them to see the dam . . ."

"R.K. and Toma took them to see the stable . . ."

"R.K. and Toma took them to see the corn silo . . ."

The informants poured in, very different one from the other, but they all talked about the fellow with the cameras, who complained that there was not enough light to take pictures and about how Toma and R.K. and even his own companions told him that he could take them the next morning.

The culminating item was that the jeep was in the village, that is, it was parked near the southern entrance. This eclipsed the news of the cameras. By now, practically every one of the villagers had found something to report.

"They're here. They're on the square in front of Cerro's. Now they've gone in."

R.K. and Toma were said to be showing them the mill, the ex-dormitory, one of the new houses. From every place where they were not came news of where they were.

"They're showing them everything. Cerro has joined them. and Widow Biliotti and Cataldo Chiesa. They're explaining one thing after another."

Then came a report on how the visitors were taking it. They looked one way, and said yes, yes; then they looked another, and said yes, yes, again. That was how they were taking it. They were saying yes, yes, yes, and nodding approval.

Perhaps by now they were bored . . .

"But they were so eager to have pictures . . ."

"Well, the photographer is still trying. But it's as if he were chewing gum. He squints into the Leica and focuses, he squints into the Kodak and focuses, but I'm willing to bet he hasn't snapped a single picture."

And someone else said that whenever he was not focusing with his cameras, he looked up with the vague expression of a shortsighted man who has lost his glasses.

For that matter, they all had a vague look about them. Our fellows boasted of the village's glories: the number of square miles cleared of mines, the area sowed with corn, the tons of rubble removed, the tons of scrap gathered up and sold; the mill, the powerhouse, the dam, the wells, the new buildings, the truck; but it was clear that their hearers were indifferent and nodded their heads just to be polite. They were even reported to be yawning. One man yawned to the right and another to the left, all except for the photographer, who buried his face in his Kodak, as if to conceal a yawn.

They could not be blamed for that, though, because R.K. and Toma did not leave them time to breathe, and Cerro and Cataldo and Widow Biliotti the same, and worst of all, Thorn, who had also joined the group. They could not seem to understand that the visitors did not care about the village's accomplishments and that it was an exaggeration to spell one another, one man taking the words out of another's mouth and giving a fuller and more exact explanation of what had already been explained to excess.

The villagers made these comments in front of the mill, after the visitors had already gone on to the kitchen. And in front of the kitchen when they had gone to the ex-dormitory, ex-church. In front of and inside the wineshop.

"They're coming," said the fellows inside.

The door and windows of the wineshop were wide open and the lights were lit, one hanging from the center of the ceiling and two strung symmetrically over the bar, although it was not yet completely dark outside.

"I wouldn't have showed them around," a man at the bar was saying. "What do we know about them? Partisans they may be, but they're still strangers. And then there are those cameras; they must have had some purpose in bringing them."

240

But they were coming to the wineshop. Every one of the group of four or five villagers standing outside the door said the same thing as he came in. From the window that gave onto an alley in the rear, there could be heard the rise and fall of voices never before heard in the village and which, in this moment of suspense, were immediately identified as theirs. Footsteps, which could only be theirs or those of the fellows who were guiding them, rang out, paused, and then rang out again.

68

The stranger was holding forth in a voice whose accent they could not place. One man said that it might be from La Spezia, another guessed at Pontremoli.

"That's the way they talk in the quarry country around Carrara," said a third, with the air of having made a discovery.

The men at the bar put down their glasses. The rear window was blocked by the strangers, as they paused in its light.

". . . With a commission from the Prisoners' Association . . ." the voice was saying, "on a visit to our soldiers who, when the armistice was signed, went over to the Yugoslav partisans but ended up as prisoners of the Albanians . . ."

One of the hunters looked in through the window. His face was ingenuously radiant and at the same time bored, so much that of a youthful recruit and the son of a peasant that he did not seem at all like a stranger.

From inside, they had a side view of Toma's face and a three-quarter view of that of the fellow with the accent of Carrara. He was not so young, indeed he had a knowing, ironical look, with his eyelids frequently half closed and a lock of hair falling over his forehead, which his thin hand pushed back periodically.

"And so we had a chance to learn about makeshift workshops and dams and other such things . . ."

He burst into laughter, so contagious that soon his listeners joined in, so loudly that inside the bar the men looked questioningly at one another. Those who had been standing at the bar divided into two groups; one group sat down, and the other moved toward the door.

At the window, Toma's face kept a serious expression; behind it, that of Widow Biliotti seemed totally uncomprehending, while they could hear Thorn's characteristic wheezing giggle.

"Workshops where they made tubes and iron shoes to be laid on a railway track and stop a train, shops where they made type, telephone apparatus, tape recorders, radio transmitters . . ."

His figure was eclipsed as he was swept on by the group of a dozen or so hunters and guides, all of them now making a clamor that died away as they rounded the back side of the wineshop and grew louder again as they approached the front entrance.

"They even took us to admire the haystacks," he went on. "We were only able to see the prisoners for an hour or two at a time, but they rammed their accomplishments down our throats for nine hours or so every day, from Wednesday of the week of our arrival to Friday of the following week, when we went away."

By now they were near the door, at the door. But our fellows who were about to leave pushed on through, as if in protest, before they could come in.

"And so," the man from Carrara was saying, "nothing surprises me very much. I'm speaking for myself, of course. And I know that, here in Italy, everything that's produced by a workers' co-operative instead of by a big businessman like Biffi or Cantagalli is like a position wrested from the enemy in war."

With these last words, he walked in, preceded by the serious-faced Toma and flanked on one side by Thorn and on the other by the the little man described as having two cameras slung around his neck besides his hand machine gun.

"Yes, yes," he concluded gaily. "At the moment, I feel as if I were back among the Albanians."

242

They had all made their way in by now, and he was laughing with satisfaction rather than mockery. Then he suddenly turned around, causing the others to come to a sudden halt right under the lamp hanging from the center of the ceiling. No one seemed to have been listening to his last words, and his laughter raised no echo. Outside, the eyes of the fellows who, for some unknown reason, had pushed their way out, were gleaming. Inside, a dozen or so men's and women's faces were raised expectantly from two tables to the left, one on the right and another in the right rear corner, tables on which there were no glasses. The newcomers were all talking together. Toma spoke to everybody, pointing to his friend Turchino and the man from Carrara as if he were a referee at a wrestling match presenting the stars of the evening. The man from Carrara had turned around on Toma's account, in order to hear him making the presentation.

"Have we nothing hot to offer these friends?" asked Toma. "And R.K. and I wouldn't say no to a bowl of hot soup if it were handy."

He turned to a young woman who stood, with amused curiosity written on her face, leaning up against the wall near the door.

"Can you do something about it, Giralda?"

Then he mentioned the fact that four of them came from Modena, introduced Turchino all over again, and then named the other three. The people sitting at the tables got up. There were handshakes and even a few claps on the shoulder.

"Wine, wine!" they called out.

Some of the old-timers began rearranging the tables, pushing two together and inviting the hunters to sit down. Some of the fellows standing outside came closer to the door, while others leaned their arms on the window sills and peered in.

The soup arrived and was served on the two joined tables.

"Hot food in this weather?" protested the man from Carrara.

"But you were the ones to ask for it," was the answer.

Toma said that he had understood not "hot" food but "cooked" food. In any case, all six of them threw themselves upon the soup, the four strangers, and R.K. and Toma, cooling

243

it with the heavy red wine that had been poured into a large number of glasses, with a tinkle like that of bells, on the bar and the tables.

"After all . . ." they said, meaning that the soup was not bad, "after all . . ." to say, between one spoonful and another, that it was actually delicious.

From a sack they pulled out tins of sardines and American smoked meat, boxes of preserved mushrooms and salami. These were passed around, and soon everyone—including those who had left a quarter of an hour before—found himself with a piece of bread in his hand, on which he heaped one or another of the hunters' provisions.

The man with the cameras, who had removed only the gun from his shoulder and laid it at his feet, raised his face from time to time from his plate and looked into his Kodak.

"Too bad I've no flash bulbs," he muttered, shaking his calf-shaped head. He kept staring into the camera and pointing it in one direction and another, as if it were the only way he had of looking at his fellow man. The people standing around him asked questions to which he never made a reply.

"Pietrino!" called out a companion sitting across from him. "Pietrino, did you hear?" This was the very young fellow, who might have come straight from a dairy farm for his army physical examination. He even kicked the cameraman under the table, repeating: "Pietrino!"

But Pietrino only lowered his head and scowled, muttering "Yes, yes . . . I hear." Or else he looked up and into the camera, pointing it at whomever had spoken to him.

All of them were talking, at the bar, the tables, the window, and the door, and from one of these locations to another; everyone had two or three conversations going. Around each one of the hunters, three or four villagers were clustered. R.K. and Toma were surrounded in the same way. And the hunters were talking among themselves and with Toma and R.K.

"What did they fall out about?" someone asked Toma.

But neither Toma nor R.K., knew of any falling out. Who had fallen out with whom?

One group of hunters with another. Those who had stayed with those who had gone away.

"We saw them with our own eyes."

"And we saw one fellow roughed up."

R.K. and Toma were staggered. Somebody had been roughed up?

Yes, and then half carried along on someone's arm and taken to the city by force in the big jeep. To see the way he was treated, it had seemed that he must be the hunters' prey.

"They must be talking about Folco Folco," Turchino put in, "the one that sprained his ankle. He wanted to stay with us, but we told him he had better go back and get the ankle attended to."

The villagers nodded agreement. But the way he had hurt the ankle, they insisted. "We saw it." There had been some sort of a falling out, and he was running after one of his companions.

R.K., Toma, and Turchino looked at one another. A falling out? They had not heard of any such thing. They turned to the man from Carrara. What did he know?

"Well, call it an argument, if you like," said the villagers.

But the man from Carrara knew nothing of an argument. There had been nothing of the kind, to his knowledge. They called on the baby-face boy. Sartorio! Sartorio! But Sartorio knew nothing of an argument either.

There were smiles on both sides. Smiles saying that there had been an argument, smiles saying there had not.

But not all of them were there, said the villagers.

"There were seventeen of you, weren't there?" They were four, and the other thirteen had gone away. The four of them had chosen to stay, and the others had wanted to go back to the city. They had been of two such different opinions that there was nothing to do but split up.

"Nothing of the kind!" was the answer. They had split up by common consent. To tell the truth, they were all a bit bored and ready to go home, except Folco Folco, the fellow with the bad ankle, and Pietrino the cameraman. The decision as to whether to go or to stay had been reached by common accord. The case was a very easy one, a little dubious, perhaps, but fundamentally simple. It involved only one man, isolated and with no defenses. Seventeen against one were too many.

On every side of the two joined tables there were by now a dozen people. Some had jumped in through the windows and made their way among those at the edge of the room, who were talking of other things, in order to get in on the more important conversation.

"You could have thought of that before."

"Of course we could." But the fact was that there were no longer many manhunts. Once they had been frequent, but now they were rare. And when there was one, everyone wanted to be in on it.

"Out of nostalgia, you might say."

"What do you mean?"

"Nothing special. Man's a natural hunter."

The face of the man from Carrara darkened. The nostalgia was for unfulfilled revenge, for justice left undone . . . But Turchino interrupted. The fact was, he repeated, that they had realized there were too many of them.

"When you began to feel bored, was that it?"

Exactly. They found themselves getting bored with hanging around for no necessary purpose; it seemed ridiculous for seventeen men to hang around lying in wait for one man. Three or four were quite enough, and then there were R.K. and Toma, who had been partisans, to help them.

"And wasn't there an argument, then?"

"Well, everyone said what he was thinking. But you couldn't call it an argument."

Someone had begun to tune an accordion. At the two joined tables there were smiles. It's Isidoro, the villagers were saying. One of them, smiling, left the neighborhood of the hunters' tables to join him, and another followed a moment later. Notes gushed out of the tuned instrument, and three or four voices began to sing:

> *"I had just got up this morning*
> *When I met a partisan . . ."*

246

The man from Carrara joined in:

"... *a partisan* ..."

As his voice boomed out the rest of the song, he got up and strode over to the corner where the accordion was playing.

"It's in your honor," his companions still sitting at the tables assured him.

Turchino smiled, and so did Pietrino the cameraman, out of the corners of his mouth. He moved restlessly on his seat, then picked up his gun, rose, and slipped across the room. Two or three villagers who had watched him fiddle with his camera followed after. Turchino stretched, waving his long arms, and Sartorio sprawled over the table, resting a cheek on one hand. The song was carried by the voices of the three villagers and the booming voice of the man from Carrara:

"*Ciao, my beauty!*
Ciao, my beauty!
Ciao, ciao, ciao!"

At the two joined tables all was peaceful. Turchino, Sartorio, R.K., Toma, and five or six other villagers drank in the music, gazed beatifically at one another, and smiled. Harmony seemed to reign. Spataro was there, and Cataldo Chiesa. Some of them had stretched out their legs under the empty chairs. Only rarely did neighbors whisper to one another. But, amid this serene atmosphere, some shot a question across a table at Toma:

"What about Ventura?"

Toma shook himself.

"Of course. Why isn't Ventura here? I was just thinking about him."

247

69

At this same moment, two men met at the wall where the villagers had spent most of the day following the movements of the hunters in the countryside below.

"Formica!" one of them called out, turning away from the darkness before him, opaque around and below, gleaming, above, with stars that peeped out, every time he raised his eyes, in greater numbers.

"Formica has gone to the wineshop," said the other. "I'm Achille."

"He's gone to the wineshop, has he?"

"Yes, and I'm going there too. Aren't you coming along? You can't see a thing from here in this darkness."

"It's black like this when the moon's about to rise."

"What time should that be? Wasn't it full two nights ago?"

"Around eleven o'clock . . . You're going to the wineshop, are you? I don't know . . . With this heat, and all the confusion . . ."

"Stay here, then. But I'm going. I can hear them singing."

"Oh well, I'll come too . . ."

He caught up with Achille, who was already on his way, and walked along at his side. But when they were within sight of the wineshop's lighted windows, he said that there was something he had to find out. Pointing to the wineshop windows, obstructed by the figures inside, he said:

"Go on in. I'm going as far as Ventura's house, and then I'll join you."

The wineshop was at the southeast end of the village. Two of the windows were on the side where, a few hundred feet away, Ventura had fixed up a one-room house for himself and his girl. The stranger seemed hesitant to pronounce Ventura's name, but he did pronounce it.

"I'm going as far as Ventura's," he said, as if he were saying "as far as the fountain, the bridge, or the curve in the road." Achille made no reply.

At the corner, he let his companion go off alone, but lingered to watch and, two or three minutes later, took the same path, which at a certain point forked, with one branch leading to the stable and the other to the house of Ventura. His companion, barely visible ahead of him, turned around again after the fork, and said:

"Formica?"

Ventura's house was a white mass behind a wall, some twenty yards away.

"To hell with Formica! I'm Achille, I told you."

"Sh!" exclaimed the other. "I got here just in time to see him go in."

"Ventura?"

"Who else? He went straight home."

"But there doesn't seem to be any light inside."

"Sh! We'd better be going along . . . He didn't even light up."

They started back, each one on his own, in the direction from which they had come.

"He went in without putting on the light?"

"Exactly. But his girl's there. I heard him speak to her as soon as he'd closed the door behind him."

"She was there in the darkness?"

"Yes. Waiting for him in the darkness."

"All alone in the darkness?"

70

"You know who they are," Ventura was saying in the unlit room. "I kept out of sight the whole day, you know that, too. I went away. So you know now for whom they're looking, who sent them, and also about me . . . There's no further need of explanation."

"You think not?" she said after a long pause.

"Besides, you've known all along. You've told me so yourself, haven't you? . . . From the very first day. I grant you the satisfaction of having made a good guess. That's all there is to say."

"Are you sure?"

Her feet rustled on the floor near the bed, as if she had just put them down.

"There's the story of the fellow on the motorcycle . . . that needs explaining. What does it signify? It concerns all of us, that's certain. You went to see him three days ago, and you haven't said a word. It was last Friday that you went."

"Isn't it easy to imagine? Can't you imagine it yourself?" asked Ventura from near the door. "He knows me, and I know him; you've seen that. Surely you can imagine under what circumstances. You can imagine the whole thing, including what I said to him last Friday, since obviously he's played his last card and reported me."

He stopped as if to give her time to say something, but he heard only the rustle of her feet, as if she were swinging them to and fro on the floor.

"Perhaps not definitively," he added. "Without telling them everything, that you people know me, for instance, and call me Ugly Mug, and so on. But enough to make their mouths water and put them on my trail . . ."

Between where he was standing in the doorway and where she was sitting on the bed, both of them in the dark, the panes of an open window reflected the lights of the village. The shape of certain objects blacker than the walls began to emerge from the darkness: the cupboard, the table, the head of the bed, and finally the figure of Siracusa, black on top and lighter below, as if she were moving. Perhaps she had raised herself to a standing position several moments before, between the first rustle of her feet and the second. In any case, now she was moving. There was the barely perceptible motion of something like a hand and, all of a sudden, the raw dazzling light of a lamp filled the room.

"Turn it off," he said pleadingly.

She complied, but not before getting a glimpse of a face as red as if it were burned and could not stand even light. Was there something like fear in the rapidity of her gestures? She continued to be silent and motionless; perhaps her hand did not move from the switch. Ventura, too, after his plea for darkness, was silent. One, two, three, four minutes went by, until the fact that neither one of them could find his tongue became unbearable. The girl, at last, spoke.

"You're right," she said. "There's no need of explanations. Everything is clear, including what the fellow with the motorcycle tried to get out of you and you wouldn't give him. You're right; you owe us no explanations."

These few words might have been all she had to say, but she went on, in a low voice, as if the silence that still lurked behind every pause must be prevented, at any cost, from occupying the ground between them.

"You're right," she repeated. "First of all, it's not our concern. We've never delved into anyone's past, and why should we delve into yours? It's your private business. If I was questioning, it was only because of your attitude toward us, the way you behaved in these last weeks. But now all this is explained."

Her discourse seemed to be purposefully inconclusive, a way of approaching and touching him. Or was it, on the contrary, intended to save her from this necessity? But there came a moment when she could no longer fall back on repetition. She was silent again, and he gave no indication of speaking. Then she gave a muffled cry, the cry that might have escaped her when she had seen, in the light, his travailed face, due partly to a natural cause, the burning sun, but largely to something more. Ventura might have taken her cry for an expression of annoyance or impatience. But, immediately after, she switched on the light again, and he realized that there was a more complex impulse behind it.

"Turn it off," he pleaded.

Again, the redness of his skin, like that of a man who has been whipped, faded away as she turned off the light. It was not the redness that was so alarming but the fact that, within a few hours, for no other apparent cause than the sun, to which, after all, he had been exposed all summer, his appearance had changed so drastically. This time she asked him if it hurt.

If what hurt, he asked her. She didn't exactly know. Was the light painful to his eyes? Ventura admitted that his eyes

251

were smarting, but he denied having a headache, or knocking knees, or shivers, or fever. She might have gone up to him and found out from her own hand whether or not he had a fever. But she only asked for reassurance, and this he verbally gave her.

So it wasn't a sunstroke . . .

She left this idea suspended and went on to say hurriedly that he should go while it was still dark and guard himself from the sun the next day. She would explain to the others. If she didn't go with him, it was only because she wanted to put things straight and to be there, in his place, until his return.

"My return?"

"The time will come when you can return."

Once more she was swallowed up in darkness and silence, wanting to be cool or at least to seem so and, at the same time, to encourage and help him. And so, in spite of his interruptions, she stuck to the same train of thought. It did not occur to her that he had not eaten all day or that something could be done to relieve the burning. She did not speak of preparing food or putting some cream on his burned skin; she did not say that he should change his clothes before going away.

"In a few months, there'll be an amnesty," she said. "And you don't have to wait for the amnesty, anyhow. As long as you stay away for a few days . . ."

"You mean I have to go away?" said Ventura.

"Of course. The man with the motorcycle sent them here. They may conduct a search, and we wouldn't be able to hide you."

"But I didn't say I wanted to go into hiding."

"What else, then? Turn yourself in?"

71

In the light, visible from Ventura's house, of the two high-placed rectangular side windows of the wineshop, they were talking about things that had happened in '43, in '44, and even for four months in '45—things caused directly or indirectly by men like the one the hunters were now after.

It was Turchino who had begun; he had moved along with the others from the tables to the bar while the voices wandered from song to song, coming back every so often to the girl who, one morning as soon as she got up, had met a partisan . . .

The action on such and such a day, Turchino recalled. The follow-up on such another day, and he told it. The song stopped, picked up again, stopped once more, and someone would say good night and go his way; those by the windows would take their leave or climb in and let themselves down by the window frames. They all dropped in, one at a time, as Turchino told on, or they said good night and went, and finally even the men who had been sitting in the far corner clustered around Turchino, even the man from Carrara came swaying toward his comrade, with Isidoro behind him still trying to squeeze a last wisp of music out of his accordion.

Then the grills were let down over the two side windows where nobody showed his face any more: one all the way—squeak, squeak—the other three quarters. And Turchino was still telling his story.

The roundup on such a day. The mass shooting on such another. He listed. He enumerated. And the other hunters, including Pietrino the photographer, and even R.K. and Toma added their bit to his account or tried to top it.

"And that day I . . ."

"And then I . . ."

For a while they all talked at once, and then R.K. managed to cut off Turchino and the others to tell of a train trip he had taken in '43. He had started out with his schoolbooks under his arm, and his trip had ended a week later as he jumped from the moving train, the wheels grinding by where he landed.

He explained: "We'd taken the plank up from the floor of the car . . . we'd had enough sense to do that early on. But when the train stopped, we were afraid of one thing, and when it was moving, we were afraid of another."

The train was made up of cattle cars, and it ran on the

Torre Pellice—Turin line; every morning he would board it at None. One day, at the next stop, Candiolo, he saw a troop train draw up on the adjacent track. It was made up of an engine, a baggage car, and a car with blackout curtains from which men of the Fascist brigades, in black uniforms, spilled out at random. They drew up alongside the cattle cars, while a sort of officer gesticulated from the engine, his words echoing from the station's loudspeakers. He kept repeating that they should close up and lock up, close up and lock up, without making an inspection because, in this lawless area, no one could waste time taking a roll call and, besides, it should be done at Vercelli, Milan, Verona, Rovereto, or wherever there was an authorized command post that wanted to do it.

"For a whole week," R.K. managed to say, "we went back and forth from one dead-end spur of track in some Piedmontese station to another little whistle stop in Emilia, or another dead end in Venetia, and from then on I saw God-knows-what take place both in the hills and in the valleys, things that, when I think it over . . . things that, when I think it over . . ."

He could not finish. Turchino suddenly stopped his hands as they rose and fell in time to his words, and called the listeners' attention to himself. Meanwhile R.K., in a blurred voice, repeated:

"When I think it over . . ."

He had lost the thread and could not go on.

Turchino, this time, did not tell about things in general but about a personal experience, and he told it in a most circumstantial way, as if he wanted to match the story of R.K.

He told about twenty-six hours he had spent at the top of a walnut tree, watching the Fascists demolish a town from which his comrades had withdrawn, forgetting him and a fellow named Cafiero who had gone to sleep in a haymow after standing guard. Cafiero tried to get away through the woods, but was struck down with a round of machine-gun fire that split his head wide open and flattened him to the ground not a hundred and fifty yards from the haymow. He, instead, got clear by climbing up the largest of three walnut trees that grew directly behind the haymow, between it and the cemetery wall.

"But at what a price, boys!" he said. "Twenty-six hours on a bloody branch watching them sack and butcher, unable to do anything except hold my breath as if all my guts had turned yellow, as if not one feeling, not a tenth of a feeling, not a fraction of a tenth of a feeling was anything but yellow . . ."

Then Pietrino the photographer, plump and squat, with two cameras and a gun hanging over his chest, managed to thread his way among the listeners until he stood in front of Turchino, who was still talking.

From the beginning of the conversation at the bar, Pietrino had been restless and had tried several times in vain to get a word in edgewise. Now, with pudgy hands, he adjusted the straps of one or the other camera around his neck and redraped his gun on his chest, seeking to have his say, to command his moment of attention.

"So what if you did feel yellow?" he said to Turchino. And he cocked his head with its walleyed look, now this way, now that, his lips moist as if he were already sure it was his turn to be listened to.

Turchino pushed him in the chest with two iron-stiff fingers and kept him at bay with little pokes for all the time it took him to tell about a squirrel, a certain squirrel that had brought his stay aloft the walnut tree to its supreme agony.

"Devil that he was, he'd run at me and then nibble the branch at my feet; then he'd look me over; every so often he'd pick the branch below mine or the one above, making a rustling sound in the leaves as he moved, or he'd zigzag back and forth from branch to branch. And he'd stare at me after every rustle; he had a cheeky face, especially when he glared up at me from the branch below, or leaned over and peered at me from the one above, as if he expected me to lose my cool and make a fatal error. Because some of the Fascists were bivouacked not far from my tree, and I boiled with rage to hear them discuss the types of animal that might be causing the sounds. It even happened that some one of them would come close; I'd look him over through a break in the leaves as he walked across the field, his nose in the air and his gun at the ready; then I'd hear him say two or three times at endless intervals that he'd seen nothing. When the creature heard him, he'd stop moving but, as soon as the man had gone back to the others, he'd start his tricks again, the bastard. He emitted sharp venomous cries, and he'd hurtle hither and yon, shaking the branches . . . No matter what *you* may say, it was no picnic."

Now he left off keeping the photographer at bay and turned to the group as a whole. "He was a Fascist, he was . . ."

But an exclamation from R.K. cut him short.

"The squirrel?" R.K. asked.

Other voices broke in on Turchino and R.K.; there was general confusion, and Pietrino, still draped in his cameras and gun, took advantage of it.

"I've photographed dozens of incidents like that and worse," he said, "dozens . . ."

His head lowered, his eyes cast down, he made his statement in a withering voice, without ever taking his hands off the straps that held cameras and gun crisscrossed on his chest. He offered to show the photographs to anyone who cared to stop by his house in such and such a city, at such and such a street address.

"Well, what, for instance?" asked R.K.

Pietrino widened his eyes, still focusing on someone's shoes, and repeated: "Well, for instance . . ." as if not to lose his listeners' attention now he had got it. Turchino and the man from Carrara and young Sartorio began to lend an ear, sly smiles on their faces, curious to hear what he might drag out. His nervousness grew, but then a smile as candid as that of a child started at the corners of his thick lips and spread over all his face, and he began to blush.

"For instance, snapshots of a squirrel, or a fawn, or a young roebuck, or whatever you want to call a creature who has his heart in his eyes the moment he feels he's surrounded."

He went on, at ease now, telling of a very young Fascist paratrooper whom he had photographed at the moment he was caught in a trap and was struggling to escape.

"We're on the fringe of a wood," he went on, "observing how many they were, and we weren't aware of him until he

256

had been moving among the trees for some time. He came forward cautiously but with his gun slung across his shoulder, and we couldn't understand what he was looking for. We set ourselves to follow him, knowing that under the circumstances we mustn't attract the attention of his fellows, and therefore we couldn't cut off his return.

"As we followed him, we heard a blackbird singing. We heard the call repeated every two or three minutes, every four minutes, with the rise and fall that mark the blackbird's song, and all of a sudden we realized that the young soldier was answering with a similar birdcall.

"Then those who were near enough looked at one another through the underbrush. We even winked, and I readied my camera for the first shot, which I took as he was whistling again, turning from the shade toward the sunlight.

"But one of our fellows had started whistling even better than the blackbird in front of him. His was a continuous warbling, and the paratrooper had been following him for a hundred yards or so into the heart of the wood when, in a pause, he heard a whistle much farther to the left, and this made him suspicious. We saw him stop suddenly, and I caught him in full alarm in my second shot, his hands unslinging his rifle and the leaves casting their dappled shadows on him in a kind of camouflage pattern.

"Terror, however, I caught on his face only from the moment when, having gone back a few strides through the hazelnut trees and the brambles, he could hear whistling from every direction in which he might have tried to pass. He no longer wore his black beret, his forehead was scratched by thorns, a sleeve was torn, and the fear in his eyes removed our last hesitation—bred of a wish not to tangle with his cohorts who were twice our number. It was a stroke of luck that the poor fool clung to the idea of saving his skin by not firing a shot; he threw down his rifle and backed up, unarmed, among the hazelnuts and brambles, repeating a formula of surrender, with us around him moving forward from one clump of underbrush or another, but never answering . . ."

Then it was young Sartorio's turn to hold forth.

He actually was not too eager to speak; he had only said a couple of times, "As for me . . ." And there was still the man from Carrara who, when the photographer was halfway through, indicated that he wanted to speak after him. He had even laughed from time to time, and no one could tell whether it was about something in the account he was listening to or about something that he had thought of in connection with his own story to come.

The interruption that reduced the photographer to silence did not come, in any event, from Sartorio; it came from the man from Carrara, who cried out, "Speaking of . . ." and launched himself, with fire and brimstone, into the re-evocation of "a day" or rather "an evening," that is to say, "one hour of an evening," of the kind a man does not forget. "Terrible, terrible," he said, chuckling the while, as if he were saying "terrible" in order to convey "marvelous," "stupendous," "extraordinary."

But Toma and the others, and Turchino too, stopped him, protesting that it was young Sartorio's turn.

"Let the boy speak," they shouted. "Come on, Sartorio. Speak up. What did you start to say?"

Sartorio had only said, "As for me . . ." and timidly at that, as if to himself. Now his expression bespoke surprise. "Well, I . . ."

But with a dig here and a dig there, they egged him on; and the man from Carrara, resentful of having been put down, let off steam by egging him on more than the others, even if he expressed himself in his usual ironical manner, which made it seem as if he were poking fun.

Sartorio turned pale: he sweated and smiled, stammered and smiled. "Well, you see . . ."

"You mean that time they exchanged you for a bundle of faggots?" they asked him.

"Precisely . . ." his face lighted up. "There were the Fascists, see, they'd taken me prisoner, and there were those Chinamen . . ."

"You mean Mongols," they corrected him.

And it was explained to the people of the village that the Germans had Mongol or Tatar auxiliary troops, pressed into service on the steppes of southern Russia during their advance between the Don and the Volga.

"Oh, yes," everyone agreed.

"But who's to swear that they were Mongols? Who knows, really? . . ."

"Well, we called them Mongols, all right. That's what we called them, Mongols."

"They were based in Piacenza. Wasn't that their base, Piacenza?"

"The Ligurians had them, all right, and they had them up in Reggio and up in Modena, yes, they had them there all right . . ."

"Savage, they were."

"Did they have to be savage just because they were Mongols?"

"The Germans were savage, too."

"Mongols?"

"Savages."

"As far as that goes, I'd say the worst were the Fascists who escaped from Florence after August '44."

"The Pisans."

"The Florentines."

"The Pisans *and* the Florentines."

Everyone agreed to everything. It was as if Sartorio had been forgotten.

But Sartorio went on talking . . . Now he was saying that while the Fascists were interrogating him, the Chinamen arrived; and his companions corrected him once more: "Mongols," and they started again to put words into his mouth.

"With a bundle of faggots?"

"Precisely . . . And first the Fascists wanted only to know where they'd found them . . ."

"Because they wanted them."

"That's what they said. They wanted them badly."

"Meanwhile, the newcomers were looking you over . . ."

"They looked at the shoes I had on my feet, they looked at my belt and its new buckle . . ."

"So they asked the Fascist lieutenant how he intended to kill you."

"Bang, bang, he told them. He's have me shot."

"But they said to give you to them."

"That's to say, they let him understand they could do me in without its costing so much as a bullet, with a knife they wore to kill sheep."

"And weren't the Fascists glad . . ."

"They liked the idea."

Sartorio stopped at every sentence. He told his story reluctantly. But this time he didn't lag, as if he were afraid his companions would bait him again. He seemed in a rage to get it over with. "And they gave me to them, in exchange for a bundle of faggots that they had wanted from the very start."

Bursts of laughter came from all around.

Someone said, "Faggots for a faggot!"

The boy searched, his eyes filled with prideful anger, for the person that might have made this remark. He even went so far as to lay an impulsively menacing hand on his gun.

"Hey!" he came in close, his face suddenly adult, and he stuck out his neck and chin.

Even his own companions tried to calm him down. It was only a play on words, they said. The neatness of it was irresistible.

At this, he started to joke and laugh. The need for jokes and laughter that had come out with Sartorio's story continued unabated, despite the anger with which Sartorio had interrupted his story. He no longer showed the slightest inclination to pick it up again and finish it. Nor did anyone else urge him to do so. Evidently, they had once more forgotten him. And the man from Carrara pushed himself forward, amid the noisy high spirits of his comrades and the others, and finally got his say:

"Well, speaking of faggots . . ."

72

He did not pick up the subject that had been dropped shortly before but started on another tack, one that seemed to have no connection with the things they had been talking about.

He talked about women. Women and girls. About how squalid the underdeveloped town was in which he lived until he had gone with the partisans. And about the women, the girls, who lived there: some squalid, some the opposite; some right in line with the underdevelopment, and some chafing at the bit; some carrying the underdevelopment in their wombs with the blue stamp of Catholic Action on their hides like the stamp on frozen meat, and some climbing the walls so as not to get caught by it, not to lose the capacity to give of their honey and to receive that of others . . .

There was, however, according to what he said, plenty of room for amusement and even embarrassment, as he had hinted when he announced: "Speaking of faggots . . ." And now there was, in fact, amusement and embarrassment around him as he spoke. "Well, well!" they exclaimed, and not only with joking incredulity but also with embarrassment. And they looked at the three or four women still present who were laughing no less than they, and with the same embarrassment.

"But why bring all this up?" Turchino asked sharply at a certain point, with a hard severe expression. "We were talking seriously . . . We weren't telling jokes."

The man from Carrara stopped and listened a second, but then, as if he had shaken off what he had heard, he began once more to talk crudely about how beautiful and clean they were, how fresh and tender and gay, their mouths like sweet-meats, their bodies pliant, generous, and so on, and so on—that's what the girls were like who had several lovers; and, instead, how pig-headed, stupid, and sour-breathed were the so-called respectable girls.

He told of experiences he had had with a girl of the first sort and with one of the others simultaneously. "So which is better," he asked in conclusion, "a sweetmeat shared with two or three others, or a turd you eat all by yourself?"

Then he redescribed his experiences on the two fronts, with more intimate, scabrous details ("underdeveloped! underdeveloped!"), although they were only concerned with the ways, stages, and levels of what is called fucking. But some few here and there muttered words of disapproval, while other looked uneasily at the women, who had not moved away. Once more Turchino interrupted. "Can't you see we're fed up?" he yelled. "Talk proper! Can't you see there are women present?"

The man from Carrara shut up with an air of stunned fury that could have presaged an explosion of laughter and rage. He did not let himself go in either direction, but his eyes flashed and his mouth was twisted. "Here," he said darkly. And he checked himself, he held himself in . . . "What we've got here," he said solemnly, darkly. "Here we've got a fine, upstanding example of the lower middle class. That's what we've got."

The faces around him turned with worried glances toward one another. Were they going to come to blows? They called Isidoro. And a few people moved into the breach between the two men, who were squaring off as if they believed they could slay each other with dirty looks.

"A fine, upstanding example of a schoolteacher-mamma's boy," they heard the man from Carrara mutter.

Turchino seemed to see him melt away before his piercing look, yet he deigned—more for the audience, it seemed, than for himself—to throw him a snippet in reply. "We've got quite a bully boy here," he spat out between clenched teeth, and would not look at him above the knees.

The other fellow swelled up again. Would he come back at him? His mouth was already open . . . But Isidoro spun out a chord on the accordion, and a thread of tender music wrapped itself around them, like a lamb, like a bellwether, then another and another and another, one high and taut, then one all trembling, then one from the bass clef.

A rush of laughter tumbled from the man from Carrara's open mouth. He turned easygoing and unaggressive.

The song was the old one of the girl who meets a partisan. "Oh, Isidoro!" someone said, as if annoyed. Would they have another song? Two of those who had been singing earlier began again. Others joined in, the women too, one at a time; and the man from Carrara stopped laughing to enter into the song in turn, his voice ringing out above the others in the second verse.

262

"O, partisan,
Take me with you,
Because I'm swooning away . . ."

But now they were annoyed all around him and showed it with gestures and mutterings. What a bore! One of them clapped his hands to his ears. Another screwed up his face and clenched his eyes as tight shut as fists. Didn't he know any other tune?

Turchino asked the barman if there wasn't a juke box in the place.

He propped his elbows on the bar and his chin on his hands as he snapped out at the barman who was rinsing glasses, "Haven't you got a juke box?"

The fellow did not understand. "Haven't you got a what?" And while he rinsed the glasses, he looked at Turchino as if he were raving, as if he were drunk.

Turchino looked about him for someone to whom he could repeat the question. Wasn't there a juke box in the place?

"Well, you know," the man next to him answered, "a juke box, now . . . a juke box . . ."

Turchino went on nervously, "Either there is one and you have it, or there isn't and you don't . . . Besides, it ought to be in plain sight . . ."

Sartorio commented, "Why should there be one up here?"

"Why not? They have them in Modena. Modena's full of them."

"Modena's a different story."

"There's not a place doesn't have its juke box in Modena!"

"Well, Modena's Modena."

"That's not true," interposed the photographer.

"And where are we?" Turchino said to Sartorio. "We're in the Modena area, not in darkest Africa. We're only a few miles from Modena. Couldn't they have a juke box? All you have to do is want one . . . All the towns around Modena are having a ball, with cafés everywhere and juke boxes singing out all over, and people walking as if they were dancing, and neon lights . . ."

"*All* the towns?"

"*All* the towns?"

"Well, a lot of them."

The photographer and Sartorio had turned to each other.

"But it isn't true that they're all over. It isn't true that Modena's full of them."

"Depends on what you mean by full . . ."

"After all, they've only started to come in this year."

"Fact is, there are a lot of them."

"In Modena? Maybe a dozen."

"Oh, twenty, twenty-five, at least."

"And with those neon lights," Turchino went on expansively, "with everybody happy everywhere, with that music pouring out of the cafés as if they were bombarding you with it, oh yes, and the girls that make you want to dance in the streets, those girls, those girls, and the boogiewoogie, the friendly boogiewoogie (blessings on the man who dreamed *that* up!), and the streets black with people coming from political meetings; oh, those sunny mornings and the crowds from meetings, those meetings, those marches and demonstrations everywhere, all over a city draped in red flags and echoing with boogiewoogie . . ."

He was not the only one to talk. There were those who went on singing to the sound of the accordion, but a good many had turned gradually toward him and kept their eyes on him attentively, even though not another word came from his lips, and not another finger did he wiggle, nor did he bat an eye. They watched him with ever-growing interest as if amazed that the things he had spoken about could actually exist.

Even among the singers, a few had fallen silent to listen to him. They had drawn near, still singing, and then had fallen silent, absorbed in what he had to say. Giralda seemed almost to be holding her breath as she kept her eyes on Turchino's lips when he spoke. And Spataro contracted the cheek muscles on either side of his mouth as if he had been drinking in one by one the words that Turchino had let fall. And every so often, Toma would come out with an "Ah!" a sound he seemed to emit automatically as one sentence or another made a particular impression upon him.

Even the man from Carrara had drawn near to the bar

and sobbed out his song, holding back his thunderous voice for as long as half a verse so as to be able to catch what Turchino was saying that made it possible for him to attract and hold such concentrated attention.

But soon murmured comments and mutterings arose from the attentive crowd. Were they agreeing? Or disagreeing?

Turchino had picked up his thread again: "Do you think you're having any fun here," he said, turning to address the man who had been rinsing glasses, "with an accordion, an ac-cor-di-on, and this caterwauling in chorus, yes cater-wauling? That was all very fine in the *maquis,* as long as guns were crackling, bombs were falling, and paratroopers were catapulting. But today, when we see what's going on, it means only living in the past. You're back in the Dark Ages, so far back that I wonder what you'd dance if you did dance: a tango? A waltz? Oh, what the devil . . . !"

73

"Right you are!" said the man from Carrara, who, like all but one of the others, had stopped singing. The man behind the bar had rinsed the glasses for the second time and did not know what to do to face up to the harangue to which he was subjected. He lined the glasses up on the bar, one in front of every face, then filled them with heavy red wine from a bottle that he took out of a cupboard below.

"Wine!" exclaimed Turchino, with annoyance on his face and in his voice as he smelled the sharp odor emanating not only from the glasses but from the wine spilled on the bar as well. "No, no. I want something cooling," and with the tip of one finger he pushed away the overflowing glass before him. "Can't you give me something else, something cool?"

The man from Carrara assented. That was the point. Wine you are!" again. "What's right is right!" he added.

The man behind the bar looked from him to Turchino. "Something else?"

He glanced, in puzzlement, at the three or four villagers who surrounded the two hunters.

"They don't want any more wine," they explained. "What have you got? They want something else."

"Exactly," Turchino and the man from Carrara insisted. The photographer and Sartorio joined in.

The hunters were unanimous, and Toma spoke up for them as if he were an interpreter.

"They don't go in for wine so much in the city."

And the hunters said wine wasn't the only drink in the world.

"Not that I don't like it," said Turchino, "during a meal and even for half an hour after. But later on, if you're thirsty, wine doesn't fill the bill."

The man from Carrara assented. That was the point. Wine was more like something to eat than something to drink. The photographer said that this wine was particularly heavy, and Sartorio observed that it was slightly acid. The man from Carrara came to its defense. It wasn't really too heavy, he said, and to his taste it was, if anything, too smooth rather than too acid. But wine wasn't the only drink in the world.

"There's Coca-cola, for instance," he said. "There's iced coffee and beer and whisky, a lot of drinks that are enjoyable in company, especially in hot weather."

The barman's face lit up.

"Shall I give them some *grappa?*" he asked Toma.

The man from Carrara had changed place and was standing beside Turchino, as if to lend him support.

"What's right is right," he repeated.

Turchino shook his head sadly.

"*Grappa?*" he muttered. "*Grappa?*"

Toma shrugged his shoulders in the direction of the barman.

"I don't know," he said. "I don't think so."

Turchino shook himself as if to throw off his glumness.

"Haven't you something really cooling?" he asked. "Like mineral water?"

The barman said to Toma that they had only to make themselves clear. Thrusting his arm up to the elbow in the cupboard under the bar, he pulled out two brownish bottles, then two more and two more, pried off their musty caps, and set all six of them in front of the hunters.

"Beer," he said to Toma.

Turchino stared at his bottle and the others with an unalterably sad expression.

"It's beer," said Toma encouragingly.

But the bottles were not frosted; they were merely wet, and Turchino continued to stare glumly.

"It won't foam," he observed wearily.

The other hunters had stretched out their hands, first Sartorio, then the photographer, and third the man from Carrara. Sartorio started to hold the bottle up to his mouth and the photographer was pouring the contents of his into a glass. The man from Carrara hesitated, grasping the bottle in his hand and wrinkling up his nose.

"And do you know why it doesn't foam?" Turchino asked.

The man from Carrara made a face as if he were biting on a lemon.

"Beer, eh?" he said to the barman.

The photographer poured it very slowly, as if trying to raise some foam.

"No use," said the man from Carrara. "It isn't going to foam."

"And do you know why?" Turchino repeated.

Sartorio removed the neck of the bottle from his mouth. He had been sucking it, like a baby, with his eyes closed. Now he reopened them, thrust the bottle away, and looked around as if searching for a place to spit.

"Soup!" he exclaimed.

Turchino nodded his head glumly.

"That's it," he said, scientific even in his sadness. "Because it's warm, like soup."

The man from Carrara said that it was unheard of to have beer and not keep it refrigerated. Was that how they drank it? Horse piss would be the same thing. Beer wasn't a finished product when it came out of the brewery; it required refrigerating. Didn't they know that the only good beer was ice-cold beer?

"It's drunk cold even in the winter," the photographer put in.

"Why does a man drink beer, anyhow?" said the man from Carrara. "Because he's thirsty. A thirsty man thinks of beer. And how does he imagine it? Cool, cold!"

"Not like this, in any case," said Sartorio wistfully. "This could be bran water."

The others threw him a pitying glance. Poor fool! He was the one to speak, after he had drunk half a bottle, nearly a whole one!

R.K. and Thorn giggled. Half a pint of bran water!

But the villagers, for the most part, concurred with what the hunters had said. Yes, beer had to be ice cold. Warm beer was no good, no better than bran water.

"I simply don't understand," said Turchino gently. "Why don't you keep it refrigerated? Or is it that you make do with wine? That must be the explanation. Otherwise you're guilty of extreme carelessness." Sorrow or weariness had softened his voice. "It doesn't take much brains to put it on ice."

R.K. giggled again.

"Ice!" he exclaimed.

He looked at Thorn, who burst into laughter, then he looked at Giralda Adorno and Spataro and at the man behind the bar.

"The fact is," interpolated Toma, "that we don't have a refrigerator."

The hunters turned around just enough to look him in the face, first the man from Carrara, then Sartorio, then the photographer and, finally the weary Turchino.

"Well!" said Sartorio. "You must have an icebox, some sort of receptacle in which to keep ice." Then, with a bewildered air, he added: "My God! How do you do it? To go get a block of ice every day, and have it melt on you before the next morning . . . That's a real problem."

"Hee, hee," went Thorn.

Turchino, the man from Carrara, and the photographer looked from Toma to one another.

"It's more than a problem," put in Spataro. "The only transportation is my truck. And I have other things to do than running after ice."

"Yes," said Toma. "The fact is, we have to get along without it."

Turchino's arms fell to his sides, and the man from Carrara left the bar to go sit on the nearest chair, clapping his long, slender hands against his thighs.

"Just the way it was with the Albanians!" he exclaimed. "Exactly! A hundred in the shade, a hundred and two in the shade, afforded by an occasional building with a corrugated iron roof, hours of walking, and on the rare occasions when there was a bar, no cold drink to quench our thirst. Beer, warm beer, like the horse piss in the square in front of the railway station of Tirana. And coffee the same, an inch of coffee, Turkish coffee, with grounds that stuck to our gums for the rest of the day. And the lemonade and orangeade, like the water in an enema bag with a tinge of artificial coloring, served at what they called room temerature. Coca-cola out of the question. And alcohol at astronomical prices in the night clubs frequented by the personnel of foreign embassies, with no chance of an ice cube to make it palatable. All this because they manufacture tape recorders and radio transmitters instead of refrigerators. Not a refrigerator in either a bar or a private house within a radius of a hundred miles. Foodstuff rotting in storehouses and water that might have been pumped from the hump of a camel crossing the desert. I tell you! . . . In Modena, every bar has its refrigerator, and in the surrounding countryside as well, every bar, café, party headquarters, workers' club, movie house . . . And here you drink only wine, as they did in the times of Noah. Just like in Albania. As if you were Albanians. Here we are, fifteen miles from Bologna and twenty miles from Modena, but you're a bunch of Albanians . . ."

Slapping his thighs again, he shot up from the chair and rejoined his companions at the bar.

"Do you know what I say?" he shouted. "That we get out of here! That we pick up and go!"

He strode up and down, with the lock of hair falling over his forehead, in front of the men leaning against the bar. The business we're involved in is dubious, ten to one it's a

269

farce. We all know that, don't we? I thought as much from the start, and I said so . . ."

He wheeled around, staring at the villagers, one by one.

"We know nothing about him, whether he's a hare or a hound, fair-haired or dark, old or young, much less what he's wanted for. They gave us a job that's a pig in a poke. An informer's supposed to come point him out, like Judas kissing Jesus Christ on the forehead. The whole business depends on him; he was supposed to come at noon, and now, at eleven in the evening, he still isn't here. That's why I say let's get going . . ."

Then, turning to his companions, he went on:

"Come on, boys! What are we waiting for at this hour? Let's go. We've waited five hours longer than the others, but now it's time to leave. Or else I'll go by myself; I'll take the jeep and clear out."

"Take it easy," said the photographer. "If we've hung on for five hours we can hang on for ten. We may as well wait until tomorrow morning."

"Do we have to stay thirsty until tomorrow?" roared the man from Carrara. "Not me, I can tell you. Within twenty minutes we can be back in civilization, with a glass of beer or Coca-cola in front of us . . . and I'm supposed to stay here with a parched tongue all night? All on account of a fellow who may or may not be guilty . . . That is, if he's really here, if he isn't a creature of dreams or imagination . . ."

The photographer shook his big head, and Sartorio stared at him, opening and shutting his mouth. Turchino seemed to be gazing at him from a distance, through a haze of fatigue. He leaned back, bracing his elbows on the bar.

"Never again for me, boys," said the man from Carrara. "Never again . . ."

One, two, three of the villagers lowered their eyes, while a fourth turned around and spoke to Turchino.

"Did you go to all this trouble without even knowing who you were looking for?" he asked.

Turchino vaguely waved one hand without detaching his elbow from the bar, as if to dispense himself from speaking. His face brightened, and he smiled as he repeated the gesture,

270

without saying a word. Finally, the photographer was the one to speak.

"We do know something," he said.

And he said exactly what they knew, with words that might have been and probably were borrowed from Turchino.

"Where he was, for instance, and what happened there . . ."

74

The moon shone, now, into the dark room. A rectangle of light appeared, little by little, on the wall opposite the window, forming a sort of second window which divided, above the bed, the darkness that surrounded Ventura and that which surrounded Siracusa. For a long time before this she had said nothing; perhaps her last words—"So what are you going to do?"—still echoed in his ears. He had not told her, he could not; he had only answered that he did not know, and that was not the point, anyhow. Then he had talked at length, entering into all the things that, at the beginning of their long night, he had said required no explanation.

"What am I telling you?" he said brusquely at a certain point. "I'm not Carità or Koch, I'm a nobody, but it's just as if I were one of them, I know; I've learned that . . . That's why I said I needn't explain. I did say that, didn't I? I didn't want to explain. Because even if you have forced me into it, the fact remains that anything I may say is a sort of justification. And I don't want to justify myself. The very idea disgusts me. I saw the miserable show they put up when they defended themselves, when they even beat their breasts and said they were sorry. Maybe they were, but the upshot was that they were defending and justifying themselves, looking for excuses. We ought to keep quiet, that's all. Only if a man is silent does he admit that he was wrong. There's even a proverb: 'Silence means consent.' But how can I be quiet if you say nothing?"

He was silent, then, for a couple of minutes. Was he really waiting for her to talk? Perhaps his talking had as its only purpose to shake her out of her silence. Every now and then he broke off and waited.

"You want me to go away," he went on. "I wouldn't talk any more if I did, that's sure; I'd have nobody to talk to. But I'd be at the same point where I was when I joined you people last year, only worse off. I don't know if I'm making myself clear. Before this year, I could have gone along considering myself out of luck. I knew that every man's hand was against me, and the odds I had to combat gave me a certain satisfaction, almost a reason to live, even when I was most tired of the struggle. But you've pulled this support out from under me, you've led me along a road where I've lost it and, without you, I'd be back where I was before, without the reason to live that I had then . . ."

He paused again, as if waiting for her to talk, to demonstrate in words what she thought of what he was saying. But still she said nothing; nothing came out of her; she might have been only a memory in the room. His pause and his thwarted expectancy took on an element of irritation, and every time he started talking again it was in an increasingly harsh voice.

"Not that you've made me so tender-skinned. But it's one thing to flee from something you think of as revenge and another to run away from something that the people whom you have joined look on as sacred. You do consider it sacred, don't you?"

At this point he was shouting, but he did not pause to let his shout weigh in the silence. He went on, as if by talking he could control the resentment boiling up within him.

"When there was war, my only concern was to be good at it. As far back as the Spanish War. A man can commit himself even to something he's pushed into almost accidentally. There was a time when it was a question of staying at my post or running away, and I thought I was proving myself by staying. All the rest was a consequence of that. I thought I was proving myself . . ."

He attempted to keep his voice even but all of a sudden he interrupted himself with: "What did you say?"

The girl did not repeat what she had said. But had she really spoken? It did not seem so, after all; perhaps it was only a sound from outside, and he did not repeat the question, but merely added: "I thought you said something."

Then he continued, at length, carried away by what he was saying. He said that it could happen to anyone to be unable to withdraw from something to which he was committed. "A man should see a thing more clearly before he commits himself, that would be the only other way."

He was more and more excited, and the girl's silence was more and more unbelievable. Once more he paused. It could not be that for so long a time she had not opened her mouth. She must have at least murmured a word or two while he was speaking.

"Do you agree?" he asked.

He seemed to hesitate for a moment between two courses of action: to explode against her silence or to go on talking in order to keep himself under control.

"That was my mistake," he continued, "not to have bothered to find out what it was all about. Years and years I was in it without looking at it closely. I didn't look at all . . . Whereas, if I had scrutinized it, I'd have seen that there was something else behind it, something difficult to accept, and I'd have realized that . . ."

His voice trailed off, as if he were disgusted with what he had just said and what he was going to say.

"There I go again, justifying myself," he exclaimed resentfully, and a moment later he returned with assurance to his previous train of thought, repeating how miserable it was to defend and justify oneself and look for excuses. If a man has made a mistake, that's all there is to it. But beneath his words, there was impatience with the fact that she did not pronounce herself. His voice betrayed exasperation.

"Or do you consider it more than a mistake?" he insisted.

And he seemed to move forward from the foot of the bed in the direction where he knew her to be or to have been. Actually, he continued to stand still, with only his hands in motion. Was he repressing the impulse to approach her? He dug his hands into his pockets and pulled something out, dug them in again and pulled out something else. This was how he had suppressed the anger in his voice, talking as if every word were dug up from deep down inside.

"You said I wouldn't have to stay away more than a few days," he dug up, "that after that I could come back. I don't know whether you really meant it, whether you really want me to return, or if you said it just in order to get me away. There's a doubt in my mind. Would you say it again?"

With this abrupt question, he recapitulated everything he had been trying to say.

"Would you say it again?" he repeated. "If you do I won't doubt any more."

Thus he betrayed the fact that he had been hoping all along, beneath his anger and resentment. That he had hoped and feared, and that at the same time he hated himself for his hope and fear. After repeating the question and its corollary, he followed it with another, apparently irrelevant.

"Do you want to smoke?"

It was in order to pull out tobacco and cigarette papers that he had dug into his pockets. He took an inordinately long time to roll a cigarette while he was digging up the words of his question. Now the cigarette was ready and, even in the dark, she could imagine how he would have handed it to her and lit it. This seemed in some way to frighten her; it was harder to bear than words. The smell and taste of tobacco might have made her feel sick to her stomach and prefer speaking to smoking. Was this so? Seconds went by, and Ventura heard no answer. But her feelings were not limited to mere repugnance. And how could she choose among the various sorts of repugnances that assailed her? Seconds continued to pass, and then Ventura suddenly heard her crying.

With the passing of the seconds, he might have thought that the offer of a cigarette required no answer, that she was waiting for the cigarette finally to arrive in her hand. He stepped forward from the foot of the bed, causing the floor boards to creak. It was that moment that he heard her crying. He stopped short, and indeed stepped back.

"You don't want to, I guess," he said, as if he were concerned to cover up the new sound that replaced the silence. It was covered, momentarily, with the renewed creaking of the floor-boards, and with some sentences that perhaps he was not even conscious of pronouncing.

"Because it's so late; I understand."

"Because, quite naturally, you want to sleep."

Then he held his breath, as if he had just the opposite concern, as if he wanted to retrace the sound and hear it again from close by. Because he could not be sure that the heart-rending sound was still there. And so the words that he continued to string together, between pauses, took on an urgent and nostalgic tone.

"You always wanted to smoke when I was smoking. In fact, I got the habit from you . . ."

He lit the cigarette, and the light of the match played upon his face. Did the girl see it? She had cried out when she glimpsed it in the light of the lamp a couple of hours before. If she saw it now, it might have seemed more familiar. But perhaps she did not dare raise her eyes and could gather only from his voice that his face was not all that terrible.

"I have learned a great deal from you people," he said with bitter humility. Struggling, instinctively, to raise himself above his frustrated hope, he added: "Is it that you don't want to or that you can't?" He was still inclined to anger, to shouting, to calling for reasons, but every time he fell back into discomfiture and bitterness.

"I mean smoke. Is it that you don't want to or that you can't?"

He seemed now to fear rather than to demand an answer. There was no more urgency in his words, no more expectancy in his silence. He seemed to be talking in order to wipe out the effect of his silence, and to be silent in order to wipe out the effect of his words. At the end he said no more, content that, at least, she had stopped crying.

One last time, the tip of his cigarette shone out in the dark. Then they both looked at the glow of the butt as it went out on the floor where it had fallen. After that, they thought only of each other; he of her and she of him.

75

How long did all this go on?

Behind the bar of the wineshop, a clock hung on the wall. The case was a black iron rectangle, painted red; the round face was white, with black numbers. It had no pendulum and did not strike the hours, and no one ever consulted it for the time. But in the rare intervals of silence during a conversation, it could be heard ticking faster and faster, and someone might look at the position of the hands.

So it was that we heard it said: "Why it's half past eleven!" After which we heard that it was after midnight, twenty-five minutes after, and a quarter to one.

The man from Carrara was no longer talking, as if, because he had said so many times that he was leaving and then lingered on, he was ashamed to make himself heard. Turchino said only "Yes," "No," and "Oh, well . . . ," and then only when he was asked a direct question. Sartorio talked on but with long pauses, and so did the photographer. The villagers tried to draw them out and occasionally exchanged a few words with one another, but relapsed into long silences, broken only by the suddenly loud ticking of the clock. Their desultory conversation shifted from one subject to another.

First, the hot weather. The villagers asked what went on in the cities, in Bologna and Modena, on hot summer evenings. But the hunters were noncommittal; they mentioned one thing and another, but without enthusiasm, and the subject languished.

Second, moving-picture theaters. The villagers wanted to hear about those in the center of the cities and those on the outskirts, about the outside of them, the entrance, the projection room, the seating capacity, the audiences, the kinds of films shown, the stories, the backgrounds, the actors. But the hunters confined themselves to generalizations; they gave the names of the theaters—the Orpheum, the Excelsior, the Modern, the Triumph, the Garibaldi, the Emilia—and said that the films were American. And so this subject, too, was exhausted.

They passed on, after a long silence, to dance halls, public parks, political meetings, party headquarters, markets and what was on sale, shop windows and what was on show, newspaper stands, ice-cream vendors, restaurants, and gasoline stations. Every time it was the villagers who broached a new subject and kept it going with their questions, while the hunters made brief or vague replies, cutting the matter short or letting it drop. Actually, the subject was always the same: the city, and the life of the city since the end of the war. The hunters began to feel that they had covered every detail and were sick and tired of the whole thing.

The barman was alone at the bar, leaning over it as from a balcony, propped up on his elbows, with his chin in one hand. The others were sitting at the tables, in groups or singly. Turchino was alone and so was the photographer; the villagers sat alone or together in twos and threes, but all of them were linked in an all-embracing conversation, which rose, died away, and rose again from table to table, while every now and then the ticking of the clock seemed to grow louder and closer.

"It's one o'clock!" someone exclaimed.

They began to talk about the hunters' sleeping arrangements.

"One could sleep in the upper room of the wineshop."

"We have a spare bedroom."

"We could take two in a double bed."

"Who else will volunteer?"

"I'll take Turchino."

"And I'll take Sartorio, if it's all right with him."

"Then the other two can stay here."

But nothing was definitely decided. The man from Carrara was dozing or seeming to doze on his chair at a table at the rear of the room. Turchino had got up and was strolling around, first in a wide and then in a narrow circle; then he sat down again, but at a different table. A subject that they had covered already came up again and ran from a villagers' table to a hunters' table, making the rounds.

Now they were discussing the political parties and how many of them there were. Six or seven, or only two—the reactionaries and the Communists—as seemed to be the case, according to the hunters, in Modena and Bologna?

Sartorio joined the photographer in making reply. Turchino put in a word every now and then, to corroborate or correct his companions, but without committing himself too deeply. Toma, R.K., and Spataro, as the best informed of the villagers, put forth opinions that were more in line with those of the hunters than with those of their fellows.

Yes, there were seven parties or, if you counted all the smaller groups of the south, even more. But if you analyzed the differences among them and divided them into those that were substantial and those that were trivial, it came out that there were really only two.

At this point, the question arose as to how the villagers voted. Who raised it? Sartorio, the photographer, Turchino? By this time, personalities no longer counted. The hunters, on their side, and the villagers, on theirs, spoke with a single voice.

"How we vote?"

Subdued laughter traveled from table to table.

"That's a good one!"

"How *do* we vote?"

Then they said there were no parties in the village, and they voted every day. They voted for Whistle. But, among the jokers, a few men spoke up seriously. How could they vote if they weren't registered? Should they desert their work and the harvesting and go all in a body to straighten out their registration? The hunters were amazed.

"Do you mean to say that you don't vote?"

They were all amazed in the same manner, looking at one another and repeating the same words. Even the man from Carrara raised his head and came out of his cantankerous retirement at the back of the room, his eyes as sharp as if he were listening with them.

"You mean to say you've never voted?"

"Not even for the referendum that led to the choice of a republic over a monarchy?"

Now it was the villagers' turn to be amazed, including Toma and R.K. and Spataro.

What? Was there a republic?

There had been a referendum, and the republic had won?

Alongside the discussion between the hunters and the villagers, there was another, among the villagers. Many of them rose to their feet. Just think of it! They could all remember that before the village had come into being, before the end of the comings and goings, years ago, there had been talk of how the king really ought to be got rid of and his place taken by a republic. And now it was done. They talked among themselves, heedless of the hunters, excitedly yet without wanting to display their satisfaction. The man from Carrara had got up, pushed away his chair, and was holding forth, as if distance made him tower above them and he were speaking from a pulpit.

"I knew it," he intoned. "I saw it from the start; I felt it in the air. In these confounded co-operatives, they have only one thing on their minds. Poor idiots! One can only be sorry for them."

He came forward, moving lazily, but with darting eyes, circling an empty table to the right and another to the left, and all the time continuing his harangue. The "poor idiots" exchanged murmurs and recriminations. But, face to face with the hunters, they joined together in their excuses.

When they went to buy and sell in the neighboring villages, they were too involved in their own problems to pay attention to what people were saying. For a while they had picked up a newspaper, but no one read it, no one had time, and finally they had stopped buying it. At this point, they asked for confirmation of what they had just been told. Was it really true? Then, as if ashamed of their doubts, they said again: "Just think of that!" "Well, well!" "They actually did it!"

The discussion between the hunters and themselves fell again into a dichotomous pattern, as if behind the many voices it were a dialogue between two persons.

"Yes, we 'did it,' " exclaimed the hunters. "And we didn't merely vote, either. It was a long struggle. Every day on the streets. A test of strength every day, for months on end. And after the voting as well."

The hunters mostly talked, quietly telling how it had gone,

279

and the villagers mostly listened, making restrained comments. The man from Carrara had sat down beside his companions and put in a word at intervals, quite calmly.

"Having the republic doesn't mean that we can just sit back and take it easy," said the hunters.

And they took it up from there: the republic was just a beginning, a point of departure, an iron in the fire that must not be allowed to cool, that had to be beaten and forged and shaped.

The villagers spoke of it in the same terms, saying "we" and including themselves among the builders of the republic. If they mentioned the status of the village with its adjacent land, it was as if it were only an episode or an aspect of the common effort required to maintain the republic's existence. Of course . . .

But the hunters inclined to keeping themselves apart. They said "we" in a way that excluded the villagers. "We" this and "we" that . . . As they quietly puffed themselves up, they became once more aggressive. "We created the republic," they said. "And you not only didn't contribute to the making or vote it into being, you weren't even aware of the necessity of its creation."

76

What were they driving at?

The villagers wavered for a moment, as if about to rebel; then they met the accusation in the tranquil spirit that now reigned in the room, returning to the mortified manner of a short time before.

"True, true," they admitted. "You're quite right, and we have nothing to say. That's the way it was . . ."

"And what good did it do you?" the hunters insisted. "What satisfaction have you had? There are thousands of cooperatives . . . Of course you consider yours very special, and you did build it up under unusual circumstances. But what's the net result? What do you have, if it isn't just a co-operative like another?

"Yes, you dug up the mines, at your own risk, over an area of a thousand acres. But now that the government provides men and tools for the same purpose, that doesn't make much sense. Nor does all the rest—the houses and other things that you broke your backs to build because you didn't have the know-how . . .

"Just weigh the energy you spent against the results you've obtained. There are a lot of you. A hundred and fifty or sixty, perhaps. And by working sixteen hours a day you do the job of three hundred. Like a factory with three hundred workers. That means a total of a hundred thousand working days, eight hundred thousand hours. You've put eight hundred thousand hours of work into throwing up or patching up a few houses, building a small dam and digging irrigation ditches. There's not much to show for your efforts, economically speaking, especially if you include the ploughing and sowing and reaping . . .

"There's the wheat, of course, and the corn, but not much more than enough to meet your own needs. And if you wanted to sell it for an amount commensurate with your labor, you'd have to ask eight or nine times the going price. Eight or nine times! While America, which sells it to us at half the local market price, manages, even so, to make money. Wheat! God knows why everyone has such big ideas about wheat; you'd think it was gold! If we can't gather it in at the rate of a ton every half hour, the way they do in America, we'd better let the Americans supply us . . .

"Yes, we've got to fit in our production to that of other countries, limit ourselves to making things that don't cost more manpower than elsewhere. Faucets? Very well, then, faucets! Dustcloths? Dustcloths! Because the economic world is one. If anyone tries to be self-sufficient, he misses the bus, or even finds himself running behind it.

"In your village economy, you haven't produced in a year the equivalent of what ten factory workers produce in a month. You're running behind the bus. How can you go on this way? You'll burst your lungs if you don't stop.

"If at least you had the conveniences: iced beer, hot water, electric light strong enough to read by, a juke box with boogiewoogie! But you have none of these. You've built an old-fashioned village. There's a collective oven, but it's wood-burning and a woman has to stoke it, when what you need is bottled gas. And you have collective toilets, like those on the balconies of tenement houses in the last century, when they had no idea of hygiene . . ."

The villagers made no objections; they did not even correct the exaggeration of certain details. They put in a word now and then to keep up with the hunters, but what they said was: "True, very true," to every point that the hunters scored. There weren't very many of them, perhaps eleven or twelve in all, scattered among the tables, but it was with the easily won assent of a crowd that they submitted to the accusations and admitted their shame.

"That's the way it's been," they said. "We have to admit that we never gave these things any thought."

And the hunters (whether it was the man from Carrara or Turchino, Sartorio or the photographer) went on implacably:

"You're not just a family; there are a hundred and fifty of you and, with your sixteen hours a day, you've done the work of three hundred. Like a factory with three hundred workers. Just compare what three hundred factory workers produce in a year compared to your production. Yours is laughable; it's nothing. You've put out the energy of three hundred workers, a hundred thousand days, eight hundred thousand hours, and you've got no more for it than what ten workers obtain in a month . . ."

"Correct," said the villagers. "Digging with a teaspoon isn't like digging with a pick and shovel . . ."

"Pick and shovel? Say a high-compression drill, a bulldozer! Work is money. Just like raw material and the tools of production, like both together. It isn't to be thrown away. And you can't make up for a lack of equipment with extra work. It's uneconomic. Today, work is the measure of an object's economic value. Work in itself; work represents effort, and it has to have a maximum value put on it. At maximum selling prices to meet maximum needs. Just think how much you'd have to sell to compensate for your labor! At an average price, say, or even a low price . . . Eight or nine times as much as the price in the market."

"True, true," said the villagers.

"And then there's the night work, that should earn overtime pay. If you think of the time that it took you to dig up the mines, and the risks involved . . ."

"That has no market price," the villagers admitted.

Here there was argument. This was the nature of a peasant's work. The things produced did not bring a high price, but they were essential, even if it took ploughing and sowing and reaping to produce them.

"There have to be peasants, even if they aren't paid their due."

Hadn't it always been so?

Did this mean, asked the hunters, that there have to be those willing to live worse than others?

"Who knows if it *has* to be. We've lived this way for five thousand years, but maybe it's time to call a halt. Maybe it's no longer necessary."

"We're sick and tired of it, that's certain. I'm a peasant's son, and I've had enough. And so has every other peasant's son."

"But who cares? Whether it's necessary or not, those who want to live this way are welcome to do so if they like it. Do you like it? Then you can't be peasants! Or else you wanted to prove a point. Because you wanted to make arable land out of mine fields."

But was that the point?

"The point isn't whether to do it or not to do it, but how to do it. There are countries whose agriculture is run in a different way. Take Russia, take America. America sells us wheat at half the local price and makes money on it. The Americans harvest a ton in half an hour. Everything's motorized. A man on a reaper for every three hundred acres. Whereas with us, the cost of reaping wheat is out of all proportion. We sow and reap as if we were taking part in a sacrament. Wheat! The economic world is one, and if we can't produce wheat as efficiently as the Americans, then we may as well let them supply us."

Again the hunters were repeating themselves. One point

after another they had hammered in by sheer repetition. And the villagers, too, repeated what they had said before, that it was all very true; they went so far now as to admit that they might have made a mistake when they undertook an enterprise that offered no other prospect than tilling the soil.

"Right, right!" said the hunters triumphantly. "Of course you made a mistake . . . If you'd at least make an effort to fix the place up in such a way that it would fit the needs of the present day . . . Instead, it's in a practically prewar condition . . . The collective oven is all very well, but it's wood-burning, just as if bottled gas hadn't been invented . . . And you drink your beer warm because you have no refrigerator . . . To say you made a mistake is an under-statement!"

By now, the villagers looked bewildered as well as mortified. They bent their heads to listen. They said it was all true and bent their heads. Their heads sank lower and lower, as if they were withering away on their chairs. Including Toma and R.K. By degrees, they hardly spoke, muttering, "Weeelll" or "I never!" or "Think of that!" while the hunters rambled on about everything under the sun, important and unimpor-tant, of matters political and nonpolitical. To put out effort on a village was a waste of time, they said, because a village was on the edge of things, not at the center. Something achieved at the center sooner or later got out to the edge; life moved from focal points and crossings into the capillaries, and not the reverse. Effort should be concentrated in the cities, factories, labor unions, party headquarters, and public squares. These were the seats of political power; by bringing pressure to bear on them, such results as the creation of the republic, to which, in spite of their hard work and courage the villagers had contributed nothing, were achieved.

At this point the hunters spoke again of their cities, Mo-dena MODENA, Bologna BOLOGNA, and of the festivities in honor of the new republican national holiday which had begun in early June and gone on indefinitely, as if festivity were inherent in the republic and made it festive to go to work and come away, to lean out of a window, to go up or down stairs, to call out to a passing friend, to stand around a bar, to light a cigarette; with music pouring out of every door-

284

way, with every shop and house window lit up from dusk to dawn with neon or bright lights, with every street made into a garden of red and red-white-and-green flags hanging from every floor, with loudspeakers which filled the arcades at six o'clock every evening with the din of an assembly on the Piazza Ducale, the Piazza Duomo, the Piazza Santo Stefano, the Piazza delle Arche, or the Piazza Maggiore, with the flux and reflux of other individuals on the run, and mingling with groups that bumped into one another in the same way, so that where there was at first one man there were soon two, five, fifteen men, and nobody was left on the street alone . . .

Their eyes gleamed as they talked, with nostalgia for the things they had been describing and regret that they could not, this very night, enjoy them. Far from their thoughts were the man whom they might hunt again on the morrow, the hunt and the pleasure of the hunt. Yes, the gleam in their eyes was for the pleasures of every day, every night, which on this particular night they were missing.

Soon the villagers' eyes gleamed for the same reason.

"Look here," said R.K. "Could a man make a living in the city if he were to go there? . . . Would he find work?" And, as if he were not sure he had made himself clear: "Would he find a job that would enable him to eat and to buy clothes and so on?"

77

In the dark room, a long time had gone by in which Ventura and Siracusa had no other thoughts but of each other, his thoughts of her and hers of him, of how he was and how she was, of what he was thinking and what she was thinking . . .

Yet there had been a moment, at the beginning, when it seemed as if Ventura had begun to talk to her again, in detached sentences, like single thoughts to which he gave voice among the multitude of thoughts that he kept to himself.

"Yes . . . It would be very easy . . . While they are still in the wineshop, as if offering me a chance . . . and our fellows are entertaining them because they seem to be doing their patriotic duty . . .

"I can't stay here . . . And I can't go away, like a dog whose leash has been taken off to leave him free . . .

If only they weren't the four stupid idiots that they are . . ."

Then the girl realized that he was dead tired and his legs had crumpled. She could hear him continuously wriggle his feet. Together they heard sounds from outside. A cock crowed from the fields that were still mined, an animal that might have been a rabbit scuttled across them. Behind these there was a vibration in the air, and the rustle of water flowing over the dam. Then the muffled roar of a train and again the crow of the cock, now calling and answering his fellows.

Finally, Siracusa heard Ventura move from where he was and throw himself down on the side of the bed opposite the wall against which she was standing. At the same time, a door slammed somewhere in the village and R.K.'s voice rose and fell among the houses, above another, lower voice. For a minute, they heard only these two voices, always in motion, so that Siracusa almost thought that she was walking with the two voices at the same distance behind her. Then the two voices continued to move, neither closer nor farther away, without ever arriving. Could it be that they were circling the house and her inside it?

When the voices were no longer to be heard, she might have thought that she had arrived safely and that the door which closed on the two voices had closed on her. Then she could hear the heavy breathing of Ventura, who had fallen into a deep sleep, and imagine that she too was sleeping, and let herself sink into this thought until the room was devoid of every capacity of hearing and thinking.

If anyone had looked in in the light of the dawn, two hours later, he would have seen Ventura, sleeping flat on his stomach, with his trousers on and his shoes on his feet, while she, in her white nightgown, huddled up against the wall.

After July, it is light at half past five or six o'clock in the morning. But they did not change position even when a ray of sun fell on the water in a carafe and lingered there, like a bird, returning every morning to disport himself for a quarter of an hour. The sun's warbling was of light rather than of sound, but it filled the room with equal presumption. It was incredible that Ventura and Siracusa could go on sleeping.

At this hour they were usually up and about. And theirs was, this morning, a strange sleep. Ventura might have seemed drunk or drugged, and Siracusa, her feet drawn up close together, one arm under her head and the other over her face, gave the same impression of having been drugged or perhaps tied up and gagged.

At intervals she heaved, arching her back and straining her legs, as if she were trying to free herself from some constraint. Or she moaned in a way that might have seemed to denote suffocation. In any case, she was the first to wake up. Outside, a wheelbarrow creaked as it went by. She sat bolt upright, looking around and becoming aware not of the sun but of the presence of light. Staring down at her arms and hands, she decided to plunge them into a basin of cold water. Then she put on an apron, threw open the door, and stood in the doorway. A big white cloud was rising from the southeast, with the sun peering through it, at the point where she was accustomed to seeing it around eight o'clock or half past eight.

"What's going on?" she murmured to herself.   For the village, a hundred yards away, did not look the way it usually did at six in the morning, but rather the way it looked at nine, with all the doors and windows open, people walking rapidly by and children at play. She ran to the stable and found that it had already been cleaned, with fodder in the troughs, fresh straw on the ground, and the cows quietly chewing their cud.

"What is it?" she thought again.

For at a second glance, the scene was not exactly what it should be at nine o'clock. Children were playing, to be sure, but the three or four persons whom she had thought were passing by were gathered in a cluster between the black rectangle of an open door and the black square of an open window and were talking earnestly together. This never happened in the morning. What could it mean? She looked in the direction of the light amid the white cloud, but it was gone, and she lowered her eyes to see the wheelbarrow, which was again creaking near by. A woman was pushing it, an old woman, Widow Biliotti.

"What's the matter?" Siracusa called out. "I'm late, but you could have called me when it was time to milk the cows."

"We forgot about it," said Widow Biliotti, "in the confusion when they went away."

"They? Who?"

"The hunters . . ."

"They've gone?"

"Yes. They must be in Modena by now. They had more than enough of being here."

"And the man they were searching for?"

"They're mere boys. They were fed up and didn't want to hang around any longer. R.K. went with them . . ."

"What?"

"He went with them to Modena. He was carried away by their talk. So was Toma . . ."

"Has Toma gone away too?"

"Yes, and there are others that speak of going. Giralda Adorno, Spataro . . ."

"What for?"

"To live there. It seems there are jobs . . . They say this is a dungheap, that our efforts are wasted, that only in Modena or Bologna is work worthwhile. R.K. and Toma were carried away. They packed up their things and left."

Siracusa turned around and hurried back into the house. Before she was through the door she was calling:

"Ventura! Ventura!"

Still flat on his stomach, as he had been when the ray of sun came into the room an hour before, and when Siracusa had got up fifteen minutes ago, Ventura remained motionless, with his head under the pillow. Siracusa shook him.

"The hunters . . ." she said. "The hunters . . ."

"What's that?" said Ventura, stirring.

He pushed the pillow off his head, turned over, raised himself until he was leaning on one hip, with an elbow sinking into the mattress.

"The hunters . . ." she repeated.

Ventura fell back, looked up at her, and then closed his eyes.

"Let them come," he murmured.

"But they've gone away," she shouted.

Abruptly Ventura sat up.

"Gone away?"

He could see that she was excited, but he gave no sign of emotion.

"They've given up," she said. "They're not looking for you any longer."

Ventura fell back again. He had a faraway look, as if nothing mattered except the fact of being in bed and enjoying the long sleep he had dreamed of for so long.

"And do you know what's happened?" Siracusa added.

Ventura stared at her with a total lack of curiosity while she told him about R.K. and Toma.

"What do you know about that," he murmured.

Then she told him that there were others (she didn't know how many) that wanted to go too. Something must be done, she said, to stop them, however few or many they were.

"Get up!" she said. "We've got to talk to them."

He stared at her with something like surprise, then finally sat up again and threw his legs over the edge of the bed.

"With the passion they had for hunting!" he exclaimed.

"They got over it," she said. "Perhaps they weren't such famous hunters, after all . . . All they did was criticize, and create discontent . . ."

She moved about impatiently, while he continued to sit on the edge of the bed with his head between his hands.

"What more can I say?" he asked.

Then, instead of putting his feet on the floor, he unlaced his shoes and took them off.

"What more can I say?" he repeated.

She was still quivering with excitement, but he lay down on the bed. Finally, she calmed down and no longer even looked at him.

"That's right," she said, and went out, alone, but only to close the door behind her and sit on the doorstep.

EPILOGUE

78

Time passes, time has gone by—autumn, winter, March, June, August, and autumn is here again—1947, 1948, the Cold War, the Marshall Plan, a Christian Democrat government, the Berlin Airlift . . . Rita Hayworth has come and gone, and so has *The Third Man* with Orson Welles; faster planes than the Dakota fill the skies, Vespas and Lambrettas obstruct the roads; three crops of wheat have been reaped, workers in heavy industry have a new national wage scale, an attempt on the life of Togliatti has been followed by a general strike and the general strike by police repression; a new body of police, the *"Celere,"* is rough-riding over the sidewalks in jeeps, capital has flowed back from abroad, millionaires have reopened their villas on the lakes, supermillionaires come off their Panama-registered yachts to dine in the night clubs of what used to be fishing villages, young people are dancing the samba instead of the boogiewoogie, and the beaches are crowded with girls in bikinis.

Uncle Agrippa is still riding the trains, just as he did in 1946, from Bologna to Milan, from Rome to Villa San Giovanni, up the west coast to Genoa and down the east coast to Brindisi, via Piacenza and Alessandria to Turin, via Mestre to Udine and Trieste, along the Arno from Florence to Pisa, and from Bologna to Rimini and Pesaro.

Stations and trains are not what they were. Stations have been repaired or rebuilt in a new architectural style. Train cars are new or repainted, some of them are in aluminum instead of wood or iron, and the compartments are joined by a lateral passageway. Neither stations nor trains are crowded with people carrying sacks, baskets, knapsacks, and shapeless bundles. Now that they are no longer looking for relatives from whom they had been separated by the war or dealing in black market goods, people are either going north to look for six months of work in factories or going south to sit out six months on the doorsteps of their native villages.

The way of traveling is different also. Young people have infiltrated the ranks of the disarrayed war veterans and refugees in the mountains, and stamped out their memories. Their opinions, tastes, and claims prevail, spreading among everyone under forty. Only a few survivors, with obstinate purposes, fail to be aware of the change and continue to see things in 1948 and 1949 the way they saw them in 1945 and 1946. Uncle Agrippa is just as he was in 1945, and Carlo the Bald is just as he was in 1946, both of them unchanged in a changing world. They still meet, between Modena and Bologna or Bologna and Florence, as they did before; they greet each other in the old way and talk of the same things.

"My daughter . . ."

"That mountain settlement . . ."

Carlo, however, does have something to say about how the settlement is different from what it used to be.

"A quiet place. Everyone making payments on his house and turning in the required percentage of his crops. A warden who distributes the mail and keeps a public telephone; a bus passing every day between Bagni della Porretta and Bologna, electric current from the regional powerhouse . . ."

"And a school, no doubt, and a doctor . . ."

"Those are in the larger village to which they are administratively attached, ten miles down in the valley. They didn't have him before the war, either, when there were a thousand people . . ."

"A doctor, you mean?"

"Or a school, either. The school is a real problem. They'll get one eventually, but for now they have to make do as they did before."

"Sending the children ten miles away?"

"There are no more than a dozen children of school age. Most of the families up there don't have children."

"But for a while they had a school. You told me so yourself."

"Yessir, in 1945-46. If you could call it a school . . . God knows what was taught there . . ."

"But it was better than nothing."

"Do you think so? Nothing isn't always the worst."

"Well they got taught their ABC's, didn't they?"

"There's a priest, now, to teach them."

"Oh, they have a priest, do they?"

"Yessir! With the church, that we restored to its function, and a baptismal font and a rectory . . ."

79

It is April, summer, winter . . . They meet and talk again while traveling as they did before, but among very different travelers, young, self-assured, and presumptuous, who know where they are going. Another April and another August, and they begin all over, amid the same lights and shadows and glimpses of the same landscapes, speaking of things that have changed, in a manner that makes it seem there has been no change.

"So you got the agreement you were after?"

"That *I* was after? Perhaps not even the landowners really wanted it. All they care about is money coming into their pockets. I'm paid to do a job, but I'm free to have my own opinions. But order has been restored, yes, and the rights of ownership . . ."

"They're back on the tracks, is that it?"

"More or less. And without any need of forcing their hand, without any unpleasant incidents. Just letting things come to a head and ripen in their own way . . ."

"Like pears, you might say."

"Like pears, yes."

In October, and in the flatlands a layer of mist swathes the trunks of the mulberry trees, fills the ditches, hovering over some fields and not over others. The bridge across the mist-covered Po River clanks with the passage of the train. The Po valley is a white forest and, in the unheated railway cars, we feel a penetrating chill in our anklebones. October is half, three quarters gone; the mist climbs up the Lombard poplars, envelopes Lodi, and sneaks up, like icy smoke, upon the suburbs of Milan. The conversation proceeds, or perhaps it falls back to the line it followed in August, when the corn stood high, and in May, when poppies shot up among the blond wheat, or in March, when the fields were masses of cabbages. Or perhaps the line it follows is the same as it was in the mists of the year before or the year before that.

"When did it happen?"

"I already told you. It would have come out this way in any case, as things are going, with industry developing and cities growing and the countryside regressing."

"Still, anyone that has land doesn't want to lose it. Just look at your employers, for instance . . ."

"My employers! That's natural enough; it's a matter of principle. But I'm not speaking for them. It isn't that the land brings in less income, especially because, everywhere, since the war, they're growing things that yield a bigger price. I'm talking about the life the peasants lead as compared to the life of a factory worker."

"You talk about a lot of things."

"There *are* a lot of things. Take a two-hundred-acre farm and one of four thousand acres. The first, even if the soil is good and it's expertly cultivated, yields crops and nothing more. But with four thousand acres, there's the possibility of financial profit, of taking out loans and conducting all sorts of operations . . ."

"But we were speaking of that settlement in the mountains."

"Do you think I'm talking off the top of my head? I've gone back there."

"Last year?"

"Last year, and this year."

"But if you concluded the agreement . . ."

"That wasn't really my doing, I told you. The question resolved itself . . . My little game of a couple of years ago was aimed at putting the fear of God into a certain person— you know whom I mean—and at getting him out of the village. But what happened is that he stayed and the others went away . . ."

They talk and talk, of him and the others, him and the others, from misty season to misty season, across the fields of cabbages, and the wheat intermingled with poppies, and the corn, and the fields burned after the corn is in, of him who was the chief stumbling block, and of the others who, without him, would have been less of a stumbling block, and of how he, alone, had become meek as a lamb whereas the others, without him, would have given trouble. So that it was just as well that Carlo's little game had had the unexpected effect of sending away not him but the others.

They talk and talk, of what caused him to stay and the others to go, or, rather, of why he had not gone, of why, for some reason, he was not intimidated and why he had not broken away.

He and the others. He and the others. Uncle Agrippa has reservations about the phrase "the others." But Carlo patiently explains. By "the others," he meant those who came first to the village. Who stayed there, with him; who dug up the first mines, with him; who built the first houses, with him. Not all of them of course. Not the women from Messina, because they stayed; not some of the other men, because they stayed too. But the others who had started out with him, and worked at it with him, in the same resolute spirit, until the last minute, when it came out that there was a difference between them, when they were able to make up their minds to go away and he was not able to make up his mind about anything.

80

The conversation is repeated, dropped, picked up again, and sometimes Uncle Agrippa or even Carlo the Bald says: "Too bad!" And sometimes there are digressions such as there were in 1946, when they traveled in the darkness between one point of light and another, cigarette butts which were lit, extinguished, and lit up again, until they finally went out for good. At that time Carlo did most of the talking. He told how the whole group, "men, women and children," were working at pulling up the mines. They were committing an abuse, he said; they were outside the law and practically stealing. And yet, he said, they were good people; they were doing something of positive value, and their way of life was logical enough, in fact it was the best possible under existing conditions.

Now Uncle Agrippa recalls these words. You said this, and you said that, he reminds him. He is the one to talk now, during the digressions that flower between one gust of mist and another until they come to a city and a station platform.

"You had a good opinion of what they were doing."

"That I certainly did."

"The feeling of community . . ."

"The commune, let's call it, the commune that it was in those days . . ."

"In those days?"

And Carlo, now, recalls, point by point, what it was, with an enthusiasm such as to make it seem that he had fought to save it rather than to destroy. Uncle Agrippa does not catch him up on this contradiction.

"Too bad!" is all he says.

"Too bad!" Carlo echoes.

But the other people in the compartment are not interested in the subject as they were in the railway cars of two, three, or four years ago, with the wooden seats and the central passageway, and the travelers who wanted to hear the whole story and voice their opinions. Now Uncle Agrippa and Carlo might as well be talking statistics for all the curiosity they arouse. The compartment and the passageway outside are filled with noisy young people; they are talkative, all right, but only among themselves, as if they did not even hear anything that was said outside their age group.

Sometimes they sing snatches of choruses to which they invent the words. At the top of their lungs or in falsetto voices, two or three of them putting their heads together on one side and two or three on the other. Or else they laugh. One of them murmurs a story, keeping a straight face, and the others laugh until tears come to their eyes. Until the train stops and all of them, seated or standing, rush to the windows.

"Castelfranco?"

"Yes, Castelfranco."

There is nothing but mist outside, but the name is all they want to know as they push out through the doors, disappearing in the white vapor before the echo of their voices has died away. A smell like that of a cellar blows in. And new young men invade the compartment, like miners coming out of the mine, occupying seats and standing room and raising nodding faces above the frosted lapels of their jackets.

Or else, we journey between mountains and sea, from Genoa to Rome or Rome to Genoa, always crossing the Maremma in the early morning, amid fields of burning stubble, in view of either the smoke of an approaching fire or the smoke of a fire that is retreating, with a man standing to warm his hands beside it.

Here Uncle Agrippa often finds himself among totally inattentive young men.

soldiers getting off at Grosseto,

sailors and workers bound for La Spezia,

sailors and workers bound for Leghorn,

students going to Pisa or Rome,

workers going to Orbetello,

workers going to Rosignano Solvay;

all of them joking and laughing among themselves from where they get on to where they get off.

In vain, he searches among the laughing faces for someone he might know, he tries, persuasively, to make a new acquaintance. None of these new people is curious about what he might have to say. They may answer his first remark, and smile, but then their eyes wander and they return to the general clamor, unaware of the fact that he is still talking

. . .

Is he still talking?

Yes, he does not give up so soon; he gets out a second, a third, a fourth sentence, but his voice grows weaker and weaker until it is only an echo that sounds inside him. On his worried face his whole life story is written, from the time when he was the newborn baby of Sicilian peasants, left without his mother's milk for twelve hours at a time, to shiver and pee into his diaper. The black beams from which his cloth cradle was suspended have disappeared from his memory, and so has his mother's dark nipple to which his mouth finally found the way after she had come home. But everything that he has seen remains imprinted on his face. Perhaps this is what gives his face its character of old age, this mark left by everything he has seen and seen so many times over. Bread that is always bread, a train that is always a train, from the time when he first saw it to now, with the view out the window of a station, a tree, a field of smoking stubble, seen on a hundred times three hundred and sixty-five occasions and always the same—a station, a tree, a field of smoking stubble, viewed from a window that is always a window.

And yet, on these railway lines far from the axis of the Apennines he does, sometimes, run into people he has met in the years when everyone traveling by train knew him. There are still old people, and they turn up; Chicken, for instance, and Rosina, or Carlo the Bald. He meets Carlo on the Adriatic coast, when he must get off at Porto San Giorgio, or on the coast of Etruria, when he must get off at Follonica. He has to stake out the lots for new real estate development on the shore; this, says Carlo, is his new job. And they celebrate together their meeting at a place where they have never met before; they are completely taken up with each other, and now they are the ones to shut themselves off from the other travelers. The newcomers ignore them, as usual, but they are ignorant of the fact that they are ignored; they talk on and on as they did in the times when everyone hung on their words, as if what they are talking about were the most important of the problems and interests of the day.

81

Carlo is almost nostalgic for the first year of the mountain village, and Uncle Agrippa is quick to detect and foster his nostalgia. He gives no sign of seeing any inconsistency between Carlo's praise of the village on the one hand and his taste for what he calls "law and order" on the other, the division of the fruits of the land between the owner and his tenant, the warden who supervises the telephone and the priest who sticks his sacraments into personal and family relationships. Carlo is, indeed, happy with the way things are now going. He continues to go there and see how everything is progressing. A billiard table has been installed in the headquarters of the agricultural workers' association, and he goes there to play on occasional Sundays.

Does he play with the man he wanted to drive away, the one who stuck it out after all?

Yes, with him, among others. Only the fellow's no longer any good; he no longer puts his heart into it. But he has played with him. Once he even dragged him out of bed for a game. Ever since Carlo has ceased to have any responsibility for the village, he goes back to feel its pulse, to check up on the mood of the villagers.

Is it to see whether the mood is better or worse than before?

Carlo looks out of half-closed eyes at Uncle Agrippa. Yessir, he admits. And he admits that it is better. He thinks it over before he says it, then thinks some more and repeats it, every time with greater enthusiasm. Better, yes. How could it be otherwise? Definitely better.

They have neon lights and shops: a grocery, a bakery, a general store, all of them with neon signs. Even the shed that served as a workshop when they were building has a sign that says "CARPENTER," and the letters are lit up with blue at night. The same man still runs it as a private business. And the former wineshop is now a real bar, with a red-lighted sign on the façade, yellow lights over the door, and a string of vertical blue lights at the corner that say "Motta Ice Cream," the same trademark that is imprinted on the white metal case near the door and on every rectangle of ice cream that is taken out of it. The "M" of "Motta" is the "M" of Milan.

Behind the bar there is a refrigerator and beside it a pinball machine where, if you chalk up fifteen points, you have the satisfaction of seeing an astronomical figure light up in the mouth of a siren. Music pours out of the bar, and the agricultural workers' headquarters beginning at three o'clock in the afternoon; the two tunes clash and echo in the middle of the street between them.

Not that Carlo is so very keen on the juke boxes. He would prefer something more subdued and more melodious. But they are unmistakable signs of prosperity.

"Well . . ." says Uncle Agrippa.

He does not really know what a juke box is. He lives on trains and knows nothing except that which can be found on trains or in railway stations. Nevertheless, he accepts the virtue of everything that Carlo points to as a good sign. Carlo is pleased with the way things are going in the village, and Uncle Agrippa shares his pleasure. Just as well, he says, just as well.

But Carlo is discontented also. Thinking it over and over, he curls up his lips and shakes his head.

There are always fewer people, he says. Newcomers have settled there, peasants from higher up in the mountains and lower down in the valley, day workers who go from one land-owner to another, but the total number of inhabitants has fallen. Many of the younger men have gone away, including those of the peasant groups that came after the arrival of Antonia. All the young people are restless, and every growing boy or girl wants to go to the city, and most often goes and stays there.

So that although the village has cold beer and hot music, there are no more inspired people, no willing arms for hard work, no fresh, eager faces. Except for the women of Messina, who seem to be waiting to smell mold before they let themselves grow as fat and lethargic as if they had gone back to Sicily. And a few middle-aged people, who accept the mold because they do not want to repeat their former exertions. And except, of course, for *him* . . .

The fellow who stayed instead of going away?

"You know who I mean . . ."

"That fanatic?"

"A fanatic when he was with fanatics . . ."

"The stumbling block, the hard nut to crack . . ."

"Until he turned out to be just the contrary—soft, lazy, a sort of Bohemian, without any wish to get away . . ."

"That is, after he had decided to stick it out."

"But what made him stay? There was always this side to his character, you see. He knew that if they found him, he was done for."

"Done for?"

"In those days, with everyone so full of resentment . . . The younger they were, the more intemperate."

"And if they had taken him?"

"Oh, if they had . . . It makes me laugh—I'm sorry. I was sure that he'd react, that he'd be scared and beat it. How could I know that he'd risk his skin rather than budge?"

"Well, everything turned out for the best, I grant you."

"Everything, or nearly everything. Where he's concerned, it might have been better if he'd cut loose and run. Of if they'd taken him and killed him off . . . When I think of the way he is now, inert and without any ambition, a fellow that once could command a whole regiment of engineers . . ."

82

The conversation may have some of its ramifications in a railway cafe, in the station at Rimini or the station at Bologna. Here Uncle Agrippa and Carlo talk from one table to another. One of them walks in when the other is already seated and sits down, not beside him but at a table nearby, one of the many empty among the few that are occupied, where often there are still the dirty cup and the bottle and the glass of water of the man who was there before. Everybody shouts for what he wants: "Waiter!" "My coffee!" "Make it snappy!" Three yards are like a mile in this subterranean cavern, with its vast empty spaces. The voice that sets the key is that of the loudspeaker announcing the arrival and departure of the trains. Uncle Agrippa and Carlo must raise their pitch. Their conversation proceeds in a singsong, from one table to the other.

"At least if he'd run away, he might have found himself involved in some other historical event!"

"Historical?"

"Like the establishment of the village in August 1945 and into the first months of 1946. I can't explain. But from hearing about it over and over, I have some idea of what the word means. Some things in life are historical—they belong to history—and some aren't."

"Was the war an historical event? And what *isn't* historical? The peace in which we're living, for instance?"

"I said I couldn't explain. I'm no schoolteacher. But just look at him the way he is now, and tell me if it wouldn't have been better if he'd run away and latched on to something of interest, or if he'd been bumped off when they were looking for him . . ."

"You said that before."

"But I don't seem to have made my point. The point is that if either of those things had happened, he'd have stayed involved in what people call history. Whereas the way things are now, he's out of it, removed by a thousand miles . . ."

"I don't see what it matters whether a fellow's in it or out of it, myself."

"But history's important. There are people who'd say it's a matter of to be or not to be."

"So you've turned philosopher! And what about ourselves? Are we in it or out of it?"

"I don't know about you . . . First of all, you're retired. But as for me, I consider I'm in it. I buy, sell, trade, cut down trees, build. I work for someone else, of course. But there are miles that used to be covered with pine woods where now there are summer houses, and all because of my efforts. Then there's what I did with that village. I belong to something constructive, whether for good or for ill, but something that's moving. And what does he belong to? . . ."

83

One train pulls in and another pulls out.

A train from the third world of the south to Switzerland spews forth a confused crowd of men in shirt sleeves who invade the station café and rush for coffee, beer, orangeade, and sandwiches, men from Apulia and Calabria who work for the Swiss colonial empire. They overturn chairs and tables, breaking a cup or a glass here and there, and dividing Uncle Agrippa and Carlo until their next meeting a month from now, or six months, or perhaps the next day.

Once more the conversation is interrupted. But there is no danger of its remaining incomplete. Everything has been said, a bit at a time, over and over and over.

"What does he belong to?"

"Well, to the village, you might say. And the village is something. It has its neon lights, its nylons, its consumption of heat in the winter and ice in the summer, all things that it didn't have before. It has its improved crop production, the agricultural machines that are on the way. It has people that want to live there and people that want to go away. It makes its dent, small as that may be, along with other villages . . ."

"But does he belong? It's something small and miserable, a nothing. And can he be said to belong to this nothing? a nothing. And can he be said to belong to this nothing? When I go there and ask for him, they seem hardly to know who he is. As if he were someone who had been there but who is practically forgotten. Nobody sees him every day. Ventura? Ventura? I have to call him Teresa's husband before they catch on. All of them know Teresa; she does most of the work in the fields, she goes to market to buy and sell. Siracusa, they used to call her, not because of where she came from but because of an ancient coin she wears around her neck like a religious medal. Now she's Teresa. She knows she's only a peasant and her wasted efforts are of no particular importance. Ventura's only Teresa's husband. He's gone to seed, but he doesn't know how to be a genuine peasant or how to be a nonentity. Because that's what he is, a nonentity wasting his life in a mountain village, with a wife that supports him.

"Oh, he spends some hours in his own field. He ploughs when it's the season for ploughing, and scatters the fertilizer. Every morning and evening he milks his cow in the stable. But it's as if a shadow were ploughing and milking . . . The way he is when we play billiards together, a wet rag. Oh, he scores, all right, but without seeming to notice. He isn't interested in scoring any more than in anything else. He might as well not score. His heart isn't in it. Teresa has to tell him what to do from one day to the next. To remind him, and urge him on.

"Otherwise he'd stay all day at the window, or lie on his bed, smoking. In the winter months he never sticks his nose outside, to go to the bar or the agricultural workers' headquarters, or to take the bus to the city or to a market or fair in one of the neighboring villages. In summer he doesn't go anywhere, either. He never thinks of improving the land. Of terracing the hillsides and growing vines and irrigating them in the dry season, of trying out a new crop and new ways of making it flourish.

"Once upon a time, nobody was his equal in all these things. When he was an engineer during the war, and in the early days of the village. As long as the land was worked in common, until August of 1946, he was the guiding spirit, commanding the rest of them like an orchestra director. While now that he has only the one field that belongs to him and his wife, a vision purely his own of today and tomorrow, he floats like a half-collapsed balloon on a sea of indifference. Just the contrary of what usually happens.

"As if we knew what was usual and what was the contrary! You'd expect that when everyone had his own piece of land, he'd put his heart into working it. But nothing of the kind has come to pass. Everyone squeezes out of his land as much as he can. But you can't say that he puts more effort into it than before or gets more out of it.

"Once upon a time they were really something! But now you can't say that he's the only one to have collapsed. The place is pathetic. The land, as land, has lost its importance.

The neon lights and the Motta ice cream don't conceal the reality of the situation. It's funny, isn't it, that there shouldn't be a single example of what you might call the usual and expected thing. Not even the women from Messina, who grow fat and plant grapevines. Not even Teresa, who pulls Ventura along like a wagon. She's not the Siracusa that she used to be; she's a housewife, trying to get a good price for her milk and putting up preserves for the winter.

"Of what, then, is he the contrary? I'm angry enough to say what I think—that he *is* the contrary. But the contrary of what? Tell me that, if you can!"